GUN FOR HIRE

A stranger approached the table. The man was tall, lean, and hard-looking. At a distance of three feet, the man stopped. "I hear you're lookin' to hire some men."

"We are. We need men good with their guns. Your name?"

"Jaeger. Gus Jaeger. And what might yours be?"

"I am Victor Spectre, these gentlemen are my partners—Ralph Tinsdale and Olin Buckner. Take a seat, Mr. Jaeger."

Jaeger took one of the straight-backed chairs and tilted it back away from the table. "What exactly do you have in mind?"

"There is a man. He needs killing."

Jaeger looked them over with a puzzled frown. "There's three of you. Why don't you do it yourselves?"

"Because this man is a rather accomplished gunfighter."

Jaeger smiled. "Well, then, you needn't worry about any other applicants. There's not anyone around that's better than me. You've got all the gunhand you'll need. By the way, who is this gunfighter?"

"It's . . . uh . . . Smoke Jensen," Spectre said regretfully.

Jaeger's chair banged noisily back to the floor and he swallowed hard. "If only a quarter of what I heard is true. . . ."

"It's wise to have a healthy respect for an adversary," Spectre stated. "Do you think you can conquer your awe of Jensen long enough to make an end to him?"

After a long moment of careful thought, Jaeger replied, "If I have three or four good boys to back me up."

Victor Spectre replied almost primly. "We were thinking of more like twenty. . . ."

WILLIAM W. JOHNSTONE

SPIRIT OF THE MOUNTAIN MAN

ZEBRA BOOKS
KENSINGTON PUBLISHING CORP.

ZEBRA BOOKS are published by

Kensington Publishing Corp.
850 Third Avenue
New York, NY 10022

First Printing: January, 1996

Printed in the United States of America

One

Sliding languidly, in big, oily swirls, over a few submerged sandbars, the red-brown surface of the Colorado River glided past the low, native stone buildings on the isolated knoll. The complex rested well above the sandy, ochre flood plain, beyond the maximum high water mark. According to the Army engineers who designed the structure, it made the ideal location for a prison.

For that was the purpose of this high-walled, forbidding construction. Yuma Territorial Prison; it housed the hardest of hard cases, the most unrepentant road agents, bank robbers, and highwaymen, the wife and baby killers who had escaped from other institutions to kill again and never show a flicker of remorse. At the quarry, guards' shrill whistles announced the noon hour and the men working on the rock pile lowered their hammers and drills. They shambled wearily through the shimmering mid-day desert heat to find what solace they could in the shadows of an overhanging wall of the strip quarry. Among them, three men stood out from the rest.

Victor Spectre could never be mistaken for a drifter or a highwayman. A graduate of Yale, he had the look about him of a businessman, albeit one who kept himself in excellent condition. Trim, with hard muscles, in his mid-forties, he had only the beginnings of a pot belly. The latter had developed quite a lot during his seven years in various prisons.

He used to be the brains behind, and leader of, a large outlaw gang that operated in Missouri, Kansas, and Colorado.

He had lived the good life, in luxurious splendor, in a fancy St. Louis hotel, and directed the actions of his vast gang from there. That is, until his greed and the viciousness of his underlings attracted the wrong sort of attention. That's when he met up with *trouble*. And it was spelled; *Smoke Jensen*. They had a series of violent encounters.

Since that time, Spectre's thick shock of black hair had a white streak to the left of his part, caused by a bullet fired by Smoke Jensen. The slug had knocked him unconscious and saved his life. His eighteen-year-old son, Trenton, had not fared so well. Originally sentenced to hang, Victor Spectre's money and influence got his death warrant commuted to life in prison. With icy green eyes and thick, bristly brows which met in the middle of his forehead when angered, he quickly became the head cock on the yard at any institution in which he had been incarcerated. It also earned him frequent transfers when enemies and rivals among the prison population turned up mysteriously dead. No different from previous occasions, Victor Spectre had assumed leadership over his two companions.

Ralph Tinsdale was a contemporary of Victor Spectre. He had a thick build, going somewhat to pot with advancing years and a starchy prison diet. He used to be a big land speculator, who obtained prime ranches and city properties by the simple expedient of having the owners killed and dealing with the widows. He had been in the process of acquiring from a silver-haired dowager a choice square block in the heart of the business district of Denver when he discovered that the late Harrison Tate had been a close personal friend of one Smoke Jensen.

Quite quickly, Smoke Jensen wrote *finis* to the evil machinations of Ralph Tinsdale. In their final confrontation, Smoke had left Tinsdale for dead, at the bottom of a deep ravine, with two bullet holes in the belly. Tinsdale had survived with large scars and a permanent limp. Smoke found that out when called to testify at the trial. When the guilty verdict came in and the judge sentenced him to life in prison, Tinsdale cursed Smoke hotly in language unbecoming the stylish clothing the swindler wore. His time in prison had failed to mellow him. Tinsdale had grown slack behind bars, so that his once lustrous hair had turned a mousy brown, poorly cared for, and his once natty pencil-line mustache had been replaced by a scraggly wisp of its former self. Only his hatred of Smoke Jensen gave him a semblance of youthful vigor. Enough, though, that he was accepted as second in command of the unholy trio.

Olin Buckner had nearly ten years on his associates. His auburn hair, which had faded to mostly gray, was worn slicked back tightly on a long skull. He had a porcine appearance, enhanced by a jowly face, with a pug nose and small, deep-set black eyes. An over-large mouth and big ears added to the illusion. He had already developed a middle-aged spread. Once, though, he had been trim and almost compulsively active. He had owned an entire town in south-central Montana. Most of it he had acquired by unlawful means, and he ruled with an iron fist—until he tried to drive out the daughter of a mysteriously and recently deceased friend of Smoke Jensen.

Smoke went after Buckner with a particular vengeance. Olin Buckner replied by hiring an army of gunfighters, putting a bounty on the head of Smoke Jensen, and sitting back to enjoy the results. Buckner might have been a fine, skillful fisherman, but he had never hooked a shark before. When Smoke Jensen got through with him, he had lain in a hospital bed for five months before he could stand upright, and another three before he could be brought to trial. Like the others, his residual wealth and influence bought him a commutation of sentence. The hangman was cheated and Buckner went to the worst prisons in the west. He ended up in Yuma and soon found a common bond between himself and the other two.

Now, this trio of the lowest form of human debris stood quietly in line to take a bowl and tin cup in turn, and shuffle past the trustees who dispensed the mid-day meal. Each inmate received a large dipper of a thin soup, purported to be chicken, but lacking even the sight of a speck of meat, and half a round loaf of sourdough bread. Then they retreated to the blessing of shade. As always, the topic of conversation among Spectre, Tinsdale, and Buckner centered on Smoke Jensen.

"I hate that bastard," Olin Buckner spat. "I've not been able to enjoy a day or night without pain since Jensen shot me. I want him dead—no, crippled and suffering would be better."

"You both know I have ample cause to despise Smoke Jensen," Ralph Tinsdale spoke in precise tones, as his stomach cramped and growled in protest to the food. "I was a man of consequence and ample means before Jensen thrust himself into my affairs. Since then, I have not been able to eat a meal without terrible agony. And prison has further destroyed me."

Victor Spectre gave a snort of amusement through his nose. "And you have destroyed a few of them, from what I hear."

Tinsdale sniffed disdainfully. "I was not afforded the respect I deserved."

"Well, whatever," Spectre muffled through a mouthful of bread. "I have no reason to love Smoke Jensen, as you well know. He maimed me and murdered my son, took everything from me. The only this is—"

"Quiet down there," a guard snarled. "No talkin' among the prisoners. You three know the rules."

After the guard turned away, Victor Spectre repeated himself. "The only thing is, there is not a thing we can do about it from inside here. Smoke Jensen is free as a bird to go and do anything he wants, with no harm to him."

"I'd give a hell of a lot to see it otherwise," Buckner growled. He spooned the thin soup into his mouth.

Ralph Tinsdale studied Victor Spectre while he munched on the chewy sourdough bread. "Are you proposing we find a way to get out of here?"

"I think that would go a long way toward accomplishing our mutual goal, to bring an end to the career and life of Smoke Jensen."

"It won't be easy," Tinsdale offered.

"No," Victor Spectre agreed. "And, as I said, we can't do it from here. We will have to find a way to escape."

Suddenly the guard rounded on them, his Winchester no longer on his shoulder, but held competently at high-port in a menacing manner. *"No talking among prisoners!* I warned you three jailhouse lawyers once. This is the second time. There won't be a third. You'll be taken direct to the Sun Box."

Silenced by that most effective threat, the three master criminals froze in silence. They knew all too much about the ingenious variation on solitary confinement employed at Yuma Territorial Prison. Four coffin-like boxes of sheet iron and rock had been constructed in the center of the Yard. They were so small a man could not lie down, could not even sit properly with the door closed and locked. The only openings were tiny, barred, holes in the upper part of each door. Each of the recent arrivals at the institution had heard the screams, wails, and blubbering of men driven mad in the heat of a Sun Box. Finally, the warden turned away to snarl at other offending prisoners.

Buckner, by far the most devious of the trio, leaned forward and whispered. "Find some way this afternoon to be sent to the infirmary. We can talk freely there."

* * *

Spring had awakened new buds on the aspen trees of the High Lonesome, which had unfolded into tender, pale green leaves. The meadows and pastures of the Sugarloaf had turned emerald. Warm, soft breezes called longingly to those with sufficiently sensitive natures. One of those was a tall, broad-shouldered man with faint streaks of gray in his hair. He breathed deeply and savored the winey fragrance of renewed life. Then he set his coffee cup on the plank flooring of the porch and came to his feet.

"I think it's time to go fishing," he told the lovely woman beside him. "I'll take Bobby along and get in three or four days on Silver Creek, and over Honey Spring way."

His wife looked up with a frown of protest on her forehead. "That boy has yet to finish his studies, Smoke."

Smoke Jensen smiled a wide, white smile in a sun-mahoganied face. "Sally, there's a universe of learning out there in this magical country. He can learn biology, botany, even weather studies."

Sally Jensen broke her stern visage with a giggle. "Also a lot about rainbow and brown trout, I'll wager."

Smoke took her outstretched hands and raised her from the wooden rocking chair. He remained amazed that she had never lost her youthful figure. The years and five children should have done some damage, yet he could detect none at all. "And right you would be, my dear. The last day we'll catch a mess and bring them home to you. Have some fresh biscuits waitin'. And a pie. We have to have a nice pie."

"I've a Mason jar of cherries left, and a couple of blackberries. Which would you prefer?" Sally asked sweetly.

Smoke patted her on one shoulder. "Whatever you pick will be all right with me. Now, I'll go get Bobby and we'll round up our gear."

Bobby Harris had been living with the Jensens since he became an orphan at the age of ten. His stepfather had been beating the boy's pony and Bobby had been tearfully pleading with the drunken brute when Smoke rode up to the small homestead outside of Thatcher, Colorado. Smoke Jensen could not abide any man who would harm an animal and watched in growing anger. When the abused critter stumbled to its knees, the lad became hysterical. Smoke stepped in when the stepfather decided to turn the length of lumber on Bobby.

After a thorough beating, administered by the hard fists of Smoke Jensen, the drunken sot had gone for Smoke with a pitchfork. Bobby's shouted warning saved Smoke's life and cost that of the stepfather. Smoke was on the way to give assistance to old and true friends in Mexico at the time and at last decided on sending Bobby and his pony north to the Sugarloaf. A year later they made it official by adopting the orphaned boy. He was bright and energetic, although at times a bit forgetful of the limitations of a small boy. He was doing such now, risking any future progeny on the saddle of an unbroken mustang, when Smoke came upon him at the big corral.

Sugarloaf riders had located the wild horses a month earlier, still snowbound in a box canyon. They patiently constructed a barricade across the mouth of the chasm and waited. When the snow melted and the animals calmed somewhat, flankers along the herd's edges brought them in to provide a new bloodline to the prize horses raised by Smoke and Sally on the Sugarloaf.

Grunting and squalling, the wild bang-tail crow hopped and sunfished under the small, tightly gripping legs of Bobby Harris. Smoke rode in close and held his peace, gloved hands folded on the saddlehorn of his big 'Palouse stallion, Thunder. Two more jumps and a tornado spin later, Bobby tasted corral bottom. The spunky lad came to his boots after only a lung-jarring grunt, dusted off his jeans and chaps and spat grit from his mouth. "Damn," he followed it with. Then he saw Smoke Jensen. "Oh, sorry Smoke. I—ah—" He grinned sheepishly.

"What's a damn or two between two friendly men?" Smoke asked lightly. Bobby literally glowed. He wore his hero worship of Smoke Jensen for everyone to see. "I thought you might be in a mood for something a little less strenuous."

"Like what?" Bobby limped to the fence and squirmed through the two lower poles.

Smoke teased him shamelessly. "My nose and my mountain man instincts, tell me it's time to go hog out a few rainbows. Think you'd like that?"

Bobby dusted his hands together, then adjusted the angle of his pint-sized Montana peak Stetson. "Would I? You bet, I would. Where would we go? How long?"

Smoke raised his chin and spoke as though just thinking of it. "I thought we'd angle up Silver Spring a ways, then head over toward Honey Spring. Be gone three, four days."

Bobby's eyes went wide. "That's stupendous, Smoke, I'll git ready right away."

"Stupendous?" Where the hell do they get these words? Smoke wondered silently.

Grinning from ear to ear, Bobby Harris turned in the saddle. "This is really great, Smoke." He breathed deeply, filling young lungs. "It smells so good up here. I can tell pine an' blue spruce, grass a-growin' like crazy. There's water up ahead, I can smell it, too. We never had nothin' to smell around Thatcher, excect dust."

"Whoa! Get a rein on that enthusiasm. And remember the grammar Sally has been drilling into your head."

Bobby made a face. Along with Miss Grimes at Punkin' Head School," he lamented. "Study, study, study. That's all we do."

Smoke pulled a wry expression. "Then how'd you manage to come home with that big bag of marbles at snow closin' last winter?"

Eyes fixed on the skirt of Thunder's saddle, Bobby slid out his lower lip in a pout and dug at his pug nose with a knuckle. "We only got to play during our nooning, Smoke, honest."

"Then you must be the best marble player in all of Big Rock."

"I'm . . . good, right enough. Sammy an' me played some when I boarded at his folks' house."

Here, in a land of big and early snows, school was held on a reversed schedule, from the fifteenth of April until the fifteenth of October. Tutoring made up for the other three months of class work. Sally Jensen, who had taught school at one time, held group lessons for Bobby, the children of ranch hands, and neighboring youngsters. It vexed her students mightily, Smoke knew, yet they showed up and behaved extraordinarily well. A broken leg had prevented Bobby from starting in Big Rock this April and, now out of his cast, cabin fever had set in.

What else would account for the boy undertaking the hazards of breaking mustangs? Smoke asked himself. Well, in a week, two at most, he would be headed for Big Rock and the little red schoolhouse at the end of Main Street. It had been arranged for him to live with his best friend, Sammy, and the Weisers expected him no later than that. For all Bobby's protestations, Smoke noted, he and Sammy had managed to get enough time away from the classroom the last summer to acquire a decent browning of their hides. A faint yellow-brown tinge of high altitude tan still colored Bobby's cheeks and forearms. Given this summer, he would be free forever of the unhealthy pallor which had accompanied the boy to the Sugarloaf. The high altitude sun soon cured normal skin like leather, with about the same color.

"We gonna build a lean-to or sleep out under the stars?" Bobby asked.

Smoke smiled back. "We can do whatever you want."

An animated face answered Smoke. "Then can you tell

me some stories about you and Preacher? About back when you were my age?"

Smoke leaned over and lightly tapped Bobby on one shoulder point. "I didn't know Preacher when I was your age. I was fourteen, I think, when I would up lost out here and on my own."

"So? Go on."

"Tonight, over fish and biscuits."

"That's a promise, Smoke?"

"Promise."

Toward mid-afternoon, Smoke Jensen called a halt to their journey. A small stand of silver-barked aspen beckoned. On his own land, Smoke could be certain of being safe, yet training and experience compelled him to pass up that inviting shelter. Instead, he used a short-handled axe to cut down a dozen forearm-thick saplings, bundled them and tied them off behind the packhorse. They traveled on to a moderate clearing, with plenty of grass for the horses, and shaded by a big old blue spruce.

It towered a good sixty feet into the air, and had, for at least 250 years, miraculously escaped the attention of the fierce lightning that crashed through these mountains and valleys each summer. With Bobby's help, he quickly constructed a roomy lean-to and covered the long, slant back and square sides with overlapped layers of pine bough. They stood back, hands on hips, and admired their handiwork.

"Not bad for a couple of amateurs, eh?" Smoke opined teasingly.

Bobby made a face that indicated he knew his leg was being pulled. "Awh, Smoke, you must have made hundreds of these before."

"Thousands, more like," Smoke agreed. "Now, it's your job to fetch firewood, while I bring stones from the creek for the fire ring."

Bobby cocked an eyebrow. "Who says we're gonna catch anything?"

"We have to cook *something,* don't we?"

"Yep. But who says I've got to get the firewood?"

"I says. Is that good enough for you?"

Bobby gave a fake gulp. "Yes, sir, yes it is."

He scampered off to do as bidden. Smoke turned toward the creek, located a suitable distance from their camp to muffle its noisy gurgling. As he neared the bank he heard lazy splashes from the sparkling water of Silver Creek. The rainbow trout would be thick enough to almost walk on, and hungry after the long winter.

An hour before sundown everything had been laid out in readiness. Outfitted with a Mason jar of live dragon flies and some of the newfangled artificial dry flies hooked into their shirt collars, man and boy set off to the east bank of Silver Creek.

At first sight, Bobby almost forgot himself and cried out in excitement. The water swarmed with mossy green backs. Hundreds of finny creatures filled the stream. Their deep color faded along their sides to the dividing line of rainbow colors. Beyond that their white, speckled bellies flashed brightly when one or another would roll gracefully after surfacing to snap up a winged insect. Bobby's eyes danced.

"Let's get to work," Smoke suggested.

Within half an hour they had a dozen pan-sized trout. The larger ones they had unhooked and thrown back. Those they caught tomorrow would be filleted and smoked. This intimate time together would teach Bobby many mountain man tricks. Smoke got the fire going while Bobby cleaned the fish. Smoke made biscuits and put the pot of beans he had put to soaking over the fire on a trestle arm. Bobby looked on and asked endless questions about camp cooking, while he peeled onions brought from the root cellar at the Sugarloaf headquarters, washed and sliced potatoes, and put a large skillet of them on to fry. At last, when the coals undulated with just the right red-orange glow, he put the fish on to fry.

They ate it all, wiped the skillets with biscuit halves, belched and patted full bellies. Then Smoke leaned back and lighted a thin, hard, dry cigar. Bobby returned to his first interest.

"Tell me about you an' Preacher."

"Oh, my, where to begin? I had to be about fourteen when Preacher hooked up with me and Pa in Kansas. Now, mind, we did not hit it off at the first. Preacher was old. Nearly as old as God, the way I saw it. He was crotchety, set in his ways, and about as foul-mouthed as any ten men could get. He could fill the air with blue smoke when he took to cussin'." Smoke paused to consider. Yep, Preacher had been all of that, and much, much more, too. "He was the best friend anyone could have, man or boy."

"Preacher was also kind, loyal, astonishingly intelligent, and absolutely convinced that life, as he lived it in the High Lonesome, was the best sort of life anyone could ever have. He took me in after Pa died."

"Tell me about one of you and Preacher's famous gunfights, Smoke?" Bobby interrupted.

Smoke sighed. "All right. Just this once. I recall the time when Preacher and I had to fight off eleven tough outlaws, the last of a gang that had been preying on immigrant trains along the North Platte. It was in the 'Sixties then, and the Army had mostly gone back east to fight for the Union. So, boarder riff raff grew bolder and bolder. This particular bunch had holed up in one of the trading posts they had also victimized. Preacher an' me had to go in after them. . . ."

. . . Preacher eased his head up over the fallen log and peered closely at the tumble-down shack that housed the eleven vicious highwaymen. This weren't no dance for a seventeen-year-old tadpole to jine into, he reckoned. But Smoke was here and rarin' for a fight, so what could he

do? He cut his eyes to where Smoke Jensen crouched between some fat granite boulders, some twenty yards away.

Good boy, Preacher thought approvingly. He'd learned the
lad about not bunchin' up right early in their time together.
"The main idea is to give whoever is shootin' at ya more
air than meat for targets," the mountain man had explained
to a wide-eyed boy of almost fifteen. "Fact is, they's always
more air than meat, as you'll find out when you are on the
give side of that equation."

That had been near four years ago. Now all the lessons
on surviving in the Big Empty were about to be put to the
test. Preacher fervently wished that Charlie Three-Toes and
some of those other never-quitters among the trapping fra-
ternity had come along for this showdown. Best to have all
sides of a building covered. Whatever, there was nothin' for
it now. Preacher slid the barrel of his .56 Hawken over the
fallen tree and took aim on a square of thinly scraped hide
that served as a window pane. Behind it, kerosene lamps
and flickering candles projected the head and shoulders of
a human figure. Preacher eared back the hammer of the
Hawken.

Sure, he could have hollered out for these scoundrels to
surrender, to come out with their hands up, but he reckoned
that such a move would only bring him and his young companion to more grief. So he fined his sight picture and
squeezed the trigger. The Hawken made a sharp, clean report and shoved into Preacher's shoulder. The conical bullet
went straight and true.

From his vantage point, Smoke Jensen saw a small black
dot appear in the skin window and a moment later the human figure popped out of sight as though pulled by a rope.
As instructed, he fired at the doorway when the flimsy pine
board panel flew open. An unseen man screamed and then
Preacher bellowed at the top of his lungs.

"That's two down! You men in there best come out and
surrender. We've got you surrounded."

Well, at least on two sides, Preacher eased his conscience over straying from the whole truth.

"Like hell we will," came a belligerent reply. "We been watchin'. There's more of us than you."

By then Preacher had his Hawken reloaded. "Not for long," he bantered back as he again took aim on the window.

A crash and tinkle, and one clear, bell-like note followed his shot. To Preacher's right, Smoke put a round through the open doorway. His reward came in hurried orders.

"Drag Rafe back out of there, we've gotta close that door."

Weak, though clearly audible to Smoke Jensen, Rafe spoke from the floor of the shack. "I'm gut-shot, Doolie. I ain't gonna make it."

Anger, colored by fear filled the reply. "Then crawl outten that door so's we can close it."

"It hurts too much, Doolie."

The crack of a pistol shot answered him, then Doolie's growl. "Now, drag that body outten the way an' let's get to business."

Preacher had trained him well. Smoke was ready for that. He winged another man who bent over the dead Rafe. The hard case made a yelp and a startled frog-leap obliquely to the doorway. "Oh, dang, they got me in the cheek, Doolie."

"Can't be much, you can talk all right," the outlaw leader muttered.

"It's the other cheek, Doolie. Oh, damn, it hurts."

"Stop yer belly-achin'. We got to get 'em. By my count, they's only two. I say we rush them."

Doolie and his henchmen did not get the chance. Preacher's next blind shot through the opaque window shattered a kerosene lamp and the whole shelter went up in flames. Clothes afire, two men ran from the doorway, their weapons forgotten. Preacher dropped first one, then another with a pistol ball from his Model '60 Colt. Smoke fired at a third who went to one knee, shot through the side. Smoke's rifle sights still had him shooting low. Doolie and a couple more stubbornly insisted on fighting it out from inside.

When it was all over, only five of the eleven remained alive, all wounded. The shack burned to the ground with Doolie in it. And that's how Preacher handled that. . . .

Smoke Jensen looked down at Bobby Harris to find the boy with his head on one crooked arm, eyes closed, breathing deeply in a sound sleep. Smoke chuckled, then asked himself aloud, "Was I that boring?"

The boy did have a long, hard day of it, he reasoned. Tomorrow there would be more adventures. Smoke settled in his soogans and closed his eyes under the starry sky.

TWO

Darkness lay in a heavy blanket over the Yuma Territorial Prison compound. Droopy-eyed guards stood watch in the eight turretlike towers atop the walls at each corner and in the middle of each span. The two on the river side would be their targets, it had been decided. When he judged that alertness had sufficiently drained from the sentries, Victor Spectre forced a spate of coughing that would signal the other two to put their plan into operation.

Spectre's plan was simplicity in its most distilled form. They would incapacitate the turnkey, get out of the cell block, knock out the guards and pitch them over the side, then follow them on ropes made of torn blankets. To that end, when the cough ended, Buckner began to bang the bars of the cell he shared with Tinsdale with a tin cup. When he received no response, he called out.

"Hey! Hey, turnkey. There's a man sick in here."

No answer. Not even a light at the end of the corridor outside the open-fronted cells. Buckner, the most guileful, drew breath and yelled again. "Damnit, I mean it. He's powerful sick."

At last a light came, weakly from a hooded kerosene lantern. "Stow that racket."

"My cell-mate is powerful sick," Buckner wheedled. "It's that rotten pork we had at supper. He's about to die on me."

"Have him report to the infirmary in the morning."

"He is not going to *last* until morning, Boss. Please,

come take a look for yourself. He's all gray and green, eyes are rolled up. Hurry!"

Grumbling, the turnkey complied. He had a rolling gait, a leftover from his years before the mast on a clipper ship. When he had left the clipper ship service, he swore he never again wanted to see a body of water he could not hurl a rock across from bank to bank. He wound up here, at the top of the Rio Colorado delta, where the river ran a mile wide. He muttered to himself about the whims and petty annoyances of his charges as he approached the cell. He looked inside and saw a man who could indeed be on the edge of death.

Unadvisedly, he unlocked the cell and stepped inside. To his credit, he locked it behind him before he crossed to the bunk. He had no way of knowing that the pale, gray-green face had been achieved by mixing whitewash powder with scrapings from an ancient copper deposit in the quarry. When he bent to get a closer look, Olin Buckner snaked an arm around his neck and began to squeeze.

In less than two minutes Buckner had quite thoroughly throttled the prison guard. Ralph Tinsdale took the man's keys and helped to lift him onto the bunk in his own place. They gathered their makeshift ropes and slung the coils over both shoulders. Then Tinsdale unlocked the door and stepped out under the overhang of the second tier catwalk. Buckner followed and they locked the cell behind them.

They went directly to the cell that held Victor Spectre. Spectre waited for them at the bars. His cell-mate had awakened and suddenly realized what was at hand. "Take me along," he pleaded. "Hell, man, I'm doin' life like the rest of you. You gotta take me."

"We do not have to take you anywhere," Spectre told him coldly.

A crafty light glimmered in close-set eyes. "You don't take me, I'll make a fuss, get you caught. It's a floggin' an' another five years for attempted escape. Best be takin' me."

Resignation blossomed on the face of Victor Spectre. He nodded curtly, and gestured toward the cell door. "You win. To prove there's no hard feelings, you can go out first."

A lust for freedom glowed in pale blue eyes. "Now, that's mighty white of you."

When he stepped forward to stand at the door, Victor Spectre slid a hand-fashioned stone shank out of the sleeve of his shirt, gripped the cloth-wrapped hilt, and drove the needle point deep into the right kidney of the other prisoner. Swiftly he slashed from side to side, withdrew it and destroyed the second vital organ. The man would bleed to death internally in less than four minutes, Spectre knew.

"Let's get going," he commanded as he eased the rapidly becoming corpse onto a bunk.

Once outside, the trio headed for the barred stairway at the opposite end of the corridor from where the turnkey had appeared. They moved on tiptoes to reduce any chance of discovery. Fortunately for them, the prison authorities insisted that all metal objects be well tended and frequently oiled, to insure swift entry into the yard or cell blocks in the event of trouble. The key turned noiselessly and the bolt slid back.

Stealthily, the three escapees traversed the stairs and came upon the first guard in his corner tower. His chin rested on his chest and soft, wet snores rumbled up from his throat. Buckner bashed him in the side of the head to insure he would not awaken for a while, then hoisted the slumped body and dumped him over the side. The other pair crawled along the parapet to the middle watch post. They found this guard staring out toward the river, contrary to his standing orders to look inward at the prison.

On a signal from Spectre, they swarmed over him and knocked him out without raising any alarm from the other watchers. In a second, he joined his fellow guard at the foot of the wall. Spectre motioned Buckner forward and began to fasten one end of his rope to a roof support of the midwall tower. Tinsdale did the same as did Buckner when he reached them. They slid down the rampart with surprising ease, only to find their ropes some fifteen feet short. The barrier had been footed in bedrock and the yard was that much higher than the ground outside.

Not liking it, though liking the alternatives even less, Victor Spectre let go and dropped to the rocky ground below. Good fortune went with him. He did not twist an ankle on any loose stones. Tinsdale came next and hit on his rump with a solid whump. Lastly, Buckner let go and plummeted to earth. Sharp pain shot through his left ankle.

He had severely sprained it. "What do we do now?" he bleated.

"Go on as planned. Ralph and I will find a boat, bring it here, and pick you up."

Twenty minutes later, the blunt prow of a river punt came into view through the limited starlight. Biting back shafts of pain, Buckner hobbled to the gunwale and his companions hauled him aboard. Cloth-padded oarlocks moved with a soft rumble and thump as they pushed out into the stream, leaving the guards behind, one with a broken neck. They headed northeastward, although Mexico lay a scant few miles the other direction. It had been Tinsdale's contribution that they would stand a better chance by going the long way, which would be least expected, rather than south into sure capture by the Rurales in Mexico. All in all, it proved a clever twist in their plan.

On this third day of their fishing trip, Smoke Jensen sat on a large, water-smoothed, flat rock and watched Bobby cast his line in lazy serpentines across the surface of Honey Spring. Smoke leaned on one elbow, took a puff on a cigar, and reflected on their time alone together as the gray white streamers drifted upward from his mouth. He felt he had made some progress with the boy.

Bobby had opened up to him, more so than any time in the past. For the first time the boy had released the pent-up sorrow and horror over his mother's death and freely grieved for her. She had not abandoned her son, as Bobby fantasized, rather she had been taken away by Rupe Connors. Rupe had been a brute and a sadist and had turned out to be a coward. He had abused the woman and the boy and in the end he had killed her with his fists and boots. And, for his cowardliness, as much as his savagery, Smoke Jensen had killed Rupe. Bobby understood those things more clearly now. Sally had been right, as usual, in saying that Bobby had transferred his large store of unexpressed love and hero worship to Smoke. The last mountain man only hoped that he had enough years left to see Bobby grow into a man. A sudden movement on the water brought Smoke abruptly upright.

A big old brown broke the surface and went for the man-made dry fly at the end of Bobby's line. The boy was a natural fisherman, more so than Smoke. He knew instinctively just when to set the hook, how hard to yank and how long to play the catch before landing it. He was in the process once again of doing so when his bare foot slipped on a mossy rock and with a shout, Bobby fell into the water.

"Ow! Ouch, my ankle," Bobby cried immediately. Then, "Get him, Smoke. Hurry or he'll get away."

Trout, line, and pole had started away from the shore of the pond. Smoke bounded into the water and snagged the cane rod by the butt, yanked and retrieved enough to fight the fish. Over one shoulder he called to Bobby. "Get out of the water. Now. You'll catch your death."

" 'Kay, Smoke, if you say so. Oh! Ouch. That really hurts."

"Don't be a baby," Smoke teased.

Bobby glared at him. "I ain't a baby. But, I'm cold, an' my foot really hurts."

Dripping, Bobby climbed from Honey Spring pond and

stood on shore, which prompted Smoke to be bossy again. "Get out of those clothes and wrap up in a blanket. I'll build a fire after I catch your blasted fish."

Twenty minutes later found them drying off beside a hat-sized fire. Bobby's teeth still chattered and he had a blue ring around his lips. Water dripped from his longish blond hair and the sharp points of his shoulder blades could be seen through the blanket that covered him. All of that did not keep him from a fit of giggles when Smoke described what he had been forced to do in order to land the brown trout. The titters dried up and Bobby looked seriously at Smoke.

"It's sure too bad that these mountain waters aren't like those around Model and Timpas. I mightily long to go for a swim."

Smoke sighed. "That's something you'll have to live without in this part of Colorado."

"Awh, darn." Then the boy brightened. "Don't you think, maybe by July, the water'll be warm enough? It is in Big Rock."

Shaking his head, Smoke patted Bobby on one shoulder. "It might be for you, but to me it's too dang cold. Now, get to work at warming up."

When the shivers ceased, Smoke examined Bobby's ankle. What he saw troubled him. "I don't think it's broken, but that ankle is swollen too much to get it back in your boot. Get dressed while I think on what to do next."

"Yes, sir."

When Bobby had restored himself in his clothing, he turned an anxious face to Smoke. Smoke Jensen rubbed his jaw with long, thick fingers. "You're not going to be able to keep on out here. Thing to do is turn back to the Sugarloaf."

Bobby frowned. "What about the fish you were going to smoke?"

"I figure they'll get smoked like we intended."

"How?"

Smoke smiled and explained. "I figure since you know where the house is from here, and you're big enough anyway, you can ride on in by yourself."

"Really?" Bobby squeaked. "You mean it?"

"Yep. That's the long and the short of it. I'll help you load up and see you on your way, then come back and pull out a nice mess and get to it. Tell Sally I'll ride in late the day after tomorrow, right before supper."

Bobby all but jumped with excitement. "I really get to ride in by myself? It's—it's . . . stupendous!"

Fifteen minutes later saw the injured boy on his way. Bobby had a .38 Colt Lightning tucked in his waistband and his Stetson sat at a jaunty angle on his straw-colored hair. He waved confidently to Smoke, who chuckled and waggled his hat in the air. Smoke wanted very much to give the lad confidence in his ability to care for himself. After all, he was thirteen now. *"He'll do fine,"* Smoke said gruffly to himself. "Just fine."

Early morning revealed that not only humans had responded to the siren call of early spring. While Smoke fished the shore of Honey Spring for big browns, a shaggy, ill-tempered grizzly awakened from his hibernation. Belly rumbles prompted him to crawl out of his cave and go in search of something to eat. Instinct aimed him toward Honey Spring.

Alone now, and content with it, Smoke continued to fish into mid-morning. When he made a dozen casts and failed to get a single rise, let alone a strike, he decided to quit until evening feeding time. He had already smoked two dozen and would set his morning's catch to a smudgy aspen and hickory fire right after his noon meal. With what he could catch this afternoon, he would have a fair supply to take home the next day. With his mind made up, he began to roll the line onto his pole. With his gear packed up, he turned to head for his camp.

Right then, a very hungry bear, fresh out of hibernation, ambled down to the water for something to eat. Its small, myopic eyes did not at first take in the figure of a lone human. The grizzly snuffed the wind, grunted and tossed its head in bad humor. That sure put Smoke in a dilemma. A fishing pole was no defense whatever, and a handgun— even a hefty .45 Colt—would hardly be enough to take on a bear. A moment later, the bruin discovered Smoke.

In its ill-tempered mood, the grizzly saw the man as a threat to its territory. With a thunderous roar the animal charged.

Far from being a starry-eyed animal lover, Smoke Jensen had never seen any purpose in the wanton killing of animals. So, he took flight, his creel and pole left behind. It soon turned into a close racc, with the speedy grizzly closing ground with each bound of its oddly articulated hind legs. Smoke won, though only by a hair.

He scaled the first twelve feet of the slender pine without even a grunt of effort. Once beyond the reach of the bear, he dug in his heels and shinnied up five more feet, grabbed the lowest branch, and pulled himself higher. With a powerful swing of his strong body, Smoke swung himself up to where he could straddle the branch. Now the sweat broke out. Smoke found himself panting for air. Below him the grizzly roared and assaulted the tree.

It made a good five feet, then began to slide back from sheer weight. Snuffling and tossing his head, the bear began to circle the pine. Above him, Smoke hung on and tried to think of something good happening.

After a third pass around the trunk, the bruin followed his nose to the wicker creel of trout and ripped it open. Voraciously it consumed every one, then went to the shore of the pond and waded out a ways. Competently, its long, sharp claws began to flash under the surface and come back out with a fat trout that flew sparkling through the air to land on the grassy bank. A disgruntled Smoke Jensen sat where he was and watched the bear work for an hour.

When it had its fill, perhaps it would amble away, Smoke reasoned. That would give him time to get down, get Thunder, and get the hell out of there.

Nightfall found the grizzly still there. He growled, yawned, grunted in frustration, stomped the ground, and made frequent trips from tree to pond and pond to tree. Smoke hung on and sweated. He removed his belt and fastened it around the trunk and retreaded the buckle. At least he would not fall asleep and become bruin breakfast. The ursine grumbling went on until a thin sliver of moon appeared to float majestically through the plethora of stars in an inky sky. At last, he fell asleep. So did Smoke. His last thought echoed in his head. *Maybe tomorrow will be a better day.*

A squat, bow-legged man, with grizzled, thinning hair, looked up from his kitchen table at the sound of a hollow thump that came from the small dock he had constructed out into the Colorado River. Visitors. And wouldn't you know it, right at breakfast time. Hiram Wells cut his eyes to the cloth-draped larder. He knew by heart what was within it.

Plenty of slab bacon. Only two eggs. Chickens had been acting offish lately. Flour for biscuits. Cornmeal, too. It would serve, and he could come out of it with a few cents in hard money. That would come in handy. Hiram pushed back his chair and came to his feet as he heard boots thud on the planks of his dock. He reached the door in time to count three men approaching at a stiff gait. One of them, he noted, limped. Too long in a boat, Hiram judged.

Yeah, but from where? And all night? The questions plagued him while the strangers approached. They came straight on, not even a howdy. The one in the lead nodded pleasantly.

"Mornin'. We'd be happy to pay if you could fix us something for breakfast."

Hiram pondered a moment. They stood and carried themselves like men of quality. Businessmen or the like. Yet they wore the thread-bare pull-over shirts and butternut linsey-woolsey trousers, with the broad black stripes that marked them as escaped convicts from the prison down-river at Yuma. A sudden chill struck him. Had he let them get too close already? Hiram decided to hedge.

"I'm a tad light on supplies, gentlemen. But I reckon I can whip up some bacon and some scrambled eggs. Biscuits or cornbread. I've some honey."

"Fine, fine," the apparent leader said rapidly. "Anything will do. We're rather hungry."

He had that cultured way of speaking, Hiram noted. Could be he was mistaken about the clothes. They might be some back-Easty fashionable hunting togs. "Come on in, then," he invited.

Hiram went to the stove and turned his back to them. That way he failed to note the quick exchange between the trio. His cartridge belt and six-gun hung on a peg in the wall. Above it hung a shotgun and a use-shiny Winchester. Hiram heard a soft footfall and then the strident click of sear notches as a hammer ratcheted back.

Hiram did not hear the bark of his Model '60 Remington conversion revolver. The bullet beat the sound to his head by a split second. Hiram Wells slammed sideways into the wall and fell dead to the floor. Quickly, Ralph Tinsdale undertook the duties of the cook. He provided a warm meal in minimal time. Victor Spectre had to cut Olin Buckner out of his boot, then all three sat down to consume the food hurriedly. They included that which the late Hiram had prepared for himself.

With their bellies full, they took the flour, cornmeal, sugar and salt, a tub of lard, and the remaining portion of the bacon slab. Done up in a flour sack, the provender accompanied them as they went to the small barn in search of horses. An hour after sinking their escape boat, Victor Spectre and his partners rode off without a trace.

Morning found Smoke Jensen still literally up a tree. He awakened to loud growling—from the bear and from his stomach. He had not eaten since the previous noon. Smoke opened gummy eyes and rubbed them, then looked down to find the grizzly reared back on his haunches, staring up He had a hungry expression. A night in a tree without even a blanket had induced a lot of stiffness. Smoke hoped that it would not make him a quick snack for the bear. Abruptly, the bruin came to all fours and resumed his circular post around the pine tree.

With each pace on the left side, the grizzly emitted fearsome growls. Each with the right, disturbing rumbles. Smoke looked on and considered his chances of killing the creature with six loads. At least he might incapacitate the animal and not have to track it down later. He had about resigned himself to having to shoot the creature when it stopped pacing abruptly and reared on its massive hind legs.

Its small, pig-eyes stared myopically while it turned its head from side to side, as it listened to slight sounds as yet unheard by Smoke. Gradually, Smoke made out faint hoof-beats and snatches of conversation. The bear's ears twitched, the black muzzle pointed in the direction of the sound. Dropping to all fours, the animal bolted for hiding in a lumbering gait as two riders cantered into view. Within three minutes, Smoke recognized them, grateful for the help, yet wishful that it had been anyone else but these two.

A laughing Monte Carson reined in under the tree. His face wreathed in mirth, Hank Evans sat beside him. "Hoo-haw! Look what we have here!" Monte chortled. Mid-morning sunlight winked off his sheriff's badge.

"What do you suppose got him up there?" Hank asked through a titter of laughter.

"Couldn't be that bear, could it?" Monte queried rhetorically. "That big ol' grizzly bear?" He held his sides and howled with merriment.

"You mean that little-bitty fur ball that got scared off by our horses?" Hank kept up the badinage.

"That's it. That's the one," Monte guffawed.

"This is it!" Smoke corrected, while he brandished a big, knobby fist. "This is the one that will smack you right between the runnin' lights when I get down out of this damned tree."

"Oh, why, come right ahead," Monte taunted.

Smoke glowered at them. "Do you think you two could stop cacklin' like a barnyard full of hens long enough to give me a hand getting down?"

Hank snaked a rope up to Smoke, who draped it over the limb. Then the last mountain man released himself from his emergency sling, restrung his belt and swung one leg over the branch. Balanced sideways, he inserted a boot toe in the loop of the lariat and turned around to hang from his hands.

"Lower away," he gave the sign.

In less than a minute, Smoke had returned to solid ground. His mood had not improved the least while Monte Carson and Hank Evans plied him with questions about how he had been caught off guard by the grizzly. Hank laid a fire and filled a coffeepot with fresh water. He set that to boil and broke out Smoke's skillet.

"I'll bet your hungry, right?" he asked of Smoke dryly.

"Don't even mention it."

"Bacon, eggs, an' fried tatters?" Hank prompted.

"A pound of bacon, a dozen eggs, and two pounds of potatoes with onions, if you please," Smoke answered calmly. "And that's just for starters." Then his temper caught him out again. *"And I don't like bein' done for!"*

His voice echoed across the water in the silence that followed. As though on a signal all three men broke up in side-splitting laughter. Finally, Smoke choked out a sensible reply. "I'll tell you about it after the first cup of coffee."

Monte stepped forward, extending a silver flask in one hand. "I've got a little rye to spike it with."

"Good," Smoke grumped. "Damn good. Then you'll hear it all."

Three

After Smoke had recounted his incident with the bear, with frequent interruptions of sniggers and out-and-out hee-haw braying laughter, he got around to asking Monte what had brought the lawman out from Big Rock. Monte took a pull on his coffee, rubbed his chin in a contemplative manner, and turned his sky-blue eyes on Smoke.

"Well, it might not mean anything at all. It's something I picked up from the telegraph. Only, the names were familiar, and I did want an excuse to sample some of Sally's great pie, so I rode out to tell you about it."

"Well, then, stop chasin' around Murphy's barn and do it," Smoke responded in mock irritation.

"All right, I will. Three men have escaped from Yuma Prison."

It left Smoke unimpressed and unconcerned. "There's more than that has gotten out of there."

Monte ignored Smoke's teasing interruption. "These three went together. Beings as how you put all of them behind bars, I got to thinkin' that maybe you should know."

"Who are they?'

Monte named them. Smoke listened and shook his head. "I remember those three right well. I had no idea they had gotten together in prison. How'd a thing like that happen?"

Right at home with this sort of situation, Monte called off the list. "Attempted escape can get a man transferred. So can a killing inside prison that a certain convict cannot be proven to have done. Or just being a constant pain in the ass. There's plenty of causes. And, considering the Territorial Prison at Yuma is the hellhole of the entire system, no doubt the worst all wind up there eventually."

Smoke nodded affirmatively. "You've described Buckner, Spectre, and Tinsdale perfectly, Monte. They are all killers, they would no doubt contrive to escape, and beyond any doubt, they are all huge pains in the ass."

"There's more. They badly injured one guard, and killed another and a turnkey on the way out."

"Yep. I had no idea they'd been put together, like I said, but with these killings, it makes it clear that they're up to no good. Now, let's put out this fire and go look at a piece of that pie."

After the noon-hour rush, business had slackened off at the Grand Canyon saloon, in the Arizona town of the same name. Five cronies sat around a green baise-topped table playing a desultory game of poker. The hands took forever to be played and the largest bet was half a dollar. At another table, one sequestered in a shadow-darkened corner, Spectre, Tinsdale, and Buckner sat conducting business. They had been in the settlement on the rim of the Grand Canyon for less than a day. They had as yet to pay any notice to the spectacular view. Bored with the lack of activity, Buckner nodded toward the card players.

"Last of the big-time spenders."

Victor Spectre studied him over the rim of a whiskey glass. "I'd not sneer, were I you. Up until we killed that old man on the Colorado, the most you've had in your pocket for the last fifteen years is lint, Olin. You would have sold your soul for fifty cents cash money."

Buckner flushed deep red. That had hit too close to home. He had sold his soul, or at least it seemed like that, when he was younger and his need for tobacco had become overwhelming. He had stolen it. The first theft of his life. He lost his chance to make a testy reply when a tall, lean, hard-looking man approached their table. The stranger appeared to be in his mid-twenties, and did not remove his hat or act in the least servile, Olin Buckner noted. At a distance of three feet, the man stopped and cleared his throat.

"I hear you're lookin' to hire some men."

"We are. Are you, by chance, interested?" Victor Spectre responded.

A fleeting, icy smile spread full lips. "Not by chance, by lack of other employment. What is it you are hiring for?"

"We need men good with their guns. And I like to know the name of any man I'm talking business with."

"My name's Jaeger. Gus Jaeger. M'given name is Augustus, but it's a lot to work your tongue around, so I shortened it. And who might you be?"

"I am Victor Spectre, these gentlemen are my partners in this little endeavor. Ralph Tinsdale and Olin Buckner. Now, Mr. Jaeger, take a seat and we can discuss this a little further."

When Jaeger took one of the straight-back chairs, reversed it and seated himself, Spectre signaled the bartender for a round. When that had been duly delivered and the apron absented himself, Spectre steepled his fingers on the green table and spoke in a low voice.

"It did not take much initiative or effort for us to do a little research. I suppose your current unemployment has something to do with the three years you spent in prison for stagecoach robbery, Mr. Jaeger. The others in the gang got considerably more time, am I correct?"

Gus Jaeger went white from anger and clinched a fist before answering. His cold, hazel eyes burned under black brows. "You're right about that. The reason is I hadn't pulled as many jobs with the boys as they got caught for.

What business is it of yours to go snoopin' into a man's past?"

"Oh, we did not do anything so shady, believe me. We simply went through some of the sheriff's old wanted posters and reviewed past issues of the newspapers. Your name came up, along with some others. We left invitations in their postal boxes, like the one you received. So far, you are the first to respond."

Jaeger's full, fleshy lips pulled wide in a rueful grin. He removed his Montana Peak Stetson, revealing thick, black hair, and sailed it toward a row of hooks on the near wall. It caught and held. By then he had recovered himself enough to speak calmly.

"I'm surprised there has not been more interest. What exactly do you have in mind?"

"There is this man. He needs doing away with," Spectre evaded.

Jaeger looked them over with a puzzled frown. "You want to hire a killing? There's three of you. Why don't you simply find him and do it yourselves?"

"It's—well, it is not quite that easy," Spectre still tried to avoid naming the target.

"Why not? Is he a gunfighter?"

"Yes, Mr. Jaeger, he is."

Smiling, Jaeger knocked back his whiskey and tilted his chair away from the table. "Well, then, you needn't worry about any other applicants. There's not anyone around that's better than me in a one-on-one shoot-out. I could even handle two to one, if necessary. If you gentlemen are satisfied, you've got yourself all the gunhand you'll need. By the way, who is this gunfighter?"

It's—ah—Smoke Jensen," Spectre regretfully gusted out.

Jaeger's chair legs banged noisily back onto the floor and his jaw sagged. Belatedly, he closed his mouth and swallowed hard. "If I weren't so hard up for work, I'd tell you just how crazy you are and high-tail it out of here."

Tinsdale responded dryly. "You've heard of him, I gather?"

"*Heard* of him? I grew up readin' penny dreadfuls about Smoke Jensen. If only a quarter of it was true, he's pure hell on wheels. Not anyone I'd want to go up against alone. Hell, I'd be afraid to even try to back-shoot him."

"It is wise to have a healthy respect for an adversary," Spectre stated flatly. "Though hardly good to fear someone you are engaged to dispose of. Are you sure you can conquer your awe of Jensen long enough to make an end of him?"

After a long moment of careful thought, Jaeger made reply. "Of course I can. Especial, I've got me three or four good boys to back me up."

Victor Spectre responded almost primly. "We were thinking of more like twenty. Very well, Mr Jaeger, consider yourself hired. We will, naturally, pay for your hotel accommodations and meals, with a two dollar a day stipend until we are ready to move on."

"Is Smoke Jensen here, in Arizona?"

"Not that we know of. We assume we will need to do something to flush him out of his high valley ranch in the Colorado Rockies. Until we are in a position to do that, we must build up a sizable gang to make things happen as we want them to. Now, you can do us a first service. Spread the word to those of like inclination. Tell them we are prepared to be most generous." He paused a moment and pinned Jaeger with his cold eyes. "Only don't tell them who they'll be facing."

After Gus Jaeger departed Olin Buckner spoke what was on all their minds. "A good thing that old man was a miser, or we'd not be able to be so generous."

"Yes, quite," Spectre answered. "We will have to act

quickly to replenish our purse after our recruiting is ended here, Olin."

"What did you have in mind, Victor?" Tinsdale asked.

"We have engaged the services of an expert highwayman. I think we should find out all we can about the stage lines coming into here and what they carry."

Buckner brightened. "Yes. And there are banks along the way, too. By the way, where are we going?"

Spectre spoke in a tone that suggested he had been thinking on the subject for a long while. "North. Perhaps as far as into Wyoming. There's a place there guaranteed to make Smoke Jensen come to us."

"Where's that?" Tinsdale demanded.

"Later. You will all know when the time is right."

Over the next three days, they learned all that could be expected about the stage lines. Spectre and his partners also interviewed close to twenty-five men. Among them certified hard cases, murderers, and a number of outlaw wanna-bes. They rejected all but two of the latter, and one of the killers, who had an odd cast in his eye that made him appear to be studying them for the best method of making their deaths long and excruciating. That left the trio of vengeance-hungry felons a total of seventeen gunhands.

"We'll get more along the way," Spectre advised them philosophically.

"Why do we need more?"

Spectre smiled patronizingly. "Simple, Olin. We have to have a veritable army to take over an entire town."

Eyebrows climbed Buckner's forehead. "What town?"

"In due time, Olin. At the right moment, everyone will know. Please, do not bring up the subject again. Uh—Mr. Jaeger, notify the others that we will be leaving early tomorrow morning."

"Right away, Boss. And—ah—call me Gus, everyone does. And I can call you . . . ?"

"*Mister* Spectre," Victor interrupted.

An hour after first light, the eighteen hard cases rode out of Grand Canyon with the partners. They left by twos and threes in order not to attract unwanted attention. Twenty miles out of town, where the trail disappeared around the curved base of a large hill, Victor Spectre called a halt.

"Men, Gus here has considerable experience at holding up stage coaches. Miller and Brock, as I understand, have some acquaintance with the technique also."

An erstwhile thug named Huntoon screwed up his face and, in an Appalachian accent, asked a baby-faced gunfighter named Carpenter next to him, "What's that feller say?"

Carpenter cut his pale ice-blue eyes to Huntoon. "He says Jaeger, Miller, an' Brock have robbed themselves a few stages."

Brow furrowed, Huntoon considered this. "That a fact?"

Spectre ignored the aside and went on. "In a short while, a stage, heavily laden with the payroll for the Valle del Cobre mine will be coming around that curve. We are going to rob it. In order to do this, you will follow the orders of Mr. Jaeger. Misters Miller and Brock will direct the two phases of the operation. Obey them as you would myself and we shall all enjoy the spoils."

"We gonna split it up share for share?" Huntoon raised his voice to inquire.

"No. My partners and I shall use the proceeds to pay you your new wage of ten dollars a day."

An excited murmur ran through the outlaws and thugs. The only objection came from Huntoon. "Now that's mighty generous, Mr. Spectre, but we'd prefer equal shares."

Victor Spectre's face flushed dark red. Fury burned in his green eyes, and sparks crackled in his voice. "And would you also prefer to be left stone dead beside the trail?"

"Uh—no, sir. Not at all, nosir."

"Then leave the financial affairs of this jolly band to your betters, Mr Huntoon."

Huntoon's mouth almost got him dead after all. "What d'y'all mean my betters?' Y'all may talk lak a dandy but you ain't nothin' more than another jailbird on the run. I done seed the flyer in the post office."

Thunder rumbled and lightning flashed in Spectre's harsh rejoinder. *"We are your betters,* you hillbilly trash, for the simple reason that we can read and write and we do not dally with our cousins and sisters."

Had it been any other man, or had he not seen Carpenter, a feller he thought of as a friend, put his hand on the butt of his Colt, Huntoon would have dragged iron. Instead he lowered his eyes and spoke softly as he would to his father. "Yes, Boss. Your right, Boss." It didn't keep him from brooding on the idea of a future feud.

Victor Spectre did not even attempt to hide the smirk on his lips. "Very well. Gus, divide the men according to your needs and get them in position. We haven't much time."

Twenty minutes later the keener ears among the gang picked up the faint jingle and slap of chain and tack over the rumble of hooves and crunch of iron-shod tires. Before long the creaking of the coach could be heard. It surprised Victor to see the nervousness of so many among his band of desperados. He trusted that they would perform better than it looked like they could.

The flying manes and outstretched necks of the coach horses came into view around the curve. At once, men rode out of the brush and trees to either side of the trail and fired at the men on the driver's bench. Others blocked the roadway and two of them reached for the lead horses. A shotgun boomed and one of the outlaws screamed horribly.

More gunshots crackled from the robbers and the guard slumped dead.

A moment later, the driver dropped the reins and threw up his hands. He pitched forward over the dashboard and fell to the tongue. The horses came to a calamitous halt, the hind four ramming forward into the rumps of those ahead. Swaying wildly, the coach juddered to a halt. From inside, a lone passenger fired a futile, unwise shot. Three rounds answered him.

Silence followed. Then, the unseen passenger groaned as the masked men walked their mounts to the coach. Fin Brock dismounted and opened the door. The wounded passenger leaned outward and two highwaymen helped him from the stage. They sat him against a boulder and ignored him thereafter. It took little time to discover the three large strongboxes filled with gold and silver coin.

Men cheered at the sight. At the direction of Gus Jaeger, the stage horses were unhitched and their harness altered to serve as pack bearing tack. One iron-banded crate went on each of three, alone with some of the load from the gang's pack animals. With loads lightened, the hard-faced men removed their bandana masks and rode off without any thought for the wounded passenger.

Four

Spectre, Tinsdale, and Buckner remained very much on the mind of Smoke Jensen as he rode into Big Rock to telegraph the prison for more details. An emergency breeched foal and other ranch minutia had prevented him from returning to town with Monte Carson. Now, a week later, he dwelled on the circumstances of the men whose criminal careers he had interrupted. There wasn't a one of them who did not get what he deserved.

With such dark broodings filling his head, Smoke ambled spotted-rump Thunder onto the northern end of Central Street, the main drag of Big Rock. The recent craze for naming every street in the small community amused Smoke. He considered it *pretentious,* one of the fancy words Sally had taught him. He did not think what he discovered halfway down the first block of the business district to be pretentious, nor did it amuse him.

A burly man, a stranger to these parts, stood between the driver's seat and dashboard of a heavy wagon. Muscles rippled in his thick shoulders as he plied a whip to lash the daylights out of a pair of scrawny, sway-backed mules, trapped in the harness of the overloaded rig they pulled.

"I'll learn ya, gawdamnit, you stubborn, stupid critters. When I say haul, you by damnit haul. Now git to movin'."

Smoke Jensen just naturally bristled at this unnecessary cruelty. He eased his 'Palouse stallion closer and tipped the brim of his hat back on his head. For all his sudden anger at this abuse, he kept his voice polite.

"Excuse me." The huge teamster ignored Smoke. "I said, excuse me. I don't think you will achieve the results you expect by beating these starved, worn-out animals any longer."

The burly driver turned to face Smoke. "Mind yer own gawdamned business. These lazy bastids, all they do is eat and sleep and crap. Hell, they even sleep standin' up. Now, git on outta here and leave me to what I have to do."

When the teamster turned away and applied his whip again, Smoke edged Thunder closer to the wagon. He reached out with one big hand and lifted the man off his feet. With a touch of his heels, Smoke backed Thunder clear of the buckboard and released his grip on the astonished wagoneer. Then Smoke calmly dismounted while the astonished lout dropped to his boots in the dusty street.

Blinded by rage, the foolish man went at Smoke with the whip. In one swift move, Smoke deflected the lash with his left forearm, grabbed the braided leather scourge and yanked it from the man's grasp. Smoke's right hand got right busy snapping short jabs to the thick lips of the dolt. Rocked back on his heels, the errant teamster belatedly brought up his arms in an effort to end the punishment. Smoke Jensen merely changed targets.

Hard knuckles dug into the puss gut of the abusive dullard. Coughing out air, the man did manage to land one blow that stung Smoke's left cheekbone. Smoke responded with a looping left that opened a cut on his opponent's right brow. A red curtain lowered over the teamster's right eye. He uttered a bull-roar of outrage and tried to grab Smoke in a bear hug.

Smoke danced back from it, and popped his target on one fat jowl. He felt teeth give beneath the layer of fat. Then the stranger tried a kick to Smoke's groin. Smoke side-stepped it and grabbed the offending leg. He gave it a quick yank upward.

"Phaw!" the teamster bellowed when his rump contacted the hard-packed street.

Smoke closed with him and battered his head seriously. Groggy, the owner of the mules tried to stand. Smoke knocked him flat on his back with a left to the jaw. Satisfied that he had taken all of the fight out of the man, Smoke turned his back and strode toward Thunder. He barely heard the scrabble of boot soles on the pebble-strewn street as the battered man came at Smoke with a knife.

Bert Fowler had never been given such a humiliation in his entire life. Always big for his age, he had bullied and brow-beaten even children older than himself. As he grew, he had filled out, both in muscle and in flab. Bert loved to eat. Six eggs, two pork chops, a couple of slabs of cornmeal mush, and a half dozen biscuits he considered a light breakfast. He routinely ate a whole chicken when he sat down to be serious about it. That came with the better part of a serving bowl of mashed potatoes, a quart of gravy, and more biscuits to mop up the run-over. Bert liked his run-overs.

By the time he was a man full-grown, he stood an inch over six feet and weighed 257 pounds. When Smoke Jensen lifted him off his wagon, he had increased that to an even 300. Now, bruised, cut, and bleeding, his ribs and gut aching pools of fire, Bert got set on revenge. From his boot top he retrieved a long, thin-bladed dagger and pushed himself upright. Wiping blood out of his right eye, he went directly for the back of the man who had assaulted him so viciously.

Smoke heard the rush of boot soles at the last moment. He jumped to one side and slapped instinctively at the hand that held the knife. Bert Fowler staggered a bit off course, but whirled in time to confront his enemy. Smoke Jensen saw no reason to kill this lout. Even though faced with the danger of a knife, he eschewed the use of his trusty .45 Colt Peacemaker. In the fleeting instant when both men stood in locked study of one another, he decided to give the errant teamster a taste of his own medicine.

Cat-quick, Smoke bent at the knees and recovered the handle of Fowler's whip. He came up with the lash seething through the air in a backward motion beside his ear. He sensed when it reached its maximum extension and brought his arm forward. Fowler screamed when the nasty little lead tip he had affixed to his bullwhip bit into the flesh of his right shoulder.

He retained his grasp on the knife regardless, and lunged forward with the tip extended toward the heart of Smoke Jensen. Smoke cracked the whip again. This time he cut through the front of Fowler's shirt and left a long, red welt on pallid flesh. Fowler howled with pain. He took two more staggering steps toward his hated opponent.

Smoke met him with another rapid, three cut criss-cross that opened the entire front of his assailant's shirt. Blood ran from the rent flesh. Fowler reversed the knife and made to throw it. Smoke Jensen sliced the dagger from his hand. Relentlessly the flogging went on.

Smoke moved from side to side, the strap cut into the bulging shoulders of Bert Fowler, tore away the remains of his shirt and began to checker his back. He bent double, intent now on merely protecting his face. Smoke had no intention of marking him there, and laid on the flail with unemotional exactness. The trousers came next.

Long gaps in the trouser legs showed equally white human legs beneath, albeit stout as beer kegs. They did not remain so for long. By the time Smoke Jensen had cut the cloth away at mid-thigh, in the manner sometimes worn by small boys, those legs had become rivers of blood. This would be one beating Smoke determined the man would never forget. Fowler went to his knees, howled pitifully, then finally cringed into a whimpering mass of cut and bleeding flesh. Smoke Jensen relented.

Stalking over to the badly mauled teamster, Smoke tossed the bloody whip into the wagon box and stared down at the product of his efforts. "Tell me," he asked politely, "Did you enjoy feeling like your mules must have?" Then he turned away, remounted Thunder and rode off down the street.

Smoke Jensen tied off Thunder outside the telegraph office at the railroad depot in Big Rock. His boots rang on the thick two by six planks of the platform as he crossed to the door. Inside, the telegrapher sat in his bay window that overlooked the tracks. Coatless, he had sleeve garters to hold up the long sleeves of his light blue shirt with the white vertical pinstripes. Three cigars protruded from the upper pocket of his vest. A green eyeshade obscured his face. He looked up as Smoke approached the counter.

"Afternoon, Mr. Jensen. What can I do for you?"

"I'd like to send a telegraph message."

Rising from his chair, the telegrapher came to the counter. "Do you have it written out?"

"No. I'll do that now."

An octagonal-faced Regulator clock ticked out the seconds while Smoke wrote his query on the yellow form. It was clear, concise, and direct. He hoped the answer would be the same, and come quickly. When he finished, he handed the missive over to the telegraph operator, who glanced at it and raised an eyebrow.

"You—ah—expecting company, Mr. Jensen?"

He remembered when the famous Smoke Jensen and Monte Carson had stood back to back and battled a nest of outlaws in the streets of Big Rock. They had cut them down mercilessly and driven the remainder out of town. The village had been right tame since then.

"I don't think so. And, I'm going to do my best to see nothing unusual happens."

Relief flooded the face of the railroad employee. He counted the number of words. "That'll be two and a quarter. I'll get this out right away. If a reply comes in soon, where can I reach you?"

"I'll be over at Monte's office." Smoke paid him and left.

Back astride Thunder, Smoke ambled along the main street to the low, stone building next to the town hall. He looped the reins over the tie-rail and gained the stoop. Inside the stout, thick door, Monte Carson sat at his desk, a report form from the night man in one hand, a steaming cup of coffee in the other. He glanced up as Smoke entered.

"Didn't take you long to decide to look into that a little more, did it?"

"No, Monte. It just sat in my head and gnawed until I had to find out all I could."

"Pour yerself some java. Herkimer just got in some fresh beans over at the Mercantile." Then he noticed the disarray of Smoke's shirt. "What did you get into?"

Smoke snorted and tugged at his shirttail. While he poured, he told Monte about the stranger and his mules. Monte listened, nodded at the proper spots, and then rendered his judgment. "It's a wonder the feller didn't get himself a sudden case of the deads."

"If he had pulled a gun, instead of that knife, he would have."

"That's cold Smoke, downright cold," Monte said with a twinkle in his eyes.

They drank coffee and talked about the latest goings on in Big Rock for a quarter past an hour. Monte was in mid-sentencing, telling Smoke about how Bluenosed Bertha, one of the bar girls at the Follies saloon, had gotten her finger caught in a mousetrap when the door swung outward.

"What's this?" the lawman demanded.

In the opening stood a boy of about eleven or twelve.

Barefoot, he had a thick thatch of carroty hair above a balloon face of rusty-orange freckles. His unfastened trouser legs ended at mid-calf, which gave him the look of an urchin. "For Mr. Jensen, Sheriff. We got an answer back from the folks out in Arizona Territory."

Smoke took the folded, yellow form and handed the boy a dime. The lad's eyes went wide. "Oh-boy! A whole dime. Thank you, Mr Jensen."

He scampered off down Central Street, no doubt to the general mercantile and those inviting glass jars of horehound drops and rock candy. Smoke opened the message and read from it. His eyebrows rose and he whistled softly at the conclusion. He gestured toward Monte Carson with the sheet of paper.

"They've learned a bit more since that first telegram. The warden verified that they killed two guards and seriously injured another in their escape. The search has been fruitless in Mexico. But a hermit, by the name of Hiram Wells, who lived up-river from the prison was found murdered and his horses missing."

"That fits with what the warden says a trustee told him. Which is that the three of them formed an alliance to get revenge on some unnamed man responsible for them all being in prison. A man who lives somewhere up in the mountain country."

Monte Carson looked hard at Smoke Jensen. "He didn't have a name, huh?"

"That's what it says. Although it doesn't take a whiz at arithmetic to add up one and one and get two."

Brow furrowed now in concentration, Monte reached a conclusion. "I think you an' me, an' a couple of good deputies had ought to ride up to the Sugarloaf and fort up. That's what I think."

Smoke shook his head. "No offense, Monte, but I don't think that's such a hot idea. No sense in bringing the fight home with us. In fact, the farther I can keep Spectre, Tinsdale, and Buckner from the Sugarloaf, the happier I will be."

Genuine concern for his long-time friend colored Monte's words. "What do you have in mind?"

"I reckon to head into some friendly territory up Wyoming way. Say, maybe Jackson's Hole. I can settle in, make my presence known, and let the word get out. Then let them come."

"Think they'll do it on their own?"

"No, Monte, they'll bring along help. Spectre used to run a large band of outlaws, numbered around forty. He's known along the Owl Hoot Trail. If he feels the need, he can get all the men he needs."

"Why do you single him out as the leader of all this, Smoke?"

"Because I came close to blowing out his brains in the showdown we had. And I killed his only son. But, look at it this way. When they come for me, and they will, I'll have these would-be avengers on ground I am well familiar with and they know little about. That'll go a long way toward evening the odds."

Monte could not let it go. "I hope you're right. I sure's hell do."

Hanksville, in Utah, hovered on the edge of Ute country. As yet, the native dwellers of the sparse ground had not been corralled and driven onto a small, unpromising reservation in the southern corner of Colorado. They roamed free. It was doubtful that more than a handful of politicians in Washington knew that they existed. Not until the arid land they occupied offered something of value would they come under the scrutiny of the Bureau of Indian Affairs. Hanksville had a white population of fifty-seven and a scattering of Mexican and halfbreed residents. It also served as a transient haven for men on the run.

Victor Spectre came there to recruit more guns for his gang. He had little difficulty in achieving that. Eleven hard cases signed on. Men with shifty eyes and a day or more growth of beard, they found the pay acceptable and the promise of a bonus for killing just a single man satisfying. There were no saloons in Hanksville, so the outlaws drank in their rooms and Victor ordered a quick departure when he had all of the reinforcements he could expect to obtain. So far their travels had paralleled the Colorado River. Here they would make a change.

Five miles outside of town to the east, he halted the growing band and gathered them around. "We're heading north from here."

"How far north?" one fellow with an over-fondness for the desert asked with a gimlet eye.

"Quite a ways."

"Thought you said this feller we're to kill lives in Colorado?"

"He does, but we're not going there."

Upon hearing that, Fin Brock looked hard at Spectre, doubt clear in his narrow face. "Then how are we gonna get him?"

Spectre's answer was simple enough for anyone. "We make him come to us."

Farlee Huntoon got in his nickel's worth. "Easier said than done, I reckon. 'Specially if he finds out how many of us there is."

Others agreed. Huntoon pushed his luck. "One man alone, he don't have to come up again' us, lessen he chooses to."

Victor Spectre's voice crackled in reply. "There are ways, Mr. Huntoon, to make a man do anything you want him to. If you weren't such a dolt, you'd know that."

"Say what? Was you tryin' to insult me, Mr. Spectre?"

Victor spoke lightly, his face unreadable and his tone dry.

"No, Mr. Huntoon. I was praising the remarkable lack of genius engendered in the terminally inbred."

"Well—ah—okay, I reckon that's no insult then. Ain't often I get praised."

"No, I expect not." Spectre turned away.

One of the new men, Judson Reese, better spoken and dressed than the average, touched his hat brim in a sort of salute. "If we cannot have the exact location, can you at least give us a general idea of our destination?"

Spectre beamed at him. "I admire a well-spoken man. Yes, I'll answer that, since you've put it so nicely. In the short term, I feel you men need some recreation. Especially after being in that straight-laced place. We shall pay a visit to the Utes. I hear there is a prosperous trading post not far north of here. Then we will be going on to Wyoming, perhaps even Montana. But, rest assured, wherever we go, Smoke Jensen will come to us."

Back on the Sugarloaf, Sally Jensen knew something had gone terribly wrong for her husband the moment he rode up the lane to the main house. His usually high, smooth brow wore lines of furrows. He kissed her somewhat absently, then hugged her tightly to his chest as though it would be the last time.

"What is it, Smoke?"

Neither he nor Monte Carson had mentioned the real cause of Monte's visit to the ranch a week earlier. Now Smoke found himself at a loss as to how to explain. So, he used the time-honored tactic of husbands everywhere. He evaded.

"It's nothing important. I'll tell you over supper. And—ah—ask Bobby to take supper with us, too, please."

That worried Sally even more. Good wife that she was, though, she remained quiet about it. She fixed them a choice rib roast from a steer recently slaughtered out of the

small herd kept for that purpose—Smoke would like that—
and mounds of mashed potatoes—Bobby would like that—
with pan gravy, turnips, and a half gallon, blue Mason jar
of wilted lettuce put up last summer. She had already baked
a pie.

They ate and Smoke related only the gossip he had picked
up in Big Rock that he knew would interest Sally. Then,
over a second piece of pie and a cup of coffee, Smoke
grudgingly drug out the topic he least wanted to discuss.

"Sally, do you remember when Monte rode out here a
while ago?"

"How could I not? It was only last week."

"What you are not aware of is why he came." And he
went on to give her a highly edited version of the escape
and the backgrounds of the men involved. When he had
finished, Sally sat with her hands in her lap and stared at
the checked tablecloth. At last, she raised her head and
spoke somewhat shakily.

"What is it you are going to do?"

Smoke frowned. Now came the hard part. "I am going
to be gone for a while. It's me they want, not you, or the
hands, or even Bobby. Odds are they are unaware he exists.
I'll put some distance between us and then let it be known
where I am. The word will get to them. They'll come. And
then I will take care of them the way I should have the first
time around."

Sally said it plainly enough that its tone of resignation
nearly broke Smoke's heart. "You'll kill them."

"If that's what it takes." He broke his hazel gaze from
her steady, demanding eyes. "We can hope it ends otherwise."

Bobby suddenly charged into the conversation. "I want
to go with you, Smoke."

"No. That's out of the question. I have to do this alone
and not endanger anyone else. Monte even offered me depu-

ties and his own help to defend the Sugarloaf. I told him no. My way is the best."

"I'm big enough," Bobby protested. "You've gotta let me come. I can shoot and I've been practicin' with rifle and six-gun. Ike says I'm a far above average shot, even from horseback. And you taught me how to live in the mountains."

Smoke needed little effort to sound stern. "Not another word, young man."

Sally got right to the most painful item. "When?"

"I'll leave first thing tomorrow morning."

Tears swam in Sally's eyes as she cleared the table, and she brushed them away angrily. He was her man and he would do what he thought best. Though if he would listen to anyone, it was she. Sally tried to use that power sparingly. His feelings hurt, Bobby excused himself early to go to the bunkhouse.

That night, laying in bed, Smoke reached out and tenderly took Sally in his arms. She came eagerly and they had a long, tender, passionate parting. The one in the morning would be a facade, a formality for the hands who would witness it.

Pale gray hovered over the eastern ridge as Smoke Jensen came from the kitchen door and took up the reins to his pack horse and Thunder and turned back to the open doorway. Sally hesitated only a second, then lifted her skirt and apron and ran to his embrace. He held her tightly and she did a remarkable job of holding back the tears.

Stuff and nonsense, she thought angrily as she felt the burning behind closed lids. She had seen her man off to danger a hundred times before and not acted so childishly. She pulled back and they kissed hungrily.

"You take care of yourself, Smoke Jensen."

"Yes, ma'am, I'll be sure to do that," Smoke said with wry humor.

They kissed again and Smoke swung into the saddle. He looked around, wondering why Bobby had not come out to see him off. With a light-hearted wave he parted from his wife and set out down the lane to the main gate of the Sugarloaf. As he neared it, he saw a forlorn figure waiting for him there.

Bobby did not argue or even plead. His looks said it all. His throat worked to fight back the lump, his big, blue eyes pooled with tears. He worked lids rapidly to fight them back, determined not to shed them in a shameful display. After all, if he was going to prove he was big enough to go with Smoke, he had to be too old to cry like a baby. Hope died hard in the breast of a thirteen-year-old. It crashed suddenly and swiftly for Bobby when he heard Smoke's soft, sincere words.

"No, Bobby, you still can't go. I'll see you when this is over."

Bobby had to force the words past the thickness in his throat. The effort caused his hat to fall from his head and hang by its string. "Wh-When will that be, Smoke?"

"Only the Almighty knows that, son."

"Then don't go, Smoke. Please don't go."

Smoke Jensen shook his head at the intensity of the boy's concern. "I have to, Bobby, there is really no other choice. Some day, something will happen in your life and you'll know for yourself. Now, goodbye."

Fear clutched Bobby's heart. "No. Don't say that. Just say so long."

Smoke reached out and ruffled Bobby's snowy hair. "All right. So long, pardner."

Then he turned Thunder's head and rode off to the north.

Five

Smoke Jensen no sooner got out of the basin that sheltered the Sugarloaf than he discovered that the word had gotten out on the owl hoot telegraph. It came at him in the form of two proddy young gunhands who trotted along the trail toward him. They reined in and touched fingertips to hat brims by way of greeting. Then, the one on the right who had carroty hair and buckteeth below pale green eyes the color of arctic ice, spoke with the over-confident sneer of youth.

"You familiar with these parts, old-timer?"

Old-timer? Although there was a touch of gray in his hair, Smoke hardly thought of himself as an old-timer. It brought forth a testy response from him.

"I might be, depends on who's askin', sonny-boy."

Chill eyes flashing, the punk leaned toward Smoke in a threatening manner. "I'm askin', old man, and you'd best be answerin', hear?"

There was that word again. Damn! "What is it you'd like to know?"

"We were wonderin' if you might know where we can find a man we're lookin' for."

Smoke shoved back the brim of his Stetson with his left hand, Thunder's reins held slackly in the fingers. His right hand rested lightly on his thigh. "It would help if I had a name. There's not many folks this far from town."

"Yeah. We done asked at Sulpher Springs. A gent in the

saloon said the man we want lived down this way. His name is Smoke Jensen."

Smoke tensed, but didn't let it show. "Might I ask what you want with Smoke Jensen?"

That bought him a surly answer. "That's none of yer business, you old fart."

That did it! Smoke dropped all pretense at civility. "Well, I just happen to think it is my business, being that I *am* Smoke Jensen."

The lout beside the orange-haired one cut his eyes to his partner. "Gol-dang, Lance, what do we do now?"

"Go for it, Lonnie!"

That had to rank as the stupidest mistake Lance had ever made. He had barely closed his fingers around the butt-grip of his Smith .44 American when he looked down the muzzle of the .45 Colt Peacemaker in the hand of Smoke Jensen. His eyes went wide and his mouth formed an "O," though he yanked iron anyway.

Smoke shot him before the cylinder of the tilt-top revolver cleared leather. The bullet punched through Lance's belly and burst out his right side. Reflex fired the Smith and the would-be gunfighter shot himself in the leg. Smoke swung the barrel of his Colt to cover Lonnie. The kid had his Merwin and Hulbert .44 clear of leather, but not aimed. Smoke's second round ripped through the youth's liver and angled upward to shatter a portion of rib before exiting from his back. Desperation fought long enough for him to trigger a round.

At such close range it was nearly impossible to miss a man-sized target, but Lonnie did. Hot lead cracked past the right side of Smoke's chest and splattered on a granite boulder behind him. Smoke fired again and pin-wheeled Lonnie in the breastbone. Shards of bone slashed the young lout's aorta on the way through to break a vertebra between his shoulder blades. He was dead before he hit the ground.

Bleeding profusely from stomach and thigh, Lance forced

himself to draw his left hand gun for another try. Smoke reached out and batted the weapon from the wounded thug's hand.

"Give it up, Lance," he told the adolescent. "You're dying as it is."

Lance's defiance came through gritted teeth. "Go to hell, Smoke Jensen."

Smoke ignored it. "Out of curiosity, why did you draw on me?"

Lance swung his good left leg over the saddle, put both hands on the horn, and slid off his mount, his face white with agony. His right leg gave and he slumped to the ground. The horse jittered and danced a few steps away. Through the entire brief and bloody action, the only movement Thunder had made was to twitch ears at each gunshot. Smoke dismounted and ground-reined the 'Palouse stallion, then knelt beside the dying saddle trash.

"You might as well tell me and go off to the Almighty with a clear conscience."

"You taken to preachin' sermons lately?"

"No, but the man who raised me was called Preacher. He taught me to shoot, too,"

"Did a—a damn fine job of it."

"Save your breath to answer me. Why did you pull iron on me?"

Lance turned those icy green eyes on Smoke. "The word is out that a whole lot of money will be paid for your head."

Smoke had a fair idea he knew who had made the offer, though he had to ask. "Who's supposed to pay?"

"A man named Vic . . . tor . . . Spectre," Lance choked out before he died.

High up along the Colorado River, in the corner of Utah, the gang led by Victor Spectre and his partners found the Ute Indians. Their number had grown to twenty-eight. They hungered for whiskey and women in this strict Mormon land. From a distance they eyed the low, brush lodges of the Utes and the square outline of a trading post. The trader would be the Indian agent, Spectre had told them.

"I suggest that three or four of us ride up there first. We can size up the place and distract the agent. The rest of you be ready to come on full tilt when I give the signal," Spectre told them.

Gus Jaeger and several others nodded sagely. Gus prompted, "Do you want me to come along?"

Victor Spectre cut his eyes to the lean outlaw. "No. You stay here, lead the men."

"Good enough."

Spectre picked two of the gang, then he and Tinsdale rode off toward the distant building. The remainder of the gang waited behind a low ground swell.

When they reached the front of the building, which faced east, they saw two burros tied off out at the hitch-rail. The four outlaws dismounted and entered, to find only three white men occupying the trading post. Two of them had the look of prospectors, the third wore a white shirt, with sleeve garters, dark trousers and a string tie. The agent/trader, Spectre judged. Three Indian women stood at a dry goods counter, haggling with the proprietor over a bolt of cloth. No problem there, the gang boss thought. Spectre stepped up to address the Indian agent.

"I say, sir, might you have some whiskey we could purchase?"

"Nope. Ain't allowed where there's Injuns."

Spectre cocked his head and gave the fellow a "man of the world" look. "Oh, come now. My companions and I are fairly parched after being a week in Utah. Surely you must have a little—ah—private stock set aside?" A hand in one pocket, he let the jingle of gold coins sound clearly.

Avarice glowed in the gray eyes of the trader. "I might be able to find something. It'll have to be after I get rid of these wimmin. Can't have them knowin' there's liquor around. They're Utes and their bucks would burn this place down for a swallow apiece."

"Very well, then." Spectre crossed to the door and stepped outside. From a vest pocket, he took a highly polished gold watch and lined the open face cover up with the sun. The flash could be seen clearly by the waiting outlaws.

They came down on the trading post like the Tartar warriors of Gengis Khan. By then, Victor Spectre had reentered the trading post. He crossed to the agent/trader and grabbed him by the front of his shirt.

He put his face close to that of the suddenly frightened man and growled at him. "Your strongbox. Where is it?"

Consternation registered a moment before anger washed it away. "You are going to rob me? You'll not get much, and you'll not get away with it. Harvey, Lem," he called to the sourdoughs at the small bar across the room.

Harvey and Lem could do little to help him. They faced into the drawn six-guns of Ralph Tinsdale, Nate Miller, and Judson Reese. Squawking like pudgy hens, the Ute women made for the door. Victor Spectre dragged the spluttering trader across the room and rammed him against a wall.

"Tell me now and I might let you live."

Raising a trembling hand, the meek Indian agent pointed to the bar. "There, under the counter. It just has a key lock."

"Where's the key?"

"In it, during business hours. It's where I keep my whiskey."

Spectre motioned to Reese and Miller. "Clean it out."

That's when shouts of alarm in the Ute language came from outside. The outlaws swarmed around the agency trading post and began to shoot down the helpless Ute men, who were armed with only lances, bows, and arrows. Women screamed and the children ran in panic.

Laughing, Farlee Huntoon took aim on a boy of about nine and shot him between the shoulder blades. He eared back the hammer to pot the child's little brother, then yelped in pain as an arrow creased the upper side of his left shoulder.

"Owie! That damn buck done drew blood," he bellowed as he turned to one side and fired into the face of the Ute who had shot the arrow. "Owie," he repeated for emphasis.

Those among the Ute men who had not already been killed or seriously wounded began to flee. They dragged along what women and children they could. The gang spread out and methodically began to exterminate the remaining males. The old women they let go. The young ones they corralled in the Council lodge, a large brush shelter. Back inside the trading post, Victor Spectre examined the booty.

"You were correct about one thing. There isn't a lot of gold here," he said to the proprietor. "Too bad. Had there been money enough, I might have been persuaded not to do this," he added casually as he lifted his revolver.

"No! Oh, please, no!" the Indian agent pleaded. "There's— there's more whiskey. In the root cellar," he bargained with his life.

"We'll find it," Spectre assured him, then shot the man dead.

By the time the two prospectors had been killed and stripped of their small pouches of placer gold, the last of the Ute men had run off with the women and children they had rescued. Gus Jaeger gathered the gunhawks and tolled them off by twos to make their pick of the young Ute women and girls. The female population of the Ute village began to shriek and wail the moment the first pair were dragged from the Council lodge.

Sally Jensen sat in the old wooden rocking chair on the front porch at the Sugarloaf. The rocker played a game of tag with the tail of a plump, orange-and-white tabby that lay at her side. So far the cat was winning, the wooden bow had not yet made contact as the tail whipped in and out beneath it. She glanced up at the angle of the sun. The hands would be in for supper before long.

She looked across the open yard to where the ranch cook bent over his pots of spicy beef stew, thick gumbo, and New Orleans-style rice and beans. A Cajun who had drifted north and west of his native bayous, he had proven to be a natural with the hearty fare of the High Lonesome country. Though where he obtained the okra she would never know. The summers were too short and mild to grow it here. He looked up and saw the expression she did not know she wore. A wide smile flashed in the swarthy Acadian face and he spoke with what he hoped sounded reassuring.

"Won't no harm come to Mr. Smoke, Miss Sally. I gar-ron-tee it."

How did he know I was worried about Smoke? Sally gave a little shiver and looked expectantly toward the direction from which the hands would ride up on the headquarters as she answered him.

"I know that, Jules. I was . . . only thinking."

"He be one brave mon, Miss Sally. Smart, too. He not be steppin' in front of some *sacre bleu* outlaw bullet." Jules Thibedeux nodded his head in confidence and understanding and went back to his cooking.

Sally heard hoofbeats then. She came to her boots and marched to the head of the steps. She paused on the second one, her face lighted by the gold-orange of a lowering sun. Riding beside Ike Mitchell she recognized the slender figure of Bobby Harris.

Bobby had taken to sleeping in his old room in the main house in the five nights since Smoke's departure. His attitude bothered her. He had not as yet returned to school in Big Rock, and although content to teach him at home, she worried about his adjustment to children his age.

Impatient with herself, she banished the thought and put a smile on her face. Bobby would be moody enough, let alone he saw her worried about Smoke also. She ran fingers through her dark hair and tossed the curls to give them springiness. Then she stamped her foot in vexation when a tiny voice in her head asked her where Smoke was right then.

Smoke Jensen drifted into Wyoming that day at midmorning, near the small town of Baggs. He had been slowed because of a pulled tendon on his packhorse. The normally sure-footed animal had stepped into a prairie dog hole and badly strained its canon tendon. It limped and fought the lead. He would have to rent another one or trade off at the livery in Baggs.

With that decided for him, he stopped thinking about it. The skyline of Baggs seemed to grow out of the tall, waving prairie grass. He saw the tall spire of a grain silo rearing on the horizon, then the slender one of a church. The town had grown since he had last passed through. Then the blocky shapes of the business district crept above the rim of the world. At a half mile distance, Smoke heard the barking dogs. Shrill cries of children came next. A cow mooed in a backyard. A wagon, badly in need of axle grease, shrieked its way along the main street. Smoke counted half a dozen new houses.

Smoke felt his initial tension sloughing off. Too early, he realized as he swung off of the trail onto a maintained roadway. Two local farmers, their wagons stopped opposite one another to swap tall tales, looked hard at him with open suspicion. Beyond them, at the first house on the edge of town, three children, barefoot, shirtless boys, stared solemnly. The youngest popped a thumb into his mouth as Smoke rode by. A buxom woman rushed from the side door to scoop them up and hurry them inside. Something, or someone bad had been here recently, Smoke reasoned. He guided Thunder to the livery first.

He found it where it had been before. The same bent, stooped old man came forward to take the reins of Thunder when Smoke dismounted. The sturdy, buckskin-clad gunfighter nodded toward his packhorse.

"I've got a horse with a strained tendon. I'd like to trade him or rent another if I have to."

"You got his papers?"

"Sure do. He's prime stock. Raised him myself."

"Say, you've been here before, ain'tcha?"

"That's right. Last time about two years ago."

Thumb and forefinger massaging his whiskered chin. "As I rec'llect yer name's Johnson, Jennings, something like that?"

"Jensen. I breed horses down in Colorado."

A light gleamed in aged eyes. "Yeah. Do a fair bit of gunfighting, too, as I recall."

"Huh! Let's keep that between the two of us, all right?"

Thin lips spread to reveal toothless gums and the old man cackled. "I ain't got any problem with that. M'lips are sealed." He went to the roan gelding and ran an experienced hand down the forelegs. He lifted a thick lip and studied the teeth. His keen eyes noted that even with the heavy pack load, the back remained straight and firm.

"If he comes from your stock, you've got a deal, Mister—ah—Smith." He pointed to the corral beside the livery barn. "I got me a fine little mare out there. I'll let her go for the swap and thirty dollars. She's a Morgan an' been broke to a packsaddle."

Smoke gave him a genuine smile. "I've been wanting some Morgan blood in my remount herd. I'll sign the papers over and we can seal it with a drink on me."

"Fine as frog hair by me. My name is Issac Rucker. Put it on the transfer an' I'll get you Debbie's papers." He winked. "I could feel it weren't broke. I had me a sharper dope a horse with a broken leg with laudanum and try to pass it off as only a strain."

Their transaction completed, Smoke and Issac walked toward the saloon at the corner of Spencer and Lode streets. The Bucket of Blood looked exactly as it did when Smoke last paid it a visit. Green and white bunting decorated the balcony railing. Cut out letters of green blotting paper spelled out *Erin Go Brah!* above the center of the backbar. The piano tinkled mournfully, playing *The Minstrel Lad.* It had been *Danny Boy* when Smoke had been here last. A huge, portly, handlebar-mustached man stood behind the mahogany, a spotted white apron folded double and tied around his ample middle. He saw Smoke and recognized him immediately.

"Ah, faith an' it's Kirby me lad. C'mon me boyo, cozy up an' take a wee dram. Jensen may not be a name from the auld sod, but yer an honorary Irishman whenever you are in me darlin' place."

Smoke winced. If he had any hope of going unrecognized, Sean Doolin's big mouth had ruined all that. If anyone in here connected the name Kirby Jensen with Smoke Jensen, the word would be all over the town in five minutes. He and Issac Rucker crossed to the bar. Doolin slapped down two large, fish-eye shot glasses and poured them with pale amber Irish whiskey and added a tot to his own. He set the bottle aside and raised his glass in a toast. Smoke and Issac joined him.

"Up the Irish!"

A surly punk halfway down the bar raised his head and glowered at them "Up their backsides, I say."

Smoke turned to stare at him. He saw a long-haired, trashy piece of barely human refuse, of about twenty-two years, whose lank, greasy hair showed no familiarity with brush or comb. He had a snotty sneer smeared on his thin-lipped face and a two-day stubble of pale, yellow beard. He wore a six-gun slung low on his right thigh, secured by a rawhide thong. The holster, an old, worn military one, had its cover flap cut away to give quick access to the butt of the .44 Colt Frontier it held. Probably considered himself a gunfighter, Smoke appraised.

The sad thing was that he would most likely die without ever knowing how wrong he was. Smoke looked again at the hateful expression, tiny, mean eyes, and unshaved jowls, then decided he might as well try to enlighten the lout.

"Who or what are you?"

Smoke's words hung in the air a long moment before the punk worked his mouth and deliberately spat tobacco juice at Smoke's boots. "If you don't know, you've got a treat comin.' I'm Tyrone Sayers. Folks here-about generally tremble when they learn that."

Smoke slid into his black, leather gloves as he forced his voice into a high, squeaky register. "Oh, I am trembling. Don't you see? As far as I can tell, your name is spelled S-H-I-T."

"Back me, Norvie!" Tyrone Sayers erupted in instant violence. His hand dropped to the butt of his revolver and began to yank it free, while Sean Doolin grabbed up a bung starter and started for Sayer's companion. "Take it outside, boyos," he commanded.

Sayers ignored him. He had not cleared the back-plate of leather when Smoke went into action. Instead of drawing, he rapidly stepped forward and slammed a hard right fist into the punk's mouth. Sayers flew backward and the small of his back smashed into the top rail of the bar. His gun-arm continued moving and he freed the long-barreled Colt. That's when Smoke hit him again. The revolver thudded on the sawdust-covered floor. His friend went for his gun then.

A loud *thop!* sounded as Sean brained Norvie with his wooden mallet. He went rubber legged and slumped to the floor, his head resting on a spittoon, while birdies sang in his head. Smoke did not even hesitate during this one-sided exchange.

He waded in on Sayers. His elbows churned back and forth as he worked on the exposed gut of the stupid lout. Sayers wheezed and gasped and tried to escape along the bar. He stumbled over his fallen comrade and had to duck fast to escape a sledgehammer blow to his head. Lightning fast, Smoke recovered and smashed a vulnerable nose.

Blood flowed in twin rivers from Tyrone's mangled beak. His eyes watered and he pawed at them to clear his vision. Smoke went back to Tyrone's middle again. Tyrone decided he had had enough of that. From a soft pouch holster at the small of his back he drew a stubby .38 caliber Herington and Richards and whipped it toward Smoke Jensen.

Chin down to protect himself from any retaliation by Sayers, Smoke did not see the little gun coming until it lined up with the middle of his belly. "Smoke, look out!" Issac Rucker shouted.

Smoke reacted instantly. With his left he batted the small revolver out of line with his body. It discharged through empty air in the same moment that Smoke Jensen drew his .45 Colt and jammed the muzzle into one ruined nostril on the face of Tyrone Sayers.

He didn't have to say it, the tiny .38 was on the way to the floor already, but he did anyway. "Drop it."

Through his pain-dulled mind, Tyrone Sayers finally made the connection between names. "Jesus Christ! Smoke Jensen!"

"Nope. Its just Ike Rucker . . . and Smoke Jensen," the liveryman said through a chuckle.

All of the strength went out of the legs of Tyrone and he sagged to the floor. He barely caught himself on the edge of the bar. "I didn't know. For the love of God, *I didn't know!* Please, Mr. Jensen, don't kill me."

Smoke eased off a little. "I think you've learned some manners. Get a hand on your partner there and clear the hell out of here."

Tyrone Sayers could not take his eyes off the six-gun

burrowed into his nose. "Yes, sir, anything you say. Yes, sir, right away."

With a grunt he came to his boots, grabbed the unconscious lout beside him by the shirt collar and dragged him to the bat-wings. When they disappeared through the bat-wings, Sean Doolin slapped a big palm on the bar.

"By all the saints, that was a sight to behold. Another round on me."

By the time Smoke Jensen had consumed a substantial meal to rid his head of the buzz brought on by the Irish whiskey and ridden out of Baggs, Tyrone Sayers had cleaned up and his friend had regained consciousness. Tyrone was full of plans which he quickly shared with Norvil Yates.

"Norvie, dough dit Billy Beterson nund br'ng hip here." Tyrone talked funny because he had twin fat lips, and two rolls of cotton batting stuffed in his nose with a heavy layer of tape to hold them in place.

"What do you want Peterson for?"

Tyrone explained in his mushy voice. "There's a bounty out on Jensen. Big money we're gonna collect it."

Right then, it seemed to Norvil Yates that his friend would not fare well in the prophet business.

Six

Back at the sugarloaf, a worried Monte Carson dropped in on Sally Jensen. He stood on the porch, hat in hand, and related what he had learned the previous day in Big Rock. His expression revealed the level of his discomfort.

"I have some more news about those escaped convicts."

Sally nodded. "Not good from the looks of you."

Monte tugged at one side of his walrus mustache. "That's a fact. They have cut a bloody path across Arizona, following the Colorado River. It is suspected that they are in Utah now."

Sally had seen outlaws come and go, had faced terrible odds herself. For some reason she could not bring herself to be overly concerned about these men. "Just how much havoc can three men create, Monte?"

"It's not three anymore, Sally. They have a regular gang. There's more than twenty of them. And it appears they are heading northeast. Could be to here. I'd feel better if you came into town, where I could keep an eye on you."

"Honestly, Monte, I don't think that's necessary."

"Smoke would never forgive me if something happened to you."

Sally forced a light laugh she did not quite feel. "And I would never live it down if I picked now to turn delicate and vaporish."

Caught on the horns of the proverbial dilemma, Monte fingered his hat nervously and brought up a lame excuse.

"Well, if you hear from Smoke, pass along what I told you." He took his leave and cantered off down the lane.

After Monte had ridden out of sight, Sally remained standing on the porch, looking after him. She ran over in her mind what he had said and his offer to provide protection. Then she looked through the curtained window into the living room. A golden oak shelf clock ticked steadily, its brass pendulum hypnotic in the stillness. The hands would be in soon, she mused. She would take Bobby aside and tell him to be cautious. She might even tell him why, Sally decided.

Twenty minutes later a loud clatter arose in the barnyard. Hungry hands tied off their mounts to a corral rail and made for the row of washbasins along one side of the bunkhouse. Sally made herself keep her peace until all had eaten and some sat back with quirleys sending ribbons of blue-white tobacco smoke into the noon sky. Then she went out and gathered in Bobby Harris.

They walked a distance from the hands before Sally spoke what was on her mind. "Something has come up that makes me feel I should caution you to be very careful when you are away from here. In fact, I think I will rescind my rule about wearing a gun. Take your Colt Lightning when you go out this afternoon."

"Why? What's happened?" the boy asked eagerly. "It's Smoke, isn't it?"

"No," she hastened to assure him, then read the disbelief in his clear, youthful face. "Well, yes, somewhat." She had allowed herself to be mousetrapped and it angered her. Reluctantly she related all that Monte Carson had told her. Fire blazed in Bobby's eyes when she finished.

"I should have gone with him," Bobby said stubbornly.

"No, Bobby. Smoke is not hurt. We don't even know if he is in danger." Unwilling to hurt the boy, she unwittingly did just that. "Believe me, there's nothing you could do to help him more than staying here, being armed and keeping a sharp eye."

Bobby's face turned red. *"Yes, there is!"* He turned away from her and started for the house. "I'm takin' my stuff back to the bunkhouse."

Suddenly apprehensive, Sally called after him in a rush. "You don't understand, Bobby. I'm asking you to keep a watch out for me as well as yourself."

Bobby turned his head to throw back a hot retort. "I can do that well enough from across the ways. Right now, the hands are better company than you are."

Gus Jaeger crawled back down the slope of the ridge to where the gang waited. The long, thin wisp of hairs that descended from his lower lip moved in agitation when he spoke. "There can't be more than three families living there. They've got 'em a palisade around the houses and barns. Brats runnin' around in the yard. Didn't see sign of but two grown men."

Victor Spectre showed his appreciation of such skill with a big smile. "You did a good job. How far are we from the Great Salt Lake?"

"It's about fifty miles north and a bit west," Gus answered.

Spectre nodded. "This must be one of those outposts— what do the Mormons call them? Desseret Towers?—that are strung across Utah. That means they will have quite a lot of valuables. No handy bank to go to after closing shop for the day. Get the men ready, Augustus, we'll take them, like we did those Utes."

Twenty minutes later the outlaw band stormed down on the Mormon encampment. Too late, they discovered the place to be a regular fort. Their rude awakening came in the form of a screeching in the air, followed by an explosion some thirty yards in front of the lead element of the gang. The heavy roar of an artillery piece followed.

"B'God, they've got a six pounder in there," Gus Jaeger accurately named the weapon.

Spectre reined in when the outlaw foreman did. He frowned, perplexed. "Does that mean trouble?"

"If they have any grapeshot or canister, it sure as hell does," Gus opined.

So far the residents of the small community had not bothered to close the gate in the stockade that surrounded their dwellings. Another shell burst close by and the cannon roared again. A staggered line of smoke clouds rippled along the parapet and rifle balls cracked through the air around the hard cases. Some looked around nervously.

In their trade of banditry, they were not accustomed to organized resistance. These Mormons had quickly proven that they were nothing to be trifled with. Victor Spectre studied the next volley of fire from the wall.

"How many grown men did you say?" he asked Jaeger.

"Two's all I saw. There could have been more inside buildings."

"Looks to me like everyone over the age of ten has a rifle and knows how to use it. We had best come up with something better than a frontal assault."

Gus Jaeger considered that a moment. "They can only point that cannon one direction at a time. And if they're puttin' all their guns on the side opposite us, it could be we should ride around the place like Injuns and look for a weak spot."

"Good thinking," Spectre approved. "See to it. I'll take five of the best sharpshooters and keep them busy over here."

Jaeger liked that. "Now you're talkin', Mr. Spectre."

He had it set up in two minutes. While Spectre and his two partners and the marksmen provided covering fire, Gus started off with the remaining twenty-three gunmen. Again the cannon opened up. This time, tiny plumes of dust spurted upward from the hard ground in the midst of the riders who fired at the walls as they angled across the defended portion of the wall. Grapeshot.

Three horses went down shrieking, their riders and two other men wounded by the one inch balls. One of the outlaws sat slumped in his saddle and tried to put his mangled intestines back inside his body while he groaned horribly. While the attackers recovered from this new turn of events, the gate swung closed. Shouts came from inside and the crack of a whip. Slowly the black nuzzle of the cannon appeared as it rolled up an incline and leveled on a rammed earth platform, the barrel protruding over the spiked tops of the barricade.

In frustration, two of the sharpshooters fired on it. Their bullets rang on the cast barrel and flattened, to moan off harmlessly skyward. With only poor targets to choose from, the snipers had little effect. Victor Spectre watched the gang disappear out of sight around a corner of the stockade.

At once a fusillade erupted as more rifles joined the defense. "Who are they?" Spectre asked rhetorically.

Again the cannon spoke. The grapeshot crashed into the earth less than ten yards from where they had positioned themselves. It made Spectre's skin crawl. He made a quick, disappointing estimate of their chances. He rose in his stirrups and called to the marksmen.

"This will never do. We're too far outnumbered. Ride clear of that place and then join the others. We're breaking this off." The cannon barked again to give his words emphasis.

When the withdrawal began, the gate opened and armed, mounted men swarmed out. Considering himself fortunate to have escaped with such light casualties, Victor Spectre increased the gait to a gallop and streamed after his gang. The Mormons obliged him by doing the same.

It became a horse race, rather than an assault. One which

they barely managed to win. Victor Spectre was pleased to discover that Gus Jaeger had correctly anticipated him and led the gang away to the north. He and his partners streamed along in their wake. The crack shots along with them turned to fire at the angry Mormons.

Gradually the distance closed between the leaders and the outlaws. When Spectre got within hailing distance, he shouted gustily, "Keep going. Take that notch ahead. I don't think they will follow us beyond that point."

"You had better be right," Gus Jaeger said through gritted teeth, softly enough not to be heard.

A vast sea of tall, lush grass extended to the north, east, and west for as far as the eye could see from the last ridge that overlooked the Great Divide Basin. Smoke Jensen made camp in a small clearing in the midst of a large stand of lodge pole pine. To his northwest lay the small town of Wamsutter, Wyoming Territory. After hobbling Thunder and Debbie, he set about gathering windfall for a cookfire.

Rabbits bounded away at his footsteps and a quail called his mate. A rookery of crows turned a gnarled old oak black with their bodies and the air blue with their grating complaints. The air smelled sweet and clean. To his satisfaction, Smoke did not detect a hint of wood smoke. No one else shared this empty place with him. He could do with it that way for quite a while.

Smoke Jensen had always been a loner. At fourteen or so, Smoke Jensen had, in mountain man parlance, been to the mountain and seen the elephant.

His early life had been hard. A hard-scrabble farm that grew more rocks than crops, always being hungry, and never enough clothing to keep warm in winter had been his lot. But then, everyone else had lived the same during the Civil War, especially in Missouri. Young Kirby had never eaten a juicy steak or a grapefruit. Didn't even know what the latter was until years later when he had seen one in the breakfast room of a fancy San Francisco hotel.

No, his past life had not prepared him for elegance. It did teach him to survive. So he took up a notch in his belt and began to trudge along the trail with Preacher . . .

That had been a day to remember. When Kirby first saw Preacher, the man looked to him like one of the horrors out of a story by the Brothers Grimm. Preacher hadn't shaved in several days and a thick, dark stubble covered his cheeks and chin. He was dressed all in skins, with Indian beadwork on the shirt, which he wore loose, outside his trousers, kept in place by a wide, thick leather belt. From that latter hung a tomahawk, the biggest knife the boy had ever seen, and a brace of revolvers in soft pouch holsters. A possibles bag hung over one shoulder by a rawhide strap, and a bullet mold dangled below that.

There was a brass compass tied to it by a thong, and a powder horn. Preacher wore buckskin leggins over trousers of the same material, with high-top, lace moccasins. The uppers of those had been done in ornate quill and bead work.

Preacher wore his hair long, and lockets of other human hair had been braided into the fringe of his shirt. A skunk-skin cap covered the crown of his head. His mustache was months overdue for a visit with a pair of scissors, and covered his mouth in a shaggy droop. Had young Kirby Jensen been four or five years younger, such an apparition would have made him pee his pants. Then he saw the twinkle in those flinty eyes and the mouth opened in a white smile.

Preacher took him under his wing and saw to his upbringing, and his education. Before a year had passed, Kirby had read from Shakespeare and from the *Canterbury Tales* of Chaucer. He had improved his ciphering to the point he could deal with fractions in his head. He also learned to trap beaver, mink, otter, and raccoons. He proved to have a natural eye and became an expert marksman within two years. He could ride a horse nearly as well as a Cheyenne boy born to it. All in all, he concluded as he arranged tinder and kindling in a ring of rocks, he had a well-rounded education. . . .

For which he would be eternally grateful, he vowed as he lighted the fire with a Lucifer. When the twigs blazed merrily, he fed thicker chunks of wood until he had enough, then left the small fire to find himself some fresh meat for his supper. It didn't take long. In a land rich in animal life, Smoke soon found a covey of plump quail.

With a cunning learned from Preacher, he called them in close enough to swiftly grab up three and wring their necks. He took them back to camp, plucked them, gutted the carcasses and threaded them on a green sapling to roast over the coals. Then he made biscuits. He had some dry hominy, which he had put to soaking when he first reached his chosen site. All that he wanted for was some gravy. To achieve that, he put the tiny giblets of the birds to boil with some wild onions and some crumbled sage leaves. Coffee came next.

Smoke's stomach began to growl as he smelled the savory odor that rose when the sparse fat on the birds began to drip into the orange glow beneath them. He poured coffee the minute it boiled enough. Sighing, he sat back against his saddle and sipped with lowered eyelids.

Tyrone Sayers peered through a thick screen of gorse and blackberry brambles at the man who laid in the clearing in such confident repose, his saddle for a pillow. Tyrone knew they would find him. A wide smile spread on his face, which made him wince as the cuts in his mangled lips split open again. *You're gonna git yers, Smoke Jensen,* he thought in triumph as he slid back to where the others waited.

Despite the distance and the obvious fact that their target was catching a quick nap, Tyrone mush-mouthed his announcement in a whisper. "Fellers, we've found us Smoke Jensen."

Billy Peterson's brow furrowed. "Yeah? Where?"

Billy's patch was shy a few punkins, Tyrone reflected, but he did what he was told and didn't give any back-talk. That moderated the erstwhile leader's outlook toward the awkward lout.

"Jist beyond that little ridge, Billy. He's camped in this little clearing in a stand of pine. Right now, he's takin' a snooze. So, what we're gonna do is split up, take our time at it, an' work our way through those pine trees until we're right on top of him. Then we're gonna make ourselves rich men."

Billy could not suppress a giggle. "You sure talk funny, Tyrone."

"Go suck an egg, you little shit!" Tyrone fought to gain control over his mangled mouth and succeeded in part. "Listen to me. We got a chance at this."

Not understanding, Billy continued to press for details. "How we gonna capture him? I hear he's mighty fast and a whole lot mean."

Tyrone looked at the younger boy with disgust. "We ain't gonna capture him, dummy. When we git in place, we open up and fill him full of holes."

Wonder filled Billy's eyes. "We gonna call him out?"

"No, peabrain. We git him while he lays there."

"Tyrone, that ain't right," Billy protested.

Anger succeeded where willpower had failed before and Tyrone spoke almost clearly. "Look at me. He did that to me. Do you think I'm gonna let him get away with it?" Then he quickly outlined where he wanted them to take up position. Then he concluded, "I'm gonna kill Smoke Jensen if it's the last thing I do."

Pleasant smells from the cooking quail gave Smoke Jensen another stomach rumble that pierced his light sleep. He came to his boots and carried the soaking hominy off a ways to drain it. Then he set about finishing his meal.

Lard from a paper tube melted in a cast iron skillet. It would serve to make the biscuits and fry the hominy. It would provide for gravy, also. Smoke worked with an economy of effort and movement that marked his mountain man upbringing. He soon had dough mixed and the hominy sizzling in the pan. He put the biscuits in a Dutch oven, popped on the lid, and hung it low over the coals on a trestle arm. Then he poured more coffee. For a short while, he forgot about what had brought him so far from home. Everything seemed to have been put here just for his enjoyment.

To the west. a flood of gold had spread from north to south, and extended up to the bloated red ball of the sun. Birds called in the distance. His horses grazed on the thick, green shoots and made low, whuffling sounds. A doe and fawn stepped timidly from the treeline and the female turned large, black eyes on the man by the fire. Smoke watched them till they moved out of sight, then ladled up his meal and began to chew in a mood of contentment. The peacefulness lasted through the meal.

When the last dark, tender flesh of the final quail disappeared down his gullet, Smoke bent to mop up the last of the gravy with a biscuit half when a bullet cracked out of nowhere, slammed into the bottom of the skillet, and ripped it out of his hand. Pain shot up to his shoulder. The sharp report of a rifle quickly followed, accompanied by the detonation of at least two other weapons.

Seven

Another bullet barely missed Smoke's head and threw a shower of sparks from the fire. A third slug moaned off the rounded surface of a boulder beyond the fire pit. Hand stinging from the impact of the first round, Smoke propelled himself backward and landed on his shoulders. He had his Colt free and it bucked and roared in the direction from which the first shot had come. The hot lead smacked solidly into a tree. A flicker of movement put his second round right on target. A scream answered him.

Then, "Oh God, Tyrone, he got Billy! Billy's bleedin' like a stuck hog!"

"Shut up, ya idiot! He can find ya from your voice." Smoke's next round clipped a small branch from an aspen right over the head of Sayers, who yelped in alarm. "See what I mean?"

Smoke came to his boots and ran after the second shot, as had his would-be assassins. He dived behind a large boulder and picked his next target from the blunder through the brush. His .45 Peacemaker spit flame. The first, high, hysterical voice shrieked again. "Yiieeee! He got me now."

"Shut up, Norvie!"

Smoke's keen hearing let him refine his sight picture a little. Norvie Yates did not leave this world with a bang, but rather with a whimper. Shot through the throat at the tender age of eighteen, his last intelligible words were a gurgle of self-pity. "Mommy, help me, Mommy."

Tyrone Sayers, would-be gunfighter, emptied the cylinder of his six-gun in panic. He hit exactly nothing.

"Goddamn you, Smoke Jensen!" he ranted, mush-mouthed. Goddamn you to hell."

"Give it up, punk. It's not worth dying for," Smoke advised him coldly.

"You're the one who's gonna die. You're gonna make me a rich man."

Smoke did not reply. Silence he knew had its own strong medicine. Instead he moved again, to come to ground at the base of a large pine. The magic of his sealed lips began to do its work.

"Answer me, goddamn you. I'm gonna collect the bounty on your head."

By then, Tyrone Sayers had reloaded and came out of the brush in a bound that landed him beside the fire. He slip-thumbed four rounds from his Smith American before he discovered he had ventilated an empty bedroll He slowly turned on one heel, his face a mask of confusion.

"Come out. Show yourself like a man. Face me, you bastard," Tyron wailed through puffy lips.

Smoke Jensen stepped out into the clearing behind Tyrone Sayers. "Surprise."

Sayers spun and brought up his .44 Smith. Smoke had emptied his right-hand .45, which he wore low on his leg, and now drew his second revolver from the holster slanted across his left hip at belt level, butt forward. Before Tyrone Sayers could trigger his .44, Smoke completed hauling his iron. He lined it up, squeezed the trigger, and blasted a pinwheel hole through the heart of Tyrone Sayers.

Sayers rocked back on his heels. His eyes began to glaze. He squinted as his life swiftly ebbed away, and tried to focus on his target. His arm would not raise. Then his knees gave way. He sank down hard on the ground and teetered for a long second. Then with a faint gasp, he rocked backward and fell, to land on his head.

Ever cautious, Smoke Jensen made a careful check to determine that only the three had come after him. Then he reholstered his Peacemaker and addressed his remarks to the corpses.

"Only damn thing is, now I have to gather up the bodies, lift them by myself and strap them on a horse." They would serve as an excellent message to anyone who might follow.

A rabbit munching its way through the clearing awakened Smoke Jensen in the still, gray light of pre-dawn. The bunny froze when Smoke rolled onto his back, threw off covers, and sat upright. He yawned and stretched, then drew on boots. The furry critter missed becoming breakfast by its second instinctive alternative. It decided to flee.

Smoke stood up, stretched again and headed for the kindling to build a fire. While the coffee built, he considered what to do. He would take the other horses and all of the weapons and ammunition. His pack horse could easily carry the load. It might be better not to travel the main roads. If word of Spectre's price on his head had traveled this far, the less he saw of anyone, or they of him, the better. The sooner he got to Jackson's Hole, the quicker his trail would grow cold. Smoke fried bacon and mopped up the grease with left-over biscuits. He drank three cups of coffee, used the dregs to drown his fire, then buried what was left. He broke camp twenty minutes later and rode out.

At mid-morning, Smoke noticed a thin white column rising beyond the near ridge. He crested the rise and looked down on a tidy little cabin, located on the shore of a small lake, formed by Lost Creek. A low barn and corral had been built against the shelter of a round-topped knoll. Smoke rode in cautiously and stopped fifty yards from the buildings when a stoop-shouldered oldtimer stepped out on the narrow porch.

"Hello, the cabin," Smoke called out in a friendly tone.

"Hello, yerself," came the reply. "Be you alone?"

"That I am."

"If yer friendly, ride on up. I've coffee on the stove an' I'm cookin' up some eats for noon. Yer welcome to partake."

"Obliged." Smoke rode in and introduced himself simply. "My name's Jensen."

"Morgan Crosby. It's nice to see a friendly face. Don't get many folk out this way often. There's water at the barn. Tie up yer critters there and come on in."

They sat at a linoleum-covered table and Crosby told of moving to this part of Wyoming after the War. His slight Southern accent put a capital on the word. "Yep. I rode with ol' John Mosbey and the boys," he remarked on his service for the Confederacy. Crosby gave Smoke a cold eye. "I suppose you was with the Union bluebellies?"

"No. I didn't take sides in the war. I've lived in the High Lonesome since I was a boy. I never developed feelings for one side or the other," Smoke informed him.

"Well, now, that sounds mighty fine. You headed anywhere in particular?"

Smoke considered it only a moment before answering. "North. Up around the Yellowstone River."

Crosby poured them more coffee. "I never lost anything in that country, so I've no reason to want to go there."

"It's beautiful. Quiet and peaceful, and what people do go through there are, for the most part, friendly."

A light twinkled in the eyes of Crosby. "Then there's a few others that ain't?"

"Like everywhere," Smoke agreed.

Morgan Crosby roused himself from the chair. "All I've got's some fatback an' beans, creamed onions an' taters." An elfin twinkle came to his eyes. "But I had me some dried apples I put to soak early this mornin'. Made me a pie."

"Sounds good," Smoke encouraged him.

After they had eaten, with both men working on a second

piece of dried apple pie, Smoke Jensen stiffened with the fork halfway to his mouth. A split-second later, Morgan Crosby did the same.

"Seems this is the day for visitors," the old-timer muttered.

"I make it to be four or five of them," Smoke advised.

"Yer hearin's keener than mine," Crosby admitted. "I wonder what's on their minds."

A moment later, they found out. "You in the cabin, come out with your hands up."

Smoke moved to a window with fluid speed. He peered around the corner of a scraped hide pane. "Is it the law?" Crosby asked.

Unlimbering his .45 Colt, Smoke shook his head. "Not unless the law around here looks like grave diggers. There's five of the scruffiest saddle trash out there that I've seen in a long time."

"Not friends of mine, then." Then Crosby added, "You seem to attract the most unpleasant sort of company."

Ruefully, Smoke had to agree.

"We'll give you two minutes, then we fill the walls with holes," came the warning from outside.

She had looked everywhere. Early that morning, Ike Mitchell, the foreman, had come to the house to tell Sally Jensen that Bobby Harris had not slept in the bunkhouse the previous night, nor had he shown up for his work assignment. Immediately she checked upstairs. His bed had not been slept in either. She expanded her search to the area around the ranch headquarters.

That had been an hour ago and still no sign of Bobby. Sally went to the corral and slipped a hackamore bridle on her sturdy mare, Blue Bonnet. She led the animal out and fetched a saddle.

"Blue, girl," she told the horse, while she saddled it,

"we've got some searching to do." She retrieved the reins and swung astride.

Sally rode in widening spirals out from the Sugarloaf headquarters. Noon beckoned from close by and still no sign of the boy. Sally began to wonder if he had taken it into his head to go after Smoke.

"Surely he wouldn't," she told herself aloud for more assurance.

Her survey took her in the general direction of a low knoll with an ancient, huge, blue-green Douglas fir atop it. How the inviting target had escaped a lightning strike for the more than hundred years it had grown, neither she nor Smoke could guess. While she approached it, with Blue Bonnet rutching in protest to such prolonged activity after two days of idleness in the corral, Sally began to make out the shape of a figure at the base of the tree. At first it appeared to be a jackrabbit hunkered down in the low grass.

After a while, Sally could tell that more was attached to the earlike shape than a mere rabbit body. At fifty yards, she could see the profile of a human face. Closer still, she recognized Bobby's pug nose and slight frame. His horse grazed peacefully down the reverse slope and his bedroll lay rumpled at his side. Relief swallowed anger but, even so, she spoke harshly when she rode up and he did not even acknowledge her presence. In fact, he deliberately turned away to gaze off toward the 14,000 foot peak that towered to the west.

"Young man, what possible right do you think you have to put us to all the effort to find you?"

"I was right here," Bobby told her through his pout, tears formed in his big, blue eyes.

"That's not even a reason." Sally dismounted and walked to his side. "You have your duties with the hands. Also, you are entirely too old for this sort of behavior."

Bobby turned to look at her then. It was immediately obvious to Sally that he was about to lose his battle with his tears. "And I'm old enough to have gone with Smoke, too," he stubbornly maintained.

"No, you're not!" Sally snapped back, small fists on her hips. The split skirt of her riding habit swirled violently as she resisted the urge to stomp a foot. "This fantasy of yours has gone on long enough. I'm sorry, Bobby, but you are going to have to look at this realistically." She softened her tone, surprised at how harsh it had grown. "If you intend to remain on the Sugarloaf, as our adopted son, or even as merely a ranch hand, then you have to learn to face facts.

"You must take responsibility for your acts." She paused, sighing. Was he absorbing any of this? And most of all, to obey orders given to you. Smoke and I both love you, and we don't want to see any harm come to you."

"Then maybe I won't stay," he answered coldly, then stomped away to his horse.

Smoke Jensen and Mogan Crosby found themselves under siege as rifle slugs cracked through the thin hide windows of the cabin. Smoke strode to the door, yanked it open and made a quick response. A yelp of pain answered him. Then four slugs slammed into the thick log walls. Horse hooves clopped in the barnyard.

Smoke moved also. At one window, he lifted a corner for a quick look. He caught two of the hard cases in the act of entering the barn. That left three more. One no doubt wounded. They would be taking up positions also. He cut his eyes to Morgan.

"I got me a good shotgun an, a bag of buckshot," the old man suggested.

"We're in for a siege. I'm more worried about water and food."

Crosby chuckled, a sort of squeaky *he-he-he* sound, and pointed to a squarish wooden structure on one end of the sink counter. "I dug me my well first, then built the cabin around it. 'Tweren't nothin' but Injuns out here then. I spent me many days and nights forted up in here. I've got a tunnel to my root cellar, too. And another to the barn."

Smoke raised an eyebrow at that. "That's one you might live to regret."

"Oh, you mean them fellers out there? Won't be any problem. The door is built into the bottom of a grain bin an' locked from this side. I keep just enough grain in there to hide it."

Smoke scratched his head in wonder. "Where did you come up with all these ideas?"

"I went to Europe when I was young. Saw what they did in all those castles. Some of them, those with wells, were never taken by siege."

"I am impressed. Now, our only real problem is if they send the wounded man for reinforcements. It would be nice to know where they came from."

"Yep. I allow to as how it would, though the Basin has been crawlin' with proddy fellers for the last four, maybe five days. Dependin' on whether they're locals or not, could be we're in for a rough time of it."

Ace Delevan had been a liar and thief all of his life. He became a killer at the tender age of twelve. Since then he had killed thirty men and maimed twice that number. He figured that made him an ideal choice as the one who would get Smoke Jensen. Though a vicious thug, none would say Ace Delevan was stupid. That's why he brought along four of his cronies. Now Hank had a nasty bullet scrape on his upper left thigh and sat in a stall of the barn whining like a baby.

Maybe it hadn't been a good idea to come on like lawmen? They had heard in Baggs that Jensen had passed through. And that three local punks had gone after him—and hadn't returned. Delevan and his friends rode on until they came upon a horse overburdened by three corpses. They backtracked the animal and picked up the trail of a man who had to be Smoke Jensen.

Although Smoke Jensen was reputed to have been on both sides of the law at one time or another, Ace Delevan knew that he most often sided with the law. Which gave him his big idea. If Jensen thought them to be lawmen, his respect for the breed would get him out in the open so they could blow him to doll rags. Ace accepted that one or two of his partners would buy a bullet. But he knew himself to be fast and accurate. At least as much so as anyone he knew. *He* would still be the one to collect that reward on Jensen's head. A silhouette moved across one of the vellum windows and he fired in reaction.

A hole popped in the scraped animal skin. No response from a wounded man. One thing bothered Ace. He had no idea how many men were in there. Jensen for sure, he had gotten a glimpse of a broad-shouldered, ash-blond man in the doorway. A man so quick and steady he put a slug along the side of Hank Graves's thigh. A groan came from the wounded man as Ducky Yoder finished bandaging the limb.

"How's he doin', Ducky?"

"I'm doin' miserable, Ace," Hank answered for himself.

"He can ride, if that's what you want to know," a surly Ducky Yoder growled.

Ace Delevan slitted his eyes. "Who said we were gonna ride anywhere? Smoke Jensen is in there an' we're gonna git him."

Ducky cut his eyes to the open barn doors and the cabin beyond it. "Who says that's Jensen in there?" He meant, "besides you."

Ace chewed on the drooping left end of his mustache. "I say it's him. For that matter then, you tell me what man could fling open that door, jump into the openin', bust off a cap, an' pop back outta sight without even gettin' a shot at him if it ain't Jensen?"

That silenced Ducky for the moment. Ace eased through the shadowy interior of the barn to where he could see through a crack. Burl Winfree and Pauli Hansel had taken up good positions that covered the front door. They had the back covered. A clapboard add-on had been tacked to the rear, to allow for a kitchen and wash house. The door to that hung open a slight bit. Ace sighted in.

A billow of gunsmoke obscured his results for a while. When he could see clearly, he found only a neat little hole. He fired again. Something made of glass broke inside. There followed a shout of anger, then a cloud of wood splinters that cut at his face. The boom of the shotgun got drowned in his curses.

Ace plucked a splinter from his cheek as he turned to the other ruffians. "There's at least two of them in there."

"Then we'd better think up some way of getting them out or us in," Ducky Yoder suggested.

Ace shook his head. "We ain't gonna do that, just the five of us. Hank, can you ride well enough to go round up the Joiner brothers an' Wally Eckert?"

Hank winced. "I reckon. Iffin I can reach my horse."

"Might oughtta find Jake Brock an' Jose Suarez, too."

Ducky Yoder put in his two cents worth. "Jeez, that's scraping the bottom of the barrel, isn't it?"

Ace blinked. "Ya mean Jose?"

"Naw. I mean Jake. He's a hopeless drunk."

The trio laughed. Ducky helped Hank to his feet. "Go out the side door an' cut through the corral. Your mount is at the water trough," he told Hank.

"We'll lay down cover fire," Ace offered.

Hank hobbled away at the best speed possible under the circumstances. When he reached the double door to the corral, he swung it wide, ducked as low as the pain in his leg would allow, and made straight for the far side. Ace and his companions opened fire. Hank made it to the rump of his horse when Smoke Jensen drew a fine bead and let go with a round from his Winchester.

Hank's head exploded in a shower of blood, bone, and brain tissue. He went rubber-legged and fell in a pile of smoking horse manure. From beside him at the back door, Morgan Crosby let go with first one barrel, then the other. Double aught buckshot slashed the plank wall of the barn.

"You bastard," Ace shrieked. "You put two pellets in my left arm."

In answer, he got three fast rounds from a Winchester. This was going to be one long afternoon, Ace thought bitterly.

Smoke Jensen shoved cartridges through the loading gate of his Winchester. He had seen movement in the corral and tracked the wounded thug to his horse. He had managed to finish him and get back to the semi-detached kitchen in time to give the others a nasty surprise when one of them shouted at Morgan Crosby. Now if that saddle trash out there would only do something else stupid, Smoke considered.

He weighed the safety of their position and made a suggestion in the form of a question. "Morgan, don't you think we're a little exposed out here? Those clapboard walls are nowhere near as thick as those of the cabin."

Crosby pondered on it a while. "Yep. I suppose yer right. But we've still got us at least two in the barn. Which reminds me, if it's only two, where's the other pair?"

Smoke had already gone into motion. "Out front, no doubt."

He reached the front room of the log structure moments later. Right in time, Smoke discovered, to watch the man Ace had called Pauli Hansel get brave.

* * *

When no return fire had come from this side of the cabin, Pauli correctly deduced that no one was guarding it. A recent immigrant from Germany, a former Bramen dock waif turned killer, he had fled from the German police. It had been natural enough for him to throw in with the criminal element in New York. Ace Delevan had proven a good leader, and when things got too hot, Pauli had agreed to move west with the gang leader. So far it had been easy.

There were fewer stores to rob, but the banks bulged with gold. And people out here were all so trusting. Pauli compared it to stealing from children. Only this time they had come up against someone a whole lot tougher than most residents of the frontier, and a whole lot meaner. From his vantage point, Pauli had seen what happened to Hank Graves. When the firing increased from the back of the building, it convinced Pauli that he could close in on the defenders from their blind side and finish it once and for all.

He had not counted Smoke Jensen into his equation. Pauli Hansel had taken three long strides toward the building when he saw a slight flicker of movement at one window. He swung his rifle to his left shoulder as a tongue of flame licked outward in his direction. Something hit him hard in the chest, with enough force to drive him to his knees. Pauli tried to contain the fiery ache long enough to sight in. He had the target lined up, palms sweaty, breath in short, agonizing gasps, when another hammer blow smashed into the butt-stock of his Marlin .38-40. The slug rammed through and blew away the lower portion of his jaw. A cascade of lights went off in Pauli's head and his shot went wild, a good five feet above the roof-tree of the cabin. An instant later, he fell dead in a welter of his own blood.

"Hey, Ace," Burl Winfree shouted. "They done got Pauli."

Nothing for it but to rush the cabin, Ace thought. He

relayed his plan to Ducky Yoder. Then yelled to Burl Winfree.

"Burl, listen to me. We're gonna have to take this place damn fast. When you hear us open up, blast the front of that place and take the door. You got that?"

"You gone crazy, Ace?" Burl protested.

"No, I ain't. But at this rate, they're gonna git us one-by-one. Jist do it, y'hear?" This had indeed turned out to be a terrible afternoon.

Eight

This was more like it in Smoke Jensen's book. When the volume of fire increased, he made ready. Braced at the edge of the window, protected by two-foot thick logs, Smoke shoved the muzzle of his rifle out the edge of the sash. He had not located the remaining hard case, only had a general idea from the sound of the voice. Smoke expected the man to charge for the front door when those in the barn opened up. That Burl Winfree did not choose to follow his orders to the letter nearly cost Smoke his life.

When the thugs in the barn began to blast furiously at the rear of the house, Smoke Jensen stepped away from the protection of the thick wall and tore apart a square of the window covering. At the same moment, a bullet snapped past his right ear. It took Smoke a fleeting second to locate the shooter. When he did, the Winchester tracked onto target and bucked in Smoke's hands. It had been a hasty shot, one Smoke did not expect to be fatal. The hot lead did tear through the shoulder of the charging hard case. He bit off a groan and kept coming.

Burl had emptied his rifle magazine and shifted the Marlin to his left hand. The Colt in his right bucked and roared as he advanced, somewhat falteringly as blood soaked the back of his shirt. Smoke Jensen crouched below the window, waiting. Boot soles thudded on the small stoop porch and the weight of a body crashed against the door.

It shook and rattled in its frame, but the latch held for

the moment. Increased effort cracked the slide bar and it began to splinter on the third powerful kick. Smoke exchanged his rifle for a .45 Colt and waited. The door, which ordinarily opened outward, vibrated violently and cracked apart at the middle, between two upright planks. Another kick and a muffled cry of pain followed and the divided halves flew inward.

At once, a man followed. Smoke raised his six-gun and fired. "Good," he told his target. "But not good enough."

Burl Winfree slammed back against the doorjamb, an astonished expression on his suddenly pale, grayish face. Slowly he slid down the side post to a sitting position. He left a glistening red trail behind. With effort he worked his mouth and breathy, gurgles came from deep in his chest.

"Are . . . you . . . Jensen?" he asked with his last gasp.

"Yep. One and the same."

Smoke Jensen watched the man until he died, then hurried to the aid of Morgan Crosby. The old man did not seem in much need. He had the remaining pair pinned down. One lay sprawled behind a feed bunker, badly wounded in the left shoulder by a load of buckshot. He kept up a steady fire, though, that crashed through the kitchen and smacked the cabin wall. The other man was not in Smoke's line of sight.

Then a rifle cracked in the hay mow and Smoke found his target. Two fast rounds from the Colt drove Ace Delevan away from his vantage point. He went down the ladder hand-over-hand and zigzagged his way to the big, open doors. Morgan Crosby fired at him as he cut away at a sharp oblique angle. The shot column hissed past inches from his chest.

Smoke Jensen fired at the movement also, with greater effect. His bullet took Ace low in the gut. Ace doubled over in blinding pain and stumbled into a pile of burlap sacks. Those gave him a softer landing than he expected. Biting on his lower lip, Ace rolled over and swung his six-gun toward the threat from the cabin. He was seriously hit, though not as badly as it could have been. He waved feebly to Ducky Yoder, stretched out in the yard.

"Ducky, cover me."

"Sure enough, Ace."

Ducky opened fire, blazing away where no one waited anymore. Ace forced himself upright and began a shambling run toward the cabin. When he passed by Yoder's position, the last of his men came to his boots and followed. Both wounded, their chances for success lay somewhere between slim and none. Yet, they came on.

Three pellets of 00 buckshot, from a load fired by Morgan Crosby, tore into Ducky's left hip. Pain, suddenly numbed by icy shock, made him veer off course. Canted to one side to ease the hot agony in his abused flesh, Ducky angled toward the south corner of the house. Seeing that, Ace had a sudden change of heart. He reversed his course and ran back inside the barn. He returned with two horses.

"Quick, mount up. We've gotta get out of here," he yelled at a dazed Ducky Yoder.

"Go . . . on. I ain't . . . gonna last . . . no how," Ducky declared.

Ace used the mounts to cover himself as he ran up between their scourge and themselves. He jammed the reins on one bang-tail into the hand of Ducky Yoder and used that big ham fist to literally toss his last companion into the saddle.

"Keep low," Ace declared as he swung atop his horse. Following his own advice, Ace spurred his mount to a fair to middling run and they raced away from danger.

After five minutes, Smoke Jensen and Morgan Crosby came out into the yard. The old man went from one dead piece of trash to another. At last he shook his head, massaged his chin with one gnarled hand and looked Smoke hard in the eye.

"B'gosh, we done did it. Run them right off. By the bye, they ain't local."

"I've handled more," Smoke confided without bravado. "And alone for that matter."

Crosby knew he had to ask. "Humph! I figgered that. You know, the name Jensen is a right common one, sure enough. But, this little fight's put me to wonderin'. Mighten you be *the* Jensen? Smoke Jensen?"

Laughing, Smoke nodded in the affirmative. "None other. And, I'll say it was a pleasure to fight alongside someone who can handle a shotgun in so masterful a manner."

"Careful. Talk like that'll git me a big head," Crosby grumbled good-naturedly. "Well, seein's as how you are Smoke Jensen, I'm obliged to let you know that there is something in the wind that don't blow good where you're concerned. It'd be best if you watched your back-trail real close. An' to check every curve before you round it."

"I appreciate that, Morgan. I've heard something to that effect before."

Crosby spit a long, brown stream of tobacco juice. "This ain't in the past. I'm talkin' about the here and now. I reckon these proddy little pissants were lookin' to collect on that money's been put on yer head."

"No doubt. Some others tried just yesterday," Smoke informed Morgan. "And I do know who's put up the bounty."

Morgan Crosby cackled and slapped a thigh. "I figgered you did. A feller in your position don't live as long as you have, lest he's mighty smart. Now, you take care, Smoke Jensen. I'll deal with these bodies."

"You could use a hand digging holes," Smoke offered.

"I ain't that old that I need help. Besides, who said I was gonna bury them? We've got plenty hungry coyotes and buzzards around these parts. All I have to do is drag the bodies away from here."

Smoke took his leave. "Thank you for the good meal and for lending a hand with this trash."

"It's me who's thankin' you," Crosby came back. "I haven't had me that much excitement in a long time. Makes me feel twenty years younger."

With an exchange of friendly waves, Smoke Jensen turned Thunder down the lane and rode off northward from the cabin. Morgan Crosby bent to fix a rope around the crossed ankles of the late Hank Graves to make ready to drag the corpse out of sight and smell of the cabin. He'd harness up old Rose. She was steadiest for chores like that. It had indeed been a good day, he thought with a crooked smile on his lips.

"So this is Dutch John," Ralph Tinsdale declared as the outlaw gang rode into the outskirts of a small town nestled in the Uinta Mountain, located in the northeast corner of Utah. "What are we stopping here for?"

Victor Spectre told him at once. "When I was last here, they had recently opened a nice little bank. I figure by now it should be rather prosperous. What some of you are going to do is make a withdrawal."

Tinsdale's eyes scanned the streets. Every man in sight wore a six-gun or had a rifle or shotgun close at hand. Even the purses of some of the women bulged in a suggestive manner. More Mormons, he reckoned, still shaken by the ferocity of the fight they had been forced to run from. From what he saw here, these people seemed equally competent. He made his unease known to Spectre.

"Are we all going to be in on it? These people can handle themselves. We could be caught in these streets, trapped here while they cut us down to the last man."

Victor Spectre gave him an encouraging smile. "Nothing to be alarmed about. We'll designate six to ten men to rob the bank, while the rest of us avoid the business district and ride out of town a ways. There we will prepare a greeting for any posse that might follow." He reined in and turned to the other side.

"Gus, pick nine good men and split off from the rest. You'll enter the main part of town up ahead in twos and threes. Do nothing to attract attention. At precisely eleven fifty-nine, you will enter the bank with five men. Close and lock the doors, draw the blinds and then take everything."

"How come we gotta do it right then?" Farlee Huntoon blurted out.

If looks had the capacity for murder, the thunderous expression Victor Spectre turned on Farlee Huntoon would have had him dead and buried, six feet deep, and a headstone erected. "For one thing, Mr. Huntoon, you will not be going along. However, I'll answer your question for the benefit of any others who might be unaware. In these small communities, every business, with the exception of eating establishments and saloons, closes down over the noon hour. The bank will be no exception. That should give you the better part of an hour to thoroughly loot the place."

Fin Brock and Judson Reese rubbed their hands together in anticipation. Grinning, Reese spoke for them both. "I like that. Just take our time and git it all, eh?"

"Precisely, Mr. Reese," Victor told him. "The five who remain outside will provide a delaying action once the robbery has been discovered. Those carrying the money will ride by the most direct route to the northern edge of town and take the high road in the direction we have been following. You will know when you have caught up with us."

Brock sniggered. "We'll know it even more when any posse catches up."

Spectre suppressed a smile. "That we will. Now, Gus, pick the men you want and we will start off. Those participating in the ambush will take varying routes out of this residential area, with none, I repeat, none entering downtown. Good luck."

"And good fortune," Olin Buckner added with a jaunty salute.

Walter Higgins looked up from his large, roll-top desk as two men entered the double front doors of the Merchant's Bank of Dutch John. Through the open doorway of his private office he could see the large hand on the clock click over to 11:59. With perfect timing, the chief clerk intercepted the rough-edged customers.

"I'm sorry, gentlemen. We are about to close for the dinner hour. Can you possibly come back at one this afternoon?"

The better dressed of the pair spoke in well-rounded tones. "We won't be long. I promise you that."

It was then that Walter Higgins noticed three more men crowd in behind. They had the disreputable appearance of saddle trash. *Oh, God,* the banker thought, *we are going to be robbed.* Sure enough, the last one in turned around, shot the bolt, and drew the blinds. Higgins sent an unwilling hand to the drawer that contained his revolver.

That is when weapons appeared in the hands of the desperados. The softly spoken one put steel in his voice this time. "I wouldn't finish that reach, Mr. Banker."

For some unaccountable reason, Walter answered through trembling lips. "Higgins. My name is Higgins."

"Now, that's quite all right, Mr. Higgins. You see, we've come to make a major withdrawal." Gus Jaeger gestured with the muzzle of his Colt to the teller cages. "Get to it, boys."

To add insult to injury, the outlaws stuffed all the cash and coin into canvas bank bags and secured the leather tops to buckles by their straps. Although he had never had his bank robbed before, Walter Higgins felt certain that he was behaving in the proper manner. If only he could keep his mouth shut.

"You'll not get away with this. The Mormon Militia has an outpost not far from town. They'll hunt you down, you know."

Two of the lowlives sniggered. "Watch us tremble, *Mister* Higgins," Jaeger sneered.

This could not be happening. The tall, thin one who had been speaking, pushed through the rail that divided the working part of the bank from its lobby and went directly to the vault. Walter Higgins half-rose from his chair.

"There's nothing in there," he blurted in a chill of anxiety.

"Let's let me find that out for myself." Gus continued to advance of the big, walk-in safe. "Oh, my," he announced a moment after entering. "If it wasn't your job to protect your depositors' valuables, I would be quite angry at you for lying," he informed Higgins. "As it is, I'll simply ask you to come help me fill up a few bags."

Higgins raised a hand that shook as though palsied. "I cannot. It would make me . . . culpable."

Jaeger's head appeared around the two-foot thick brick wall of the vault. "That's a new word for me. What's it mean?"

"It means, that if I help you, in the eyes of the law it would be as though I robbed my own bank."

Gus Jaeger smiled nastily. "I'm sure you would find some way of explaining it. Now get in here or I'll blow you clear to Kingdom Come."

Walter Higgins wanted to sob. Shoulders slumped, he got up on his high-button shoes and shambled to the opening. For a wild second he thought of slamming the vault door on the outlaw and thus trap him for the law. Then hope died as he realized that it took two men to close the door. Inside, Higgins meekly held the bags, while the robber scooped stacks of banded bills off the shelves. A sickening sensation spread from his middle. There had to be at least 25,000 dollars here. A vast fortune. And he would be held responsible. He wanted to speak out, to refuse. One look at those cold, hazel eyes convinced him not to. At last it was over. Three sheaves of five dollar bills remained.

With a nasty smirk, the robber pointed to them. "I'll leave a little seed stock. Thank you for your contribution."

Back in the usually sane, silent, stable world of the bank proper, the gathering up had been completed. A hard hand touched his suit coat from behind. He shrank from it. With a push, Jaeger urged Walter Higgins toward his chair.

"Take yer seat, Mr. Higgins. We'll be leaving now. Nobody poke a head out or make a sound for at least ten minutes. If you do, you'll be hurt . . . and badly."

After they left the bank, Walter Higgins folded his arms on his desk, lowered his head, and began to sob softly. Faintly, from the street, he heard the drum of many hooves. It did not make him feel any better.

Sheriff Atwater sipped coffee from a tin cup and leaned back on the back legs of his chair, tilted against the wall of his office. A growing commotion outside drew his attention. At last, Parker Evans, the bank guard, rushed through the doorway. Eyes wide, hair in disarray, Evans looked like he had seen the Devil himself.

Atwater, a calm easy-going man, did not even lower his chair front to the floor. He merely gestured with the half-full cup and spoke in a lazy drawl. "What's got you all excited Parker?"

"We've been robbed, Sheriff! The bank. Five men came in and took every last cent. They ordered us to stay inside, but the minute they rode off, I snuck out the side door and ran for here."

Now the chair banged to the floor. "Five men, you say?"

"Yep. But from the sound of the hooves, I'd judge they were twice that number."

"Go spread the word, Parker. I'll be getting a posse ready. We'll ride out at once with however many I can buttonhole.

You follow with what more you find soon as you can. Oh, by the way, you're deputized."

Sheriff Atwater followed Evans out the door. He headed directly to the eatery on the corner where he knew his three duty deputies would be. He rounded them up, and seven others in for their dinner. They went next to the feed and grain store and acquired five more men. The last stop, at the livery stable, produced three more. A small boy with black hair, cornflower blue eyes, and a dusting of freckles ran up with a message from the bank guard.

"Mr. Evans says he has fifteen men rounded up and they will be ready in ten minutes. He says that the ones you're after left town to the north."

"Thank you, Tommy," Atwater replied as he swung up to the saddle after swearing in the volunteers. "Well boys, we know where to go now."

He turned the head of his horse and led the way out of town.

The only northern pass out of the Uinta Mountains narrowed some fifteen miles out of Dutch John to a steepwalled canyon. Three waterfalls, spaced from two to five miles apart, thundered in silver streams from high overhead, curtains of mist around their bases. Crystal clear water, icy cold to the touch, ran from these spectacular displays of nature. Aspen, cottonwood, hickory, and cedars put splashes of green in the crags of the ochre gorge.

In the midst of this spectacular scenery, Victor Spectre chose to set up his ambush. Out of sight around a curve, he put a team of outlaws to falling trees, while others dug out at the base of boulders, to roll them onto the trail. Satisfied when he saw that project showing progress, he turned to the inactive hard cases.

"Pick yourselves a good location on the slopes beyond the barricade. Dig yourselves in. Then fix a place for at least one other man who is working on the road. We have no way of knowing how many will be coming after us. This could be a desperate battle. One we cannot afford to lose. We must turn them back decisively. I have every confidence in you."

"Sounds jist lak a gen'ral don't he?" Farlee Huntoon said in a not-too-quiet aside to Dorcus Carpenter.

"You got any complaint with what money we've made so far?" Carpenter asked acidly.

Huntoon had to think about that a while. "No. Now you put it lak that, none at all, at all."

Believing it important to appear entirely in control, Victor Spectre chose to ignore the babbling of the hillbilly. "They will be here before you know it, so you had better get started. Make sure you have plenty ammunition. Then, remember how hard those Mormons hit us outside Grand Canyon and hit this posse twice as hard."

Thus inspired, the hard cases went to it with a will. They dug out shallow pits and tamped piles of dirt and rocks in front for a firing platform, then some of the more enterprising among the usually lazy criminals concealed their efforts with cut branches. From a distance of twenty yards the leaves nicely hid the raw earth.

An hour later, everything lay in readiness. A lookout posted back down the trail rounded the curve at a brisk canter. He had his hat in his hand, waving it above his head. "They're comin'! They're right behind me."

He slowed and angled his mount beyond the barricade, then disappeared into the low-hanging branches of a big cedar. Moments later, the sound of drumming hoofbeats reached the ears of the waiting outlaws. In the blink of an eye, Sheriff Atwater and two others rounded the bend and rendezvoused with history.

Twenty-three rifles crashed, but only three slugs plucked at the loose woolen jacket worn by the lawman. Behind him, his deputies likewise went unscathed, with only damaged clothing. By then the rest of the posse crowded onto them from behind and the fight became a wild melee.

Sheriff Atwater looked on in helpless dismay while some members of his posse dismounted and sought shelter among the boulders and from behind the overhanging lip of the creek bank. At last he found voice for his worry.

"Don't dismount! Stay on your horses, men. We've got to pull back."

"They can't shoot through rocks," a haberdashery clerk shouted up from behind a huge granite mound.

"Why pull back?" another greenhorn at the lawman game asked. "We got 'em trapped."

"It's more like we're the ones trapped," Atwater muttered to himself.

At least, more slugs on both sides passed through air than flesh, he observed gratefully. That gave them an even chance, or would have if the suspected ten outlaws had not turned into a regular army of them. From the relative safety of halfway around the curve, he counted enemy muzzle flashes. Atwater came up with twenty-eight, which meant ten more shooters than he had. The way they all consumed ammunition, the sheriff reasoned, they would soon be down to knives and fists.

That speculation proved wasted effort five minutes later when the second half of the posse arrived in a cloud of dust. Townsmen and local ranchers shouted and milled in confusion until the presence of more men banished the fear in the timid and a decision was made to attack the hard cases behind the barricade. When they did, all hell broke loose.

Nine

Victor Spectre watched the arrival of the second posse with considerable apprehension. When their dash toward the barricade his men had erected turned to milling confusion, it raised his spirits a good deal. He clapped his partners, Ralph Tinsdale and Olin Buckner, on their shoulders and nodded toward the quandary below.

"Looks like they are doing our job for us," he stated heartily.

Tinsdale studied the disorganization a moment. "Can't we take advantage of this?"

Spectre thought about that. "Yes. Have the men slow their rate of fire and take careful aim. A few bodies falling off of horses should do wonders for that posse."

His words went out quickly. The steady crackle of rifles and six-guns dwindled gradually, until individual shots could be counted. That's when the bank guard, Parker Evans, decided to have his contingent charge.

"By God, they're coming at us again," Buckner blurted.

Spectre remained calm. "All the better, Olin, They have to slow down to get around the barrier. Our men can slaughter them."

All three escaped convicts looked on in astonishment as six of the more adventurous among the possemen raced directly at the barricade, guns blazing, to jump the obstruction. They cleared it with hooves dragging, and surprisingly, shot their way clear of the gathered outlaws, to win safety on the far side. The rest of the posse stalled out against the mass of dirt, rocks, and tree trunks.

"I don't believe that," Ralph Tinsdale gasped. "How could anyone have missed them?"

Gus Jaeger joined the trio at their vantage point on a small knob. "Simple, we weren't expecting it. We'll be ready the next time."

Having the charge broken finally allowed Sheriff Atwater to gain the attention of the entire posse. He stood on a rock part way up the slope of the canyon wall on the right-hand side and raised his arms over his head to signal for quiet.

"This isn't over by a long way. We haven't even hurt them, but they haven't beaten us either. We're going to have to do some thinking on this."

"Wish I'd have brought some dynamite," the owner of the General Mercantile grumbled.

Atwater looked at him with disdain. "What, and have us all deafened? No boys, that's not the way. What I want is for about ten of you to ride back to the nearest ford across this creek. Then walk your horses up this way under cover of the neigh bank. From what I've seen of it, the overhang will give you cover up past where those robbers are holed out. We've got six fellers over there already. When you get up with them, position yourselves so that any stray shots from us won't hit you. Then fire a shot to signal us. We'll attack them together."

Several heads nodded in understanding and agreement. "That should work," Parker Evans spoke for them all.

Not one for rousing speeches, Sheriff Atwater looked hard at the posse and gestured with one pointed finger to the downhill ford. "All right, then, lets get to it."

Parker Evans picked ten men who had come with him and set out for the water crossing. Sheriff Atwater watched them out of sight, and then muttered softly to himself, "I sure hope this works."

Parker Evans and his picked crew found the bullet-riddled body of a stranger floating in the stream at the ford. At least one of the outlaws had been hit, he thought with grim satisfaction. Too bad it could not be more. He walked his horse into the shallow water and turned uphill. Silently, the others followed him.

A quarter of a mile from the ambush site, shelving sand-bars formed a dry shelf on which to walk. It also ended the noisy splash of eleven horses walking. Cattails grew in profusion on the silt-covered higher portions of the sand-bank. The sharp-edged leaves of the water plants cut at exposed hands and one slashed the cheek of Roger Latimer. He grunted and dabbed at the incision with one hand. When it came away covered in blood, he pulled a kerchief from his pocket and held it to the wound. Evans suddenly signaled for a halt.

The faint sound of voices rode the air above the gurgle of running water. Evans signed for the others to hold fast and eased forward. He rounded the bend where the barricade had been constructed and came face-to-face with one of Spectre's hard cases. Fortunately for the volunteer deputy, he had his six-gun in one hand. Unfortunately for any hope of sneaking past the outlaws undetected, he fired it into the chest of the scruffy, long-haired thug.

"What's going on?" a voice demanded. Three shots followed.

Parker Evans fired twice to cover his retreat, then turned tail. The rest of the crew wore expressions of disappointment when he rejoined them. Roger Latimer put their feelings into words. "What did you go an' do that for?"

In his defense Evans spoke what he had been thinking. "I didn't plan on it. I just came upon this feller with the robbers. They have men down here on this side of the road-block."

"They sneakin' up on us, do you suppose?" asked one not-too-bright shop clerk.

"No, stupid, but it's plain we can't sneak by them now," Latimer complained.

Evans shrugged. "Yeah, We might as well turn back."

The pop-eyed, sandy-haired clerk belabored the obvious. "The sheriff ain't gonna like this."

Parker Evans had no intention of allowing that to be the last word. "Could be. But, he'd like it even less if I got you all killed, don't you think?" Then another thought struck him. "Nope. We're not turning back. You," he pointed to Latimer, "ride back alone and tell the sheriff that I suggest he get the posse ready to attack from the front again. When the shootin' starts, we'll come on 'em from the crick."

"It's better than goin' back with our tails between our legs," Latimer agreed.

Evans tried for enthusiasm in his words. "And it'll work, too."

Suddenly the air of the canyon turned into a hailstorm of hot lead. The posse came back at them with guns blasting into the positions prepared by the outlaws. At first, Victor Spectre could not believe it. When a twig snapped off the tree he sat under and dropped on his shoulder, he lost all doubt.

"Pour it on, men!" he shouted. "Give them a taste of hell."

If they could turn them once more, really hurt them and break the charge again, then they stood a chance to bring an end to it. At least for now, Victor amended his thoughts. Pursuit would be inevitable. But, it wasn't too far to the territorial boundary. That was definitely in their favor. Firing began from the six lawmen behind them, adding to the confusion. He saw two men fly from their horses as though yanked by ropes. Another dropped his weapon and howled, though the voice could not be heard above the bedlam of the fighting. The charge faltered.

These weren't professional lawmen, paid to risk their lives, Victor reasoned. Store keepers and clerks had too much else to worry about. Spectre brightened as the lead rank of the posse turned aside, to circle the upper end of the barrier. Another man took a bullet and turned away. Then, suddenly, a fresh salvo erupted from the creek bank. Men in overalls and business suits streamed upward, effectively flanking his forces, Victor Spectre saw. Their near-victory could become a terrible defeat.

Parker Evans surged upward over the lip of the creek bank. The front shoulders of his mount surged with power as they gained purchase on the more level ground above. To left and right he saw confused, frightened faces. Then the six men who had ridden beyond the gang charged downhill. Several outlaws actually broke and ran. This just might be it, he thought exaltedly.

Then a heavy .45 caliber slug ripped through his brain and ended the banking career of Parker Evans. Dead before he hit the ground, Evans lay atop one hard case he had killed only a second before.

When the townspeople with him saw Evans die their resolve disappeared in a whiff of powder smoke. Reining in sharply, they turned the heads of their horses toward the creek and dashed to safety. Suddenly without support, the six in the rear also swerved toward the shelter of the water. Half a hundred bullets followed them. One among the fleeing possemen uttered a piercing scream and did a back-roll off the rump of his mount.

Out in front of the wall of wood and dirt, the charge

faltered, then reversed in a panicked scramble to the protection beyond the far side of the curve. Several of the less experienced among the gang raised a cheer. Pride even swelled in Victor Spectre for a moment, and prompted him to mount up and ride down among the entrenched gunmen.

"We did it, men. I told you we would."

Even the most cynical among them looked upon Victor Spectre with renewed respect. Several among the outlaws rushed forward to urge immediate action.

"Let's go after them," one suggested.

"Right. Run them to ground and finish off the lot."

"No," Victor dashed their expectations after brief thought. "We'll wait a while, see if they come back."

"We could be well along the trail if we leave now," Ralph Tinsdale implied.

Spectre considered that a moment. "Very well. We'll wait fifteen minutes and then send someone forward to find out what they are doing."

"That does it," Sheriff Atwater spat, as he tasted the bitterness of defeat. "We'll have to turn back."

"But they've got our money," Roger Latimer protested.

Sheriff Atwater had to answer that and fast. "We'll get it back. Here's how. We will pull back a ways from this bend. Regroup beyond the ford and find out what we have to work with. While we do, I'll send two of you back to find the Militia and ask them to join in. I know," he hastened to add to forestall the protest he knew would come. "Not all of us are Mormons, but they had money in that bank, too. They'll come. When we have soldiers here, we can crush these vermin like stink bugs."

"What if they don't wait? What if they come after us, or pull out?"

"If they do, Roger, while the militia is on the way, we'll fight them, give ground slowly. Or follow along if they run.

One way or the other we have to finish this before they reach the border."

Nate Miller and Fin Brock returned after an absence of only five minutes. "They ain't there, Mr. Spectre," Miller reported. "We looked as far as the last ford and there's not a sign of them. Looks like they turned tail."

"That's fine, just fine," Spectre beamed. He turned to the eager faces of the gang. "Well, men, I think we can leave all of this behind us. We haven't far to go to be rid of the threat at any count. We will be in Wyoming within less than a day. Mount up and let's go."

Swollen with prideful success, the gang went to their horses. Encouraged by the high spirits of the men, Spectre allowed himself to expand a bit more on the theme as they walked their horses to the notch that led them to the high country of Bridger Basin.

"We're headed for a town, men," Spectre said loudly enough to let it echo back along the ranks. "And when we get there, we will send for Smoke Jensen."

Always the malcontent, Farlee Huntoon asked, "Mr. Spectre, how can you be so sure he will come?"

Eyes sparkling, Victor Spectre produced a broad, knowing smile. So confident was he of success that he did not even bother to insult the lout from West Virginia. "Oh, I'll think of something," he answered archly.

Smoke Jensen had a definite location in mind. It had been some time since he had visited Jackson's Hole. He reckoned that the high peaks around this spectacular basin would be ideal for him to work his way around whoever came along with Spectre, Tinsdale, and Buckner. He could clearly visualize a nice little cove in the Snake River where the sand washed almost snow white and the grass grew lush and thick. It smelled of sweet pine and wild daisies and the breeze blew softly with only a few days exception. He would settle in there and then scout out the country around the basin.

Surrounded as it was by 13- and 14,000 feet peaks the small "hole" served as the southern gateway to the Yellowstone country, the "Land of Smokes," as the Blackfeet, Crow, and Cheyenne called it. Beyond it, "civilization" had begun to encroach. Three towns now existed on land that had only a few years ago been covered red-black with the backs of millions of bison. Of all of these settlements, the only one Smoke considered deserving of existence was Dubois.

A quite, peaceful town, Dubois had an honest lawman, a church, and a school long before any such had existed anywhere else in Wyoming. They welcomed any among the law-abiding, with zero tolerance for beggars, criminals or trash. The reason? Smoke Jensen had helped make it that way. When Smoke's time came at last to leave, the townspeople threw a three day fandango. Colorful bunting and Chinese lanterns decorated the main intersection. There was feasting—trestle tables groaned under the weight of food, kegs of beer, and bottles of whiskey—dancing long into the night, and games for the children. Narry a feminine eye, from eight to eighty, was dry when Smoke finally rode out.

Maybe he would visit Dubois on this trip and let the word get out from there that he had come back to Jackson's Hole. Then he would return to the Hole and begin to construct some unpleasant surprises for Spectre and the gang he would bring with him. It would be necessary, he knew, because the three of them would not come alone. Even together, they did not have the courage it would take to face him. Now, halfway across the Great Divide Basin, he called an early halt for the day.

He spent two hours of the remaining daylight to check his back-trail. Smoke found it reassuringly empty. Next he turned his attention to making camp. While he worked, his mind turned back to how he first encountered and dealt with Victor Spectre, Ralph Tinsdale, and Olin Buckner. . . .

Olin Buckner had dreams of building an empire in Central Montana. He, and two like-minded associates had worked over a few years to acquire ownership of Twin Pines, a small settlement in a lush valley that contained only four ranches. Two of them belonged to the consortium of Buckner and his friends. One of these had actually been obtained through legal means. Not so the business establishments of Twin Pines. The three saloons, two eating establishments, the hotel, and the feed and grain outlet had been acquired by the simple means of brute force. Only one business, the general store, held out. It was there that Smoke Jensen learned of the methods employed by Buckner's hired guns. Smoke had come in for supplies and had nearly completed his transaction when four of Buckner's bully-boys swaggered into the mercantile.

"Yer not sellin' anything to him," the self-appointed leader brayed, a stubby finger pointed at Smoke. "He's workin' for that Luscomb woman." He knew that much, but he didn't know who Smoke *was.*

The proprietor bristled. "I'll sell to whomever I please."

"Not anymore." The reply crackled in the suddenly tense atmosphere of the room. "Y'see, that's what I came to tell you. Mr. Buckner has decided this has gone on long enough. He's buying you out as of today. I brung over the papers, all legal and such. All you gotta do is sign." Grinning, he shoved forward the papers.

Reflexively the store keeper took them and began to read aloud. " *'For the sum of one dollar, and other valuable considerations, I, Howard Leach, do agree to sell and convey all interest and claim to the property, building and contents thereof . . . '* one dollar!* I wouldn't sell for ten thousand times that sum. And I would never sell to Olin Buckner and those scum he associates with. Now, get out of here, Tyson."

Swiftly, the grin on the face of Zeke Tyson turned to a thunderous scowl. "I even brought you your dollar. You'll take it, if you know what's smart."

No question remained in the mind of Smoke Jensen as to how he would side in this matter. He eased away from the counter and faced off with the thug. "The man said he didn't want to sell."

Snarling, the hard case reached out and began to tap the chest of Smoke Jensen with one stubby finger. He made a big mistake. "Keep yourself shut of this, saddle trash. Best you get out of here and hit the road."

"Please."

"Please what?"

"Please get out. And, *please* hit the road."

Pushed beyond the extremely low threshold of his temper, the dull-witted Tyson exploded with rage. "You five-and-dime tinhorn." He looked Smoke up and down with utter disdain, noting the low-slung righthand rig, with the .44 Colt Model '60, and the other one, worn slant-wise, at belt level on the left hip, butt outward. "You fancy yourself a gunfighter, eh? You're just about to find out what that word means."

"Please, Tyson, take it outside," Howard Leach appealed.

Frothing at the mouth, the thug whirled on the merchant. "All right, Howie, we'll do just that. Then, when I'm done, I'm gonna come back in here and get your signature on that paper or spread it with your brains."

Tyson led the way out into the street. Two of his henchmen followed. They spread out, with one hard case leaning on a rain barrel across the main drag, the other some twenty feet east of Zeke Tyson. Smoke Jensen came next, with the last thug behind him. Smoke made note that the lout remained at his back. It troubled him somewhat, though not a great deal. Tyson spread thick, trunklike legs, and stood flat-footed in the center of the avenue.

His words came in a jeering bray. "Any time yer ready, tinhorn."

Smoke raised a hand in a halting gesture and took a quick sidestep to his left. "You're the one who wanted this, not I. If you want to make a play, go ahead. But, get this scum-sucker out from behind me first."

"Tally likes it right where he is. Don't ya, Tally?"

"Sure enough, Zeke," came the mocking reply from be-hind Smoke Jensen.

"Well, then, in that case, if you haven't anything more to puke out of that overworked mouth of yours, I suppose it is up to me to open this dance."

So saying, Smoke spun and dropped to one knee. His righthand Colt appeared in his hand in a blur and he shot Tally dead-center in the chest. Tally thrust himself backward and slammed into the front wall of the mercantile. Pain blurred his vision and he waggled the Merwin and Hulbert .44 in his left hand uncertainly, in search of a target.

Only Smoke Jensen had moved the moment his six-gun recoiled in his grip. He did a shoulder roll that put him ten feet from where he had started and well out of the line of fire from either Tally or Tyson. Unfortunately for Tally, the move had been made too swiftly. Zeke Tyson had fisted his own six-gun and let roar. The slug cut through air where Smoke Jensen had been and slammed into the bulging stomach of Buck Tally.

"Oh, God, Zeke, you done kilt me," Tally panted out. Gut-shot, his words came out coated in crimson. He slid to a sitting position with a mighty groan. His boot heels drummed on the planks of the boardwalk and he stiffened suddenly. A great gout of blood vomited explosively from his distorted lips and he fell over dead.

"Jesus, nobody can shoot that fast," one of the remaining toughs with Zeke Tyson babbled as he stared at the fallen gunman.

"Get him, goddamnit!" Tyson shouted. "What are you two good for?"

From his place in the center of the street, one quickly showed that he was good for dying. He tracked his already-drawn six-gun toward Smoke Jensen, who ducked below the rim of a horse trough and hugged the ground a moment. When slugs punched through the spongy wood of the opposite side and began to spill water onto the ground, Smoke popped up, sighted quickly, and blasted a lead messenger of death into the heart of the hapless hard case.

Staggered, he discharged his weapon in the general direction of Smoke Jensen and dropped to both knees. Smoke felt the heat of the bullet as it cracked past his right ear. His fourth round struck solid bone in the skull of the wounded gunman and put him into the next world. Smoke moved the instant after he fired.

Desperately, Zeke Tyson made his try for Smoke Jensen. In all his short life, Zeke had never seen anyone so fast and so accurate as this saddle tramp. His own slug cut through emptiness where the dauntless gunfighter had been a moment before. Then it was his turn to look down the muzzle of a leveled .44. He immediately did what any red-blooded, first-rate gunfighter would do. He ran like hell for the safety of a nearby alleyway.

Smoke Jensen turned his attention to the remaining henchman. Thoroughly cowed by the speed and deadliness of their intended victim, he had ducked behind the flimsy cover of the rain barrel. To his regret, it had not rained in twenty-seven days and the level in the barrel had dropped to only a couple of inches. He shot around its bulging middle and drew greatly unwanted return fire.

With the ease of a bar of lead dropped in a mud hole, Smoke's slugs cut through the oak staves of the intervening cylinder and out the other side to lodge in the chest of the crouching gunhand. Without a sound, he spread out on his back on the boardwalk. Smoke Jensen waited a moment, then approached cautiously.

Only a dwindling light remained in the eyes of the dying man. Pink foam bubbled from the holes in his chest and a spreading pool of red surrounded his shoulders. Concentrating his energy, he formed breathy words.

"Who . . . who are . . . you . . . mister?"

"They call me Smoke Jensen."

Understanding bloomed in those dead man's eyes. "I . . . I should . . . have . . . known. I'm . . . I'm dead, ain't I?"

No reason to hide the truth, Smoke reasoned. "You soon will be."

"Gawd, it . . . don't hurt any less."

"What doesn't?"

"Gettin' . . . done in . . . by the-the . . . best." Then he gave a mighty convulsive heave and died.

That's the moment Zeke Tyson chose to fire a shot from ambush. The bullet whipped by close enough to cut the hat from the head of Smoke Jensen. Smoke turned and drew his second Colt from its high holster. The muzzle tracked right and he fired into the puffball of powder smoke that lingered at the corner of the alley. It struck nothing and Smoke heard the thud of retreating boots. Prudence cautioned him that it would be foolish to go in and dig out the man. Instead, he crossed the street.

In the doorway, the merchant stood with an expression of awe on his face. "Lawsie, you did for them right sudden like. Mister Jensen, your custom is welcome in my establishment any time."

Smoke gazed on him with a hard eye. "Will it still be when I come after Olin Buckner?"

"Yes, sir. You can count on it."

When Smoke Jensen returned to town at the head of a large band of gunfighter friends and a number of oldtimer mountain man acquaintances from his days with Preacher, the store keeper stood true to his word. Although by that time, he wore one arm in a sling, the result of a savage beating he had taken from Buckner's henchmen.

Smoke had personally cleaned the ploughs of those responsible and they presently inhabited the hilltop cemetery west of town. In retaliation, Buckner had hired an army of gunfighters, put a bounty on the head of Smoke Jensen and sat back to enjoy the results. That consequence soon bankrupted Olin Buckner and cleared the way for the final showdown.

After some judicious whittling away of the odds, Smoke and his rugged band closed in on the Crystal Cage Saloon, Buckner's headquarters. The fighting grew fierce and, at one point, it looked as though Smoke Jensen and his allies might go down in defeat. Two men had gained the roof of the bank across the street from the general store positioning themselves to shoot Smoke Jensen in the back. That is when the steadfast merchant took a hand in the game. He burst through the doors to his business, his trusty shotgun in hand and shouted to Smoke.

"Smoke! Look out! On top the bank."

Smoke had started to whirl around when the shotgun boomed and the store keeper blew one of the hard cases off his feet. Smoke settled with the other a second later. Smoke waved his six-gun at the man and quickly set to reloading.

"Thanks, I owe you one," the famous gunfighter told the merchant.

"Way I figure it, I still owe you a couple, Mr. Jensen," he responded beaming.

Balance quickly shifted in the fighting. When he finally closed with Buckner, Smoke Jensen administered a thorough thrashing with iron hard fists. Bleeding and broken, Buckner lay slumped in defeat in a corner of a room above the saloon. But only for a moment. From an inside coat pocket, Buckner produced a two-shot, .50 caliber derringer. Racking back the hammer of the short-barreled, under-powered weapon, Buckner fought to get enough air to rail at his enemy.

"Goddamn you, Smoke Jensen. You'll pay for ruining me."

His first shot slammed into the thick, wide leather cartridge belt at the small of Smoke's back. It failed to penetrate, though it staggered the gunfighter. Yet, Smoke managed to turn and face his assailant. Buckner's second bullet cut a hole, front to rear, through the fleshy part of Smoke's right side. Its impact coincided with the discharge of the Colt in the hand of Smoke Jensen.

Put well off course, the slug went low and smashed the right hip joint of Olin Buckner. Dizzied by earlier wounds, Smoke Jensen stumbled across the room and kicked the now-useless pistol from the hand of its owner. Then he sat heavily in a chair, blood streaming from his side, and waited for someone to come.

Ten

It was the same when he faced Ralph Tinsdale. . . .
Smoke Jensen had been a friend of Harrison Tate for over
twenty years when he received a telegram at the Sugarloaf
from Harrison's wife, Martha. Had Smoke dwelled in one
of the glittery cities of the East, or even in Denver, his
message would have come with a black border. Harrison
had died three days earlier, ridden down by a runaway carriage. The driver had not been caught. Saddened by the loss
of a good friend, Smoke and Sally Jensen made ready at
once to take the train from Big Rock to Denver to attend
the funeral.

When they arrived, Smoke found the circumstances re-
lating to the death of Harry Tate a bit like over-ripe fish.
He also became embroiled in a minor scuffle after the funeral, at the grave-side service. A scruffy-looking individual
approached Martha, demanding to speak with her immediately. He was, he claimed, an attorney, representing a client
who absolutely insisted that Martha sell some property to
him.

Rude to the point of disgust, the lawyer kept a bland
expression as he pushed his cause. Boorishly, he shoved the
papers into the face of the grieving widow. Only the heavy
veil that covered her face prevented him from actually striking her. Sally Jensen put one arm protectively around the
shoulders of Martha Tate.

"You do not understand, madam. Women cannot inherit

property in their own right. You have no children, so you may retain possession of your husband's property for so long as it takes to dispose of it. The sooner, the better."

His untimely and unseemly intrusion sent flashes of memory through Smoke Jensen. In an instant he recalled the pressure brought against the merchant in Montana. This sounded too much like that to ignore. Smoke moved forward as the cad shoved the papers forward again.

Smoke planted a big, hard hand on the nearest shoulder of the shyster and bore down with hard fingers. "Back off, buster," the lawyer said from the side of his mouth.

Smoke swung him with such force his hat spun away and his longish hair swung in the breeze. Smoke planted his other fist solidly against the still-flapping lips, painfully stilling them, and depositing the lout on his butt in the rain-wet grass. Smoke spoke softly, yet each word bore the weight of menace. "Now that I have your attention, listen good. The lady has just buried her husband. Kindly have the decency to allow a proper period of mourning. And, while we're at it, kindly haul your despicable carcass out of here this instant."

Shaken, the attorney cut his eyes from Smoke to the widow, then back again. "I don't know who you think you are. . . ." he began to bluster.

"Oh, I know quite well who I am. My name is Smoke Jensen."

Instantly the lawyer turned the ashen color of the already dead, a greenish tinge ringed his fat, greedy, now-trembling lips. *Everyone* had heard of Smoke Jensen. Shakily, he scrambled to the soles of his patent leather button shoes and made a hasty retreat, frequently pausing to glance nervously behind him. A fresh shower slanted through the limbless trees and cold fall rain made a damp ruin of the papers clutched in one of his hands. Later he was to find out that his client Ralph Tinsdale had not heard of Smoke Jensen, and didn't care to be advised about the subject. They both lived to regret that.

Over the next five days, Ralph Tinsdale resorted to other, more vicious means of enforcing his will on the Widow Tate. Tinsdale absolutely had to gain title to a choice, highly valuable square block in the center of downtown Denver. He desperately needed it to complete a land development scheme which would make him unbelievably wealthy, with more money than he could spend in three lifetimes. Two nights later, the carriage house behind the Tate mansion on Nob Hill caught afire. Two horses died, and a third was so badly burned that it had to be put down. The next day, Martha Tate found her beloved pet cat poisoned on the back porch. Crushed anew by this added grief, Martha retreated to her sitting room, to be consoled by Sally, while Smoke attended to affairs.

At the local police precinct, Smoke quickly found that the captain and most of his men resided solidly in the hip pocket of the as-yet unnamed speculator. The reception Smoke received when he went to file a complaint on Martha's behalf was cool enough to form frost.

"Accidents do happen, Mr. Jensen," the captain said airily. Then his obvious envy turned his coolness to arctic ice. "Even to the filthy rich."

Smoke could not believe what he had heard. "Are you saying that you are not even going to investigate this?"

"I see no real need."

Ire bubbled up in Smoke Jensen as he rose and leaned menacingly over the captain's desk. *"I do,"* he growled harshly. "If you are going to ignore this, then I'm sure not. I'll look into it on my own."

Steel glinted in the flinty gray eyes of the lawman. "You do and I'll have you behind bars for obstructing justice, interfering in a police investigation, and everything short of mopery."

"How could my investigation interfere with something that is obviously being so ill-served?" Suppose you tell me how can I interfere with an investigation that is not being made?" Smoke stopped suddenly, recalled an offer that had been made to him a year ago by another better lawman than this travesty. "I'll be back here, right enough. Only not to go to jail, but to watch you eat a large helping of crow." With that he swarmed out of the office.

Two hours later, a sheepish desk sergeant knocked on the door to the captain's office. "Uh—Boss, there's a United States Marshal out here, wants to talk to you. He's—ah—been here before."

"Oh, hell, I was about to leave for the day and head for Lulu's place. Send him in," he concluded, sighing.

Smoke Jensen entered the office and the captain's jaw sagged. "Deputy United States Marshal, Kirby Jensen, Captain. I'm here to advise you that I will be conducting an investigation into the cause of death of Harrison Tate, and the attempted extortion and intimidation of a widowed woman by the name of Martha Tate. Neither you nor your men will be required to participate. But I will expect your complete cooperation. Which boils down to this," Smoke added with a blooming smile. "Keep the hell out of my way."

Smoke had left the precinct station and gone directly to the office of the district U.S. Marshal in Denver. An old friend, Marshal Slator, had first offered Smoke Jensen a permanent deputy's badge some five years earlier when Smoke had aided the lawman in clearing out a nest of highwaymen who had plagued the gold fields and storage houses of Colorado. Smoke declined at the time. Slator made the offer again a year gone by. Smoke soon found that it didn't take more than ten words to find the silver circle pinned on his vest under his suit coat. Grinning, he then returned to the police station.

Shaken, the captain began to babble. "How—where—what in the name of God did you do to get that badge?"

"Accepted an old offer from a friend," Smoke answered factually. "Now, can we begin again? I want the names of any known arsonists believed to operate in this district. Also the names of animal haters. I also want a trace put on the carriage that ran down Harrison Tate. Where did it go? Who owns it? Where is it now? Who drove it the day Harry was killed?"

"You sure want a whole lot for a man who was in here not two hours ago begging me to look into some old lady's cat being poisoned."

Smoke gave him a nasty smile. "Why, Captain, I've only begun."

That night, three window panes were shot out of the second floor front of the Tate mansion. That proved an immediate mistake. Smoke Jensen seemed to appear out of nowhere while the two, laughing, drunken men who had fired the shots staggered off down the flagstone walk. Each felt a light touch on one side of their heads an instant before their noggins were painfully slammed together.

Although dazed, one of them had the forethought to go for his six-gun, only to feel the muzzle of a .45 Colt Peacemaker, jammed into his stomach, and fired. The hot gasses blew through his intestines and did more damage than the slug. It reduced him to a writhing ball of misery. Beside him, his stunned companion gaped.

"Awh, God, Petey—Petey," he croaked brokenly. "What happened to you?"

A hard, square-jawed face swam into his view. *"I* happened to him," Smoke Jensen informed the piece of riffraff. "If you are not ready for some of the same, you'll be quick about answering some questions."

"Li—like what?"

"Who hired you to shoot up that house back there?"

"I don't know what you're talking about," the suddenly white-faced punk blurted.

Smoke Jensen showed the drunken lout the blood-spattered muzzle of his Peacemaker and tapped him on his belly. "Yes, you do."

Eyes grown wide and white, the words tumbled out. "I don't know. Some feller we ran into down at Mulrooney's."

"If you don't have a name, what did he look like?"

Eyes fixed on the threatening barrel of Smoke's revolver, the thug gave a description through trembling lips. It matched that of the discourteous lawyer at the funeral. Then he concluded with, "He offered a lot of money. A whole hundred dollars."

"Did he pay you in advance?"

"No. He said to look him u-up!"

"So you have an address. Give it."

Twenty minutes later, Smoke Jensen had the punk locked up and the corpse on the way to the morgue. With that out of the way, he summoned a horse-drawn cab and returned to the Tate mansion. In the morning he would pay a visit at the address he had obtained.

Ten minutes past nine, the next morning, Smoke Jensen let himself into the reception area of an elegant office suite in a five-story brick building on Boyle Street. The view from the top floor windows gave out onto San Francisco Bay. The calm waters, Smoke noticed, wore a plethora of steam ships, their funnels belching black streams, moved majestically through the gaggle of white dots from sail craft of varying size. Smoke knew that there existed rules of the road, so to speak, for vessels on the water, but to him all that bustle appeared to be some sort of mystical dance. At a desk, set behind a dividing rail and forbidding, low gate, sat a prim, pinched-faced young man.

He wore a high, celluloid collar, and an expression of disdain. He had removed his coat, to reveal a snowy shirt, off-set by a florid cravat that seemed to bloom up under his chin. The fellow peered at Smoke through the lenses of a pince-nez and further pursed his already puckered lips. A brass nameplate on the leading edge of the desk declared the individual to be Jerome Wimple.

"May I help you, sir?"

"Yes," Smoke answered bluntly. "Who or what is Tinsdale Properties, Limited?" Smoke had obtained the name from the gold leaf letters on the frosted glass of the outer door.

The priggish secretary glanced around the outer room, at the potted plants, long burgundy drapes, dark wainscotting, and starkly white painted walls, as though to determine the answer to that question for himself. He sighed, as though loathe to speak, and raised a narrow hand, with long, pallid fingers in a gesture of dismissal.

"We deal in real estate. Do you wish to list a property with us or are you looking to buy?"

"Neither one. I'm looking for a man who is supposed to work here."

Wimple's expression indicated that he had immediately lost interest, yet his position compelled him to continue this profitless course. "I am familiar with all of our employees. If you can give me his name, I'll be able to direct you to him."

Smoke hesitated a moment. "I don't have a name. Only what he looks like. He's about my height, heavier, maybe two hundred pounds, thick, black hair, a scar under his right eye, sort of red-faced, like a drinking man. Wears a large mustache, which he waxes and curves up the ends."

Oh, dear heavens, Brian Trask! Jerome Wimple blanched for only a fraction of a second, duly recorded by Smoke Jensen.

"I can think of no one of that description working for Tinsdale Limited."

Smoke Jensen took a menacing step toward the desk. "Oh, really? If I were to bounce you off a couple of walls, do you think it would improve your memory?"

Panic put a squeak in Wimple's voice. "You can't do that! Please leave or I shall be compelled to summon the police."

Smoke had reached the desk. With one big, hard hand, he bunched the front of the starched white shirt of Wimple and yanked him off his swivel chair. With the other he delved into his coat pocket and produced the U.S. Marshal's badge.

"I *am* the police. United States Marshal. If I cannot get any satisfaction out of you, I'll speak to Mr. Tinsdale."

"M-Mr. Tinsdale is no—not in at the present time," Wimple stammered, consumed with sudden fright. *What would Bruce say about this?* he wondered. This would never do. Jerome Wimple found himself suddenly released. His rump hit the seat of his chair with a soft splat.

"Then I'll be back." Smoke Jensen turned on one boot heel and stalked from the office.

Down on the ground floor, Smoke started out the tall front double doors when a man entering brushed him rudely aside and passed on for the stairs. Smoke caught only a quick glance. About his size, florid complexion, bulbous nose, black hair, a surly sneer on his face. Smoke had walked across the small stoop and down the five marble steps to street level before he realized who he had just seen.

At once, he swung about and started back into the tall, brick structure. Smoke took the stairs up to the fifth landing two at a time. Quickly, he strode down the carpeted hallway to the door of Tinsdale Properties, Limited. Without a pause, he yanked open the door and stormed down on the startled Jerome Wimple.

"Where is he?" Smoke demanded.

"Where is who—er—whom?" Wimple bleated.

Smoke Jensen bent closer. "The man I just described to you passed me in the lobby downstairs. He had to be coming here. I want to see him now."

"You must be mistaken, Marshal. There's no one come in here since you left."

"If you are lying to me, you'll find yourself in a cell with some mighty tough customers. I guarantee you that you'll not like it."

Smoke Jensen let himself through the swinging gate and advanced on the closed doors of offices along an intersecting hallway. Colt fisted, he threw open each portal, one-by-one. The result turned out the same at each entry. At the far end, he found an outside exit. The panel stood open a crack. Beyond it, Smoke found an exterior iron stairway, a fire escape. From far below he heard the steady ring of leather boot soles on the metal treads. His anger mounting, he returned to the office.

His hot, stinging words lashed into Jerome Wimple. "You miserable piece of pond scum, you warned him off, didn't you?"

"I don't know what you mean."

"Oh, but you do. Here's a little message for you, and for your boss. I'll be back, and when I come, I will use whatever force is necessary to get straight answers."

With that he stomped out of the office. It had been a mistake to show the badge. As a lawman, he was duty-bound not to use undue force or to beat suspects. At least not in public. Smoke Jensen consoled himself with one thing. He had not been kidding about returning.

Over the next three days, Smoke Jensen followed a twisting trail that led at last to a large, lavishly appointed brothel. His man, Smoke had been informed, would be spending the evening and night there. Smoke also had a name now— Brian Trask. From the dregs of Denver society, Smoke had learned that Trask and a crew of henchmen carried out the wishes of their boss, one Ralph Tinsdale. The same Tinsdale who dealt in real estate.

Smoke had questioned Martha Tate about the offers she had received. They had come through a lawyer, she insisted.

But not the one at Harrison's service, she added. The first before her husband's unfortunate accident. Although the police had not been exactly forthcoming with information, Smoke privately believed that Harrison Tate's death had not been an accident. Tonight he intended to verify that belief.

Brian Trask showed up at the parlor house a little after seven that evening. He was as loud and boisterous as he was crude. Smoke wondered how he had ever obtained a membership in one of the bay area's most exclusive bordellos. The parlor houses, unlike the vulgar cribs and doss houses of the waterfront, boasted private membership, elite clientele and the most discreet of parties and private arrangements. It cost a considerable amount to join, and applicants usually underwent intensive scrutiny. Smoke reasoned, correctly, that someone had bought Trask's membership for him. Smoke had shamelessly used a club card he found in the wallet of Harrison Tate, suitably altered to read "Junior," to gain admission. He spent the next two hours observing his target.

Seated in a red leather banquette, with a lovely, young hoyden under one arm, Smoke Jensen watched while Brian Trask teased and fondled several of the inmates of the establishment, and drank prodigiously. Then he consumed a mountainous meal of boiled pig's knuckles and ox tails, with a mound of sauerkraut, mashed potatoes, fried parsnips, and apple sauce. He downed it all with long quaffs of rich, amber beer. Afterward, Trask washed his fingers in a finger bowl as daintily as any Nob Hill fop. Then he took his pick from among the girls.

Smoke leaned toward the doxie he held in one arm and murmured into her ear. "The auburn-haired one there, what is her name?"

His hostess, who said her name was Vivian, peered across the room to where Smoke had nodded and saw Trask and the girl at the foot of a large, curving staircase. "Oh, that's Danielle."

"A lovely girl. But not so delightful as you." Disliking himself for what he was about to do, Smoke Jensen ordered a bottle of champagne and two glasses be brought to a room upstairs and suggested to the sweet young Vivian, who had all but crawled into his lap, that they adjourn to above floors. The bartender and waiter knew which room she used, so the champagne was there, waiting, when they climbed the stairs to the third floor. Even though the wine was brought up by rope-pull dumbwaiter, a human one was there ahead of them, hand out for a gratuity.

Smoke tipped him a three dollar gold piece and saw him to the door, every bit the ardent lover. He kept control of his desire by thinking of his beloved Sally, while Vivian removed her outer clothing and paraded before him in her foundation garment. It was a dangerous pink, trimmed in black lace, with long garter belts that suspended black, net stockings. *It might be all hoity-toity downstairs, but in the privacy of a room,* Smoke thought, *a whore is a whore.* He watched her with feigned appreciation—well, not all that feigned—and then turned away from her to pour the wine. Before popping the cork, he deposited in Vivian's glass the powdered contents of a small envelope he had obtained from the doctor tending Martha Tate. The powerful, taste-less, odorless opiate derivative would induce sleep quickly.

He filled the glasses and watched the powder dissolve, then turned back and handed one to Vivian. They toasted a "night of bliss," and drank deeply. Smoke poured more champagne and again they drank it off. Smoke removed his coat, unfastened the buttons of his vest and removed it. Then he stepped behind the willing young thing and untied the laces of her undergarment. Over her shoulder he kept close watch as Vivian's eyelids began to droop.

"Your friend, Danielle? Which is her room?" he asked softly.

Vivian blinked sleepily. She could not understand why

she was getting so drowsy so early in the evening. His question puzzled her also. "Wh-why do you want to know?"

"More champagne?"

"Ummm. I just want some happy times, Junior."

They all knew Harrison Tate, whom they considered a harmless old roue, who came for the food and drinks and the chance to gaze upon lovely young flesh. The arrival of Tate, Junior had them all excited. Vivian considered herself to have made a fortunate catch. She smiled languidly at him, inviting him to the bed.

"Champagne makes for happy times," Smoke Jensen suggested.

"Jis' a little bit. I feel fun—funny."

"Then laugh and enjoy. We have the whole night ahead of us."

Smoke poured and asked his question again. Through dimming awareness, Vivian dredged up the required answer. "She's in two-oh-seven. Tha's right, two—uh—oh—seven. Why d'you want to know?"

"I thought. . . ," Smoke told her inventing, "that when her friend left, we could slip down and get happy together."

"Really?" Vivian's eyes rolled up and her lids closed over the exposed whites.

Smoke helped her to the edge of the bed, removed her clothes and put her under a sheet. He would give it an hour, then head for the room that held Brian Trask.

Brian Trask lay sprawled naked in the satin sheets of a thoroughly mussed bed. In his usual manner, he had rapidly thrust and ground his way to explosive release twice in one hour and promptly rolled onto one side and went into a deep sleep. As instructed, Danielle had refreshed herself, dressed, and left the room. She had no need to extract her fee from the slumbering man's pocket, such vulgar matters were handled on the member's monthly billing. She had barely swayed her way to the stairs leading to the ground floor when Smoke Jensen appeared on the flight above her. He froze immediately and she went her way ignorant of his presence.

When Smoke reached Room 207, he crouched and tried the knob. The door was locked. From his boot top, Smoke took a slim-bladed knife and attacked the bolt. After a couple of tries, it slid back and the thin panel swung inward. Smoke went with it

Moonlight filtered through the open window, and the curtains billowed inward on a light breeze. The zephyr smelled of sea tang and fog. Smoke Jensen crossed the floor silently to the large, four-poster bed. Silently, he looked down on the naked man who slept there. Silver shafts dappled the pale body, revealing slashes and circles of pink that denoted old wound scars. A tough, dangerous man, Smoke surmised. He turned away, went to the door, and relocked it.

Might as well get on with it, he thought as he returned to the bed. He bent down and roughly shook Brian Trask by one shoulder. The satiated man grunted and batted at Smoke's arm as though at a fly. Smoke shook him harder.

"You want more, honey?" Trask muttered.

"Wake up, Trask."

Smoke Jensen's bass rumble shocked Brian Trask to muddled wakefulness. "Wha—who—how'd you get in here?"

"Say I am a magician," Smoke told him. Trask reached for the sheet to cover himself. "No. Leave it."

"A man's got a right to his dignity," Trask growled resentfully.

"Not in this case. I've found that a feller in your present condition is more inclined to cooperate."

"I'm not cooperating with nobody," a truculent Brian growled.

"Oh, I think you will be. I want to know where I can find Tinsdale, your boss. Remember him?"

"I don't know nothing."

Smoke jammed a stiff thumb into a sensitive nerve ganglia in the man's armpit. Trask squealed like a stuck hog. "Again. Where is Tinsdale?"

Trask had drawn up into a tight ball. "I don't know. He's out of town."

"Where out of town? You are his chief enforcer, aren't you?"

"So what?" Brian asked after he stopped gagging. Smoke had put that same hard thumb to a nerve center under his right ear.

"So you know. Where is he?" A hard backhand to the exposed cheek of Brian Trask stung his eye and straightened him out.

"He'll kill me if I tell you anything," Trask babbled.

Smoke Jensen leaned in and dug the offending thumb into a complex of nerves an inch below the navel of Brian Trask. "I'll kill you if you don't."

When his squealing cut off, Brian Trask gasped and sobbed for air. "Yer a Marshal, you can't kill an unarmed, naked man."

"I've only been a marshal for a short while. I can easily forget about ever being one. Now, talk."

Brian Trask talked. Then Smoke forced the head gunhawk to dress and frog marched him out of the parlor house. When Smoke left the room, he not only knew who had killed his friend Harrison Tate—a gutter thug named Wally Quade—but also why. And what Tinsdale had in mind.

Ralph Tinsdale planned on capturing the entire center of Denver and exacting a fortune out of rentals. He also intended to do the same with every burgeoning city in the West. When Tinsdale met with resistance, he had the objecting land owner killed and dealt with the bereaved widow. Smoke had the name of the corrupt lawyer Tinsdale used and where to find him.

And where to find the criminal mastermind. Now, it was only a matter of time.

Eleven

Baldwin & Fiske, Attorneys at Law had offices in one of Denver's most attractive and expensive office buildings. A fashionable men's haberdashery store occupied the ground floor. The impressive edifice had its own carbide gas generating plant in the basement, along with a coal-fired, steam radiator heating system. Even at night, the stark whitish radiance of gas lights illuminated several windows in the upper stories. In the rapidly growing, bustling metropolis, business went on around the clock. After booking Brian Trask into jail as an accessory to murder, Smoke Jensen went directly there. He had no difficulty setting foot in the Babcock Building by the grand, polished granite-faced main entrance.

At the rear of the lobby, Smoke found another modern convenience. An elevator had been installed when the facility had been constructed. Operated during the day by an attendant, who used a large rope pull to raise and lower the open car, the device now stood vacant. Smoke Jensen studied the conveyance awhile and worked out how it functioned. Baldwin and Fiske had offices on the fourth floor. Smoke had fully expected to have to climb the stairs to reach his immediate goal. Now he entered the cage of the elevator and reached for the rope. He gave it a yank, but the car did not move. He crossed to the opposite side of the open platform and pulled again. With a creak and groan, the floor rose under his feet.

A young man appeared suddenly from the lobby attendant's cubical and waved at Smoke. "Here, sir, let me do that for you."

"Thank you," Smoke replied with forced politeness, impatient to reach the office of the lawyers, and to do so unseen.

High-stepping to get onto the elevator, the muscular youth took up position and heaved on the three-inch rope. "We have a lot of tenants who work at night." He frowned slightly and paused before hauling again. "I don't recall seeing you here before, though."

Inventing rapidly, Smoke Jensen answered him calmly. "I was asked to come here tonight on a business transaction. To see one of your occupants on the third floor."

That information erased the frown. "Oh, yes. That would be Henning Mining. Old Mr. Harvey came in not an hour ago.

"Yes, that's it. But Mr. Harvey asked that our meeting be kept in strictest confidence."

Pausing in his attention to the rope, the young man laid an open palm on the center of his chest. "I assure you, I am the soul of discretion."

"Thank you, my man," Smoke responded with a heartiness he did not feel.

On the third floor, Smoke Jensen tipped the operator handsomely, stepped off the elevator, and turned the direction indicated by an arrow on a directory. He walked along the hallway toward Henning Mining until out of sight of the elevator. Then he waited until it started down and headed for the stairs. He climbed slowly, careful not to make any betraying sound.

Up on the next level, he located the offices of Baldwin and Fiske. Smoke paused outside the door, listening. A light shown through the pebbly, frosted glass pane in the main entrance. No sound came from within. Cautiously, Smoke tried the knob. It turned, but did not release the latch. Again,

Smoke resorted to the thin-bladed knife in his boot. The bolt gave on the third try. Smoke entered and relocked the door behind himself. Now all he had to do was wait.

While he went about that, Smoke decided, he might as well learn what he could from the files. A quick search of the outer office proved fruitless. No reference to Ralph Tinsdale or Tinsdale Properties, Ltd. Halfway down a corridor, brass lettering on a stout oak door announced the office of Lawrence Baldwin, Esq. Typical of lawyers—who were suspicious of everything, including their own shadow—it was locked.

Smoke Jensen forced entry and went to a rank of three head-high file drawers. He soon found them to also be locked. To his surprise, it took even more effort to slip the latch on the first set and slide open the drawer. He found the "T" section, but no file for Tinsdale. The second down yielded nothing also. Smoke began to suspect that he had been lied to. In the third drawer, he came across his first nugget of gold. A thick file bore the label: *Tinsdale Properties, Limited.* It consisted mostly of real estate contracts, with a small bit of correspondence as well. Not wishing to advertise his presence, Smoke took the letters out to the reception area and read them under the night light.

To his disappointment, they provided nothing useful. He returned to the office and replaced everything as it had been. The search continued. Smoke drew blanks on the last two drawers. He closed the files and smiled to himself at the click that sounded when the sprung lock snapped back into place. On to the next.

Nothing, until the fourth drawer. There, under a warning label in bold-faced red letters that read: **MOST CONFIDENTIAL,** he found his reward. *Tinsdale Correspondence* it was labeled. Smoke took the whole file out into the light. What he learned at first amazed then angered him. No question that Tinsdale and Baldwin were in cahoots in the land swindles. Tinsdale wrote candidly of using intimidation, extortion, and murder to acquire parcels of land in the heart of Denver. On one, dated the day after the death of Harrison Tate, Smoke found the most damning evidence.

"Lawrence," the letter read. "A man named Quade will be coming by later today to see you. You are to give him five hundred dollars out of the Special account, and arrange a chair car ticket on the first train out of Denver, headed west. San Francisco would do fine. As always," and it was signed *Ralph*. There was a post script that washed cold fury through the veins of Smoke Jensen, Wally Quade had been the name given him by Brian Trask the night before.

"P.S. I am sure the Tate property will be available soon. You might send Trask around to see the widow about it, eh?"

Smoke removed that from the file and dutifully read through the remainder. Nothing else came so close to sealing the fate of Ralph Tinsdale. Routinely, he searched the remaining file drawers, found nothing significant and settled in to wait for the arrival of the crooked lawyer.

He had prudently stopped off at a small street-front eatery on the edge of Chinatown and stocked up on an assortment of *dim sum,* bite-sized, portable foods that could be eaten as enjoyably cold as hot. They were in a woven sea-grass bag Smoke had carried into the building. He sat now behind the desk of Lawrence Baldwin, boots propped on the unmarked mahogany surface and reached in for a sample of the Chinese appetizers. Baldwin would be in about eight the next morning, Smoke estimated. Then he could remove another link in the chain.

Lawrence Baldwin, Esquire, respected and admired member of the Colorado Bar, confidant of the Mayor of Denver, member of the Pioneers Club—an exclusive residence club for charter residents, who had come to Colorado before it because a state, and their male descendants, provided they all had and maintained enough money to be eligible—had a routine day in mind when he entered the outer reception area of his offices. He surely did not expect anything untoward today, and certainly did not have in mind what he discovered when he opened the door to his inner sanctum.

"What are you doing here?" The man to whom Lawrence Baldwin addressed that question looked large and dangerous. "How—how did you get in here?"

"Shut up and close that door," the darkly scowling stranger demanded.

In spite of his inclination to the contrary, Lawrence Baldwin found himself doing as told. Once the heavy oak panel clicked into place, he leaned back on it for support, his knees suddenly weak, his bluster vanished. It had at last registered upon him that the unknown visitor had backed up his commands with the ugly black muzzle of a very large Colt revolver. It had been pointed at his minute lawyer's heart. Fear sweat popped out on his brow and upper lip, oily and cold.

"Come over here and sit down," came the order from behind Baldwin's desk.

Lawrence Baldwin started his habitual route that took him to the place the stranger now occupied. He cut himself short and took one of the large, leather clients' chairs. His growing apprehension caused him to sag into it. With considerable effort, Baldwin found his voice again.

"Now, could you possibly tell me who you are and what you are doing at my desk?"

"It's Judgment Day, Mr. Lawyer Baldwin," Smoke Jensen told him in sepulchral tones.

Baldwin really began to sweat now. "What do you mean? What are you talking about?"

"Tinsdale Properties, Limited. Ralph Tinsdale. A man named Brian Trask, and another named Wally Quade. That's what I'm talking about."

Ghost-white in an instant, Lawrence Baldwin swallowed

hard and fought the urge to bolt and run. He drew a deep breath, held it, let it out slowly. Took another. "Ralph Tinsdale is a client of mine. And I do represent his company. What business is that of yours?"

"Are you also his bag-man, to pay his hired killers?"

Had it been possible for Lawrence Baldwin to turn any whiter, he would have done so. "I won't dignify that with an answer. It's impertinent of you. There is a thing called lawyer-client confidentiality, you know."

"No, I didn't. But it doesn't matter in this case. I don't think this case will be going to trial anyway."

That didn't sound good, for several reasons. "What . . . case?"

"The People of Colorado versus Ralph Tinsdale, Lawrence Baldwin, Brian Trask, Wally Quade, et al. The charges: murder, conspiracy to commit murder, extortion, fraud, coercion, conspiracy and any others I can think up."

"What gives you the authority to make any charges?"

Smoke Jensen reached into his vest pocket and took out his U.S. Marshal's badge. He tossed it casually toward Lawrence Baldwin. It fell short, onto the top of the desk, and cut a long, deep gouge in the pristine surface as it skidded to a stop. Baldwin winced.

"I am a United States Marshal. And I have proof of your criminal activity in collusion with Ralph Tinsdale."

The lawyer in Baldwin took flame. "Whatever evidence you have has been gained illegally. You have no case."

Smoke shrugged. "Like I said, I don't think this case will go to trial. Now, tell me, where is Ralph Tinsdale?"

Baldwin correctly read the meaning of those words in the eyes of his visitor. Lips quivering, he tried once more to bluff his way out of it. "It won't go to trial because you obtained your evidence without a warrant."

"No. It's because of the most obvious reason a case cannot come to trial. A dead man cannot be tried for any crime." When Smoke said that, Baldwin shuddered. "Of course, if you give evidence for the prosecution, testify against the others, I'm sure something can be worked out.'

For all his earlier pomposity, Lawrence Baldwin deflated rapidly. "All right, all right, what is it you want to know?'

"I have the general idea already. What I want is where I can find Ralph Tinsdale."

Baldwin swallowed with obvious effort, shook his head. "I'm not positive, understand? He—he's trying to expand his land empire. He's gone out to Dry Gulch Canyon. He wants to gain claim to as many working gold finds as possible. He'll be some—somewhere in there."

That verified what Trask and Quade had told him. Smoke gave him a nasty smile. "See? That wasn't too hard, was it?"

Baldwin hung his head, features bland and pallid. "I feel dirty."

"As well you should, considering what you've done. Now let's get out of here."

"Wh-where are we going?"

"To jail."

"But you said . . ."

Smoke smiled nastily. "You underestimate me. I'm not so stupid as to let you run around free, knowing what I know about your operation with Tinsdale."

Baldwin's mouth fell open, yet before he could frame a reply, Smoke Jensen came around the desk in a swift, fluid motion, yanked the corrupt lawyer to the soles of his shoes and gave him a rough shove toward the door.

Dry Gulch Canyon, famous a few years ago for a fabulous gold rush, lay to the west of Denver. In the high mountain country, it could not be seen from any point except directly from above on the peaks surrounding it. Tons of ore had been mined and more tons of stream bed run through sluice boxes, producing hundreds of thousands of dollars in gold. Now only half a dozen mining companies operated here.

Modern and efficient, they each yielded better than 300,000 dollars a year. Ralph Tinsdale, in his dreams of empire, wanted to own it all. He had been advised against it by Lawrence Baldwin. The intricacies of mine ownership made impossible Tinsdale's usual tactic of killing off those who refused and coercing their heirs into selling out. Tinsdale, bloated with success, would hear nothing of it. He had been in the canyon only three days and already he had learned only how correct his lawyer had been. He sat in a dreary drizzle of rainfall, crouched over a ground-cloth sheltered fire, in a side canyon. Three of his lackluster underlings were with him.

So despondent had he become that he did not hear the clop of a horse's hooves as a newcomer splashed through the puddles into the campsite. He barely looked up when the rider halted ten feet from him. Slowly he blinked when he recognized Wally Quade.

"What are you doing here? I thought you had been sent out of town."

"I didn't want to go. And then I got arrested, Mr. Tinsdale. For killing that old codger who wouldn't sell to you. Some U.S. Marshal. Name of Jensen. Captain Yardley let me out this morning. Trask, too. And your lawyer."

Stunned, Tinsdale could only gape and stammer. "Th-th-this can't be. How—how could he know who to go after?"

Quade shrugged his shoulders. "The thing is, it happened. Lawyer Baldwin said this marshal was comin' after you next. You best make ready. That Jensen is meaner than a wildcat with his bung sewed shut."

Galvanized into action, Tinsdale came to his boots. "You hear that, men? We've got a lawman coming after us. We'll make it his last manhunt." Tinsdale spun around on one heel, looked over their camp, the terrain to all sides. His decision made, he gave quick instructions. "Chances are he will come right before nightfall, or first thing of a morning. Only we won't be here. Fix up your bedrolls to look like there is someone in them, then pick a spot where you can cover all the open ground. We'll let him get in here, thinking he's right among us, then cut him down."

Smoke Jensen arrived in Dry Gulch Canyon two hours before sundown. It took him less than half an hour to track the horse he had followed onto the soft bottom soil of the gorge. It led straight to a small, narrow side canyon. Smoke reined in and dismounted. He took a ground anchor from his saddlebag and screwed it into the turf. He tied off the reins of his horse and patted the animal on the neck.

"Stay here, Thunder. I'll be back shortly." Drawing his Winchester from the saddle boot, he started off to scout the ground ahead.

Well-trained by Preacher, his skills honed over years of practice, Smoke Jensen drifted through the trees on the inner gorge walls as invisible as the air itself. He quickly located the hiding places of two men. A ways farther into the canyon, he found another. He came upon two more near the dead end of the box canyon.

Carefully, with all the stealth he could muster, he worked his way back to the first man. His target lay prone, eyes fixed on a campsite where it appeared four men lay rolled up in their blankets, sound asleep. Smoke Jensen stepped out from behind a big, resinous pine and tapped the sole of the man's boot with his own.

"Waitin' for someone?" he asked quietly.

The hard case jerked with surprise and tried to whirl rapidly. Smoke drove the butt of his Winchester downward and smashed it into the outlaw's exposed head. The steel butt-plate made a mushy sound when it made contact. The thug twitched spastically and went still. Smoke disarmed him, tied him up, and moved on.

His second target sat with his back to a boulder. He chewed methodically on a slab of fatback in a biscuit and watched the opening of the gorge indifferently. Smoke slid the tomahawk from his belt and reached around the huge chuck of granite. With a swift, powerful blow he rapped the lout on the side of the head with the flat of the blade. On to the next.

Smoke found him like he had left him, squatted behind a bush, his knees up under his chin. A rifle lay at his side. When Smoke started his quick final approach, a hidden twig betrayed him. Its crackle sounded like a collapsing building to Smoke's hypersensitive ears. The hard case heard it too, only much less intense, so he reacted slowly. Smoke fell on him, rapidly bent him forward and rammed his face into the ground.

Mouth filled with dirt, the outlaw's shout of alarm came out a muffled grunt. Desperately, the gunhawk clawed at the butt of a six-gun in his righthand holster. Smoke lifted him and slammed his head to the ground again. And again. The six-gun came clear. Swiftly, Smoke reached for his knife and buried its blade to the hilt in the right kidney of the thug.

Wheezing, the rascal sucked air and dirt into his lungs. His body spasmed and he forgot about his revolver. Smoke reversed the Greenriver knife and drove the pommel into the base of his target's skull. The lights went out, he stiffened into a rigid parody of a scarecrow and dropped from Smoke's grasp. He would probably bleed to death internally before he regained consciousness, Smoke considered, but at least he would not feel the pain. Stealthily, he moved out to the next.

Wally Quade lay near to where Ralph Tinsdale had hidden himself in a depression in the slope of the rear canyon wall. Smoke Jensen studied his location carefully for three long minutes. At last he had to concede that no way existed for him to approach unseen. He could get close, but in the last critical seconds, he would be exposed. Nothing else for it, so he began to glide through the trees.

When Smoke reached the tree line, Quade stiffened. He couldn't believe what he had seen. How could he be here so soon? Why hadn't the others seen him and given a warning? The answer came to him with sudden, painful certainty. *They couldn't give a warning!* Quickly he filled his lungs and opened his mouth to bellow.

"Hey, Mr. Tinsdale, he's here! He's right in front—"

A hot slug from Smoke's Winchester cut his shout off in mid-sentence. The report echoed off the sheer walls. Wally Quade flipped over backward. Squalling, he clawed at his holster. The Smith American came free and he fired wildly in the general direction of Smoke Jensen. Smoke took his time and ended the babble with a well-placed round between the eyes of the murderer Quade. Then he started for where he had last seen Ralph Tinsdale.

Paralyzed with fear, Ralph Tinsdale squeezed back into the loose rubble where he lay in ambush. Impossible. No man could move so swiftly, so quietly to take out all his hired guns without giving himself away. Could he? He saw movement down the slope and fired off a hasty round.

He saw dust kick up ten yards behind the man who now bore down on him. His failure spurred him to action. Rising, he started to sprint uphill. The talus slithered and broke free under his panicked shoes. He stumbled and fell forward. Fiery pain erupted in one soft palm when it collided forcefully with the rough stone. The backs of the fingers of his right hand bled freely also, though he did not lose his grip on his six-gun. Ever so slowly, the lip of the gorge grew closer. From behind he heard the rattle and clatter of more shale as the relentless lawman pursued him. What was the name Quade had given him? Jensen?

Tinsdale's heart thudded with increased terror. Oh, God,

could it be *Smoke* Jensen? Another upward glance showed him blue sky ahead. He could make it after all. But then what? He would be afoot, without supplies or help. He would lay for Jensen, shoot him when he came over the top. His breath burned raw and too short in his heaving chest. His legs began to quiver. They felt like lead. The sounds of pursuit came from closer behind. At last he saw grass and a horizon beyond.

With a cry of relief, Ralph Tinsdale hurled himself over the edge of the canyon wall and onto the plateau beyond. Without a pause he scrambled around on the ground and faced the lip. He cocked his revolver and held it as steady as possible under the circumstances. Then he waited. It wouldn't be long. Jensen was right behind him. Time sped by. Smoke Jensen did not come. Tinsdale waited longer. Still no Smoke Jensen.

"Give it up, Tinsdale. You're out of the real estate business."

Incredibly the voice came from behind him. Tinsdale whirled and raised the Colt in his hand. Hot, stupefying pain slammed into his belly. Then again. Reflexively his legs churned on the ground and launched him out over the edge of the canyon. He disappeared from sight before Smoke Jensen could fire again.

Twelve

And Victor Spectre . . . Victor Spectre had lived for years off the proceeds of crime. Always a shadowy figure, his name was not known to many lawmen. Those in the St. Louis area who did know it kept his secret and quietly enjoyed the show he made. Those who did not looked upon him as a philanthropist, a benefactor of social projects that had a civilizing effect on the citizens of the area. He lived in luxury, in the splendorous penthouse of a fancy St. Louis hotel. Stunted trees grew in the rooftop garden along with a rainbow of vibrant flowers, rich shrubs, and leafy ferns.

It was from here that he directed the actions of an immense gang that preyed upon the banks, railroads, smelters, and industries of Missouri, Kansas, Nebraska, and Colorado. A widower, Victor Spectre lived openly and notoriously with his mistress. A flamboyant redhead with an angelic face, superb body, and long, long legs that she took special pride in displaying frequently, albeit to the consternation of the society matrons of St. Louis, she had been Victor's consort for the past five years. His household also consisted of his son, Trenton, a boy of eighteen, who had eagerly and willingly followed his father's footsteps into the criminal life. Father and son adored each other, the lad consumed with hero worship, the parent full-blown with pride. Trenton had his mother's features and coloring, though carved in a handsome, masculine style. From his father he had inherited his jet black hair and brows, and the icy green eyes.

Trenton Spectre had been educated by private tutors and · did not look forward with enthusiasm to leaving his father's burgeoning criminal enterprises to attend the senior Spectre's *alma mater,* Yale. "Nonsense," his father had objected in jest. "Many great criminal minds have been influenced and honed in the hallowed halls of Yale." Spectre had the usual bevy of butler, man servants for himself and Trenton, a cook, maids who came by day to "do for the house," and a driver and footman for his carriage. Such were the idyllic conditions in the Spectre household when Victor encountered Smoke Jensen.

Peace had fled the High Lonesome and three good men had died defending their herds of cattle from a gang of rustlers as large as the average Army patrol. The cattle, brought up to the lush, green mountain pastures, had disappeared. The outlaws swaggered about as though immune to arrest. Indeed, in some counties of Colorado they *were* immune. The local law in those places had been in the hip pocket of Victor Spectre for a long while. They seemed unstoppable. Only, the rustlers had made one big mistake. The dead men were all fellow ranchers and friends of Smoke Jensen.

Although three separate herds had been involved, Smoke suspected a common cause, and a common destination. All anyone had to do was read the sign and follow the miscreants to the delivery point. After a long, arduous journey, fraught with hail storms, a prairie fire, and a tornado, the trail Smoke Jensen followed led to the stock pens of the Santa Fe Railroad in Dodge City, Kansas. Two of the Chicago stockyard buyers gave matching descriptions of those who sold the beefs. Smoke set out to find them in the three block long "Combat Zone" of the Gomorrah of the Plains.

Even though Dodge City was a Dead Line town, the No-Guns ordinance enacted by the city council and enforced by the city marshal, William Barclay "Bat" Masterson, Smoke knew his Deputy U.S. Marshal's badge exempted him. He found the first three rustlers in the Long Branch.

"I'm looking for Cole Tyree," he declared as he entered through the ornate, stained glass-paneled double doors. Immediate silence followed his announcement.

Every eye cut to the double rig of six-guns worn by the rangy, broad-shouldered man in the doorway. From behind the bar, the apron raised an admonitory hand. "There's a Dead Line in this town, Mister. You gotta give up them guns."

Smoke reached with his left hand to flip aside the lapel of his fringed, buckskin jacket to reveal the badge pinned on his shirt. "United States Marshal out of Colorado. I want Cole Tyree."

Like all good, obedient outlaws, Cole Tyree and his two henchmen had secreted several weapons upon their persons, including at least one hide-out gun. They made effort to put them into play the moment the words left the mouth of Smoke Jensen. And that's where they made their final mistake.

Ace Longbaugh had only the cylinder of his shortened-barrel Colt free of the waistband at the small of his back when Smoke Jensen unlimbered his .44 Colt Frontier and plunked a hot slug into the belly of the rustler. Ace grunted and blinked his eyes, fighting to retain control over his badly damaged body. Meanwhile, Smoke saw movement to his left and pivoted.

This time the fight for control ended before it began. Bruno Butler took the round in his heart. Dead before he could complete his draw, he went rubber-legged and fell across a green baize table, scattering a stack of coins and a few bills. The latter fluttered to the floor while three bar girls shrieked and hugged one another. With Bruno out of

it, Smoke turned toward the main threat, the as yet unharmed Cole Tyree.

By then, Cole had his six-gun out and the hammer back.
He had just seen two of his men cut down without even
clearing their irons. Part of him rebelled at carrying this
any further, yet he knew he must. Eyes blazing, sweat oiling
his face, he drove the words out in a shout.

"Who the hell are you?"

"They call me Smoke Jensen." Smoke replied and then
shot Tyree in the chest.

Slammed back against the bar, the outlaw leader discharged his weapon into the sawdust and floorboards six
feet in front of him. Smoke saw movement from the first
man he had shot and turned for a moment in that direction.

With terrible effort, Ace Longbaugh brought his six-gun
to bear. His finger closed on the trigger a moment after
Smoke Jensen again fired on him. Hit off-center in the left
side of his chest, Longbaugh shot a hole in the ceiling of
the Long Branch before he slammed back against the piano.
It gave off a discordant jangle of notes and held fast. Ace
Longbaugh did not.

He slithered down the side of the upright and sat in a
pool of his own blood. Slowly, he gasped out the last of
his life.

Two city policemen appeared suddenly behind Smoke
Jensen.

"Hold it there, mister. You've just violated our no-guns
ordinance." He looked beyond Smoke. "And killed three
men. Hand that Colt over and come with us."

"Deputy U.S. Marshal out of Colorado," Smoke told the
aggressive cop tightly. "These men were wanted for rustling
cattle in Colorado and crossing the state line to sell them.
There's about thirteen more in town, I'd wager. You'd best
be looking for them."

It had been a long speech for Smoke Jensen, but served

to dispel some of the doubt in the policeman. "Let me see a badge."

"On my shirt front," Smoke told him.

The lawman took a quick peek around Smoke's shoulder and nodded a curt acknowledgment. "Okay, marshal. Who are these men?"

Smoke named those he had names for and described several. Working with the local law now, Smoke Jensen quickly rounded up the remaining outlaws. Only five of them were foolish enough to resist. Smoke killed three of those. The shotgun accounted for the other pair. When questioned, the ranking member of the gang let slip a single name, one Smoke Jensen would come to hear often over the next few months; Victor Spectre.

Beginning that year in May, a series of bold bank robberies swept through the Rocky Mountains, culminating in Big Rock. Sheriff Monte Carson formed a large posse, split it into two, one half to be commanded by Smoke Jensen. Smoke readily agreed. He and Sally had a large portion of the assets of the Sugarloaf tied up in that bank. Not to recover so vast a sum could spell their ruin. Like many another deputation, the volunteer lawmen soon concluded they chased a whirlwind. Not so Smoke Jensen or Monte Carson. They drove the men under them, riding from first light to half an hour before sundown.

Night came swiftly in the High Lonesome. There was little time for an afterglow. The sun went behind the peaks to the west and the world turned black. Only those majestic pinnacles, mantled year round in snow, formed glowing silhouettes that projected streamers of orange, magenta, and gold. Smoke Jensen appreciated one such display far more than others of late. During the afternoon, he had come upon hoof prints of six horses. Two of them had distinctive marks he had also seen outside the bank in Big Rock. Their freshness indicated that by the next day, the posse would be in sight of at least some of the twelve-man gang who had robbed them of their investment money and life savings.

That set well with Smoke Jensen. The strength of these marauding bands, the rustlers numbered twenty-four, and now a dozen bank heisters, put a niggling suspicion in the back of Smoke's mind that the same man, Victor Spectre, was behind it all. He went to sleep under a blanket of diamond points ruminating on that.

Around mid-morning the next day, one of the two men Smoke had sent to scout ahead rode back to the posse on a lathered, blown horse. His face radiated excitement. "They're up there. Not three miles ahead. Walkin' their horses. Lucky for us we spotted them from inside the tree line, or we could have ran right down on them. There's six of them all right."

Smoke considered a moment. Given the direction they were headed, southeast out of the mountains toward the high plain that ran from eastern Colorado into Nebraska, the other six must be close at hand. He had eighteen men with him. Three-to-one odds on the six they had located. Better than two-to-one if all twelve joined up somewhere before they could catch them.

"Oh, and another thing," the scout reported. "The one I'd judge is leadin' them is dressed right odd. He's got on a ol', high, black, stovepipe hat, with a long feather stickin' out to the back. An he's wearin' a blue soldier coat, brass buttons an' all."

"A shell jacket?" Smoke asked.

"Naw. One like an officer wears."

That settled it for Smoke. They would hit these six fast and find out, if they could, where and when the other outlaws were to meet them. Then, with himself disguised in that outlandish outfit, at least six of the posse could get right in close, while the rest would fall on the robbers' flanks from ambush.

"Heres what we'll do," Smoke spoke suddenly, then outlined his rudimentary plan. Twenty minutes later, they put the first phase in operation.

Smoke found himself well pleased with the way the posse spread out when he gave the signal. They came to a gallop and charged down on the unsuspecting hard cases. When the outlaws discovered their peril, they greeted the lawmen with a hail of wild firing that hit nothing. At a range of fifty yards, Smoke Jensen signaled for a halt.

Eighteen horses set their hind quarters and skidded to a stop. Eighteen rifles came to shoulders and fired a ragged volley. Four of the six scum died at once in a blizzard of hot lead. The other two, one wounded, threw up their hands in surrender. Smoke Jensen rode forward, his Colt Frontier keeping them covered.

Smoke put his cold gaze hard on the man in the blue coat, whom he had instructed be left unharmed. "Where and when are you to meet up with the rest of the gang?"

Equally icy, the leader tried to bluff it out. "I don't know what you're talkin' about, mister. All I know is that you are murderers. You cut these men down in cold blood."

"Only after we were fired on," Smoke countered. "And I reckon you've been around enough to know your blood's not so cold at a time like that."

"Maybe so, but I got nothin' to say to you."

Smoke cut his eyes to two of the posse. "Get him off that horse."

Roughly they dragged the man from his mount. At Smoke's direction they threw him on the ground and spreadeagled him, with the help of two more. Smoke dismounted and, as he did so, took a tomahawk from one saddlebag. He approached the man, testing the edge of the axelike weapon with one thumb. He hunkered down so his face poised only inches from that of the other man. Smoke smelled the sour odor of fear, unwashed body and stale whiskey.

"Let me tell you something. I spent a lot of time around the Cheyenne while I was growing up. I learned me some right clever ways of makin' a feller hurt. The Cheyenne said I took to it right natural like. Thing is, I haven't lost my touch over the years."

"You're bluffin'. Yer a lawman. You can't do things like that."

Smoke cocked his head as though to say "Oh, really?" He spoke to the posse. "You fellers see anything going on here?" A couple of them guffawed, the rest shook their heads in the negative. "Well, now that *that's* settled, might as well get to work." He hefted the tomahawk. "How about I take off an ear? It'll be smooth, you won't even have a headache. 'Course if I slip, you'll never have a headache again."

Fear rapidly escalated to panic. His voice increasing by octaves, he pleaded for his life. "Goddamnit, you can't do this to me!"

Grinning, Smoke reached out and plucked the top hat from the ground beyond the man's head and put it on his own. "You won't be needing this. Oh. And boys, skin him out of that coat. It would be a shame to have it messed up with a lot of blood." Smoke raised the warhawk.

Screaming in a banshee wail, the thug lost consciousness. Smoke turned his attention to the wounded hard case. One look at his unconscious comrade loosened his tongue readily.

"Look, I don't know everything. Not where we're gonna meet. Only that it is to be tomorrow. Clyde an' the others have the money. We're to take it to a bank in North Platte."

"What happens to it there?"

The thug looked at Smoke Jensen with growing terror. "I don't know. If—if Joe's still alive, you'll have to ask him." He nodded toward the supine hard case.

"He's alive." Smoke rose and went to where Thunder stood, munching grass. He took his canteen and stepped over the insensible man. He unscrewed the cap and poured a stream down into the slack face.

For a moment, nothing happened. Then Joe coughed, spluttered and jerked back into the real world. His first conscious act was to reach up frantically and feel both ears. Without giving the man pause to enjoy his relief, Smoke Jensen came at him again.

"Where are you meeting Clyde tomorrow and what are you going to do with the money in North Platte?"

Defeat washed away the relief on Joe's face. "If you know that much, there's no way I can keep you from learnin' the rest. We're gonna hook up with Clyde outside Julesburg. On this side. The money from all the bank robberies is to be put in a special account."

"Whose name is on that account?" Smoke leaned menacingly closer, the tomahawk raised and ready.

"I can't tell you."

"Can't or won't? The tomahawk caressed the craven's cheek.

"I'll be killed if I tell you."

"No, you won't. You'll be a long way from there, safe in jail."

That's when he saw the light. Eyes fixed on the marshal's badge on Smoke's shirt, he spoke softly. "Someone named Victor Spectre."

Satisfied he had the right trail, Smoke and his posse went on to kill or capture the other band of outlaws. With the bank robbers jailed and more than $80,000 returned to the banks from which it had been taken, Smoke decided to look into the background of this mystery man, Victor Spectre.

Smoke Jensen sent inquirers through the network of friendly lawmen he had developed over the years. The answers that came back were disturbing to say the least. From the U.S. Marshal's offices in Kansas City, Missouri, and

Fort Smith, Arkansas, he learned that Victor Spectre was considered an independently wealthy socialite in St. Louis. A philanthropist, he had endowed a library and had built a school in a downtrodden neighborhood of the Mississippi River metropolis. The Chief of Police in St. Louis had been even more effusive.

"It is my delight to state unequivocally that Mr. Victor Spectre is a veritable paragon of civil virtue," the mayor had written. "It has been my pleasure to frequently entertain him in my official residence. He is the champion of many charitable causes, makes an annual donation to a boy's home for waterfront waifs that is, to say the least, stupendous in size. Without him, our fair city would be much, much the poorer."

So, Smoke concluded at once, he would have to go after Spectre in a very different way than that with which he was accustomed. It would require that he make somewhat of a splash himself, so he continued planning. And it would be necessary to leave his beloved High Lonesome. Sally found out about his plan when she discovered him inspecting his dress clothes and several suits he had purchased over the years.

"Where are we going, dear?" she asked, hopeful he would say they would go back to visit her parents.

"Not 'we,' dear. I have to make a business trip to St. Louis."

Her entire adult life spent with Smoke Jensen, Sally had long ago learned how to skillfully hide her disappointment. She employed that talent now. "Cattle? Or horses?"

The Sugarloaf had only recently begun the process of changing over from a cattle ranch to a horse farm. Smoke had acquired a herd of twenty-five top quality brood mares and several stallions of impeccable lineage. Now, this conversion gave Smoke a moment of worry that his ploy had created more problems that it had solved. He had to think fast.

"Cattle. I think it is time we sold out the entire herd and I decided to try for the highest market, at a packing house that sells south, directly to New Orleans."

"And they are in St. Louis. Yes, it sounds good. I was beginning to think we would never be free of those stupid, woolly-faced creatures. Go with my blessing. Though . . . I would like the opportunity to browse the fashionable shops in St. Louis. They have the latest styles from New York and Paris."

Smoke made a face and responded with mock irritation. "If you did that, we would need to have ten, rather than a thousand head. I'll miss you."

"And I, you." Sally smiled and patted his check. "When do you leave?"

"Tomorrow."

"Be careful. Don't get yourself hurt."

"Oh, I will. I've nothing to worry about in such a *civilized* place." Only Smoke Jensen did not believe that for a moment.

Through a banker affiliated with Sally Jensen's father, Smoke Jensen found the doors to the salons of High Society open to him throughout St. Louis. He got his first look at Victor Spectre on his third nightly outing with the cream of the social whirl. It was a benefit dinner—at $50 a plate—for the campaign chests of several state politicians.

After the desert—*crepes à la flambé*—which Smoke found overly sweet and lacking in substance, like the long-winded speeches that followed, Victor Spectre made a lavish presentation of a large check to the party's candidate for Governor. He was rewarded by abundant applause and flattering words. Smoke Jensen took an immediate dislike of Victor Spectre. Even if he had not known of Spectre's secret life, it would have been the same. Oily men, with too much money, which they used to buy politicians, rubbed his hair the wrong way. Wisely, he avoided direct contact with the criminal mastermind. That would come later.

Smoke Jensen spent a day at a saloon across the street from the hotel where Victor Spectre lived and conducted his clandestine business. Saloons seemed never to close in St. Louis, there being only an hour or two respite when the swampers could clean the establishments and restock the bars. It made frontier drinking parlors seem downright tame. Reputed for their wildness, most closed their doors by midnight. Seated at a table by a front window, Smoke made mental note of those entering and leaving the hotel, who had the furtive "outlaw" look about them. If asked to put that description into words, Smoke would have been hard pressed to do so. It was more a feel, a sixth sense sort of thing, acquired over years of being around the breed. Any good lawman had it.

One peace officer, who was rapidly building a reputation for himself, Billy Tilghman, put it an interesting way. "You can dress a pig in a silk suit, but you still know it's a pig."

To his surprise, among those visiting the hotel, and presumably Victor Spectre, Smoke Jensen recognized the faces of three men. He had last seen their likenesses on wanted posters in the office of Monty Carson. The first came shortly before noon. He had been accompanied by a short, ferret-faced man with oiled, slicked-back hair and equally shiny patent leather shoes. He smelled of lawyer to Smoke. The other two came together, late in the afternoon, after the clang, hiss, and chug of a slowing locomotive had announced the arrival of the East-bound local at the depot two blocks away.

The trio must represent the brains of Spectre's operation in Colorado, Smoke surmised, since the first man and his slimy companion had not left as yet. At least not from the front door. Smoke would have given anything to be able to overhear their conversation. Not given to flights of fancy, he dismissed all such longing and ordered another beer. It would be his sixth for the afternoon. And he had consumed a lot of coffee during the morning hours. He was in dire need of a visit to the chiksale, only he did not want to give up his vigil until the three wanted men reappeared.

His bladder had reached the aching point by the time that was accomplished. They came out together, along with the unctuous attorney, who spoke to them animatedly, gesturing emphatically with both hands. Smoke had settled his tab a short while before. Now he watched them out of sight around the corner, then hurried out into the street and followed. First to break off was the lawyer. He entered the tiled lobby of a rundown office building, its facade grimed by coal smoke and dust. Smoke made a note of the address and continued after the three hard cases.

They led him to a tall, narrow building, sandwiched between two huge brick warehouses on the river front. Piers extended out into the vastness of the mighty Mississippi. The area smelled of damp mud, rotting vegetation, and fish. Smoke gave them a few minutes before entering himself. In the time he waited, his sensitive sense of smell uncovered cooking odors as well. When he passed through the doorway into a large public room, he saw the reason why.

Expensively decorated with rich wall-hangings, lighted by crystal chandeliers that depended from a high, arched ceiling at the second floor level, the establishment turned out to be an elaborate restaurant. Two tiers of balcony ran completely around the room, a mezzanine and the second floor level. A huge, horseshoe-shaped bar occupied the center of the ground floor. Thick waves of tobacco smoke, raucous chatter, and laughter rose up the walls all around. Not until he crossed an arched, oriental-style bridge did Smoke Jensen realize that the first floor had been off-set and the cellar had been given over for a ruder trade. Bargemen and tug boat crews more than likely, he suspected.

White table cloths, linen napkins, and real silver decorated the intimate settings for two, four, or six. Each table also held a crystal vase with a single red rose. Apparently

Victor Spectre must be as generous with his underlings as he was in his show of being a social lion, Smoke mused. That, or these fellows were skimming off some of the cream. He spotted the men he had followed and gave the head waiter a generous tip to be seated at a table close by. On impulse, Smoke ordered a Sazarac cocktail and then headed for the men's room.

Inside plumbing was still a novelty west of the Mississippi, even in this large city nestled on its banks. Several male patrons, out of sight of their contemporaries in the brightly lighted facility, remarked to one another on the oddity of relieving themselves inside a building. *Idiots,* Smoke thought with a flash of contempt. Don't they know an outhouse is a *building?* Back at his table, Smoke Jensen concentrated on attuning his ear to the conversation of the three outlaw leaders.

"So now it's an army payroll," one declared. "I'm not so sure I like the risk."

"Not just *a payroll,* Gage. It's *the payroll* for Fort Leavenworth, Fort Riley, Hays, and Fort Dodge. Victor says it will come to more than three hundred thousand dollars, what with two months back-pay thrown in."

Ice slid down the spine of Smoke Jensen. If Victor Spectre got his hands on that much money he would have the power to be untouchable. When a hundred dollars could buy a favorable decision from certain circuit judges, think what ten thousand could produce with even a federal district judge. He had to stop this train robbery, for that is what it surely would be, and bring down Victor Spectre before the payroll was taken by the gang. To do that he first had to learn more. That required that he listen to more of their conversation and endure a meal. To walk out now would raise suspicions.

Smoke ordered the standing rib roast, with creamed new potatoes and peas, and asparagus while the one called Gage talked about telegraphing to bring in the number of guns they would need for the job. Then he expressed concern about the Army and the Pinkertons knowing who had pulled the robbery.

"No, not as long as we do like Victor said. Have some of the men call you Jesse and me Frank. It'll be blamed on the James-Younger gang."

When his food came, the roast carved at the table, it was the most attractive and succulent Smoke Jensen had ever experienced. The meat was dark pink in the middle, the outer edge a crusty brown, and surprisingly tender. The asparagus could also be cut with a fork. The potatoes and peas so sweet as to make one think they had come from a home kitchen garden. Smoke hardly tasted a bite. It appeared the outlaw trio intended to make a night of it here, so Smoke ate as quickly as possible without attracting attention, paid his bill—a little steep he thought at ten dollars—and departed unnoticed.

He knew where he could get the fine details of this robbery. Firmly fixed in his mind was the face of the smooth shyster with the greasy hair.

Thirteen

Railford Blumquist had offices on the third floor of the building Smoke Jensen had noted before. When Smoke arrived, he found to his good fortune that a light burned behind the windows which had gold leaf letters, outlined in black that spelled out: ATTORNEY AT LAW. He entered and took the flight of stairs to the second floor two at a time. They creaked terribly, so he slowed and climbed the second ascent close to the wall to avoid unwanted noise.

Outside the door to Blumquist's office, Smoke prepared himself and then reached for the knob. His hand had not closed on it when it turned suddenly and the portal flew open. Smoke found himself face-to-face with Railford Blumquist.

Smoke recovered first. "Lawyer Blumquist, I presume." He stepped forward, forcing Blumquist to retreat into his office.

"Why, yes, yes, I am." The attorney frowned and looked upward at his unexpected caller. "May I ask what you wish? It's hardly business hours."

"I came for some information."

Blumquist screwed his mouth into a moue of disapproval. "Why don't you try the library? Tomorrow. When it's open. Now, I must go. I'm entirely too long overdue for a dinner party at my home."

Smoke took another menacing step, which compelled Blumquist to back-peddle or lose balance. "Dinner will have to wait. I'm here about Victor Spectre and three lowlife scum wanted for a variety of crimes in Colorado."

For a second, Blumquist blanched, but covered it nicely. Face blank, eyes flat brown mirrors, he spoke with courtroom primness. "I do not know who you are talking about."

"Yes, you do. You and one of the outlaws paid a visit today on Victor Spectre at the hotel where he lives. And you left with all three."

Although swiftly plunged into a state bordering on terror, Blumquist continued to rely on bluster. "You've been following me. I'll have you arrested for that."

"I think not." Smoke's words had the consistency of iron. "Come on, Blumquist, you're an officer of the court and so am I. Only I happen to be a Deputy United States Marshal, investigating a crime that is about to be committed. A federal crime. And I have reason to believe you know the fine details of that crime. If you expect to get out of this with your life, if not your license intact, you had better tell me all about it."

Although frightened, Railford Blumquist still managed to examine his persecutor with cold contempt. "You're nothing, Marshal. A badge with legs. And, like most lawmen, poor as a church mouse, I'm sure. Victor Spectre will crush you like a bug under foot."

"Then you admit knowing him?" Smoke probed.

"Let's say I know . . . of him. Come now, Marshal. Every man has his price. I'm sure I could contact Mr. Spectre and arrange for yours to be paid to you for forgetting all about this unfortunate situation." Smoke Jensen held up his left hand, fingers spread. Blumquist seized upon it. "Five hundred, is it?" He considered Smoke's silence. "Five thousand? Not even a drain on Spectre's petty cash."

Smoke produced a nasty smile. "No. Five knuckles," he declared before he closed the fingers into a fist and hit Blumquist flush in the mouth.

Slammed backward, Railford Blumquist back-peddled

until he slammed into the desk of his absent law clerk. The edge bit painfully into the small of his back. Smoke Jensen followed him up. Hard blows smashed into his chest and stomach. Agony radiated out to Railford's fingertips and toes. His head swam. Pain had always terrified him. As a child he had shrunk from the usual schoolyard and street conflicts. He lived every moment looking over his shoulder, expecting an attack.

He howled as he found himself picked off the floor and hurled through the air. His back made tormenting contact with the wall behind him.

The punishing blows began again. Tears sprang hot and stinging in his eyes. His lips mashed under the brutal knuckles and the pent-up water spilled from under closed lids. Once more Smoke picked up Railford and slammed him off a wall. Fighting for a modicum of control, the lawyer raised his hands in a pleading gesture.

"No. Please, no more. Don't hit me anymore."

Smoke stopped, hovered over the cringing, sorry excuse for a man. "Tell me about the payroll robbery. Every detail."

Half an hour later, Smoke Jensen had every last bit of information Railford Blumquist possessed. He knew where and when. He also knew where the loot was to be taken, and that Victor Spectre and his son, Trenton, would be there to receive it. All he had left to do was take Blumquist to jail, get to Jefferson Barracks, let the Army know about the robbery, and take care of the Spectres himself.

Victor and Trenton Spectre waited in the large, low barn on the abandoned farm where they were to meet the eight man escort for the wagon-loads of gold and silver coin and bales of greenback currency that would soon arrive. They had no way of knowing that the train they expected the gang to loot bristled with guns. The stock cars did not haul cattle, hogs, and sheep to Kansas City to the slaughter-houses. Rather, they held twenty saddled horses each and a troop of cavalry.

Added to that, all of the men and some of the "women" in the parlor cars and Pullmans behind were Pinkerton agents. Victor Spectre's plan called for half of the gang to board at various stations across Missouri and at the right spot, take control of the locomotive and force the engineer to stop where the remainder waited with blasting powder to open the express cars and wagons to haul off the money.

Doomed to failure by the quick action of Smoke Jensen, the raid would end in bloody slaughter for the outlaws. In anticipation of that, Smoke moved in on the anxiously expectant father and son. He approached the barn from behind, careful not to reveal his presence. When he reached his goal, he worked his way silently along one side, his ears tuned to the low conversation from inside.

"Father," an adenoidal voice of a youth spoke as Smoke ducked to avoid a window. "This is more money than any other of our enterprises has yielded."

"Yes. It will be more than enough to purchase a large, steam-screw vessel." Victor Spectre laughed lightly, his voice warm with self-pride. "The owner's stateroom will be quite lavish, I promise you. You will travel in it, to oversee our enterprises in Mexico. It is a turbulent land, I grant you. And I sometimes succumb to a father's weakness. I worry about you going there alone."

"I won't be alone, Father. I have engaged the services of ten good men. True, they are young and filled with the prospect of adventure. But they are fast, and good with their guns. But I'm faster and the best. Besides, you're sending along five of your most trusted underlings."

"The Mexican bandits can come at you with more than a hundred men, Trenton."

"Not to worry, Father. Not with that Gatling gun." Trenton paused and frowned a moment. "We should have had more money for this expansion. What are you going to do to recover our losses in Colorado?"

Righteous anger clouded the face of Victor Spectre. "Try again. Perhaps in New Mexico or Nebraska. Even Kansas. I hear the sod-busters there have banks fat and ripe for the plucking. What burns deep inside me is that our setbacks in Colorado are the doing of but a single man. I find that hard to believe, but all of the evidence and the accounts of the survivors agree."

"Who is that, Father?"

"That goddamned Smoke Jensen. May his soul rot in the vilest pit of hell."

Suddenly the smaller door, inset in the tall, wide portals of the barn flew open and a man stood framed by the jamb. He wore a fringed buckskin shirt, with trousers and moccasins of the same material. Slung low on his right hip, the butt of a Colt Peacemaker protruded from its holster. High on his left, canted at an angle, the butt of a second revolver showed in another scabbard.

"I believe someone has just used my name in vain."

Choked with rage, Victor Spectre could barely form words. "You—you're Smoke Jensen?"

"Well, I'm not God."

"What are you doing here?"

"I've come to arrest the both of you. Your gang is being taken care of by the Army and the Pinkertons."

Victor Spectre sputtered and his face turned scarlet. "Goddamn you to hell, Smoke Jensen." So saying, Victor went for his gun. Likewise, so did his son.

Trenton Spectre proved that more lay behind his words than teenage braggadoccio. He was fast and he was good. He had the muzzle of his weapon clear of leather before Smoke Jensen even reached for his righthand Colt. The .44 in Trenton's hand began an upward arc when Smoke drew with blinding, precise speed. Smoke had accurately judged that the boy would be quicker and surer than his father. The hammer fell on Smoke's .45 Peacemaker an instant before Trenton lined up the barrel of his six-gun.

A bullet from Smoke's revolver punched a hole two fingers' width below Trenton's rib cage. It staggered the stout, broad-shouldered boy and threw his shot off. The slug sent up a shower of fine bits of straw and dust from the dirt floor of the barn halfway between himself and Smoke Jensen. Smoke pivoted to confront Victor.

Slowed by age, and hampered by the long cut of his suit coat, Victor Spectre had barely freed his Smith American from its shoulder holster when Smoke Jensen fired at him. Enormous pain erupted in the right side of Victor's chest and he dropped to his knees. The revolver fell from his grasp and thudded on the hard-packed ground. Smoke had no time to waste on him.

Youth totaled the balance in the unended contest between Smoke Jensen and Trenton Spectre. Trenton managed to maintain his grip on his .44 Colt and brought it up while Smoke fired at the boy's father. Now he blinked rapidly in an effort to fight off his blurred vision and raised the long barrel of the Frontier Model Colt. Beyond the blade front sight, the figure of Smoke Jensen jumped in and out of focus. Frantically he tried with a sweat-slicked thumb to draw back the hammer. He saw a flash of yellow orange and felt a terrible impact in his heart.

Then Trenton Spectre felt nothing at all. Dead before he hit the floor of the barn, Trenton Spectre still held tightly onto his six-gun. A scream of paternal anguish tore out of Victor Spectre's throat. He grabbed wildly at his .44 Smith and launched himself at Smoke Jensen.

"You bastard!" he howled.

Smoke fired hastily. His slug cut a deep trough along the head of Victor Spectre from temple to rear lobe along the left side. The wound released a halo of blood drops and knocked the criminal mastermind unconscious. Still charged for battle, Smoke Jensen had to force himself to hesitate and take stock. In an eyeblink he realized that the fight had ended.

A month went by before Victor Spectre could be brought to trial. Smoke Jensen attended, much put out at having to leave the High Lonesome to attend court in St. Louis. The first thing he noticed when the bailiffs brought Victor Spectre to the defense table was the ugly wound he had given the man. It had healed into a mass of scar tissue, from which sprouted short, totally white hairs that contrasted with the black of the remainder like the pattern on the pelt of a skunk. Fitting, Smoke had thought at the time. . . .

That had been nearly seven years ago. Now, Smoke Jensen had to allow that instead of preparing himself for a new, reformed life, Victor Spectre had spent his years in prison honing a sharper hatred and desire for revenge. Something, Smoke knew, would have to be done about it, and soon.

With dawn still a silver-gray promise on the horizon, Smoke Jensen broke camp the next morning. He had packed away everything and had only a skillet, coffee pot, trestle, and iron tripod to cool and stow in a parfleche before swinging into the saddle. He aimed Thunder's nose into the northwest and advanced into the tall, barely undulating, green sea that covered the Great Divide Basin.

Without any wind to fight, particularly a sharp one out of the northwest, Smoke made good headway. He had his first destination firmly in mind; the Arapaho and Shoshoni encampments of the Wind River Reservation, near Riverton, on the Bighorn River. He had only the ramparts of the Green Mountains, now a low, dark line that protruded above the curvature of the earth, between himself and his old friends among the Arapaho and Shoshoni. Smoke had a notion, reinforced by his recollection of the determination and implacable evil of Spectre, Tinsdale, and Buckner, that he might have need to call upon his Indian friends sometime in the near future.

For the time being, though, he remained content to let the horses eat the miles and leave him to his thoughts. Not for an instant had he harbored any regrets for killing Trenton Spectre. The boy was just shy of eighteen, and corrupt enough to be ripe for harvest by the Grim Reaper. It troubled him far more that he had not finished off Victor Spectre. Although justice remained swift and sure in most cases, three men he had spared had cheated the hangman and now required retribution from himself. Too much money, all of it ill-gotten, had bought a special kind of justice for them. A small thing perhaps, though another chink in the armor of the rule of law. *Stop it,* Smoke admonished himself. Such hankie-twisting philosophizing was a mental crutch for the weak and the cowardly.

He didn't lack for money or the things it would buy. Only a hypocrite would criticize and condemn the wealthy while he, himself, was rich. Provided, of course, his mind mocked him, it was money honestly earned. He quickly dismissed the conundrum a moment later when he saw the figures of three mounted men across his path.

"Howdy, a feller don't see many people out this way," the one in the middle remarked when Smoke Jensen had ridden up.

Smoke gave his reins a turn around the saddlehorn and tipped up the brim of his Stetson left-handed. "Now, that's a fact. You gents headed for Colorado?"

A thick, walrus mustache twitched in a mirthless smile. "Actually, it's Nebraska. Not to pry, mister, but where might you be directed?"

Smoke took notice of the way the trio eyed his 'Palouse stallion, expensive saddle, and the heavy-laden Debbie, his packhorse. "Thought I might set a spell in Riverton."

The talkative one shook his head regretfully. "That's a

sort of unwelcoming place. Bein' all that close to an Injun reservation makes folks a mite edgy."

"True, I've been there before, know a few of the folks."

"Yep. That could make a difference. Any of 'em know you're comin'?"

Smoke smelled the danger plain as if someone had set fire to an outhouse. He decided to play it out. "No. Didn't write ahead or anything."

The spokesman cut his eyes to his companions before he replied to Smoke. "That's a might nice saddle, all silver-chased and such."

"Thanks." *Any time now,* Smoke cautioned himself.

Pale, gray eyes suddenly hardened to iron. "Much too nice for a saddle tramp like you." A gloved hand reached for the plough-handled grip of a Frontier Colt. "We'll jist relieve you of it."

Smoke Jensen sighed regretfully in the split-second it took for his long, strong fingers to curl around the butt-grip of his Colt Peacemaker. He and the highwayman drew almost as one. *This fellow is good,* Smoke acknowledged as the sear notches on his hammer clicked past. His attacker had the muzzle of his .44 clear of leather at the moment when Smoke Jensen dropped the hammer on a primer.

Bucking in Smoke's hand, the big .45 sent a hot slug flying into the chest of the would-be thief. An expression of disbelief and wonder washed one of intense pain off the face of the robber. His own weapon discharged downward and grazed the right front shoulder of his mount. The horse shrieked, reared, and threw its rider. Amazed that he still held his six-gun, the bandit hit with a spine-wrenching jar.

Fighting back pain, he raised his Colt and tried to ear back the hammer. Smoke Jensen had changed his point of aim in the short time the horse panicked. He deliberately put a round in the right shoulder of the man to his right front. Then brought his attention back to the first gunhawk.

The Colt in the hand of Smoke Jensen spat a long spear of flame as it expelled another bullet.

This one popped a neat, black-rimmed hole in the forehead of Smoke's assailant, exploding messily out the back of his head, which showered the third highwayman with gore. Convinced by this display of speed and accuracy, he let the English Webley drop back into his holster and raised his hands with alacrity. His horse did a nervous little dance and that caused his eyes to widen and fear to paint his face.

"I ain't doin' nothin'. I give up."

"I gathered as much. Control your mount, then reach across with your left hand, and pull that iron from its pocket."

With that accomplished, the youthful thief looked at Smoke Jensen. "What are we gonna do now, mister?"

"We're going to play a little Indian game of trust. You are going to load your dead friends on their horses and then take them to the nearest town and turn yourself in to the sheriff for tryin' to rob and kill me. If there's any money on your heads, tell the sheriff to hold it for me."

"Wh—who are you? Who should I say?"

"Smoke Jensen."

"Oh, sweet Christ. I never knew."

"Well, now you do."

A new idea came to the rattled gunman. "What if I don't do like you say an' turn them an' myself in?"

"Then I'll hunt you down and kill you," Smoke spoke simply.

Instantly ghostly pale, the youth worked his lips a moment before any sound would come. "I believe you. By God, I believe you would. I swear it'll go jist like you say, Mr. Jensen."

Smoke gave him a bleak smile. "Somehow, I believe you're telling the truth."

* * *

Monte Carson laid the three telegraph message forms on his desk, his eyes fixed beyond the open door to the sheriff's office in Big Rock, Colorado. The first report came from the warden at Yuma Prison, detailing the depredations committed by the escapees in Arizona. *Brutal bastards,* Monte allowed. The other two came from Utah. Swollen to a gang now, the murders and robberies grew larger in scope. The third had included the information that the gang had last been seen headed for Wyoming.

That gave him pause to think. Frowning, he rose with an anguished creak from his chair and poured coffee. Seated again, he ground his teeth in a chewing motion and once more stared far off into the dark sea of pines on the distant slopes. At last he came to his conclusion. He smacked his lips and slapped an open palm on his desk. The loud report caused the jailer, Monte's friend of years, to jump.

"Abner," Monte announced in his best snake oil salesman voice, "I think this is a good time for that little vacation I've been promising myself. Get in a little fishin', spoil myself with fancy food in Denver, visit friends."

Abner cocked a shaggy, gray eyebrow. "Like Smoke Jensen, for instance?"

Monte pulled a contrite expression. "Am I that transparent?"

A grin revealed long, yellowed teeth, and Abner nodded. "With them telegraphs on yer desk, an' Smoke headed into the same country, don't take a locomotive designer to know what's in your head."

"Right you are," Monte admitted. "Smoke's bound for the Yellowstone country. And he's the most valuable friend I've got."

Abner studied his boss. "You figger to go all alone?"

Monte pushed back and came to his boots. "I reckoned Hank Evans might make good company. If I push it, I might catch up before this mob of killers finds Smoke."

* * *

Spectre, his partners, and their gang—thirty-eight strong now—entered Wyoming by way of Flaming Gorge. Everywhere they could look, beauty surrounded them. The delicate, pastel greens of aspen and cottonwood set the air to shimmering as their foliage quaked in the steady breeze. Earth tones ranged from black loam, to yellow, white, ochre, burnt umber, and red-orange, in strata of rock and soil, that undulated along the raw faces of the eroded canyon walls. A cheery, blue stream burbled along over water-smoothed pebbles. Wildflowers nodded and bobbed in a riot of yellow buttercups, blue violets, bright red ladies slipper, and fields of white petaled daises. Birds twittered and trilled their mating calls from every point of the compass.

Sadly, all of nature's splendor went unnoticed by the grim-faced riders, who kept their heads straight ahead, eyes on the trail. Dorcus Carpenter and Farlee Huntoon vociferously ran it down, maintaining that their own mountains of West Virginia were much prettier, worth more as farm land, and produced the best white lightning in the whole United States. Gus Jaeger growled to them to shut up.

Only the scout, half a mile ahead on point, observed and appreciated this peaceful environment. For a moment, it profoundly touched his inner self. Sighing, his eyes misted slightly, he even gave thought to putting spurs to his mount and riding the hell away from this nest of vipers he had joined. Then the reality of the huge amount of money they had been offered reined in his conscience and he went about his job as expected. At half-past eleven he picked their nooning site and began to gather firewood.

After putting away a tin plate of warmed-over sow belly and beans, Victor Spectre selected seven hard-faced, humorless outlaws and called them together out of hearing of the rest of the gang.

"I have a special job for you men," Spectre informed them. "While we ride on into Wyoming, I want you to take supplies enough for eight days and head southeast into

Colorado. There, you will grab a certain woman and bring her back to the little town of Dubois. Think you can do that without any problems?"

Nate Miller drew himself up, thumbs hooked behind the buckle of his cartridge belt. "Sure, Mr. Spectre. Nothin' to it. Where is it we're going?"

"Your target is the Sugarloaf. That's the ranch owned by Smoke Jensen."

Fourteen

Soft breezes, heavily perfumed, sighed across the rippling grass on the northern slope of the Green Mountains. Smoke Jensen had located a low pass, hardly more than a gentle incline to a sway-back saddle and, beyond the notch, a rolling scarp, carpeted in rich green buffalo grass that had already grown belly-high on Thunder. In the distance, beyond the last rampart, Smoke noted a thin, gray column of woodsmoke. If Smoke recalled correctly, that would be the digs of Muleshoe Granger, an oldtimer who clung to the ways of the trappers, regardless of little or no market for pelts. Granger had a Shoshoni wife and—had it been four?—kids the last time Smoke had been through. Smiling, Smoke altered course to put him in line with the cookfire's stream.

Halting some fifty yards from the log-fronted building dug into the hillside, Smoke raised an empty right hand and hailed the bent, bow-legged figure who had paused to study his approach. "Hello, the cabin, Is that you, Muleshoe? I'm Smoke Jensen. May I ride on in?"

Delayed by distance, Granger's words reached Smoke a bit muffled. "Why, shore. C'mon in." When Smoke reached the dooryard, Granger continued. "We's fixin' to take a bite to eat. Step down and join us."

Smiling, Smoke did just that. "I'd be obliged."

Muleshoe's family had grown to seven, Smoke noted. Those under twelve were buck naked, sun-browned like berries. The youngest was a mere toddler, who clung shyly to the skirt of his mother's elk-skin dress, and peeped around her ample hips at the stranger. While they ate, Muleshoe Granger gave Smoke Jensen a fish-eye from time to time, then smacked his lips, licked the gravy from an elk stew off his fingers and gave a curt nod.

"Seems as how I should know you. As I recall, we met long whiles back. Ain't you ol' Preacher's young sidekick?"

"That I am. And, I've been through these parts several times on my own."

Muleshoe blinked. "That a fact? Well, they say the first thing goes is the memory."

Smoke gave a low chuckle, and a nod toward the younger children. "It must be true. At least it's not something else."

"What you gettin' at, Smoke?"

"Last time I visited your digs was about ten years ago. You had only four children then, as I recall."

Muleshoe laughed out loud and slapped a hard-muscled thigh. "Nope, it was three. But, by jing, you've got the right of it there. Plenty lead in the old pencil. Moon Raven's carryin' another in the oven right now."

Shyness overcome by an empty belly, the toddler had come forward, His sister, a girl of seven or so, helped him to a bowl of stew. All the while, he stared fixedly at Smoke Jensen. Smoke pointed to the youngsters with his chin.

"That's good to hear. You know, you two bake up some mighty fine-lookin' youngins."

Muleshoe beamed. "The pride of Granger Valley."

Smoke looked around. "You've named the place, then?"

"Yep. Had to. Folks is movin' in faster than fleas. Why, I've got me a neighbor all crowded up to me, cheek by jowl. He's not more'n ten miles over to the east. I had to file with the territorial government to hold what's mine."

"Civilization spoils everything, doesn't it," Smoke observed.

Muleshoe nodded. "Yep. There's powerful truth in those words. Now, are you real pressed for time? Or do you figger to stay the night? The youngins would love to hear some tales about Preacher," he coaxed.

"I'm not in that great a hurry. If you'll put up with me, I'd be pleased to spend the night."

Muleshoe gave him a thoughtful look. "That's good. Bein' as who you are and where, it might be best. From what I hear, you might be ridin' into some real danger."

"How's that?" Smoke asked.

"A friend rode through the day before yesterday, told me about a whole passel of men ridin' grim and hard in the saddle to the west of us. Says they come up outta Utah."

Smoke nodded his understanding. "That fits with what I've been hearing. You can be sure I've caught wind of them from time to time. But, tell me, have you seen anything of Three Finger Jack lately?"

With evening coming on, Victor Spectre, Ralph Tinsdale, and Olin Buckner had settled in camp stools at the front of one of the three Sibley tents they had acquired along the way. A decanter of whiskey gave off long, amber shafts of brightness in the flicker of firelight, as it passed from hand to hand. For all the outward appearance of conviviality, tension fairly crackled from one man to the next. Buckner's tone became quarrelsome as he vented his impatience.

"This protracted journey across the wilderness is becoming burdensome, Victor. I have never been much of a horseman. My rump and thighs still ache after each day's ride."

"You'll toughen up soon enough," Victor told him unsympathetically.

"I agree with Olin," Ralph Tinsdale injected. "If our purpose remains the same, to revenge ourselves on Smoke Jensen, then why don't we simply head to the Sugarloaf and kill him in his own yard?"

Victor Spectre shook his head in resignation. Small wonder these two had been taken by Jensen so easily. Then he made a final effort to explain. "For one thing, it would be too quick and too easy. I want Smoke Jensen to die slowly and hurt a great deal while doing it. Then there's the fact that Colorado is quite civilized now. There are trains and the telegraph, thousands of residents, and competent lawmen." He did not go quite so far as to admit he feared being trapped in the more populous country around the Sugarloaf. Not by the law, but rather by Smoke Jensen. Gus Jaeger approached, his face even more horselike than ever.

"Mr. Spectre, the men are getting down-right antsy. They want for the walls of a saloon around them, some good whiskey, and some wimmin to tussle with. When are we going to get around city lights again?"

Spectre sighed. "In due time. What's wrong with the liquor we've provided for them? Isn't it good enough?"

"Nothin' wrong, really. Only that they'd like someone to share it with." Gus snickered. "What's up ahead?"

"An Indian reservation. A rather large one. Which reminds me. In light of what you've said, make it clear to the men that they are not, I repeat *are not,* under any circumstances, to attempt to bed any of the squaws. Indians are quite strange in their attitude toward women. If you are their friend and a guest, they will offer you a daughter or a wife to warm your bed, and think nothing of it. But if you lay eyes, let alone a hand, on any woman not offered to you, your scalp will decorate their shield. Make certain the men are aware of this. Tell them, also, that if any of them do pester the Indian women, I'll personally kill them before the bucks have a chance to."

Jaeger frowned. "That's mighty cold . . . sir."

"It's meant to be. Now, go on and cool their ardor with a little whiskey." After Gus Jaeger departed, Victor Spectre returned to the subject of Smoke Jensen.

"This little town up north, Dubois, is ideal for what we want to do. Not so large as to be difficult to take over, yet not so small that we cannot house this little army of ours within the city limits. And, from others I've met in prison, Smoke Jensen has a soft spot in his heart for the people of Dubois. All we need do is take it over and send word. Smoke Jensen will come to us. Further, if my other little project bears fruit, we'll have a most attractive bait to dangle in front of him."

Two days later, Smoke reached the lodge of Chief Thomas Brokenhorn of the Shoshoni at midday. Small children ran naked and shrieking among the Shoshoni brush summer lodges. Cookfires sent up their columns of white, while savory odors emanated from the pots supported over them by tripods. Warriors gathered from their homes to form a silent column, along which Smoke rode to the central lodge. He could not shake the feeling that their formation exactly mimicked that of the punishment gauntlet. He banished the unease when he saw the broad grin on the face of his old friend, Brokenhorn, who stood before his lodge with arms folded over a barrel chest.

"You have come far, old friend," Chief Brokenhorn declared by way of greeting.

"So have you," Smoke responded, meaning the older man's elevation to Civil Chief. "You were only leader of the Otter Society when I last saw you."

"Thank you, Swift Firestick. Dismount and make my lodge your own. We will eat, smoke, and talk of old times."

"It would be a pleasure, friend Thomas. Although it is of recent times I am most interested in."

Brokenhorn nodded curtly. "Yes. Some very bad men rode through here yesterday. You must be seeking them." A kindliness lighted his eyes. "They are many. Come, take of the food of my woman, first, burn a pipeful, then we talk of these matters."

* * *

Monte Carson received a warm welcome from Morgan Crosby. Traveling light and fast, the lawman had made it that far in only four days. He filled his belly with some of Morgan's good cooking and settled back with a pipe he had taken to smoking of late.

Morgan broke one of their frequent long, silent spells. "I reckon you'd be interested in hearin' anything about Smoke Jensen?"

Monte took a long pull on the pipe. "I didn't come all this way for exercise. He's been here?"

"Yep. Five—six days ago. Had some right unpleasant fellers on his trail, though."

"What did Smoke do about that?"

"It's what *we* did, you should be sayin'."

Monte let a thin stream of white trickle from his lips. "All right, what did you two do about it?"

Morgan chuckled throatily before answering. "Mind now, I'd never seen Smoke Jensen in action before. He's 'bout as smooth as a well-oiled locomotive. Betwixt us, we convinced those fellers it were a bad idea to try takin' Smoke in with no more than five of 'em on their side."

A grunt came from Monte. "All right, where's the bodies buried?"

An expression of childlike innocence lighted the face of Morgan Crosby. "There ain't no bodies buried." He paused, slapped his thigh and cackled. "After Smoke rode out, I drug 'em off to feed the coyotes and buzzards. One of them got away. Though he be carrin' about six of my double-aught Buck. Big feller he was, else he woulda been critter bait, too." Then he went on to describe the fight.

Monte Carson considered this. No doubt in his mind that Smoke Jensen could have handled all five by himself. Better than even odds when they split up like that. And Smoke not getting a scratch. Typical. Monte finished his bowl, knocked out the dottle, and ground the tobacco embers under one boot sole. He stretched and came upright.

"Which way did Smoke head?"

"That-away," Morgan told him, a finger pointed to the northwest. "Up Yellowstone way."

Monte nodded. "That fits with what he told me."

"Which is?"

"Smoke's bound for Jackson's Hole."

"A feller could take on a small army if he knew his way around there," Morgan opined. "An' I reckon that's what's after him from what I've learned."

"Smoke knows the place well enough. Ol' Preacher taught him every nook and cranny." Monte turned to face Morgan, still seated on the porch. He extended his hand. "Much obliged for the vittles. Sure sets nice in the belly. There's still a lot of daylight to be used so I reckon I'll head on out. Plenty ground between here and the Hole."

"Come by any time, Sheriff Carson."

"Please, Monte."

Crosby beamed. "Make it Morgan, then. Be proud to have you stop by and stay a while. An' bring your friend with you."

"I'll try. Believe me, I will. Good day to you, Morgan."

"An' to you, Monte."

Five minutes later, Monte Carson rode out of sight of the snug, though bullet-scarred cabin.

A large, whole ribcage of elk had been properly demolished, along with stewed squash, mixed with nuts, wild onions, and berries. With signs and rudimentary Shoshoni, Smoke Jensen related the story of the Great Elk Hunt he had gone on when only a slight bit older than his attentive audience. Some twenty children from the village had gathered around Chief Brokenhorn's fire to gawk at the tall, lean white man and hear his exciting stories.

"It was a hard ride for me," Smoke recounted. "I was still little enough my legs stuck out from the sides of my pony. Some of you must ride the same way, right?" Giggles and whispered accusations rippled through the cluster of Indian youngsters. Smoke waited them out and went on. "Preacher and I joined with a whole lot of other trappers for this hunt. It would be the biggest ever. Five hands of men, in my language, twenty-five, came from all parts of the mountains. Preacher, of course, was the best hunter of them all. He was first to find the herd, first to kill a bull elk. I got to dress it out." More giggles and knowing nods.

"That arrangement didn't last long. By the third day, Preacher let me pick an elk out of the herd and take it as my own. 'First,' he told me, 'say a little prayer to the bull's High Self, askin' permission to take its life. Say that you have hunger and will be even more hungry in the long winter to come. Ask that the animal's spirit be born as the biggest elk of all.' That made my chest swell and I thought I was really something. Preacher told me he learned to pray like that from the Shoshoni."

"That's right," Tom Brokenhorn injected. "He did. In the time of my grandfather. And I remember that hunt. I was no bigger than *Chusha* over there." He indicated a boy of seven or so, squatted as close as he could get to Smoke Jensen. "Many of us joined in on that hunt and we all ate well the whole of winter."

Smoke went on to describe the surrounds each day and the shooting of elk with rifles and bow and arrow. He concluded, "Preacher told me later that three hundred bull elk and fifty young elk were taken in that hunt. We made meat for a week after."

"Tell us something more," *Chusha* pleaded.

Smoke stretched and forced a yawn. "Four stories is enough for one night. Your fathers will be wondering where you have gone. And your mothers will worry. Go on. I'll have another story in the morning before I leave."

After the last, reluctant boy had walked off among the lodges, Smoke realized he actually was sleepy. He roused himself and headed for the lodge that had been prepared for him. Tomorrow he would head to the Arapaho camp.

Seven hard-faced men rode onto the Sugarloaf early the next morning. They made no effort to conceal their approach from the headquarters buildings. Earlier, one of them had watched a large contingent of hands ride off to the horse pastures. By his count, only half a dozen remained to work around the barns and blacksmithy. Well and good, Nate Miller thought. When the Sugarloaf hands had gotten well out of sight and sound of the main ranch buildings, he ordered his crew forward.

Riding slouched in the saddle, Nate led the outlaws up the steep two mile lane from the gate to the ranch yard. He and his men made only slight nods and grunted responses when hailed by the first man to discover them. Looking neither left nor right, they rode on. Stumpy Granger looked up from the anvil, which still rang from the blows he had given a particularly stubborn horseshoe. He made them right away as gunfighters.

With most of the hands gone for the day, that did not bode well for those left behind, Stumpy considered. He wiped a black-smudged hand across his brow to eliminate the sheet of sweat that covered it, and watched silently, eyes slitted, as the hard cases walked their horses up to the tie-rail outside the kitchen door. There they dismounted. Still no one challenged them. Although they had been in several scrapes with Smoke Jensen, the ranch hands were hardly seasoned gunmen. They held back as the strangers started for the door.

They soon found they had backed off too long when two of the human debris pushed into the kitchen. At last, the six wranglers began to gather around the outlaws.

"What's yer business on the Sugarloaf?" one of the bolder hands asked.

"If it was any of your business, you'd have been told," growled a rat-faced individual, his right hand on the smooth butt of his .45 Colt.

Stumpy took up the challenge. "Mayhap you didn't hear too well. This here is the Sugarloaf. Smoke Jensen's ranch. Bein' as how we belong here and you don't, that makes it or business. What are you here for? An' who sent you?"

"Oldtimer, you really don't want to know."

A forge hammer in his left hand, Stumpy menaced the five men he faced. He was about to speak again when a loud crash came from inside the house. Wood splintered and a man yelped.

Sally Jensen looked up as the kitchen door swung open. Surprise washed over her face when she faced two unfamiliar men. "What are you doing here?" she demanded.

A lean, lanky one, whom she would later learn was named Nate Miller, asked, "Are you Sally Jensen?"

"Yes, I am."

Miller guffawed. "We've come to take you on a little visit."

"I think not. I have no plans to go anywhere," Sally retorted defiantly. "Especially with the likes of you. Get out of my kitchen."

"When we go, we're takin' you with us."

Her purse lay in the middle of the table. Sally made a quick grab for it and produced her .38 Colt Lightning. She had already begun her squeeze through on the double-action rig when she spoke again. "Get . . . out . . . of . . . my . . . kitchen."

"Look out! She's got a gun," the man with Miller yelped.

Sally came out of her chair with enough force to knock it over. One leg splintered when it struck the floor. Already, Miller had moved to the side. The other thug started to dive through the open doorway. Sally fired then. The slug cracked past close enough to the outlaw that he felt the hot wind. Sally started to squeeze off another round when Nate Miller dived at her from her blind side.

Fingers like iron slats closed around her wrist. "Gimme that, bitch," Miller spat.

She fought like a Fury. Sally's nails clawed Nate's cheek. He yowled, and clapped a hand over the quartet of flowing red lines. He managed to get the web of his other hand between the hammer and the rear of the receiver of Sally's Colt Lightning. The sharp little firing pin bit deeply into his skin. Sally stomped on his arch and then brought a knee up toward his groin. Only because he moved his right thigh did she fail to do him severe damage. Ignoring the deep gouges on his cheek, he used his bloody hand to shake her violently.

"Let go of that gun," he growled as he slammed her head into the point of his shoulder. Sally bit him on the arm. Miller grunted out his pain and punched her on the side of her head. Sally saw a wild burst of stars behind her eyes and her knees sagged. It relaxed her grip on the revolver and it clattered loudly to the floor.

Miller howled with pain as he shook his hand free of the firing pin and the weapon dropped away. Quickly he spun Sally around and took hold of both her shoulders. He shook her like one would an errant child.

"Listen to me," Miller spat furiously, flecks of foam flying with his whiskey breath. "You're coming with us. Either over my shoulder or on your own two feet, you're coming. I don't much care which it is. Bart, give me a hand."

Bart turned away from the door with alacrity and crossed the room to where Nate held the dark-haired woman. Each man took an arm and frog-marched her to the door. Nate Miller turned sideways and led the way out, dragging Sally behind him. When she appeared as a captive, the hands at last reacted. As one, they went for their guns.

* * *

When he saw Miss Sally in the clutches of the two hard cases, Stumpy Granger let fly with the hammer. Driven by the power of a blacksmith's muscular arm, the heavy object slammed into the forehead of the rat-faced thug. He went down like a slaughterhouse steer. Stumpy cackled with glee.

Already reaching for his six-gun, Stumpy chortled, "Right betwixt the runnin' lights."

A swift exchange of lead followed. One bullet cracked by close enough to cut the knot on the headband Stumpy wore. Momentarily the sodden cloth fell over his eyes. It caused his shot to go wild, to slam into the wall of the house. One of the saddle trash shrieked in pain, gut-shot by two ranch hands at the same time. Blood bubbled up his throat and formed a pink froth on his lips. He shuddered mightily and fell face first into the dirt, dead from a perforated stomach and blasted liver before he hit the ground.

"Stumpy, I'm hit," a young voice called from the blacksmith's right.

Granger yanked the cloth band free and looked that way. Young Clell Eilert knelt in the dust, his Colt held limply in his left hand. "Git down, boy. Get clear of this now," Stumpy commanded. He fired a round at the man who must have shot Eilert, and noted with satisfaction when the slug tore into the right side of the outlaw's chest. Another hand lay dead in a welter of gore. Nate Miller waved a six-gun over his head and called to his men.

"Mount up, boys. Git the hell out of here."

He roughly threw Sally onto the saddle of the dead hard case and led the way at a fast trot down the lane toward safety. Quickly his underlings broke off and followed suit. In less than two swirling minutes, the fight ended. Stumpy counted up the toll.

"One of them dead, and one of ours," he glumly reported to anyone interested in hearing. "At least two of them wounded, three of ours. What's worse, though, is they got Miss Sally. There's gonna be hell to pay for that."

* * *

"There's gonna be hell to pay for that," Ike Mitchell echoed Stumpy Granger when the hands returned, after being summoned by a shaken Sugarloaf worker.

"Damn straight," Stump muttered agreement.

Ike surveyed the scene. "Get everyone who is able gathered up, Stumpy. We'll pick a skeleton crew to maintain things here, the rest will ride after those bastards."

"Jist what I had in mind," Stumpy offered.

When everyone collected around Ike Mitchell, he outlined his plans. At once the hands who would accompany him went about making ready. It did not take long for Ike to see Bobby lead his mount to the corral rails and climb up to tie on his bedroll. Ike crossed to him.

"I'm sorry, Bobby, you're not going along."

"Yes . . . I . . . am," Bobby insisted as he tightly jerked down on a pair of latigo strings. "It's my fault anyway. I shoulda gone with Smoke. We could have stopped those guys long before now."

Taken aback by the boy's vehemence, Ike could only shake his head. "That's not realistic, Bobby. Smoke is miles from here, and these fellers came from who knows where. You cannot come with us. Smoke and Miss Sally would never forgive me."

Torment twisted Bobby's features. His words came out heavy and torn with anguish. "I've gotta go. Don't you see? *She's my mother!*"

Something ripped inside Ike Mitchell. Buried memories flared up of himself as a boy of twelve, standing over the grave of his mother, killed by Indians." All right, Bobby. Bring that little carbine of yours, and your six-gun. We leave in ten minutes."

Fifteen

Smoke Jensen bid farewell to Chief Brokenhorn early that morning. The Chief clasped Smoke's forearm and nodded toward the northwest.

"Go carefully, old friend. I will keep braves to watch the evil ones. I promise you that when you need them, warriors will come to help you."

"That could get you in a lot of trouble for leaving the reservation armed and without an army escort."

Thomas Brokenhorn gave him a fleeting, bitter smile and shrugged. "We are no strangers to the white man's trouble. Ride in peace and send word when men are needed."

"Thank you, old friend. May your lodge always have ample food."

A twinkle filled the eyes of Brokenhorn. "You go now to those snakes in the grass?"

"What a thing to call the Arapaho," Smoke said in mock chastisement.

"Old ways die hard. Old enemies even harder."

"Yes, I'm going to talk with Blackrobe. I'll give him your best."

"What does this 'best' mean?"

Smoke chuckled. "Better you didn't know." With that, Smoke Jensen swung into the saddle and rode off toward the Arapaho encampment.

* * *

At the head of the column of vengeful ranch hands, Ike Mitchell soon noted that the trail of the kidnappers led roughly in the same direction Smoke Jensen said he would be taking. He said nothing of it at the time, content to be assured they quickly closed ground. Sally Jensen was a plucky lady. He felt confident she would do anything she could to slow down her abductors.

Bobby Harris kept up well, Ike also observed. Not once did the boy complain of the fast pace or the ache that must be in full bloom in his thighs and crotch. They rode on through the afternoon. Twenty minutes out of each hour they walked their horses to keep them from becoming blown. If the outlaws failed to do the same, the chances of coming on them soon increased considerably. The western sky turned magenta and they had not yet made contact.

Reluctantly, Ike called a halt for the day. While the hands went about the setup of camp, Ike took Bobby aside. They chewed on cold biscuits while the man tried to make his most important point with the boy.

"Bobby, I want you to promise me one thing. When the shooting starts, you hold back. I want you out of the mix-up as far as you can be. Oh, you'll have a chance to get in your licks. I want you to pick a spot from which you can watch and see any of the outlaws try to escape. If they do, pot 'em."

The boy nodded thoughtfully. "Yeah, yeah, I can do that."

"Good boy." Ike resisted the impulse to pat Bobby on the head and nodded instead. He strode back to the cookfire and poured coffee.

When the last of the red-eye gravy had been sopped up with the last biscuit, and the final bit of ham had been munched contentedly, Ike Mitchell called the hands together around the fire. He informed them of the likelihood that the outlaws were headed for the same place as Smoke Jensen. He also advised that they had a good chance of catching up the next day. When the wranglers of the Sugarloaf had digested that, he asked for suggestions about what to do when they caught the kidnappers in the open.

Handy Barker had the wildest idea. "I say we rope 'em by the ankles and drag those bastards to death." Oddly enough, several hands agreed.

"We oughta get the law in on this, don't you think, Mr. Mitchell?" Perk Toller, the youngest, newest hand offered.

Fred Grimes, an oldtimer, had a sobering thought. "Remember one thing. Those fellers have Miss Sally with them. We will have to be mighty careful with any shooting we do. Best thing I think we can do is find 'em, then get around them and set up an ambush. Two of us could make a grab for Miss Sally while the rest of the outlaws are tryin' to escape the ambush."

Ike thought that the most reasonable, if a bit timid. Yet, Bobby Harris summed up their general attitude with his quiet, simple statement. "I say we kill 'em all."

Deep, rhythmic throbbing came from the big, "singing" drum of the Arapaho village. Four men sat at it, each with his padded beater, pounding out the notes of a hunt song. Shoulders hunched forward, their heads thrown back to the star-milked sky, they chanted the words of the favored piece. A huge fire burned nearby, with the chiefs and elders seated before it with their honored guest.

Smoke Jensen leaned back on a porcupine quill-decorated backrest and gnawed on a rib bone. The meat was sweet and rich. In the chill of the high plains night, smaller fires flickered in every lodge, making of themselves a vast display of huge, skin lanterns. When the gunfighter licked his fingers to signal he was through eating, Chief Blackrobe produced a pipe, lighted it with a coal from the fire, and made the six points. Then he passed the calumet to Smoke Jensen, who did the same as his host, took a long draw for himself and began to speak of his reason for being there.

"A moon ago, three bad men escaped from Yuma Prison in far off Arizona. They have taken a vow to hunt and kill me. I do not fear them. They are only three. But, they have taken a gang to themselves, dangerous men, made all the more so because they are not the best at what they do. They number many times two hands." Smoke paused to let that sink in.

"It is said that these men have ridden into this country," Smoke continued. "Though why they come here I do not know."

Silence followed for a while, during which Smoke passed the pipe on. At last Blackrobe spoke. "We have seen such men. As you say, they number many. They rode through here two suns ago. I did not like their looks, though in truth, they did no harm. So I sent young warriors to watch over their progress. I would believe that they are the same men of which you speak. If so, you could use some help. I promise to take this up with the council. If approved, men can be sent whenever you need them. Now, let us talk of other things and drink some of the coffee you have brought with you."

Bound hand and foot, Sally Jensen sat on a rock, apart from the scruffy band of thugs who had taken her captive. She was cold, hungry, and miserable, though determined not to let her captors know that. With only a faint orange glow on the horizon, one of the hard cases separated from the rest and came toward her. He carried a tin plate and a spoon.

"I have some grub here. Brung you some water, too. I'll untie your hands so you can eat, if you promise not to make a fuss."

Sally thought it wise to remain assertive. "I doubt I could keep down anything cooked by the likes of any of you."

A low chuckle sounded in the shadows. "You'd be surprised. Ol' Hank's a fair to middlin' cook. If you aim to live through this, you'll need to eat to keep up yer strength."

She recognized the truth to that. "I suppose you are right. I promise not to try to escape while my hands are free."

"I'm sure you won't. Because I'm gonna sit right here and watch you."

"Where are you taking me?" Sally asked once her hands had been freed and she held the plate.

He saw no reason not to respond. "North. To a little town name of Dubois. The boss says that yer husband will come there to get you free."

Sally frowned and iron edged her words. "If he does, you can be sure you will all regret the day it happens."

Again that irritating, superior chuckle. "I doubt that. Lady, there's thirty-eight of us. More'n enough to face down Smoke Jensen."

"Are you sure? What do you really know about my husband?"

Considering that a moment, the outlaw spoke softly. "I ain't never seen him, ma'am. But, I hear he's one ring-tail heller when he's riled."

Sally smiled to herself, pleased with this response. "That's true enough. He and three others took on more than fifty men one time. Smoke was shot twice, but he killed or wounded twenty of them by himself."

"Lord God, ma'am, if you'll excuse my cussin'. He's a bit more than most of these fellers are expectin'. Some of us is purty good, but not *that* good."

"Another time, he took on thirteen men in the middle of a street by himself. Five of them died, the other eight received one or more wounds. Smoke took a crease across the top of his left shoulder," she added sweetly.

"That's powerful good shootin', ma'am."

Sally used all her feminine wiles to sell her message. "I thought you ought to know. Perhaps it would be wise for you to make the others aware of these things?"

Thoughtful silence followed. "Ummm. Yes, I do think you're right."

A rustle of brush and crunch of a stone underfoot announced the arrival of another of the outlaws. A hulking brute, he smelled of tobacco smoke, stale whiskey, and unwashed body. A broken-toothed grin shined yellowish in the reflected firelight. Fists on hips, he took a long, slow look at Sally Jensen. Abruptly, he reached out and chucked her under the chin, his thick thumb and forefinger squeezing painfully.

"Well, now, I reckon it's time for us to get a little relief, don't you, Sam?" With his other hand he massaged his crotch suggestively.

Sally's confidant, Sam, bristled immediately. "You heard what Nate said, an' Mr. Spectre, too. She ain't to be touched." He sounded as though he meant it.

Menace bristled in the lout's words. "You callin' me out, Sam?"

"I reckon, if needs be."

Nate Miller appeared out of nowhere. He gave the surly thug a hard shove. "Get back where you belong. You, too, Sam. Once Miz Jensen is fed, anyway." He tipped his hat to Sally. "Sorry, ma'am, if Ogilvey upset you. He knows better. Or he at least should. I'll have Sam here rig you a safe place to sleep."

Icily, Sally answered him. "Thank you, you are so kind."

Silently, she hatched plan after plan on how to escape. And rejected them all. The time would come, she kept telling himself. It surely would.

Ike Mitchell sat his horse, his face a mask of dejection. The trail they had followed so far had completely disappeared. He pointed to the multiple tracks that led into a swiftly flowing stream. Early that morning they had ridden hard and fast to the north to get around the outlaws. An ideal spot had been picked for an ambush, and the Sugarloaf hands had settled in to wait.

When the kidnappers had not appeared by noon, Ike had to conclude that they had taken a new trail. He set three men southeast along the way by which he had expected the outlaws to approach. They found the camp, and a trail that lead off due west. Hastily, one returned to inform Ike. He immediately started off in pursuit of the new route. Fogging along the new path, they eventually came to this fast-flowing mountain stream. The horses they sought had entered it right enough.

Only they did not come out on the other side. Fifty-fifty chance for up or down stream. Ike considered it a while, then consulted the others. "You boys have tracked enough horses in your time. What do you say? Did they go up or down?"

Stumpy had his ideas. "I say up. It's in keeping with they goin' to Wyoming."

That did it for Ike. "I agree. Three of you trail south, downstream, for about four miles. If you don't cut any sign, turn around and join up with us as soon as you can." He eyed the gathered hands. "All of you keep a sharp eye. They can't stay in that water for long. We'll ride both sides of the banks. Make better time that way."

Monte Carson sweated bullets. Hot sun beat down on the waving sea of grass in the Great Divide Basin. He felt gratitude that Hank Evans had come along. Never complaining, that big smile plastered on his freckled face even in this heat, Hank rode at Monte's side. Bare-headed, Hank's carroty hair could be a flaming torch. They had covered considerable ground in the past two days since leaving the cabin of Morgan Crosby. Only today's ride and they would be in the Green Mountains. If all went well, they would negotiate them by the end of the next day.

Monte chaffed at any delay in catching up to Smoke. Even if he only got word of the gunfighter's passage he would feel better. *Thirty-five to forty men in the Spectre gang.* The words haunted him. Monte honestly doubted that the three of them could go against such numbers and come out of it alive. At least not all of them. Would it be Hank who got it? Or would he cash in his chips at long last?

Never once did Monte consider that Smoke Jensen might be sent off to meet his Maker. Smoke was the stuff legends are made of. He was as close to being immortal as any man could hope to be. Self-consciously, Monte forced himself off this path of introspection. Last thing he needed before going into a shoot-out was to worry about the outcome. Years as a fast gun, and more as a lawman, had taught him that. He turned to look at his chief deputy as Hank shouted over the rumble of hooves.

"What say I go off and find us something for supper?"

Monte shook his head. "Wait until we're in the mountains."

Hank patted his belly. "I hear there's some pigs that gone wild up there in the Greens. Mighty tasty."

Monte laughed. "Exactly what I was thinking. Roast one of them whole and bring along what we don't eat for tomorrow."

"A young porker would be real fine," Hank agreed.

Half an hour later, they came upon a pair of scruffy road agents who had stopped off to rob a hapless family of four who had a broken wagon wheel. Monte spotted them first, the man and woman frightened witless, hands in the air, while the human trash rifled their clothing for valuables. Two sobbing children were cowering behind the jacked up wheel. Monte had his six-gun out of leather before thinking about it.

So engrossed were the thieves that they failed to notice the approach of the lawmen. Monte got within twenty yards of the pinched-faced one before the bit of crud raised a sallow, startled face to stare at the threat of a .45 Colt. Unable to shoot because of the proximity of the victims, Monte anticipated that the outlaw would not be so inhibited.

He jinked to the right a moment before the craven robber fired. The bullet cracked past and the shooter jumped to one side to get a clearer shot at his intended target. Monte seized on the change of position to get off a round. His slug flew straight and true.

It struck the miscreant in the center of his chest, punched through a lung and severed the aorta. The thug literally bled to death before he realized he was dying. His legs went out from under him and he flopped on the ground. His partner exchanged shots with Hank and dived for the protection of the damaged wagon. Hank set more lead after him. The slug cut chips from the wagon's sideboard. Meanwhile, Monte Carson edged his horse to the off side of the buckboard and stood in place to meet the brigand when he rounded the harnessed team.

"What th' hell?" the snaggle-toothed outlaw blurted.

"Throw it down," Monte commanded.

"Hell no!" the bandit shouted defiantly.

Monte's horse shied in the instant when he fired. His bullet went wide and low, to gouge deeply into the road agent's hip. With a yelp of pain, the hoodlum dropped to his good knee. His Colt bucked and snorted fire. The slug cut a hot line along Monte's ribcage. Then his own Peacemaker barked and the highwayman flipped over backward. Monte and Hank reined in, checked the dead men and turned back to the startled pilgrims.

"Praise the Lord!" the blonde woman declared, hands clasped and upraised.

"You saved us, mister. We're much obliged."

Monte had his dander aroused. "No thanks to the both of you. Folks should know better not to be out here unarmed, or without an escort."

Icily, the woman answered him in self-righteousness.

"We do not believe in guns, mister. They're the work of the devil."

"Maudy's right, mister. We don't hold by guns and violent ways." He cut his eyes to inspect the aftermath, then added ruefully, "At least, she don't. After what happened, I've sorta changed my mind."

"Richard!" Maude bleated.

He rounded on her. "I mean it, Maudy. They might have done who knows what to you and the girls, after they robbed us, that is. You saw what a man, properly armed, could do to end their evil ways."

Still unswayed, Maude answered testily. "Such matters are best left in the hands of God and the law."

His own ire aroused, Richard narrowed his eyes and spoke hotly. "And just how long do you expect it might have taken for God to take a hand? Or the law to get here? We'd all be dead and turned back to dust before we could count on any help from them quarters. An' I don't mean to blaspheme by that. God's got other things to look after, an' the nearest law must be a hunnerd miles away."

Monte Carson cleared his throat in embarrassment. "As it happens, the law is right here. Monte Carson, sheriff of Price County, Colorado. This is my chief deputy."

Richard looked startled. "We still in Colorado."

"Nope. This is Wyoming, right enough. We're looking for a man."

"An outlaw?" Richard prompted.

Monte shook his head. "No. A friend. Tall man, lean, with broad shoulders, clean shaven. Far-off lookin' hazel eyes, red-brown hair," he described Smoke Jensen.

Richard cut his eyes to his wife. They both shook their heads. "We've not seen anyone like that," the man answered.

"Don't reckon you will, then. He should be ahead of us a ways. Can we give you a hand with that wheel?"

"I'd be right grateful. Got a spare lashed to the underside."

Within twenty minutes the new wheel had been fixed in place. Monte wiped axle grease off his hands and turned to his horse. Richard interrupted him with effusive thanks and a question. "What's to be done with those two?"

"No doubt they have a price on their heads. If you can put up with the stink, take them along and turn them in at the next town."

"Not on your life," husband and wife agreed.

Monte mounted, laughing, and gave a friendly wave. Then he and Hank rode off in search of Smoke Jensen.

Sixteen

Seen from a long, ragged bluff, the town of Dubois looked even more unimpressive than the description given of it by Victor Spectre. Three days of hard riding, from first light to last, had brought them to this point. The gang sat their mounts near the rim that dropped off sharply to a talus slope three hundred feet below. A beatific smile lighted the face of Victor Spectre. He made a sweeping gesture with a black-gloved hand.

"There it is, gentlemen. We have arrived. We will divide into four groups. Three of them to be led by myself and my associates, the fourth by Augustus Jaeger. We will then approach the town from all sides and take it by storm. The key is to minimize the amount of violence it requires to assert our control. Paramount is the disarming of the populace."

Farlee Huntoon looked blankly at Dorcus Carpenter. "What th' hell he say?"

Dorcus translated. "He says first we take away all their guns."

Spectre continued as though the interruption had never occurred. "Second is to make certain that only a selected few escape to carry word of conditions in Dubois. I would suggest no more than two or three, and separately. Lastly, is to secure all means of communication to the outside world. After that, you are at liberty to despoil the community and its citizens to your hearts' content. Mind you, that is to be in moderation, we do not want the town burned down around our feet."

Several guffaws answered this. Then, Fin Brock chortled, "Rustlin' petticoats never started no fires, Mr. Spectre. I reckon to keep my 'despoiling' to the ladies of Dubois, an' that's a fact."

Spectre gave him a cold smile. "Fine, Mr. Brock. One final admonition. You are not all to celebrate at the same time. An endless orgy is not in my plans. You must all get proper rest and sleep. We also need men on the alert to keep watch. Augustus Jaeger and Reese Judson will be in charge of a system of lookouts. Because, when he gets word, Smoke Jensen will come. And when he does, it will be as though all the Furies rode with him. Enough for now. Let us divide and prepare to conquer."

"Jeez, he talks like one of them play-actors," Farlee complained to his constant companion, Dorcus.

Carpenter nodded agreement. "I'd be a mite bit more comfortable with plain speakin', myself. Best if we be with the bunch comin' from this side. Less ridin' that way."

Farlee Huntoon laughed at that, a sort of gulping, slobbering sound. "I gotcha there, pardner."

In ten minutes it had been accomplished. Their spirits high, the gang of ruffians and deadly rabble set off to capture a city.

Irving Spaun had opened his bank in Dubois the year before a horde of outlaws had descended upon the town. Two months after their arrival, Smoke Jensen came to Dubois. After a lot of bloody fighting, the outlaws, at least those left alive, fled. Irving had proudly aided in their expulsion. He still prided himself at being good with a shotgun.

Even though he had reached the age of 55 and had a pot belly, he still got out and hunted prairie chickens, doves, and Canada geese. Many a winter afternoon, after the bank had closed, he would arrive at home with a pair of plump rabbits. It had been two years now since anyone had tried to rob the bank. On that occasion, the unlucky bandit had been blasted into eternity by Irving's trusty Parker. At the bank he loaded 00 Buckshot. On this bright, sunny day, as Irving stepped outside to lock the door for the noontime recess, he felt confident that all was, and would remain, well with his world. Ten minutes later, he discovered how sadly wrong he had been.

Seated at his usual table at Molly Vincent's Home Kettle, he awaited a savory plate of corned beef and cabbage, with potatoes, onions, and carrots. Suddenly, the double front doors flew open with enough force to shatter the etched-edged glass in one panel. Three men stood in the opening and menaced everyone inside with huge six-guns in gloved fists.

"Nobody make a sound," the one in charge commanded. "Jist sit still and don't make trouble. My friends here are going to come around and relieve all you gents of any weapons you may have. Then, I'm gonna name some people I want to stand up and come with us."

"You can't get away with this," the fat, male cook and owner, Mollson, who was called Molly by everyone, blurted.

An amused, sneering smile appeared on the leader's face. "I don't see anything around here that could get in our way. Now, don't even twitch an eyelid. Go clean 'em out, boys."

Quickly the outlaws complied. They came up with five cartridge belt and holster rigs, two pocket pistols, and a derringer—owned by Vera Pritchard, who operated *Miss Pritchard's Residence for Refined Young Ladies,* the local sporting house. Six other men, who had been taking their noon meal, including Irving Spaun, had been unarmed. Irving thought longingly of his shotgun, at rest beside his desk in the bank.

Molly Mollson continued to protest. "There ain't enough

money in this place to make it worth robbing. The risk is too big."

Eyes wide and rolling, the leader informed all in general. "Oh, we ain't here only to rob you. We've decided to settle down a while. Sort of become your neighbors."

"This is preposterous," Hiram Firks, who had bought out the general mercantile, blustered. "Why, the army would come, gather you all up and hang you."

Another sneer. "Not if we lived right in among you, in your houses."

"You can't do that, it's against the law."

That brought a belly-laugh from the trio. "So's robbin' you of ever'thing you've got. An' that's exactly what we aim to do. Right after we kill Smoke Jensen."

"Who?" Molly bluffed. "Never heard of anyone by that name."

A runty thug with squinty eyes, set too close together, pointed a crooked finger at the storekeeper. "Then you cain't read an' yer ears is stuffed full of wax. Ain't anybody don't know Smoke Jensen."

"That's enough, Farlee. Though he's right. Jensen's supposed to be the big hero around here, saved your town, ain't that right?"

Farlee Huntoon nodded idiotically. "Yeah, ain't it?"

Irving Spaun sighed resignedly. "Yes, that's entirely correct. And may I add that if he were here, you sorry trash would be running for your lives or on your way to the cemetery. Now kindly leave us to our meal."

"Sorry, can't do that," the leader contradicted. "I want the following folks to stand up. The banker, the saddlemaker, the general store owner, the lady that runs that fancy whooer house, the feed and grain store owner, the harberdasher—did I forget anybody? Oh, yeah, the sawbones whose shingle is hanging out over the ladies' wear shop, an' the lawyer."

"This is outrageous," Reginald Barclay, the only attorney

in private practice in Dubois objected. "What do you intend doing with us?"

Cold gray eyes pinned Barclay to the wall. "Killing you if you don't do as we say."

From outside came an irregular spatter of gunfire. It made the fact abundantly clear, even to dull-witted Huntoon, that the take-over did not go as peacefully elsewhere.

Hand working frantically to stuff fresh shells into the open breech of his Greener double-barrel, Percy Latimer, the Dubois barber kept his eyes fixed on the two hard cases sprawled in the street. Terrible damage had been done by the loads of double-aught buckshot he had fired into their midsections. Large, thick pools of blood had formed around them while they lay gaping at the sky with unseeing eyes. From across the street, two of the outlaws' companions continued to trash the windows of Percy's tonsorial parlor.

Fragments of glass, painted in a red-white-and-green diamond pattern, lay on the floor all around Percy. It would cost a pretty penny to replace that, he considered. He seated the final cartridge, eased shut the breech and checked the release lever to make certain it had caught properly. A figure moved behind a water barrel. Percy cocked the Greener. Exposing only part of his head and one shoulder, Percy swung up the shotgun and squeezed off a round

A shriek came from one man, who took a pair of pellets in his right arm. "Damn it, Jake, he got my gunarm."

"Shoot left-handed," came the reply from the recessed doorway to a saloon.

"I can't hit a blessed thing that way."

"But you can keep that bastard's head down while I rush him."

"Oh . . . I never thought of tha—"

"You never thought no-how, Louie. Now, git ready."

Louie sent rounds flying wildly into the barber shop. The

huge, bevel-edged mirror turned into a thousand slivers of quick silver. Percy's favorite shaving mug disintegrated in a shower of crockery. Percy winced and cursed under his breath, then raised up swiftly and caught sight of a shadowy figure. Bent low, the hard case ran along the front of the saloon. Percy brought the Greener into line and fired another load.

Buckshot from the ten gauge took out the bandit and a large portion of a window behind him. The glass bowed inward, then erupted in a wild shower. Jake went ass-over-teakettle into the Thirsty Man saloon, slammed by ten pellets of burning lead. Percy pushed the catch and opened the breech-loader. Spent brass casings popped up and he pulled them free. Humming to himself, he replaced them with fresh ones.

Percy swung the shotgun into line again and saw a shower of sparks spray from the long barrels of the goose gun. A fraction of a second later, intense, white pain exploded in his skull and his head snapped backward. The Greener clattered uselessly to the boardwalk outside.

Glee colored the words Louie shouted. "I got him Jake. I sure's hell got him. Jake? Where are you, Jake?"

Bert, the bartender, and six customers in the Yellow Gulch saloon found themselves confronted by eight armed men. Fortunately, depending on how one looked at it, three of the customers had reputations for being good with their guns. In an instant, even before any demand for money could be made, the air filled with lead. Bullets flew from both sides. Even with their disadvantage of first having to draw, the customers put slugs into a pair of outlaws and forced the others to retreat.

Hands gripped tightly on the forestock of a short-barreled ten-gauge Wells Fargo shotgun, Bert called encouragement to his assistants. "Drinks on the house to anyone who kills one of them devils."

"For how many and how long?" one of the young gun-fighters inquired.

"A whole day. From opening to closing time. An' for the one who gets the job done."

"How about his friends?"

Bert thought a moment, during which a shower of bullets cracked through the batwings. "Yeah, an' them too."

Their doom came home to them a moment later when a voice called from outside. "Come out with your hands high, or we'll throw in a stick of dynamite."

"Dynamite? Stick-up men don't carry dynamite," another of the defenders observed. "Where could they have gotten that?"

"I don't think I want to stick around and find out," the younger one declared.

"If we go out there, we're dead men, you know that," Bert reminded them. "You boys killed two of their part-ners."

"Last chance. Come out or die there."

An older man, a rancher, gave that some thought. "I'd rather die here, fightin' like a man, rather than go out there and be shot down like a dog."

Bert slammed the shotgun to his shoulder as he saw a dark figure rushing at the swinging doors. He fired in an eyeblink. The outlaw flew back into a tie-rail and spun a flip over it. Something sputtering a stream of sparks dropped between his legs.

"Get down!" Bert shouted.

A moment later, the front of the saloon blew in on top of them. Shock and sound waves bulged the walls on the sides and the windows blew out, sashes and all, before the glass could break. Bert felt himself lifted off his feet, his boots still rooted to the floor, and hurled against the back-bar. His ten-gauge spun off into the cloud of debris that rose from the plaster walls and sawdust-covered floor. His last conscious thought was: "My God, I'm dead."

All of the others suffered similar experiences. They and Bert found out after the furor ended, that they had not expired in the blast. Hard hands dragged them clear of the wreckage and roughly shoved them into the street. Gus Jaeger stood in the center of the block, legs wide-spread, arms folded over his chest.

"Bring them here," he commanded. "Put them on their knees." When they had the seven men positioned as Jaeger wanted, the outlaw leader glowered down at the helpless bartender and his customers. In the prolonged silence, the youngest gunhawk began to whimper.

"So you killed three of my men," Jaeger charged them. "Which ones of you did it?" When only their silence answered them, it irritated Gus mightily. He drew his Colt and put the muzzle an inch from the back of the head of a bar fly. Slowly he cocked the weapon.

"Tell me. Who did the shooting?"

Again they all remained silent. Gus Jaeger squeezed the trigger and blew the face of the town drunk all over the street. Still, he received no reply. He shot another of the customers. Then another. Suddenly bored and disgusted, he turned to his underlings.

"Give me a hand, boys. "We'll just kill them all."

Four more shots soon echoed off the walls of the standing buildings.

Within half an hour, a totally unsatisfactory time for Victor Spectre, all resistance had been crushed. Spectre rode in splendor to the central intersection of the community. There a windmill and storage tank provided water for the entire town. A bandstand stood there, also. Spectre dismounted before it and climbed the steep flight of steps. He faced the frightened people, gathered there and took the report from Gus Jaeger.

"All who resisted us have been killed. The rest are here. We lost seven men killed, nine wounded. Most of the injured will be up and around by tomorrow."

"Too many," Spectre stated curtly. "This was supposed to be quiet and easy."

"I'd say these folks were not aware of that," Ralph Tinsdale remarked as he joined them.

Victor Spectre shot him a hard, hot stare. "You are not funny, Ralph. Where do you suppose we will find men to replace those lost?"

Tinsdale frowned. "Smoke Jensen is only one man, Victor."

"But he will come with an army. We need ours intact to face him." He paused and turned away to study the confused and terrified people. "I have something to tell these people."

From his position in the front row, Irving Spaun got a good look at the man who must be the leader of The Enemy. That's how he looked at these invaders—The Enemy. In his mind's eye, Irving even saw the capital letters. He had noted earlier, after opening his bank to the outlaw scum, that Dr. Fred, Frederick Barbour, had been pressed into service to tend the wounded. Not the injured townsfolk, but The Enemy wounded. Irving silently hoped that Dr. Fred would hurry a few of them on to meet their judgment.

Unfortunately, Barbour was a dedicated healer. He could no more harm a patient than take his own life. Irving closely watched the exchange between the—for want of a better word, he called him the foreman—and the boss. Then the man in charge turned to face the assembled townspeople. He raised his arms to signal for silence and, when the gathering stilled, he revealed the most astonishing ideas that Irving had ever heard.

"Good afternoon. My name is Victor Spectre. I have come here for a cause that needn't concern you. Shortly, some of my men will escort you to your place of business and your homes. The purpose of their visit is to obtain every firearm you possess. And all of the ammunition."

A burly, retired rancher interrupted in an angry bluster. "We got a right to own guns."

Spectre shook his head sadly, as though faced with a truculent, but dim-witted child. "Not when they might endanger some of my men. Believe me, it is for your own good. Some of your friends and neighbors have already died because they chose to resist us. From now, until we leave this town, we are in charge. You will obey us without question or hesitation."

"Like hell we will," the outraged rancher snarled.

Spectre turned to his foreman and spoke quite casually. "Augustus, shoot him."

Faster than any man Irving had even seen, except Smoke Jensen, this Augustus fellow drew his six-gun and fired. The bullet entered the open mouth of the rancher and exited low in the back of his neck. He went down loosely, an unstrung marionette. Two women screamed and another fainted dead away. Smiling pleasantly, Spectre turned his attention back to his horrified audience.

"I will repeat. You will obey without hesitation or question. Now, another matter. Singly or by twos my men will be divided off and you will provide for them in your homes. They will have a room to themselves, and you will cook for them. In return, they will leave you strictly alone. This is to be merely a board and room situation. They are under orders to take their . . . pleasures elsewhere. Such will remain the case, unless some of you become obstreperous. In which case, my men will be free to exact recompense in any manner they see fit. Do we understand one another?" Several low mutters rippled through the people of Dubois. "I can't hear you." More replies now, some in normal speaking tones. Victor Spectre nodded meaningfully to Gus Jaeger. *"I can't hear you."*

More joined in, all cowed, unwilling to be loud enough to draw attention. To Irving's disgust his fellow citizens seemed mesmerized by this petty dictator. Their timidity had the reverse effect.

"I STILL CAN'T HEAR YOU" Spectre bellowed.

"Yes, we understand!" came a shouted reply.

"That's better. You will answer loudly, promptly, and truthfully any and all questions asked by myself, my associates, or my men. From here on, until our departure, of which I told you, this is our town."

Quickly then, Gus Jaeger designated men to take the residents to their stores and homes. Thorough searches were made. The outlaw foreman took three men along with him when they went to search the mercantile. Shortly after entering, two of the trash emerged with wheelbarrows heaped high with cases of ammunition, armloads of rifles, and half a dozen handguns. When the search ended, Jaeger escorted Irwin to the bank.

There he surveyed the vault and two free-standing safes. Satisfied, he nodded. "This seems secure enough. We'll keep the money here until we're ready to leave town. Now you take me to your home. We'll have a little look there. No doubt the mayor has the nicest house in town. Victor and his partners will stay there. As no doubt the next richest man in town, you will have the pleasure of hosting me."

"Oy veh! I am flattered and honored at the privilege," Irving replied sarcastically.

Jaeger glowered and raised his hand menacingly. "Any more smart-mouthing will earn you a fat lip."

"My wife keeps a kosher kitchen," Irving cautioned.

"I don't care what she calls it, Mr. Banker, so long as it's clean and there's plenty of grub."

Irving sought to educate this lout. *"Kosher* means 'pure— clean.' "

"Fine. Now, I want ham and eggs and biscuits for every breakfast."

Irving made bold to interrupt. "We do not eat ham or any pork."

Gus cocked an eyebrow. He'd never heard such nonsense. "Well, she'll fix it for me. You don't have to eat it if you don't want to."

"You don't understand. If my wife cooks pork in our kitchen it is no longer kosher. It will be contaminated."

Growing angry, Gus growled at the banker. "I don't give a damn about that. So long as there's not cockroaches crawlin' everywhere and moldy food laying around, I'll eat what I want and you can do the same."

Horrified at the image of filth and vermin in his home, Irving gathered the last of his reserves and spoke with defiance. "She will cook for you in the washhouse. I will not allow my kitchen to be tainted."

To Irving Spaun's surprise, Gus Jaeger began to laugh. "By God, you're a feisty son, aren't you? All right, Mister—er—?"

"Spaun. Irving Spaun."

"Mr. Spaun, have it your way. Just so long as I have my ham and eggs, biscuits, and some fried potatoes would be nice. Do you odd folks eat—ah—beef?"

"Yes, of course."

"Well, then, have the missus pick up a nice roast at the meat market for tonight."

"How is this food of yours to be paid for?"

Gus gave him a smile. "The usual way you pay for anything you buy, with your own money." With that they left for the house.

Once all of the arms and ammunition had been confiscated, Olin Buckner came to where Victor Spectre stood beside the great pile of munitions. "This has gone nicely. Men who are unable to resist must obey."

Victor nodded agreement, well satisfied. "Before long, the poor fools will find themselves totally dependent upon you, me, and Ralph for the barest necessities for survival."

"That's how it should be," Buckner replied contentedly. "The best and the brightest should rule and lesser mortals submit."

"The next thing is to pair up the men whose homes we've searched with their wives and children and place them in their houses under guard. Those who are involved in providing services in the stores, saloons, the bank, the hotel, and cafe are to be sent to their tasks."

"What about any single men?" Buckner asked.

Spectre made a show of considering it, though he had his mind made up long before entering the town. "They could provide a constant risk. We'll have some of the more hardened among our men take them off a few at a time. We can offer them the chance to join us. If they refuse, they can dig their own graves before being shot."

Seventeen

When the last of the single males refused the offer to join the gang, and had been mercilessly shot down, Victor Spectre turned his attention to the single women. Those he had kept in the central square while the killing went on. Now he summoned all of his men. Back on the bandstand, he gestured to the frightened, weeping women.

"You men have all fought well. There are some among you who conducted yourselves with outstanding bravery. It is my intention to reward you suitably for this outstanding service." He named the ones cited to him by Gus Jaeger. "Your compensation awaits," he went on with a gesture to the women. "You will each have a private room at the hotel for tonight. And, you will be free to take your pick of these lovely maidens to keep company with you."

Their loud cheers drowned out the rest of what Spectre had to say. When the designated men had made their selections and hauled off the frightened, protesting women, Spectre held his hand up to silence the other man. "For the rest of you, deserving as you are to some prize, you may pleasure yourselves with the remainder of the feminine pulchritude of Dubois for the balance of the afternoon. Have at them, good fellows!"

"Hot dang! That's for me," Dirk Jensen yelled gleefully, his long, greasy blond hair swung freely around his shoulders. He exposed his crooked yellow teeth in a lustful leer and headed for the nearest single woman, a girl of around fourteen.

Shrill screams began to rise moments later as the raping began.

Early on the morning of the second day in Dubois, Gus Jaeger stepped out on the porch of the home of Irving Spaun and rolled a cigarette with papers and tobacco from the pouch of Bull Durham in his shirt pocket. He lighted it and drew the smoke deeply into his chest, held it a while. Then he sighed it out with satisfaction. His belly was full of the sweetest ham he had ever tasted, four eggs, home fries with onions, and a platter of biscuits. Pleased with himself, he ankled down the steps and headed for the carriage house at the back of the lot.

There he saddled his horse and led it out into the alley. Leather creaked as he swung into the saddle. At a gentle walk, Gus headed toward the mayor's house, where he was to meet with Victor Spectre and his partners. He found them still at the breakfast table.

"Pour him a cup of coffee," Victor commanded the maid standing in attendance on the table. "Did you sleep well?" he asked Gus.

"Yes, thank you. That Mrs. Spaun is a great cook. I've never had beef so tender and juicy. We had roast last night," he clarified with a chuckle. "With braised potatoes and something she called asper—aspergrass?"

"Asparagus," Victor corrected. "A meal fit for a king. Well, we have a lot to do today. Wait in the drawing room, I'll join you in a minute."

Victor Spectre and Ralph Tinsdale came into the small room, made to look larger by a bay window. Spectre settled on a Louie Quinze chair, a cup and saucer in one hand. "Now then, I want you to select six men to act as messengers. I will send them out with flyers I am having printed today." His cordial smile turned bleak. "I am putting a price of twenty thousand dollars on the head of Smoke Jensen.

The posters will advise anyone interested in trying for the reward to come here to Dubois. I am also offering excellent pay, board, and room until Jensen is captured and brought to me to kill."

"That's mighty generous, Mr. Spectre. Are our men eligible for that bonus?"

"Of course, Augustus. I conceived of this idea last night. It is a splendid way to fill our ranks. Maybe tenfold of our losses. Also, it serves as insurance in the event my primary ploy to draw Jensen to us fails."

Rather than share Spectre's elation, Gus frowned. "You'll have every proddy son of a bitch in three territories crowdin' in here. Half of them won't even be able to use a gun. We'll have one hell of a time keepin' control."

"Not to worry. That's what your veterans are for. They took this town. They should have pride enough in it to keep down the rowdy element."

Gus smiled at this. "You know people rather well, don't you, Mr. Spectre?" It was more statement than question.

Victor's chest swelled and he all but patted himself. "I pride myself on that, Augustus. Now, make sure that business is conducted as usual. See that those quartered with the merchants and businessmen get their charges out and about. We can't entirely prevent people from coming into town. If we isolate ourselves, it would attract too much attention. So, I want you to arrange to have any damage covered up, make that unfortunate situation with the saloon look like a fire, and clean up the spilled blood."

Rising from the velvet loveseat he occupied, Gus Jaeger started for the door. "I'll see to it right away."

Victor Spectre allowed himself a moment to gloat as he stared out the three-sided opening of the bay window. Then he sighed out softly, "Smoke Jensen, your hours are surely numbered."

* * *

Unaware of the conquest of Dubois, Smoke Jensen dropped down from Togwatee Pass into Jackson's Hole two days after the town fell to Victor Spectre and his outlaw army. The tension that had swelled within him over the past week soothed away when he gazed upon the sheltered basin. For as far as the eye could see, lush, tall grass waved in a gentle breeze. Sunlight sparkled off the rippled water of the Snake River as it meandered through the middle of the declivity. White stones, as fine as crushed gravel, lined the watercourse. Pines and tall Douglas firs perfumed the air.

Smoke breathed deeply of the crisp, clean air, made thin and precious by the altitude. All of nature was alive with animal and bird sounds, which reached Smoke's ears in pleasant waves of tweets and warbles, the scrabble of claws, and grunts or snorts of larger creatures. Relaxing further, Smoke soaked up the peaceful feel of it all. Unbidden, his mind wandered back to the first time Preacher had brought him here to trap beaver and hunt elk. . . .

It had been a crisp early spring. Deep drifts of snow lay along the shaded western slopes of the surrounding mountains. A thin wafer of clear ice clung to the bank and exposed pebbles in the Snake River. Preacher's usually guarded expression eased into serenity as they rode lower onto the floor of the basin. Preacher waved a hand in a sweeping gesture.

"Ol' Jackson was one smart hombre, Smoke. Look at this place. The last real corner of Paradise in the High Lonesome, or anywhere else for that matter. Pure, untouched. We won't build a cabin here. Nawsir, we're gonna fix us a stone lodge. Build out of rocks is what."

"How'er we goin' to put a roof on it?" Jensen asked.

Preacher frowned. "We'll have to cut a couple of trees, I allow for that. An' when we're through with it, come next spring, we're gonna tear it all down."

All these years later, Smoke Jensen found the Hole still well-populated with elk. Huge piles of antlers had been erected by earlier visitors, and the soft ground held numerous hoof impressions. He caught sight of several dozen of the magnificent animals as he ambled his way to the southeast, in search of a campsite. Shortly he came upon the right place.

Located far enough from the Snake so that its waters burbling over smoothed rocks would not hide the sound of any approach, the small clearing would serve well for his first several night's stay. Smoke strung a short picket line, with the halters of his horses rigged so they could walk along and graze. Then he unsaddled Thunder and Debbie. Stretching out the kinks of a long day's ride, he drew a deep, rich breath and set off to locate windfall for a cookfire.

Hunger made itself known while Smoke assembled a stone ring on a bare circle of earth which he had cleared with a folding shovel. He completed the task and padded to the rack that held one of his parfleche panniers. From that he took a stout Cheyenne hunting bow and quiver of arrows. Then he added a coil of rope and a folded layer of cheesecloth. Anticipating the flavor of fresh roasted meat, he strode off to hunt for his supper. When he came abreast of the horses, he spoke softly to the 'Palouse stallion.

"Let me know if someone comes by, Thunder."

Raised around animals, Smoke had no delusion that the critters understood his words in a literal sense. Yet, like most men alone in the wilderness, Smoke found himself talking to his horses. He kept his eyes to the ground, searching for an animal trail. He soon found one. A narrow path, most likely made by deer. Hoofprints verified that, along with small, still moist droppings. The slightly rounded points of the front of the impressions pointed to the river.

When he drew close enough to hear the gurgle of the clear, swift water, he selected an arrow and nocked it to the string. Creeping now, he made a slow approach to the opening. Ahead he identified the spotted, buff side of a young deer. The graceful little creature had its neck bent, mouth in the chill water. A tiny flag of brown and white flickered as a dragonfly buzzed its hind quarters. Cautiously, Smoke moved to one side and searched for any larger hind.

He found one at once. A yearling, weighing about 125 pounds. Perfect. Exercising immense care, Smoke raised the bow and drew back the sinew string, while he appealed to the animal's spirit for understanding. The ball of his thumb touched his cheekbone and he took aim. His release was smooth. The keen-edged metal head entered flesh right behind the front leg and the shaft plunged inward to the fletching. Pierced through the heart, the yearling uttered a shrill bleat and reared, then fell, mortally wounded.

Momentarily saddened by the necessity of having to take the creature's life, Smoke nevertheless looked on grimly until the end. The fawn had sprinted away at the cry of alarm and pain. Walking carefully, Smoke stepped out onto the riverbank. Quickly he dragged the deer to a low limb and tied the forelegs together. He swung the short length of rope over the branch and pulled the creature upright.

With swift, sure strokes, he field-dressed the deer. He set aside the heart and liver, which he washed in the stream and wrapped in cheesecloth. Then he scooped out a hollow and buried the intestines. Lowering the carcass, he cleansed it in the Snake, and washed his arms. Grunting, he hefted the meat over his shoulders and started back to camp. He would eat the liver raw, while a rack of ribs and a front haunch roasted. The heart would be for breakfast. The rest, he decided, he would smoke in a rock smoker he would build tomorrow. He would hang the meat high in a tree. The hind quarters could cure for a few days, until he would be ready.

Using carefully graduated sizes of smooth, flattened rocks from the riverbed, Smoke Jensen started on his stone smoker early the next morning, after a breakfast of fried venison heart and cottage fries with wild onion. There were camus bulbs and wild turnip in the basin, he knew. He could look forward to a rich venison stew. Far from being a gourmand, nothing prevented Smoke from the appreciation of good food when he had it. Smoke had reached the fifth tier, the rocks meticulously fitted together, when he noticed a thin column of gray-white rising above the trees at some distance to the northeast.

Pilgrims. It had to be. No one who knew anything about the habits and wandering nature of Indians would be that careless. Unless, of course, the party was large enough not to worry. Dismissing it, he worked on until he had used the last of the stones he had retrieved from the water. When he waded, barefoot, into the Snake to pluck more rocks from the shallows, he noticed a barely perceptible blur in the air at a considerable stretch in the opposite direction of the column of smoke. Someone knew what they were doing, he surmised. They had built their fire under the wide spread of tree limbs, which would diffuse the smoke. Mountain men, or some like himself, who had been raised by that hearty, savvy breed. Smoke cut his eyes back to his work project.

"Well," he said aloud. "I've made my feet ache enough for one day."

He climbed out of the water, dried his feet and shoved them into boots. After he saddled Thunder, he mounted and rode out on a circuitous route around these curious signs of other humans.

After a careful search of the area around the well-tended fire, Smoke Jensen moved in close enough to see the men seated under the wide-spread limbs of an ancient pine, its branches thick with long, silken needles. At once, he recognized two oldtimers. Zeke Duncan and Ezra Sampson had been fur-trapping partners for the better part of fifty years. So adapted had they become to life in the High Lonesome, not even advanced age could separate them from it. Their hat-sized fire gave off smoke for only one reason.

Drops of liquefied fat dripped into the coals from the six squirrels they had set to slow-broiling over it. A lattice of green willow branches supported the carcasses of the tree-dwelling rodents. Although he had eaten no more than three hours earlier, the aroma of the cooking meat smelled delightful to Smoke. Quietly he edged back deeper into the underbrush and crawled a hundred yards before standing and walking to where he had ground-reined Thunder.

Mounted, Smoke Jensen rode out a ways, then turned back, angled toward the camp and howdied them loudly when he came within view. A cheery answer came back to him. "Ride on in and set a spell."

Then, when he had ridden close enough to be recognized, Zeke did a little dance step, beaded and quilled moccasins twinkling in the sunlight and called out with delight. "Why, you be that ring-tailed rattler, Smoke Jensen. So, you're the one snuck up on us a while back. That's right, you be Preacher's little friend."

They still never miss a thing, Smoke thought with respect.

"Not so little anymore, Zeke," Ezra advised. "Yer welcome, Smoke." Eyes sparkling, he gave Smoke a wink. "Be a whole lot more welcome if you've got a jug of Who-Shot-John along."

"Not with me. I have a crock along for medicinal purposes back at camp."

"Where might that be?" Zeke asked.

"Over yonder a ways," Smoke told him, pointing in the general direction.

Ezra cocked a snow-white eyebrow. "It ain't over where them dummies have got that signal fire a-goin', would it be?"

Zeke butted in. "Not likely, Ez. Preacher would have

taught him right. But, say, how come you knowed we was here?"

Smoke told them simply. "Same way I knew those others were around. From your smoke smudge."

"Naw," Ezra objected. "We've been real careful."

Smoke nodded to the fire. "Those squirrels are dripping fat onto the fire. It made a cloud in the branches of this pine."

"They're almost ready, too," Zeke advised. "You'll sit a spell and share a couple with us, won't you? There's coffee hot in the pot now."

"That's kind of you, Zeke. I'll take that coffee. And I'll eat some squirrel. I have some biscuits left over from breakfast."

"Couldn't be better," Ezra enthused.

Smoke cut his eyes to take in the whole of their camp. "Tell me, why is it fellers as smart as you are camped under the tallest tree around?"

Zeke grinned. "It ain't thunderstorm season yet. Otherwise you wouldn't find us nowhere near this giant. Now, put some daylight in that saddle and let's swap a few lies."

Smoke and the old mountain men sat cross-legged and drank coffee and told tales about Preacher for half an hour. At which time, Ezra pronounced the squirrels ready to eat. While they tore at the succulent, tender flesh, and gnawed on biscuits and wild onion bulbs, Zeke gestured to Smoke with a hind leg of squirrel.

"D'you know yer a wanted man again?"

Smoke thought on that a moment. "No. What's the story?"

"There's word out for gunhands to gather and hunt you down, Smoke. Big reward for your hide. Twenty thousand dollars. Alive that is."

Smoke whistled soundlessly. "Who has that sort of money?"

Zeke continued his tale. "There's this feller, Victor Spectre he calls hisself. He an' a whole passel of rowdies tooken over the town of Dubois."

"What!" Smoke blurted. "When did this happen?"

Ezra got in his two-bits worth. "Couple—three days ago now. From what we've heard fellers driftin' through here say, there was some powerful killin' done. Folks they spared are kept prisoner in their own homes."

His jaw seriously torqued by this news, Smoke abandoned caution. "Damn that filthy slime. This fight's between him and me. The people of Dubois are special to me."

Both of the oldtimers nodded eagerly. Zeke summed up their thoughts. "Reckon this Spectre feller knew that."

Recovered slightly, Smoke conquered his rampant emotions. "Nothing can be done about that now. He would have to have a regular army to take the town. Thank you for the warning. I appreciate it. And, thanks for the food, which was good, and the company, which was even better. I think I'll move along, see who those others are."

Zeke gave Smoke a knowing wink. "They're noisy and they smell bad. Could be you're walking into a hornet nest."

Eighteen

Having been warned over and over, Smoke Jensen needed no further urging to make a wide, slow, careful approach to the other camp in the basin. Two small, conical peaks stood between him and the unknown visitors. Smoke took advantage of that to advance undetected to within three hundred yards. The column of smoke continued to rise into the morning sky. A shower of sparks formed an ascending ball around it as someone threw something rather heavy on the fire.

Fools, Smoke thought in disgust. If there had been a war party of Blackfeet or Cheyenne in the area, or any other tribe, these idiots would already have their hair curing on scalp stretchers. Might as well advertise their presence with a brass band. He dismounted and tied off Thunder in a grove of cottonwoods. Then he wormed his way through the thicket of young trees, taking thirty minutes to do so, until he could clearly distinguish sounds from the camp. A cast-iron skillet gave off a musical ring, metal utensils clattered and the men talked volubly. Smoke made a quick count of seven different voices.

Their topic of conversation riveted Smoke's attention. "You know what I'm gonna do with the money for catchin' Smoke Jensen?"

"Naw, Polk, but I'm sure you're gonna tell us."

"Right you are, my friend. I'm gonna get me a room in the fanciest hotel in San Francisco, rent me a pair of the purtiest ladies of the night, and give the room service manager a thousand dollars and tell him to keep the champagne and food coming until it's gone. Then I'm gonna give him another thousand and get two different girls."

"Awh, you won't be able to keep it up that long, Polk."

"Tell me about it, Curruthers. What is it the gals down in Dallas call you? Ol' False Start Carruthers, right?"

A tin cup bounced noisily off the thick trunk of a pine. "Damn you, Polk, that ain't true. I don't care what that Lill told anyone who'd listen. It ain't so. I was jist a little drunk is what. An hour's rest and I sure showed her where Johnny hid the garden hoe."

Another voice joined the banter. "Curruthers, Polk, ain't either one of you with any sense when it comes to money and wimmin. I been talkin' with Yancy and Rand. They're talkin' about poolin' their shares an' buyin' land. Run a few hunnard head of cattle an' even hire men to work them. I sort of thought it would be an idee to throw in with them. Three shares buys a whole lot of cows and other people's sweat."

Curruthers sneered. "Gonna become big-shot ranchers, huh? Fat chance."

Polk sniggered. "You do, Hooper, an' we'll come rustle them beeves."

Hooper grew serious. "They hang rustlers down in Texas, Polk."

Suddenly defensive, Polk bleated in an effort to forestall any confrontation. "Hey—hey, I was only funnin'. I'd never rob from a partner. Ain't honorable." He added a shrill giggle. "Besides, I'll be in San Francisco gettin' my ashes hauled."

Another voice, silent so far, rumbled with a dash of cold water on their plans. "You heard what they did in Dubois. If we ride in an' throw our hat in the ring with them boys, and we do get Smoke Jensen, you'd best use your share to find a deep hole to crawl into and pull it after you. There'll be U.S. Marshals an' the Army, and who knows who else huntin' us down. They took a *town,* boys. They pestered the single women and killed a lot of folks. Ain't gonna be likely forgotten."

Polk jeered at him. "Ballard, yer gettin' yeller in your old age."

"Hell, he ain't thirty."

Polk's voice sobered. "For some folks, that's old."

At last, the seventh man, who had listened to all this with interest contributed his idea. "I'll tell you what we should do, if we're smart. I say we ought to find this Smoke Jensen all on our own and bring him in. Collect our reward and ride the hell out of there. Sure's my name is Liam Quinn."

Smoke Jensen had heard enough. He also noticed that for all their big talk, none of them seemed eager to move on to Dubois. Carefully, he selected several landmarks to pinpoint their locations in the dark, and moved on.

We've crossed over into Wyoming, Sally Jensen thought. She judged they had done so some two days ago, based on the change of terrain to high plains prairie. The mountains, though some were tall and rangy, had a smooth, rounded-over appearance. And, for miles one could see waving seas of grass, patches of it golden-brown remnants from last year's growth. She had yet to learn where they were going.

"We're takin' you to the man in charge," or "You'll meet yer husband up ahead a piece," was all she could get out of Nate Miller, the outlaw leading this band of ruffians. Sally had gone beyond worry or fear. Instead, a cold, hard anger built within her, one tempered by caution and experience, but deadly in nature all the same. She no longer sought a means of escape along the trail.

That would come later. Most likely when Smoke was near. She would bide her time, reinforce her anger and loathing of these unwashed border trash, and make herself ready physically and mentally. To do the latter, she reviewed incidents in which she had been involved with Smoke, or because of him. One occurrence hardened her more than the others.

It had been the time when she had been beaten, shot, and left for dead by unsavory louts who belonged to the Masters gang. She had gone to her father's home in New England to recuperate and the gang had followed to get retribution on Smoke Jensen. They had died there, in New Hampshire, and she had given birth to the twins. Louis Longmont and Jeff York had lent Smoke a hand and had been proud godfathers for the newest additions to the Jensen clan. Now, she drew on memories of the pain, the despair she had felt, her fear for the babies she carried. It forged the malleable metal of her present outrage into a white-hot bar of steel.

To maintain her physical condition, she found little she could do. She ate every scrap they allowed her, of course. And, when left unattended to take care of nature's demands, she lifted heavy rocks to maintain the strength in her arms. She walked about the camp furiously whenever untied. And she moved with snakelike sinuosity in the saddle as they rode, to tone her torso. It wasn't much, she acknowledged, but it helped. The time *would* come, and she *would* be ready to act.

Only a sliver of moon hung over Jackson's Hole when Smoke Jensen eased into position outside the camp of the gunmen. A decided chill hung on the May night, the air damp and tingly, borne on a breeze that wafted over deep banks of rotting snow. To ward off the cold, the thugs had built a large, roaring fire. Anyone this careless and stupid deserved what they were about to get, Smoke thought in indignation.

Still, he had anticipated the gigantic bonfire and smiled in satisfaction as he considered the two sticks of dynamite he had brought along. They were already capped and fused when he shoved them down the front of his trousers, behind his cartridge belt. With everything in readiness, he drew his .45 Colt and fired a round over the heads of the hapless men gathered around the blaze. In an instant they all went to the ground as one.

Smoke Jensen called to them in harsh tones. "You men don't belong here and you've picked the wrong man to go after. Saddle up, put out that fire, and get out of here while you still have your lives."

One of the men stood up. "You're not scarin' us, mister." He sent a round into the dark, in the direction Smoke's voice had come from. Only Smoke had moved. Now he raised the Peacemaker and blasted the bold gunhawk to perdition with a slug through the heart. Immediately the clearing became a scene of panic.

Three of the saddle trash made a wild scramble for their mounts, while the other trio elected to fight back. They came to their knees and shot wildly into the surrounding blackness. Night vision ruined by the bright blaze, they not the slightest chance of seeing Smoke Jensen.

Smoke howled like a wolf and moved to yet another position. He fired at the confused gunmen and moved as return rounds crashed into the underbrush where he had been. Now that he had the remaining six properly aroused, he heaved first one, then the second stick of dynamite into their fire.

Almost at once, the first exploded and knocked the defenders flat. Then threw flaming wood everywhere. The second followed a second later, the ground shaking underfoot even worse than before. Shock and blast extinguished what had been left of their fire. Smoke tracked muzzle flashes, noted that only four remain, and picked a target. The roar of his .45 drowned out the noise of the others'.

"Oh, my God, Liam, I'm shot," Polk wailed as the initial

shock of Smoke's bullet wore off and his chest flamed with agony.

At the camp of Zeke Duncan and Ezra Sampson, the two oldtimers listened to the sounds of confrontation in the distance. Zeke took a long, deep pull off the contents of a glazed, earthenware jug they had found at sundown, near the place they had taken to using on the riverbank, and passed it to Ezra.

"Well, Ez, it sounds like Smoke Jensen is paying a not-too-friendly visit to those young toughs over yonder."

Ezra cocked his head to one side, tilted up his chin and took a long swallow of the premium rye whiskey in the jug. "Does seem that way. I reckon that's why he left us off this jug, to keep us in camp. Wonder if they appreciate the call?"

They both cackled over this witticism for some moments, passed the crock around another time and grinned like conspirators when the noise abruptly ceased. The quiet grew louder. Zeke sipped again, belched and passed the container to his partner.

"Say, Zeke, you figger Smoke will swing by an' share this present he left with us?"

"Might be. You can never tell."

"I sure hope he does. I'd like to hear all about those boys who waste so much firewood." Cackling, Ezra extended the jug toward Zeke.

After he had reduced his opponents to two, he moved yet again. "You two, I have a message for Victor Spectre, Ralph Tinsdale, and Olin Buckner."

After a short, tense silence, a voice called out shakily. "We don't know anybody by them names."

Smoke's laughter mocked them. "Sure you do. You were

talking about them earlier this afternoon." He fired another round toward the cringing Ballard and Quinn.

A longer silence followed, then a weak reply from Quinn. "All right—all right. What do you want us to tell them?"

"Tell them they can hire every two-bit gunhand in the territory, and beyond, but that I'm a lot harder to kill than the best of them. I think you have found that out for yourselves." Smoke chuckled loudly enough for them to hear him. "One last thing, so there's no mistake. Where is it, again, that you are to meet Victor Spectre?"

"In—in Dubois."

"Then I'll leave you to find your way there on your own." Smoke had glided well out of earshot before the two badly shaken gunmen began to whisper to one another. Pleased with himself, Smoke faded into the night.

Monte Carson stood by the head of his horse, two fingers slipped behind the cheek-strap of the headstall. He gazed off thoughtfully toward the distant, sparkling waters of the Bighorn River. Between him and the wide, shallow stream lay the lodges of the Shoshoni of the Wind River Reservation. Three of the Indians rode his direction, one held a lance, elaborately decorated with sprays of feathers. An official delegation, Monte thought, sure of that. He turned to Hank Evans.

"Company comin' will have at least one minor civil chief along. Might not be the one who presents himself as leader. So keep a sharp eye, Hank, and see if you can spot the real chief."

Hank Evans worked his cheeks and lips and spat out his used-up cud of Union Leader cut plug. A stream of tobacco juice followed. "You're gettin' crafty in yer old age, Monte."

Sheriff Carson chuckled. "Naw. It's just a little something I learned from Smoke Jensen a few years back. Injuns don't take a back seat to the white man when it comes to diplomatic tricks. Smoke pointed that out and explained that most times it is the fault of different language or different ways of seein' the same thing that makes a parlay go sour, or a treaty fail."

Hank studied the Shoshoni representatives as they rode nearer. "If you'd ask me now, I'd say it was that older feller with the lance. His mouth looks like it's used to givin' orders. And, there's that hawk nose and them hard, bright eyes."

"Don't be in a rush. Take a little more time and be sure. It could be the difference between being welcomed or told to get the hell off their land."

"Or keepin' our hair," Hank added wryly.

Monte nodded. "There's that, too."

Close now, the riders reined in. Monte made the universal sign for peace and it was returned. Then he signed that they had coffee, sugar, biscuits, and molasses. Grinning, the Shoshoni dismounted. Before they did, the one dressed as a chief cut his eyes to his lance-bearer and received an almost imperceptible nod.

Hank Evans took note of that as he dismounted. He prepared a clear space for a fire and set out the makings for a quick brew. Water came from his canteen, coffee from a cloth sack, as did the biscuits. A small, screw-top jar held black-strap molasses. The Indians settled on their horse blankets and Monte sat with them, cross-legged. While Hank prepared their snack, Monte signed that he was looking for a man.

"What man is this?" the lance-bearer asked in fair, though accented and lilting, English. His eyes locked with Monte's.

"Smoke Jensen."

"Ah, Swift Firestick."

Monte blinked at the thick-shouldered younger man. "Is that a serious name?"

Chief Tom Brokenhorn, in his guise as the lance-bearer

of a civil chief, smiled. "No. It is a joke that Smoke Jensen shares with me." He rose and changed places with the even younger man in the middle, while Hank distributed tin cups of coffee and biscuits slathered with molasses. "From the description he gave to me, you must be Monte Carson. I am Chief Brokenhorn."

Monte cut his eyes to Hank, who gave him a "I-told-you-didn't-I?" grin. "Smoke speaks highly of you, Chief Brokenhorn."

Brokenhorn spread his full lips in a wide, white smile. "So he does of you, Monte Carson." He made the name sound like one word.

"Please, call me Monte."

"I am Tom."

"Are you Christian, then, Tom?"

A dry chuckle came from Chief Brokenhorn. "In name only. My mother was attracted to the words of the Black-robes from the Queen-Mother land before I was born. She had the sacred water sprinkled on her. And, she gave me one of your white men's names. For a while, the Blackrobes kept a mission among our people. When I was little, I went to school there, taught by the Fathers. I learned *Français* and English. Also a little of the tongue called Latin. The Fathers wanted me to become the first red man priest. But I knew I was not made to be a medicine man, I was to be chief."

Monte grinned at him. "Funny the grand ideas a feller has when he's a little boy. I always wanted to be a lawman . . . or a famous outlaw."

Brokenhorn nodded. "And we both had our dreams become real, Monte."

Nodding, Monte agreed with him. "So we did. Though I never became a *famous* outlaw, Tom. No stomach for it."

Chief Brokenhorn laughed aloud. "That is why I am a civil chief. I have taken the war trail many times in the past, was head man of my warrior society, but I never liked the stealing and killing."

"You are a wise man, Tom. Now, tell me about Smoke."

"He came through here five suns ago. Bad men came before him. Nearly eight hands—er—forty of them. I suspect that our friend, Smoke Jensen, hunted them. And I also think that they hunted him."

Monte nodded. "You're right there, Tom. That's why Hank there and me came after him."

"I have warriors keeping watch. The bad men are in the white village of Dubois." He pronounced the town's name in the French manner, as *Du-bwoah*.

A grim expression darkened Monte's face. "Then Smoke will be goin' there before long."

"Monte, Smoke told me he would be going to the basin the white trapper, Jackson, found many years ago."

"Yes. He told me the same, Tom. I'll go there first."

"I will send warriors with you, men to replace the watchers. First, though, you must stay with us a while, rest your horses and let them grow fat again. It is not known if there are more bad men coming, but our neighbors, the Arapaho," he made the name sound unclean, "say that some do, by two or three in a group. We must learn what we can before you go."

Monte nodded. I agree. Looks like Smoke's stumbled into another hornet's nest," he added grimly.

A pot of beans bubbled over the small fire on the vast breast of the mountain slope. Nearby, the whole carcass of a young antelope turned on a green wooden spit. Ike Mitchell and the hands from the Sugarloaf had arrived on the southeastern face of the Rattlesnake Hills shortly before sundown. Without being bidden, Bobby Harris began to gather dry wood for the cookfire. The small stone ring radiated heat as the temperature dropped with the coming of night. Several of the men complained over the past few days about the food.

With good cause, Bobby thought as he sat on a flat-topped boulder, staring out across an ocean of grass. The hams they had brought along had run out two days earlier. That left a slab of bacon, already green around the edges and slickly white on the rind. It smelled sour while being cooked and tasted the same way. Until today they had not taken time to hunt and dress out game for the cook pot. This afternoon, when two men had upchucked their noon meal, and three others had refused to eat, necessity had forced it.

It slowed progress. Yet Ike reckoned they had closed a lot of ground and, since losing the trail of the kidnappers, they might catch up to Smoke within a few days. They had better, and before the army of outlaws did, Bobby thought in irritation and impatience. He had toughed a lot, the boy realized. No longer did his thighs and crotch ache through the night, keeping him awake. He slept so hard now that he did not even hear the snores of the tired hands. They just *had* to find Smoke. He'd know how to get Sally back. Bobby stirred and broke off his distant stare across the rolling steppe of Shoshoni Basin when Ike stopped beside him and gave his shoulder a firm squeeze.

"A nickel for your thoughts, Bobby."

Bobby forced a warm smile. It was hard not liking this strong, silent man. "The price has gone up," he observed cheerily. "I was . . . thinkin' about Sally an' where she is. And . . . about Smoke."

Ike nodded. "Ain't a man among us that has anything else on his mind. You worried we won't find her?"

Bobby drew a deep breath. "I'm worried we'll find her all alone and . . . too late." He shuddered, his thin shoulders heaving.

"No, Bobby. I can't let myself believe that could happen.

She'll be all right. She's a tough lady. Smoke's taught her how to be a survivor."

"I hope she remembers what she learned," Bobby sighed. "And—and she's not young anymore."

Ike laughed softly. "Now, that depends on your point of view. There's men ridin' with us who'd see Miss Sally as a spry girl, compared to themselves. Thinkin' like that's for a small boy—rather than a growed-up member of a volunteer possee," he hastily added, lest Bobby explode again. "I come to tell you, grub's ready."

Bobby's blue eyes glowed in the firelight. "Yum. I can taste that antelope now."

"Over-growed goat, you ask me," Ike muttered as he led the way back to the cookfire. There still being some left, he thought, they might pop a buffalo out on the basin. Now that'd be some real eatin'.

When Buck Ballard and Liam Quinn reached Dubois, their spirits hung below their horses' fetlocks. Dirty, sweaty, faces powder-grimed, they presented a disreputable spectacle that Victor Spectre watched coldly as they paraded down the main street. They halted before the Full Bucket saloon and asked directions to locate Spectre. When they entered the lobby of the hotel, they looked even more like whipped dogs.

"We're lookin' for Mr. Spectre," Liam Quinn mumbled.

"I am he," Spectre stated icily. "Who are you?"

"I'm Liam Quinn, an' this is Buck Ballard. We're what's left of seven men comin' to sign on to hunt Smoke Jensen."

"Where are the others?" Ralph Tinsdale demanded from beside Victor Spectre.

Quinn shrugged. "Back in Jackson's Hole, dead as far as I know."

Olin Buckner sniffed with distaste. "What happened?"

"It seems, we already ran into Smoke Jensen."

Victor Spectre retook the initiative. "How do you know that?"

Liam Quinn studied his boot toes. "He—ah—sent you a message, Mr. Spectre."

Face twisted in contempt for Smoke Jensen, Ralph Tinsdale snapped, "What possibly could he have to say to you, Victor?"

Quinn told them what Smoke had said. Buckner and Tinsdale exploded with outrage. Buckner swore blackly, hate blistering the air as he called Smoke everything but a man. Tinsdale took exception to Smoke's claim to be better than the best guns they could hire. He called the last mountain man a two-bit, tinhorn, has-been. They would have said more, had not Victor Spectre cut them off in mid-tirade.

"Relax. We still hold the reins. Let Jensen think he has us off balance, quivering in our boots, afraid of shadows." He turned to Ballard and Quinn. "Do you men still intend to join us?"

"Yes, sir," Quinn answered for them both.

Spectre sniffed the effluvium that emanated from them. "Then get yourselves cleaned up. You're disreputable." He turned on his partners. "Make no mistake, we are in control. When the men with Nate Miller get back from Colorado, Smoke Jensen will come crawling. And when he does, he will die."

Nineteen

Smoke Jensen came to Dubois much sooner than Victor Spectre expected. Two nights after Ballard and Quinn reached the captive town, Smoke joined a group of would-be hard cases drinking in the Watering Hole saloon in Dubois. He stood alone at the darkened end of the bar and sipped a beer. None of the louts and trash had recognized him when he entered. He continued to taste his brew while they bragged about how ferocious they would be when they got their hands on Smoke Jensen.

Obviously amateurs, they began to amuse him. One fellow in particular: a florid-face, a fat-gut spilling over the buckle of his cartridge belt, a big, porous wart of a nose, a mouth too wide and thin-lipped, a regular toad of a man, who had a new opinion of what to do with every sloppy swallow from his schooner of beer. If only silly words counted in a gunfight, Smoke thought.

Unaware of the contempt of Smoke Jensen, the slob brayed on. "I say the first thing we do is hold him down and cut off his tallywhacker. That'll make him squirm."

Sweet fellow, Smoke Jensen thought. Another gulp and he was off again.

"Yah, then we feed it to him." That brought a lot of laughs.

"Naw, that wouldn't work," another lout contradicted. "He'd bleed to death before we could hurt him more. Mr.

Spectre wants him brought in alive. Speakin' of that, Prager, when are you goin' out after Jensen?"

The lard tub interrupted a swallow of suds to gape at his interrogator. "Me? Hell, Woodson, I ain't goin' anywhere until the free board and room and the beer run out. If Jensen wants to take me on, he can come to me."

In the silence that followed, Olin Buckner entered the saloon. He made a long sweep of the men arranged along the bar and came to an eye-bulging halt on the distant figure of Smoke Jensen. Instantly in shock, his mouth worked a second before he could sound words.

"He already has, you idiot!" he yelled at Harlan Prager, a trembling finger pointed at Smoke Jensen. "He's right down there." With tremendous will, he broke his paralysis and grabbed for the 1875 Smith and Wesson, Schofield, Wells Fargo Model .45 at his hip.

The first thing Smoke did was shoot Buckner. Then he shot out the lights. In the process of taking out the five kerosene lamps, he dived for the floor. Confusion broke out at once. Thugs slammed into one another shouting. Shots slammed the walls, echoed and re-echoed. His six-gun empty, Smoke reholstered it and drew the second. He crawled through the maze of churning legs, tables, and chairs toward the open end of the bar. Muzzle flashes continued to momentarily illuminate the scene of struggling men, all intent on reaching the corner of the bar where Smoke had stood. In a double flame brightness, Smoke found himself face-to-face with Harlan Prager. The lard-tub gaped and opened his mouth to shout to the others.

"B'god, here h——"

Smoke shot Prager in the gut. Moaning, the fat outlaw fumbled to draw his own weapon. He did, only much too late. Prager fired a round that smacked into the shoulder of a fellow hard case. Blood spouted, along with dust and bits of cloth. Prager's eyes went wide. He raised the six-gun again.

Smoke Jensen fired his second round. It bored a hole in the chest of Harlan Prager. Thrown sideways, Prager fought to keep himself erect, while his knees sagged beneath his weight. He groaned loudly, feebly raised his long-barreled revolver, and died as Smoke Jensen expended a third round on him. In the confusion, Smoke moved on.

He soon found his goal.

A black void stretched behind the mahogany. Smoke crawled into it. Sure enough, as he had expected, he soon found a "priest's hole" in the outer wall of the saloon. It soon became obvious, because of its gaping openness that the bartender had preceded him. Quickly, Smoke wedged his shoulders through the small doorway and out into the cool night. He found himself in a narrow alley that paralleled the long sidewall of the liquor emporium. Smoke sensed the presence of someone else in the passageway and had his Colt out and pressed into a yielding stomach before the barkeep whispered urgently.

"Don't shoot, Mr. Jensen. I live here an' I know you're an all right guy. I was here when you cleaned up the town. I want you to know I shot out the lamps at the ends of the bar." He breathed a gusty sigh of relief when the pressure of the six-gun eased off.

"Thank you for that."

"You'll need a way out of here. I'll show you where to go."

"My horse is out front," Smoke told him.

"I'll get him for you."

Smoke's soft chuckle sounded loud in the tense atmosphere. "He won't let you. I'll go get him. Wait here."

Thunder remained where Smoke had tied him off half a block from the saloon. Sounds of chaos still came from the darkened barroom. Smoke walked over, unmolested, and retrieved the 'Palouse stallion. In seconds he disappeared into the alley. While he accomplished this, a question occurred to him.

"Why did you wait for me in this alley?"

"I figured you might know about the priest's hole."

Smoke tipped back his hat while the barman led the way away from the saloon. "I'm flattered. What I want to know is why did you have one handy?"

"I'm a Catholic, so I knew about them from church history. You know, the persecutions in England and Holland a long time ago? So, I had one put in the Watering Hole when I bought it."

"Clever."

A half dozen twists and turns later, the bartender pointed down a long, dark residential street. "Keep goin' along there and you come to the edge of town. My name's O'Roarke and it's been an honor to assist you."

"Thank you, O'Roarke. I'll never forget a fellow student of history."

Smoke went on alone. He would be exiting on the south side of town, but he could easily swing west and then north, to head back toward the Absaroka Range and Togwatee Pass. The Hole lay just beyond.

Early the next morning, Spectre's army of riffraff and thugs forced the citizens of Dubois to assemble at gunpoint. The place where they gathered was before five houses on the downwind edge of town. After a long wait, Victor Spectre stepped up onto the porch of the middle structure and addressed the crowd.

"The reason we are here this morning is for you to witness an object lesson. This is in payment for the audacity of Smoke Jensen to actually enter this town and brazenly create a riot in a respectable saloon. To show you and him that we are serious about maintaining order in Dubois, we are going to burn these five houses to the ground."

An elderly, white-haired man, back bent with age and rheumatism, stumbled forward out of the press of people.

"No, please. Don't do that. It cost me every cent I had to build that house. It's for my sunset years."

Victor Spectre stared icily at him. "It's too bad you picked such a unruly town in which to settle. Torch them, men."

Wails of anguish rose from the victims as the flames spread. Their neighbors consoled them as much as they could, being under the guns of the outlaws. When the flames reached the roof-tops, Victor Spectre and Ralph Tinsdale moved away. Spectre caught the eye of Gus Jaeger and signaled him to join them.

When they had gathered off to one side, Spectre spoke quietly to them. "Until now, we have given no thought to going after Smoke Jensen. Now he has come to us without the bait even being in place. Furthermore, with Olin Buckner in bed, gut-shot and not expected to live, I think the insult is great enough that we should take the battle to him. Augustus, I want you to select a dozen men and send them after Jensen. Pick up his trail. It will be devious, but it can be done. I suspect he is hiding in Jackson's Hole. Have them pursue him relentlessly. I do not want a repeat of this sort of thing. Tell them to pin him to the ground and send word. We will come wherever they are and kill him there. If that is not possible, have him killed on the spot."

Anticipating pursuit, Smoke Jensen made it easy for the outlaws to find his trail and follow him. At least he did until mid-morning, the next day, when he reached the foothills that led to the sheer peaks of the Absaroka Range that buttressed Togwatee Pass. From there, the signs of his passage became few and far apart. It would, he felt assured, whet their appetite for finding him. Some two miles short of the summit of the Pass—which formed the transition from the Absarokas to the Gross Ventre Range, that surrounded Jackson's Hole—Smoke halted and explored a tangle of dead-fall and boulders located fifty yards up-slope from the pathway.

With his Winchester and ample ammunition in place, Smoke returned to the trail below, and created signs that led past his picked spot and on toward the notch. Then he left the traveled roadway and wiped out all indications of his presence. With that completed, he returned and settled in among the rocks and tree trunks. He had a long wait.

Smoke munched alternately on a cold biscuit and strip of jerky, the sun slanted far down in the west, when a trio of hard cases cantered into view over a down-curve in the trail. More quickly followed, until Smoke counted an even dozen. He let them get right in close, then sprung his ambush.

During the long, lonesome day, he had taken the time to rig a dead-fall, which he let fly first. Then he yanked out the three sticks that propped up a loose boulder, which rolled down with amazing speed on the surprised outlaws. The swinging tree trunk cleaned two riders from their saddles. Only one had time to yelp in pain and surprise. The huge granite stone jinked at the last moment and crushed to death three men who had abandoned their saddles, certain that their horses would be struck.

With five hard cases taken out of action, Smoke Jensen opened up with his Winchester. Another member of Victor Spectre's outlaw army threw up his arms and uttered a pitiful shriek before he fell forward over the neck of his horse. Panicked by the unaccustomed weight and the smell of blood, the animal went berserk. Squalling, it crow-hopped and sun-fished until it dislodged the morbid burden, then sprinted off down the trail. It crashed into three mounted border trash. Their mounts reared and one man lost his seat. He hit the ground hard and bounced once.

By then, the human rubbish had recovered enough to return fire. Their slugs screeched and moaned off the mound of granite boulders. Smoke had shifted slightly and began to shove cartridges into the loading gate of his rifle. When he had filled the tubular magazine, he shouldered the weapon and began a rapid fire salvo that pinned the gunmen to the ground. Surprise had served him well enough at the outset. Now, the remaining seven men recovered enough to think through their situation.

Quickly they split up and began to move obliquely up the hill toward Smoke's position from different directions. Their rush caused Smoke to draw back to his secondary position in a jackstraw pile of down-fall, where he would make his final stand.

"By God, there must be a dozen of them up there," Farlee Huntoon yelled in confusion as he worked his way up the slope.

Liam Quinn, who knew from experience, answered him. "Nope. Just Smoke Jensen. Sure an' he's one heller with a gun."

"Cain't be," Farlee objected, unwilling to face the truth. "Any one man shoots that fast cain't hit nothin', nohow."

"Jensen can," Liam assured him, then ducked as another fusillade cut twigs from the brush beside his head. From behind him, Liam heard a man yelp and go down to thrash in a tangle of wild blackberry.

Farlee Huntoon groaned in fear. "Awh, gawdamnit, that's six of us he's kilt already an' we ain't even put a slug in him."

Liam Quinn, who knew only too well how efficient a killing machine was Smoke Jensen, mocked the frightened lout from West Virginia. "Well, why don't you just go up there and do something about that?"

Huntoon drew himself up, smarting from the contempt in the Irish outlaw's voice. "All right, I will."

He started forward when two others decided the same thing. One went down without a sound, the second fled for the protection of a pine trunk. Farlee Huntoon hugged the ground and shivered violently.

Smoke still held his own against the remaining five outlaws. A moment after he broke the charge of the incautious pair who had risen from the grass, he paused to feed fresh cartridges to his Winchester. When he did, one of the crew managed to flank him and knelt behind the trunk of a fallen pine. He rested his elbow on the rough bark on the top and took aim at the side of Smoke's head. Oblivious to the danger, Smoke remained ignorant of the gunman's proximity until he heard a meaty smack, followed a moment later by the flat report of an old, long-barreled Sharps buffalo rifle.

Smoke cut his eyes to the left, where the danger lay, in time to see a shower of hair, skin, blood, and bone as the sniper lost the back of his head. The shot had come from uphill. Everyone went motionless as they took in this new factor. Then another old Sharps opened up on the group on Smoke's right.

A big, .56 caliber slug took down another of the thugs. His piercing screams echoed through the pass as he writhed on the ground, gut-shot and dying. A second later, Smoke Jensen's Winchester barked and Farlee Huntoon flooded his trousers as he desperately tried to sink into the turf. The hidden marksmen with their Sharps rifles knocked over two more hard cases and the resolve of the remainder vanished.

Three of the rabble turned back to form a rear guard. They died at almost the same instant, as Smoke and his unseen allies fired nearly as one. With Farlee Huntoon far in the lead, Liam Quinn and Dorcus Carpenter fled.

Smoke sent a .44-40 slug after them, then came out into the open. Shading his eyes with his hand—his hat had been knocked off by a close bullet—he stared up-slope toward the positions of his rescuers. With the exception of the one who had tried to blind-side him, he could have handled the twelve men easily. That did not diminish the depth of the gratitude he felt for his helpers. While his gaze roved over the rising ground, two figures rose from the underbrush, Sharps rifles held over their heads in a sign of victory.

Zeke Duncan and Ezra Sampson long-legged it down to where Smoke waited for them. Zeke began cackling while still fifty yards away. "Them fellers musta filled their britches 'fore they could get out of here."

"Most likely they did," Ezra agreed, sniffing the air.

"I owe you two," Smoke announced as they came up to him. "I owe you big."

Zeke worked his whiskered mouth a moment before replying. "Well, we was enjoyin' it mightily, watchin' you clean their plows, but then that dirty little sneak tried to pop you from the side. So we figgered it best to take a hand."

Smoke nodded shortly. "Glad you did. I'd be dead as these fellers." Smoke made a sweeping gesture.

One of the supposed corpses groaned. "I ain't dead yet, you bastard."

Ezra Sampson reached him in three swift strides. He roughly jammed the muzzle of his Sharps under the thug's nose. "Don't you think you oughtta call him Mr. Jensen, before he comes over and finishes the job?"

Herman Ogilvey tried to brazen it out. "Go ahead, shoot me, you old fart."

BANG!

Ezra Sampson gave him what he wanted.

Smoke Jensen winced, but spared no more sympathy for the dead man. Instead, he asked the question that had been at the forefront of his mind since he first had an inkling of whom had come to his aid. "What brought you two out here?"

Zeke and Ezra exchanged embarrassed glances, two school

boys caught by the school marm peeping in the girls' side of the outhouse. Zeke studied the toes of his boots. "Thing is, we came over to thank you for the jug of the other night and found yer camp empty. We sorta figgered what you had in mind, so we decided to tag along and see how it all worked out."

"We also wanted to thank you for the hind-quarter of venison you gave us," Ezra added, as though that had anything to do with it.

Smoke broke out a genuine grin. "You two old frauds. You reckoned I'd need some help. And as it turned out, I did. For which I shall always be grateful. Now, let's gather up these weapons and get on back to the Hole."

Shortly before sundown, the self-appointed posse of Sugarloaf riders reached the Wind River Reservation to find Monte Carson already there. Ike grinned sheepishly when he shook the hand of the lawman.

"Seems we had the same idea, Monte. When did you leave?"

"About two days before you, I'd judge, Ike," Monte answered with a chuckle.

Tom Brokenhorn escorted them to places by the council fire. "We are meeting to decide what to do," he explained. "You will not understand our words, so I will tell you what we discuss. I am worried that our friend, Smoke Jensen, is in more trouble now than even he can be aware of. I have asked the council to reach a consensus on sending a war party to give what help we can." He paused and gave a fleeting smile. "I have only two more to win over."

A protracted debate followed, in the musical Shoshoni language, ripe with its Athapaskan root origins. At last, the single hold-out lowered his eagle-wing fan and gave a curt nod. Smiling, the chief turned back to his white visitors. "It is done. I will immediately select a war chief and he will gather men to ride north to the Snake Basin. You may go with them, if you wish."

Monte nodded thoughtfully. "I think that would be good. Especially if the army stumbled on your braves. As a lawman, if I accompany them, I can give lawful reason for being off the reservation."

"It is as though Smoke Jensen spoke those words. Thank you, Lawman Carson." To the Sugarloaf hands, he added, "I will give you a beaded belt as safe passage through my people scattered on the reservation. I wish you all well."

Twenty

Nate Miller and his motley crew rode into Dubois half an hour before sundown. Word had not yet reached the town about the defeat of the gunmen sent after Smoke Jensen. Many of the hard cases hooted and called insults to Sally Jensen as the rabble gathered to gawk. Nate Miller pushed his way through the mob, to clear a path for Sally to follow. Her protector on the journey, Sam Hutchins, took her gently by one elbow and escorted her beyond the slobbering louts.

"Pay them no mind, ma'am, they're nothin' but trash."

And what are you? Sally asked herself silently, then gave him a brief smile. "Thank you, Sam. And, thanks for the support. I'm afraid I'm a little stiff after being tied to my horse all this time."

"It'll go away. I heard Mr. Spectre tell Nate jist now that he'll put you up in the hotel. A room to yourself."

Sally could not resist a flash of sarcasm. "How very thoughtful." Then she relented on Sam's behalf. He had been respectful, even kind, during the long trek. "What do you know about this monster who so cavalierly orders men to kidnap a woman and bring her to him?"

Sam frowned. "I wouldn't call him a monster, ma'am. He's a good leader. Has this whole thing thought out real clever. Why, look at this town. Don't look like a shot was fired when they took it over."

Sally seized on that at once. "What sort of man would

want to take a town away from the people who rightfully own it, it's residents?"

A big smile grew on Sam's face. "You ever hear of politicians, ma'am?"

Blushing at being outsmarted so easily, Sally put on a good front. "Besides them, then, if you will."

"Now you have me there, ma'am. All I know is he said it was necessary in order to get your husband to come at him."

Sally smiled sweetly. "I thought that was why I was kidnapped."

Sam looked glum. "Yeah. There's that, too."

Stopping abruptly, Sally stamped a foot. "Doesn't he realize that whether I am here or whether he has the town or not, Smoke will come after him?"

With an effort of mental gymnastics Sam rejected the truth of what she said. He chose to change the subject. "Come along, ma'am, I'll see you to the hotel."

Victor Spectre waited for Sally Jensen in the lobby. Ignoring her foreknowledge, Sally hotly demanded to know for what reason she had been brought there. Smirking, Spectre allowed as how it surprised him that she had not figured it out already.

"You have a special role in my immediate future. You are my cheese."

"Cheese?"

"Yes, dear lady, cheese. As in mousetrap. In this case the mouse is your husband, Smoke Jensen."

Thinking it wise, Smoke Jensen moved his camp south to a smaller portion of the basin. Double Peak thrust up due east of him. Once he had set up, he sighed regretfully over the duplicated work he faced to rebuild his smoker. And he needed to get another deer.

He hunted with a bow again, disturbing little in nature.

with his kill. A larger animal this time. Smoke dressed it and hung it in a tree, then set about the thankless task of building a new smoker. He had no idea how much longer he would be there, and any meat he had left over, he could give to Zeke and Ezra. Sundown caught up to him and he fried some of the liver. He would finish tomorrow.

Near noon the next day, Smoke stretched to his full height after lighting a smudgy, green wood, hickory fire in the chamber to one side of his smoker. He froze at the faint crackle of a stepped-on twig near by. It took only one stride to retrieve his Winchester. He held it cradled loosely in his left arm when a man's head appeared over the tops of some low, new-growth aspen. The stranger held his rifle up by the stock, a white cloth tied to the barrel. Smoke surmised it might be a napkin.

"Hello the camp. You be Smoke Jensen?"

"I am."

"I'm comin' in under a flag of truce. Will you honor that?"

"I will. Ride on in."

From the looks of the man, up close, Smoke wondered how he had ever been able to find the camp. He wore a derby hat, cocked jauntily to one side, a striped suit, with a collarless shirt, made gaudy by wide, vertical red stripes, separated by thin white ones, and carriage boots, with the cuffs of his pants stuffed in. A city dude, Smoke put him as being.

"I have something to show you, Jensen," he declared.

Smoke motioned him to the picket line. "Tie off and I'll take a look."

After the cityfied thug dismounted and secured his horse, he came forward with his saddlebags over one shoulder. He opened the buckles on one side and delved within. He came out with a fine gold chain, from which hung a cameo. It was one Smoke Jensen knew only too well. Next came the .38 Colt Lightning Smoke had purchased for her when they had first become available in Denver. It took every bit of Smoke's will to keep his face impassive. When the gunsel reached into the bag for something else, Smoke raised a hand to halt him.

"I've seen enough. Where is Sally?"

Over-confident, the rogue made a stupid decision to taunt Smoke. "Who?"

An instant later he found his shirt-front bunched in one powerful fist of Smoke Jensen, his feet off the ground, dangling. "Where . . . is . . . my wife?"

"All right—all right, leggo me. I'll tell you what I was told to say." When Smoke released him, the suddenly nervous, smaller man fussily adjusted his clothing in an effort to regain his composure and get the quaver out of his voice.

"Make it good. And, make it fast," Smoke growled.

"I was told by Mr. Spectre to tell you that if you want your wife to live, you will ride into Dubois within two days. You are to come alone and unarmed. If you bring help, she will be killed on the spot. Remember, two days. Come in by then, or on the third day, your Sally dies."

Without a word, Smoke took Sally's possessions from the messenger, spun him around and roughly shoved him toward his horse. "Get out of here, you outhouse rat, and don't look back."

After the messenger departed, Smoke reviewed the brief, fateful message. Fat chance of either of them surviving if he believed any of that, he considered. He would have to get Sally out of there on his own, then bring in help to deal with Victor Spectre. To do that, he needed a better look at Dubois.

In camp, outside Togwatee Pass, Bobby Harris sat apart from the hands who had treated him like an equal for more than a year. On their journey northward, his pose of manhood had slipped as time wore on. The boy had been buoyed up by a spirit of adventure alone for the last two days. Now he rested an elbow on his knee, his chin cupped in an open hand. His lower lip protruded in a typical little-boy pout. Ike Mitchell found him there as long shafts of orange speared through the trees and the eastern sky turned from blue to purple.

"You're looking sort of glum. Want to talk about it?"

Bobby looked up rapidly, his face an open bloom of hope. "Yes—er—no. Yes, I do, Ike," the boy concluded, his features crumpled into despair again.

"Well, then, where do you want to start?"

"At the beginning, I guess. I should have gone with Smoke."

Disappointment clouded Ike's eyes. "Don't start on that again."

Bobby darted out a hand and put it on the foreman's arm to stay further complaint. "No, please, Ike, let me tell it my way." At Ike's dubious nod, he went on. "I wanted to show Smoke and everyone that I was big enough to do a man's job. So, I should have gone, because afterward I got to feelin' like the other hands were laughing at me. That I was nothing but a little boy to them. Then, when those men took Sal—Mom, I couldn't stand it any longer. See, if I had gone with Smoke, we would have moved a lot slower than him alone. We could have been close enough to take after those bas—devils right away."

"They went the same way Smoke did, you said so. We might even have run into them on the way, fought it out, and they would never have taken m-my mother." He paused, eyes begging for understanding. "Anyway, I could have been more useful . . . than . . . I am now. And, I'm worried about her. I'm afraid something bad will happen." Bobby's eyes filled and he sniffled softly in a fight to keep back the tears.

Reminded of his own turmoils at the threshold of puberty, Ike impulsively reached out and hugged Bobby to him. With rough compassion, he ruffled the straw-blond hair. Smoke knows you are a big man now," he spoke reassuringly. "Smoke'll be almightily exercised over you coming along, but he'll know it was your worry over Miss Sally."

"He's got the right of that, boy," Monte Carson, who had come up quietly behind them during the painful exchange, said gruffly.

Setting aside the tin cup, Smoke Jensen praised the coffee, then turned to the real reason for his visit to the camp of Zeke and Ezra. "Could you two carry a message for me?"

"I don't know why not. Who's it go to?"

Smoke answered tightly, unsure how they would receive the news. "There's two people, really, Chief Tom Brokenhorn of the Shoshoni, and Chief Blackrobe of the Arapaho. They are camped on the Wind River Reservation. I'll write it out for you and you can leave in the morning."

Zeke cocked an eyebrow, pursed lips. "Kin they read writin'?"

"Tom Brokenhorn can. You'll have to tell Blackrobe."

"All right. What's this gonna say, this message?" Zeke accepted.

"That they are to send as many warriors as possible right away. They are to meet me to the east of Togwatee Pass, on the plain, ten miles from Dubois."

Ezra pucked his lips, which made his mustache waggle like a furry snake. "We—ah—sorta reckoned to get in on that affair."

"You still can. Ride back here with the Indians and you'll be in plenty of time."

Zeke asked for both of them. "What are you fixin' to do now?"

"I leave this afternoon to get another look at Dubois."

Ezra whistled softly. "Sounds to me like you're a sucker for danger."

A cold, bleak look filled Smoke's yellow-brown eyes. "Could be *I'm* the danger."

Smoke Jensen left the eastern grade to Togwatee Pass shortly after the moon rose. Its pale, silver light washed the land with enough brightness to see. He would be close to Dubois before mid-morning, Smoke estimated. Thunder trotted along the well-used trail, which ran five miles north of the camp where Monte Carson and Ike Mitchell slept through the night, eager to reach Smoke's camp in Jackson's Hole the next day. Neither the ex-mountain man or the posse knew of the others' presence.

And Smoke could have used them, had he but known.

Over the past three days, fourteen more gunfighters and bounty hunters had drifted into Dubois, which brought the total to well above fifty-five. They dozed late into the mornings, and lounged in the saloons through the afternoons and each night. With the town in the hands of the man who had hired them, most had not known such peace and security since childhood.

Much to the disgust of Tim O'Roarke, most of the outlaw horde made the Watering Hole a sort of headquarters. Fully three dozen lounged in the saloon on a lazy, warm afternoon. Half a dozen more had gone upstairs with some of the soiled doves. Most of them would be down before long, Tim knew. For all their bragging about what bad actors they were, and what gifts they were to womanhood, they were actually more like little boys with short fuses. How different they were from Smoke Jensen.

That thought gave O'Roarke pause. He wondered where Smoke was right then, what he was doing.

* * *

Nestled down into a depression outside Dubois, a pair of field glasses to his eyes. Smoke Jensen slowly swept the lenses along the buildings nearest to him. For two blocks they were residences. All of them had two things in common, Smoke observed. No one worked in the flower beds, the gardens, or went to and from the stables at the rear of the lots. Only two had lank washing, that fluttered listlessly in an indifferent breeze, on lines in backyards. Yet each house had a scruffy-looking hard case propped back in a chair on the porch. He went back over them again, then a third time.

The people who live there are prisoners in their own homes, Smoke realized as he looked on. Then he changed his point of focus to the first of the commercial buildings. He at once noted a greater density of outlaws among the people on the street he viewed now. They swaggered through the vanquished residents, who scurried away with furtive backward glances. Smoke spotted several faces he recognized from earlier encounters with Spectre's minions. He would have to move to sweep the main street.

Fortunately a shallow ravine ran parallel with the face of the town where Smoke observed. After he satisfied his curiosity enough, Smoke shifted into the fissure and worked north along it until he reached a culvert where the main roadway crossed it. There he removed his hat and raised up enough to scan the main street with ease. What he saw deeply troubled him. In the same heartbeat it relieved him of an earlier anxiety. At least now he knew where Spectre held Sally.

Heavily armed outlaws, in roving patrols of two and three, alertly prowled around the hotel. More sat in chairs on the balcony and under its canopy on the boardwalk. The saloons received good play also, he perceived. Small wonder. A collection of this sort, used to some space between themselves and others, needed an outlet for the tension their closeness would surely create. Easing down, Smoke took out a sheet of paper and began to sketch in the location of each nest of hard cases with a stub of pencil. With that accomplished, he moved again.

Throughout the remainder of the day, Smoke timed the movements of the outlaws, entered the positions of look-out posts and the length of the watch duty. No doubt Spectre thinks their presence will keep him from getting rough when he made his move to save Sally.

"How little he knows," Smoke said wryly to himself.

When he withdrew, well into the night, he had an idea of where every lookout had been placed, where Spectre himself spent the night, and how many men could be expected in the saloons. With however many guns he had at his disposal, Smoke decided he would go in after Sally at the time specified. That would provide time for the warriors to get here. Once he had her clear of town, Spectre and his gang would be swept out of town in a way that would give nightmares for the rest of their lives to any who survived, Smoke vowed silently to himself.

Without warning, the door to the room where Sally Jensen sat staring at her lamp-lit reflection in the windowpanes made mirrors by the blackness outside. She tensed slightly, back unconsciously arching in preparation for a spring to flee or to attack. She was convinced that these rabble could sink to the lowest, vilest of crimes, given only the slightest provocation. Slowly, she turned her head to see who her faithful guard, Sam, had let enter.

It turned out to be Victor Spectre. In one hand he held a tray with covered dishes. "I thought I would bring you your dinner. I brought a plate for myself, as well." He started for a small, sturdy, drop-leaf oak table.

"Thank you, but I am not hungry," Sally replied absently.

Brushing aside her rejection, Spectre began laying out the plates. "You must eat to keep up your strength, my dear. It's roast loin of pork, with potatoes and gravy, some garden greens, and even a slice of cherry pie. The cherries are locally grown and put up by my temporary host, the Mayor's cook. I've brought an appropriate bottle of wine, and there will be coffee after."

Sally put ice into her voice. *"I said I am not hungry."* A sharp pang in her stomach put the lie to that. Reluctantly, she had to admit the accuracy of his words. "Although I suppose you are right. I must maintain my strength in order to fight you vermin."

She went to the chair he held out for her. After seating her, Victor Spectre fussed about the table like a prissy waiter in a French restaurant. At last, he took his place and raised knife and fork. Then he hesitated.

"Ah—perhaps you would prefer to give a blessing first?"

Sally Jensen pulled a wry face. "Considering the circumstances, I hardly think I can be thankful for this food."

"Uh—yes, I follow you. Well and good, then. You might as well commence, we do not want it getting cold."

Hesitantly, Sally began to eat. Throughout the meal, she noticed that Spectre seemed oddly fascinated with her. He eyed her askance for the most part, yet occasionally Sally would look up from cutting a piece of meat to find him staring. She held her peace through most of the meal, determined not to make this a pleasant occasion for her captor. His continued behavior finally broke her silence.

"Tell me, Mr. Spectre—"

"Victor. Please, call me Victor."

"Very well, Victor. Tell me, has it been a while since you shared the company of a lady?"

Spectre's school-boy fascination faded into a scowl. "Your husband saw to that. I have been forced into the close company of only men for the past five and a half years."

"Didn't your wife visit?"

Sadness replaced the bitterness. "My wife—my wife passed on the year our son was nine." Suddenly the anger flared again, and Spectre let it all spill out. "That's why I'm here. That's why I am doing this. Smoke Jensen murdered Trenton. He killed my son."

Sally could not hide her expression of shocked disbelief. "Surely that can't be so. There has to be something you are not telling me, perhaps something you don't even remember about the—incident?"

"No, nothing. I was there. I witnessed it. The boy was already wounded, could not offer further resistance. Then your husband turned on me. His shot went high. . . ." Unconsciously, Victor Spectre raised fingers to the white streak in his hair. "I was knocked unconscious. When I awakened, days later, Trenton had already been buried."

Sally touched her napkin to her lips, mind searching for something with which to mitigate the indictment against Smoke. "Couldn't the shock of being shot, and knocked unconscious, distorted your recollection of how events transpired?"

Oddly impacted by this unconventional suggestion the turmoil it created could be clearly read on the face of Victor Spectre. He considered it a moment, then hardened his features again. "Not at all. I know what I saw. That is why I have shown such fascination with you. You are so refined, such a lady, that I wonder how you can live with so notorious a murderer as Smoke Jensen?"

Sally's compassion for this tormented man vanished. Icily, she responded to him. "Smoke Jensen is not a murderer, and I do love and live with him quite nicely, thank you."

"Sorry, you don't understand. What I want to know is what Smoke Jensen is like as a husband?"

"Don't be impertinent," Sally snapped.

Spectre forced a grin. "It is not idle curiosity, and I did not intend it to intrude on a husband and wife's conjugal privicy. Yet, the fact remains," he went on to add sneeringly, "you will be a widow soon, and all you will have is memories of Smoke Jensen. When that is the case, you will find that you have certain needs that—yes—that I will be more than able to fulfill."

Sally Jensen sprang to her feet and snatched up the tray and its unfinished meal, which she hurled at Victor Spectre. Then she slapped his face with a resounding smack.

Twenty-one

Well satisfied with his survey of Dubois, Smoke Jensen returned to his temporary camp in a hidden canyon five miles from the town. To his surprise, he found fifteen Shoshoni warriors waiting there. Running Snake, their war leader, turned out to be a grandson to Chief Tom Brokenhorn and spoke English well.

"We have been watching the bad men who camp in the white village. When that happen, I send message to my grandfather to have warriors come if you need."

Smoke found it hard to see Brokenhorn as a grandfather, yet he was already one as well. "I will probably need, right enough. When did you send for warriors?"

"On the day we see White Wolf sneak into town," Running Snake said with a grin.

That meant Zeke and Ezra would run upon them on the trail, Smoke reasoned. The Shoshoni's next words surprised him and brought to mind a question he had for a long while.

"I also have word that some worthless dogs of the Arapaho are a hand's span of sun behind us. They will be here in the morning."

Given that the two tribes had been traditional enemies for centuries, Smoke could never figure out why the Government, in its infinite wisdom, had put them together on the same reservation. Maybe the land-greedy politicians hoped they would wipe out one another? He gave off worrying it to make his guests coffee, with lots of sugar, then put meat on the cookfire.

"We will have coffee and talk," he told Running Snake in Shoshoni. "Then we eat."

"It is good. When you last visited our camp, I was not yet born. There are many things I would like to know."

Smoke Jensen cut his sharp gaze to Running Snake "Like what got these fellers riled up at me enough to tear into that village?"

Running Snake nodded. "Yes, there is that . . . and other things."

Morning brought the aroma of brewing coffee and frying bacon. It also brought twenty-eight Arapaho warriors, Zeke and Ezra along with them. That surprised Smoke, who made quick to ask about it. A grinning Zeke explained.

"We ran into these fellers just south of the pass. They tole us that they had been following a large party of Shoshoni and white men for two days. So Ez an' me figgered ever'body what was up for this tussel were already accounted for. We rode along."

Ezra took up the tale. "Then, when we got to the pass we cut sign of Injuns an' whites ridin' together. We left a stone cairn tellin' them where to come. Should be here some time today."

That gave him a larger force than Smoke had hoped for Even so, he frowned. "I don't have any more days to spare Today's the deadline. I have to show myself in Dubois or Sally will be killed tomorrow."

Zeke questioned that. "You don't really think that feller would make good on his threat, do you? Why, he'd lose his advantage."

"You and I know that, and so does he. But, I'm afraid the one in charge is unable to think clearly right now. He might consider it just desserts for me, even though he would die in the process."

Ezra spoke encouragingly. "I make it a good sixteen white men, and about thirty Shoshonis."

Smoke sounded grim. "He'll die then, no matter what happens to Sally."

What jolted Smoke even more came when the mixed band arrived shortly after noon. Smoke almost blew the head off his foreman when Ike Mitchell and the Sugarloaf hands sprinted ahead of the approaching Shoshoni warriors into the box canyon. He received yet another surprise when he saw Monte Carson and Hank Evans along. He vigorously shook his old friend's hand and led him to the cookfire.

"I have to leave soon, Monte, but there's time for a cup of coffee."

"Leave? For where?"

"Dubois. Victor Spectre has given me two days to turn myself in to save Sally's life. This is the second day."

Monte had heard about Sally's kidnapping from Ike. He had cursed and kicked rocks and slammed a fist into a pine trunk at the time. Now he let go a low, rumbling swear word and fire lighted his eyes. "You're not going alone?"

"That's what he expects, but I don't think so. This many people on hand calls for a change of plan."

Monte and Ike looked wary. Ike was first to take up the burden. "There's one person along you may want to cook up some special plans for, Smoke."

"Who's that?"

"Bobby."

Smoke exploded upward to land hard on his boot soles. "What the bloody blue hell did you let him come along for?"

Ike gritted his teeth, knowing the ire of his boss to be justified. "I—ah—didn't exactly 'let' him come along. He insisted. The kidnapping of Sally was sort of the last straw for him."

Before Smoke could hunt down the boy and unload on him, Ike took him aside and told him of his conversation with Bobby. It cooled the anger Smoke had built. Carefully he thought over what he would say while he sought out the lad, who had wisely decided to avoid Smoke's notice. Smoke found Bobby at the picket line, industriously brushing out his horse.

"Bobby, I am not happy with this. You can be sure of that. Although I think I understand why you came along."

"Yes, sir. You're going to send me back."

Smoke softened his expression with a fleeting smile. "No. You may stay. But you'll have to stay behind in this camp until the fighting's over. Having Sally's life in danger is enough, too much in fact. The risk of putting you in harm's way is more than I could bear. I—well, at first I thought of you as a nuisance. Since then, I—I've come to love you every bit as much as my own natural sons." *There, I've said it,* Smoke's expression declared.

Bobby's eyes went wide and round. "You do? You really do? I thought—I thought you looked at me as nothing but a little boy, someone to take fishing and teach about ranching."

Impulsively, they found themselves in a tight embrace. Smoke seemed reluctant to end it, pride in Bobby's indomitable spirit filling him. At last he let the boy go. "I have to do some planning with Monte, Ike, and the war chiefs."

"Then what, Smoke?"

"I'm going to Dubois to get Sally."

With Zeke's admonition that Spectre would not be crazy enough to eliminate his one insurance policy by killing Sally the next day fresh in his mind, and in light of the large number of men on hand, Smoke made drastic changes in his plans. If he did not show up by the deadline, it would put them further off balance, he reasoned. Smoke figured that a little havoc in Dubois might also have a beneficial effect. Shortly before dusk, he and Zeke rode out of the canyon mouth and started for Dubois. Already confused by Smoke's failure to appear in town, Spectre and his underlings would not be in good shape for a dawn attack after a sleepless night. They reached a spot from which they could observe everything going on along the main street. Patiently they waited out the long hours until alertness slackened.

Then they made their move. Smoke had earlier pointed out to Zeke several sentries who dozed off. Silently, moccasins replacing boots, Smoke and Zeke ghosted in on a pair of these. Solid blows, with the flat of tomahawk blades, quickly rendered the thugs unconscious. Smoke and Zeke each dragged their man off into the grass, to bind and gag them. Then they set off after another group of laggards.

"Over there," Smoke whispered in Zeke's ear. "There's two of them."

At a creeping pace, Smoke and Zeke closed in. When they came within ten yards, they could hear muffled conversation.

"By dang, I'm gettin' sick and tired of this. Who'er we watchin' out for?"

"Smoke Jensen, of course."

"Would you know him to see him? I don't blame him for not comin' in today. A man'd have to be a fool to ride into a town bristlin' with guns like this one." He laughed softly. "I'd kinda like to come face-to-face with him. Shake his hand and tell him how smart I think he is for keepin' outta Spectre's clutches."

A voice answered him from out of the darkness. "You kin, if you want to, Yonker. He's standin' right in front of you." Zeke chuckled softly a moment before he clonked the other outlaw over the head with his tomahawk.

Galvanized by this disclosure the first gunhawk came to his boots. "You are? Smoke Jensen? Where are you?"

"Right here," Smoke told him as he slapped the lout alongside the head with his 'hawk. Abruptly rubber-legged, the gunman went down in a heap.

Again, they dragged the senseless burdens out into the tall grass and tied them securely. Zeke edged over to Smoke. "I reckon that's enough, don't you?"

Smoke's breathy chortle lightened his words. "Yeah. On this side. We need to take a few more."

By two o'clock in the morning, they had taken out seven more lookouts. Then Smoke and Zeke split up and moved to positions on opposite sides of the town. Late hangers-on in the saloons soon found themselves listening to a timber wolf chorus. The eerie wails echoed off buildings and floated in the streets in such a way that no one could pinpoint their place of origin.

Judson Reese, deep in his cups, summed the experience up best. "They seem to come from everywhere at once, and entirely too close."

None of the dolts, who had been reduced to blurry vision and stagger-legged stumbles volunteered to go out and find the wolves. When one of the cries changed from wolf to the cough and yowl of a mountain lion, several tough hombres paled noticeably and slunk away to upstairs rooms in the saloon for the night. Suddenly a shout of alarm came from one of the still-conscious sentries outside.

"Fire! There's shed afire on the edge of the town."

Tongue thick with whiskey, Farlee Huntoon voiced the question many wanted an answer for. "Gol-dang, what caused that?"

Nate Miller gave him a cold gaze. "Smoke Jensen. What else could it be?"

Guffawing at the quandary of the lawless trash, Smoke Jensen and Zeke Duncan pulled back into the darkness to get some sleep before the big attack. Behind them, the aban-

doned, tumble-down shack continued to burn until first
light.

Smoke Jensen and the vultures continued Durango's
fat supply of ammunition. Jeff Atteberry lay low, off
to the right somewhere at the north-east angle bank of the

From her confinement in the hotel, Sally Jensen had
heard the commotion outside. It cheered her more than anything had in a week. When the animal calls began, she
rushed to the small barred window of the jail from the chair
in which she had been sitting. She had been brought to the
cell-block at sundown, when Smoke failed to appear. Now
she knew why Smoke had not come in earlier.

Smoke was out there now. Sally knew that as certainly
as she knew her heart still beat. He hadn't given up, and
he would not make some useless sacrifice of himself to
save her. The time would come soon. She had to be ready
to act. Yet, in the back of her head, she worried for Smoke's
safety.

Her worry increased when Victor Spectre burst into the
marshal's office and stormed into the cell-block. He ordered
her cell unlocked and entered in a barely contained fury.
Roughly he shot out an arm and grabbed her elbow in a
steel grip.

"This is all your fault," he accused irrationally. "Smoke
Jensen is on a rampage out there and it is all because you
are here."

Sally glared at him stonily. "And who is it that had me
brought here?"

Coldly, Victor Spectre ignored her. "Your husband is being a nuisance and has to be taught a lesson. It is a pity
that you have to be a part of that lesson. I had decided to
give him more time," Spectre lied smoothly. "Now, that is
not possible. Tomorrow morning, at eight o'clock precisely,
you will be taken out on the balcony of the hotel and shot
to death."

* * *

Dawn's light had not yet turned pink from gray when Smoke Jensen and his volunteers approached Dubois. At his suggestion, the Shoshonis and Arapahos kept well out of sight, spreading out on the north and south flanks of the town. From a distance, Smoke swept the streets with field-glasses. He spotted a few sleepy hard cases on the streets. All drooped from lack of rest. All looked in a low state of readiness. Smoke made a quick decision to attack at once.

"We won't have a better time," he told Monte Carson. "Surprise is still ours. We'll swing through this group of houses and take the main business section in a wide sweep. If it will make you feel better, Monte, we'll call out to them to surrender. At the least sign of resistance, we kill them where they stand."

"What about Sally?" Monte asked seriously.

"I'll find her. As a matter of fact, I have the notion Spectre will bring her to me."

Monte checked the face of his turnip watch. "Time to be doing it."

"I agree. Hank knows what to do?"

Monte nodded. "He'll attack from the far side when he hears the first shot."

That first discharge did not take long. Three hard cases came on the run from houses along a neat, tree-lined street. One of them, who had seen Smoke before, yelled to the others.

"By God, that's Smoke Jensen! Get him."

In the lead, Smoke took a hurried shot. His slug went a bit wide, to punch through the shoulder of one outlaw before the gunman could clear leather. Another appeared to trip over an invisible rope and sprawl in the gravel of the road, blood spewing from a gaping wound in his back. The third brigand, the one who had given the alarm, hastily re-holstered his six-gun and threw his hands in the air. Those in the lead went on by him. Someone at the rear would gather him in. From the far side of town, Smoke could hear gunfire.

Hank Evans and the remainder of the Sugarloaf hands would be streaming through to the business district. Another block and those on this side would join them. Then they would see. Smoke could only trust that it went the way he had planned it. Ahead he could see the balcony of the hotel. Three small figures stood on it. The one in the middle was that of a woman. Ice abruptly filled Smoke's stomach.

Another half block and the features became identifiable. Much as he wished otherwise, the woman was Sally. Smoke recognized Victor Spectre to one side. He held the muzzle of a Smith and Wesson American to her temple. At once, Smoke gave the signal to halt.

"Take it easy, Spectre. I came to see my wife was safe."

Spectre snickered. "Why wouldn't she be?"

"You said that if I did not come in within two days, you would kill her the third."

Feigning astonishment, Spectre spoke mockingly. "Why, I believe you are right. But, now you are here. If you are prepared to gave yourself up, we can discuss the release of your wife."

"If I believed that, you could also sell me the Washington Monument. Release her now and we can talk about my surrender."

"No, Smoke," Sally blurted.

"She is right. The answer is no. Whether you cannot count, or you are arrogant, I made up my mind. I decided that she dies at eight o'clock this morning. Now that you are here, the situation has changed again. That gives you . . ." Spectre fished his watch from a vest pocket while his henchman held Sally. "An hour and forty minutes. You have that time to pull back your men and give up to me, or she dies as scheduled."

* * *

Smoke Jensen led the way out of Dubois. To Monte's urgent questions, Smoke said only to wait and see. Smoke met first with the Shoshoni and Arapaho leaders. Running Snake listened to Smoke with interest, made a couple of suggestions and then asked how Smoke expected to make it work.

"It all depends on getting Zeke and Ezra into position to cover the hotel. From there on, we'll have to play it by their lead. All you need worry about is to be ready when I get Sally away from Spectre."

At ten minutes prior to the appointed time, Smoke Jensen walked Thunder down the wide main street of Dubois. An eerie silence held over the town. Residents looked away as Smoke rode by, ashamed in their helplessness. That would change, he reflected, if all went the way he intended.

Smoke had instructed Ike to have the men take all surplus arms and ammunition and provide them to the populace as the hands fought their way through the residences of Dubois. The citizens had fought to recover their homes once before, he had little doubt they had changed in only a few years. This time they had the added impetus of having the outlaws quartered among them. No one would like that sort of thing, Smoke reasoned.

And they would be given an opportunity to even the score. When he reached a block's distance, Smoke saw Sally once again on the balcony. This time two hard cases held her arms, well away from her body or the reach of a well-aimed foot. Smoke saw that two of those responsible for this situation had chosen to gather on the covered porch of the saloon, before the double bat-wing doors. No doubt they had come to gloat and claim his head, he surmised. As promised, Smoke appeared to be unarmed, his holsters empty. Victor Spectre stepped forward as Smoke Jensen reached the corner of the intersection.

"There has been another change of plans, I regret to say," Spectre declared, a nasty smile on his face. "We thought it to be too delicious an irony to overlook. This bright morning, you are going to get to witness your wife being shot to death. Then, you shall be killed with the same weapon. Only slowly, with each of us placing bullets at likely places. Your ankles, wrists, knees, elbows, hips, shoulder joints, your abdomen, the right side of your chest, then the left, and last, your head. By then, several days will have passed, during which we shall enjoy ourselves enormously. You recall my associate, I am sure. Ralph Tinsdale. Unfortunately, you shot Olin Buckner. He is looking on from his sickbed in the hotel above. We are three men whom you have terribly wronged. And, for that wronging, you must now pay."

Smoke Jensen tensed as he edged even closer. Through tight, thinned lips he made his response to Spectre. "Get on with it, you windbag son of a bitch."

According to his plan, Smoke had drawn near enough to the balcony for Sally to easily jump to the rump of Thunder. Smoke cut his eyes to those of his wife in a meaningful glance a moment before two meaty smacks sounded in the strained silence of the intersection. Instantly, Sally jerked free of her suddenly lessened restraint and darted toward the rail as the reports of two distant Sharps buffalo rifles rippled through the heated air. The two outlaws fell dead on the balcony floor. In a blur, then, she vaulted the railing and dropped to the skirt of the saddle on Thunder's back.

"Stop them!" Victor Spectre shouted, though not before Sally Jensen yanked her .38 Colt Lightning free from the rear waistband of her husband and fired on him.

Victor Spectre and Ralph Tinsdale sprawled in an undignified manner on the worn boards of the porch. By then, Smoke had freed the .45 Colt, which had also been concealed at the small of his back. He fired in a blur of speed. His first slug cut the hat from the head of an astounded Victor Spectre. Every thug present went for his gun. Hot lead began to crack and snap close to the two Jensens. Sally held onto Smoke with one hand and gamely discharged two rounds that quickly wrote an end to the checkered career of Fin Brock. Then the Arapaho and Shoshoni warriors whooped and hollered to create a diversion that allowed Smoke Jensen to take advantage of an opening in the gathered ranks of criminal slime and bolt through.

Arrows moaned their distinctive melody to strike flesh in the chests, stomachs, and throats of many a hardened rogue. They went down screaming as Thunder gained momentum and drew a wider gap between the human garbage and the priceless cargo the 'Paloose stallion bore. More gunshots crackled as the Sugarloaf hands invaded the residences of Dubois and shot down the toughs who had elected not to watch the destruction of the wife of Smoke Jensen. For all their villainous ways, they had retained their respect for women. It did them little good, as the vengeance-hungry ranch hands poured round after round into their hastily assembled ranks. Some broke and ran, escape a higher priority than any reward they might receive.

In all this confusion, Smoke and Sally quickly rode to safety. The entire confrontation had taken less than three minutes, Smoke discovered when they cantered across the small bridge at the west end of Dubois. Not bad at all. Behind him the volunteer fighters pulled back to make ready for the final assault. Not a one of the three responsible for this encounter would escape alive, Smoke Jensen had decreed.

Twenty-two

Victor Spectre raved in fury at this debacle. He refused
to look at it as a setback, let alone a defeat. When Ralph
Tinsdale offered some platitude about their still holding the
town, and that Smoke Jensen would be compelled to come
to them, if he intended to do anything about it, Victor Spectre rounded on him, face carmine with rage.

"That is exactly the point. Smoke Jensen will absolutely
come after us now. His wife is safe, he has those damned
Indian allies and nothing to lose."

Tinsdale tried to calm the outraged Victor Spectre. "Quite
the contrary, I would think. Taken from Smoke Jensen's
viewpoint, why do anything more. He has his wife, safe
and sound, why not simply pack up and go home?"

A malevolent glow burned in Spectre's eyes. "Because
Smoke Jensen does not play live and let live. *He will come.*
He has a large enough force and we have taken losses. He
knows that. When he came after me, he had no way of
knowing Trenton and I would be alone in that barn. Yet,
Jensen came without a single other man."

Peevishly, Tinsdale snapped his opinion. "We should have
killed that woman when we had the chance."

"No, Ralph," Victor Spectre answered more calmed now.
"Then we would have had a furious man on our hands to
deal with. One who would not have stopped at burning
down the entire town, if necessary, to get to us. What we
should have done was to have Smoke Jensen back-shot and

not stand around to gloat. The fact remains, Jensen will be coming. I want you to have the men ready for an attack at any time. And see that Olin is made as comfortable as possible. If he is up to it, give him a rifle he can use from his sickbed. We need every gun we can muster."

"Mom! *Oh, Mom!*" Bobby ran to Sally Jensen with outstretched arms, his light, blond hair flopping on a round head, hat spilled off in his excited discovery of his adoptive mother among those who returned from town. Mother and son hugged delightedly and shed copious tears. Then Sally broke the embrace and stood the boy before her.

"You disobeyed Smoke and myself alike. I'm disappointed, Bobby. No, that isn't true. I'm truly delighted to see you. For a while there, I didn't—didn't think I would ever see you again."

Smoke walked over and cleared his throat gruffly. "We're going to have to stop meeting like this, my dear. People will begin to talk."

Sally feigned anger. "Is that all you have to say to me? Not hello? Or glad to see you?"

"No, it's not all," Smoke said through a grin. "If you'd had the muzzle of that Lightning any closer to my head when you popped off three rounds at the Lammer brothers, we wouldn't be having this conversation." Then he grabbed her and gave her a mighty hug, that lifted Sally's feet off the ground. "It's so good to have you here. For a while there, I actually worried that it wouldn't work."

"What? The famous Smoke Jensen worried about a little thing like that?" Sally teased. For a moment her eyes swam with more tears. "Oooh, Smoke Jensen, I love you so. I never lost hope that you would come for me."

Smoke was serious this time. "Coming for you is one thing. Getting you out unscratched is quite another. I've heard about it from Ike and the hands, but tell me, how did it really happen? How did you let it?"

Sally made a pained expression. "Darn it, they caught me at the sink, away from my purse and gun. If they would have come twenty minutes earlier, while I was shelling peas, there isn't one of them would have left there alive. As it is, a couple of them didn't. And, there's one I owe a lot of gratitude to. His name's Sam something-or-other. If you can spare him, do so." She described Sam Hutchins and told Smoke how he served as her protector when the others wanted to have their way with her. Smoke agreed that he deserved to live if possible. Then he excused himself and joined the other leaders for a short conference on how they would finish the remainder of the outlaw army.

"I don't need to tell you that we have to hit them hard. And all at once. First the sentries on the edges of town. Then we close off the only streets that lead out and move in on the center of the business district." He went on to give various assignments of specific buildings to the Indians and ranch hands. Zeke and Ezra he again positioned where they could bring long-range covering fire on the hotel. With that accomplished, and satisfied that the outcome would be in their favor, Smoke called for a good, hot meal before they went back to Dubois.

Running Snake looked across the expanse of tall grass to the village of the white men. He had grown up longing to do what he would in a minute be doing. As a small child, he had sat at the feet of the elders listening to their exciting tales of sweeping raids through villages; Arapaho villages, Absaroka villages, Sioux villages, and even white villages. They sang songs of the far off Tishmunga, Assinaboine, Modoc, and Hurons, who burned to the ground many settlements, villages, and even towns of the whites. The descriptions of flames leaping high thrilled him. Even with the admonition from Smoke Jensen to leave the people and their wood lodges alone and fight only the outlaws did not detract from Running Snake's expectations.

This day, he vowed, would be sung about for many seasons to come. He waited only the signal to attack. The men had painted for war, their ponies whore feathers and ribbons braided in their tails and manes. Hand prints, circles, and lightning streaks in warpaint protected the animals from the bullets of the enemy. When the signal at last came, they would all know greatness.

And then it came!

Five shots blasted across from them. Running Snake raised his lance above his head and threw back his head. Mouth open wide, he uttered a chilling war cry and heeled his pony in the ribs. With a snort and grunt, the close-coupled mount sprang forward. Behind him twenty-eight warriors shrilled their own challenges and urged their horses to a gallop. Ahead, gaping residents of Dubois pulled back into their houses and ducked low, or flattened out on the floors.

To their utter amazement, the charging Indians rode on past without firing a shot. At least not until a handful of outlaws offered resistance. Then, bows twanged and arrows moaned. Old trade rifles barked. Ancient percussion revolvers, their brass fittings worn thin, snapped in anger and put balls from .36 to .44 calibers into the chests and faces of the enemy. Three of Spectre's vermin died in the first hail of lead. Another took an arrow in the thigh and dropped to one knee. Before he could raise his .45 Colt to fire again, Running Snake drove the long, leaf-bladed head of his lance through the vulnerable chest. The flint point burst out the dying thug's back, a foot of the shaft with it. The force of the powerful arm of Running Snake and the galloping pony rammed the tip into the ground and pinned the writhing ruffian, an insect specimen on a display card.

Abandoning the spear, Running Snake waved his arms to direct warriors into intersecting streets. Before he knew

it, the Shoshoni leader found himself at the edge of the
business district. Outlaws swarmed in confusion. Dust rose
to obscure everything. Powder smoke wafted heavily on an
indifferent breeze. Quickly he dismounted and brought his
Spencer carbine to his shoulder. When the angry, shouting
face of an armed white man came into the sights, Running
Snake squeezed off a round.

It blew away the lower jaw of the outlaw and sent him
reeling away down the street. Another quickly filled the
empty space, face contorted by rage, who charged toward
Running Snake with flame spitting from a six-gun, while
the Shoshoni worked the lever action to open the breech
and insert another paper cartridge in the breech. With too
little time, Running Snake tried to bring up his weapon as
a club, only to not have a need.

Smashed down by a tomahawk in the hand of Bright Sky,
the thug splashed the roof post of the saddlery shop with
his blood and brains. Running Snake completed loading,
added a percussion cap to the nipple and looked around.
To his surprise he saw they had advanced half a block. It
would not take long now.

White Beaver could hardly contain his Arapaho brothers.
Several curvetted their ponies in nervous circles. He vaguely
believed it to not be right to have to wait for the white men
to start the fighting. Especially two times. White Beaver was
unaware that his thoughts echoed those of Running Snake.
It would be so easy to race through these white lodges and
burn everything. Why kill only some of those in the village?
And why fight as ally to the Shoshoni? A spatter of gunfire
lifted the restraint on his warriors and they streamed into
town from the north.

To the right of White Beaver, one outlaw gaped in astonishment and shouted the news to his friends. "M'God,
it's Injuns! We're bein' attacked by Injuns."

White Beaver swung his right hand and arm across his body and shot the outlaw with an old Dragoon pistol that had belonged to his father. The .44 ball smacked loudly into the left side of the thug's chest and tore its way through both lungs. Constantly advancing, White Beaver did not see him fall. Nor did he see a local resident dash out behind the line of Indians to retrieve the weapons of the human trash. Instead, he snapped his arm right and upward to aim at a man in the second floor window of a house.

For an instant, his eyes locked with those of the gunhawk. White Beaver read fear there. Then the white renegade's face washed into an expression of deep regret as he saw his death coming. The hammer fell on the Colt Dragoon in the hand of White Beaver. To the surprise of the Arapaho, the man was propelled forward by an unseen person to crash into the glass a moment before the bullet struck him in the neck. A voice followed.

"That'll learn ya not to pester my littlest girl." Quickly followed by, "Oh my God! That Injun shot him."

More surprise awaited White Beaver as the dying outlaw fell through the air, his trousers around his knees. He hit the ground hard and did not move. The Arapaho war leader rode on. Another block and he signaled his warriors to break off and enter other streets, to close off the center of the village.

Victor Spectre, or someone working for him, learned quickly from mistakes, Smoke Jensen observed. Several marksmen with long-range rifles had been stationed on the roofs of two-story buildings in the downtown area. From there they could make things uncomfortable for those closing in on the outlaw band.

At least until one got careless and exposed himself to the still-keen eyesight of Ezra Sampson. Dust puffed up from the vest of the hard case and his head snapped back. Only

a fraction of a second later, Smoke heard the report of
Ezra's Sharps. Immediately, two of the sharpshooters turned
their attention toward the old mountain man.

Ezra's next shot went far wide of the mark and Smoke
knew he had been nicked at the least. No such condition
afflicted Zeke Duncan, who promptly accounted for another
of the roof-top shooters. The man's back arched and he
flopped face-first on a slate roof, to slide down to the edge
and off. He landed on the ground with a loud plop. Four
of the gunmen turned their fire on Ezra's position. Ezra
gave them a taste of the same with a .56 caliber ball that
took off the back of the head on one outlaw. Then Smoke
heard a faint cry from Ezra.

"Dangit, you done hulled my shoulder."

Emboldened by this, the remaining marksmen incau-
tiously showed themselves to jeer the injured men. They
quickly learned, much to their regret, that it took more than
a scratch or a hole in a shoulder to stop one of the mountain
breed. Two balls dropped as many men and the remainder
scurried for cover.

A third suddenly yowled and went down with a Shoshoni
arrow in his thigh. Smoke gave a slight nod of appreciation
and moved to another vantage point, where he could study
the ever-narrowing area where Spectre and his henchmen
could still find shelter. Two thugs broke cover from inside
the Watering Hole saloon. With Smoke Jensen looking on,
Ike Mitchell spun around the alley-side of the general mercantile and shot one rogue through the breastbone.

"Over here," Smoke shouted at the other when Ike's six-
gun cylinder hung up on a backed-out primer.

Obediently, the fast-gun turned toward the sound of
Smoke's voice. His eyes widened when he recognized
Smoke Jensen. Smoke also registered an eye-squint of surprise when he saw the features of Whitewater Bill Longbaugh. No slouch as a gunfighter, Longbaugh had been
rumored to have gone into the land swindle game and left

gun-slinging behind. Perhaps the amount of the price on Smoke's head, or the chance to up his sagging reputation by claiming that head had been too tempting for Whitewater Bill.

Whatever the case, it became instantly obvious that Longbaugh lamented his decision. He crouched low, knees bent and torso leaned forward, as though already gutshot, and his face took on a pained expression. His thick lips worked and his voice came out cramped and weak.

"Awh, shit!" Then Longbaugh added in a whine, "Uh—Smoke, we don't have to do this."

"It's you came here lookin' for me. Now it's time you started the dance."

"There's no other way?" Whitewater Bill pleaded.

At the negative shake of Smoke Jensen's head, Whitewater Bill Longbaugh made a desperate grab for iron. He almost made it. He had his sweat-slicked fingers on the fancy pearl grips of his Smith and Wesson Scofield when Smoke cleared leather. Longbaugh gave a yank and the grips slid free of his insecure grasp. Instantly an expression of wild alarm washed over his face as he corrected and made another try.

Smoke had his barrel leveled and the hammer back when Longbaugh managed to draw the cylinder clear of his soft pouch holster. The barrel came out as Smoke's hammer fell. A powerful blow struck Whitewater Bill in the gut as he looped his thumb over the hammer. Staggered by the impact of the bullet fired by Smoke Jensen, he wobbled into the middle of the intersection. With great effort, he raised his wheel-gun again and fired a round. It turned out to be the closest to good luck Longbaugh had since he had encountered Smoke.

Fire erupted along the side of Smoke's left shoulder. The shallow wound had no effect on the outcome, since Smoke Jensen already had a second slug on its way to bury itself in the chest of Bill Longbaugh. Bright lights exploded behind the eyes of Longbaugh on impact. Quickly the shower of sparks faded into the eternity of blackness he would endure. Without regret, Smoke turned away to seek out another of Spectre's henchmen. He had no trouble finding one. One that came at him from behind.

Slobbering as usual, Farlee Huntoon rushed through the bat-wings of the Watering Hole. "I gotcha, Jensen, by God, I do," he chortled.

Smoke had barely started to turn when Huntoon raised his Merwin and Hulbert .44 to make a back-shot. Even with this head start, Smoke beat Huntoon to the first round fired. The fat .45 slug sped from the muzzle of Smoke's Colt and slammed into the protruding gut of the hillbilly outlaw. Huntoon's mouth and eyes went wide and round. Enormous pain erupted among his organs. In spite of that, he managed to trigger his weapon.

Huntoon's bullet entered the side of Smoke's whipcord jacket and bit into flesh, to form a short tunnel right below the skin. Fire radiated through the body of Smoke Jensen and he took a single, staggered step before he eared back the hammer again and put another deadly projectile into Farlee Huntoon. This time the hot lead destroyed the lower lobe of Farlee's right lung. Choking on his own blood, the West Virginia trash triggered yet a third cartridge.

With a shower of splinters, the slug buried itself in the boardwalk, between the widespread boots of Smoke Jensen. A black scrim, harbinger of things to come, settled over Farlee's vision. He worked numb lips and tried to gulp back a fountain of sanguine fluid that threatened to erupt out of his mouth. He partly succeeded and panted out a few words from a body rapidly weakening.

"I . . . think . . . I've . . . died."

Smoke Jensen watched the Merwin and Hulbert drop

from fingers no longer able to hold it, stepped in close and spoke with whimsical assurance. "Not yet, but you will."

A flurry of shots from the general mercantile drew Smoke's attention. Leaving the dying Huntoon behind, he headed that way. Six Sugarloaf hands had some Spectre's minions pinned down inside the store. Before Smoke could reach the establishment and size up how to drive them out, Stumpy Granger let out a yowl and began to hop on one foot, holding the other in a gnarled hand.

"Bastit in there shot off a couple of my toes," he yelped to anyone who wanted to hear. Then he dropped the injured foot to the ground, took aim and fired at a wisp of dark shadow that crossed behind the shot-out display window. The heavy crash of a body striking the floor told the result. Stumpy cackled and reloaded his shotgun.

Smoke made a quick assessment and spoke to his hands. "There's seven of us now. Three of you take the alley. Go this way, there's no windows along that side, and head around back. Stumpy can stay here and lay down covering fire on the front. Perk, Buford, Handy, when you've had time to get in place, fire a shot and we'll charge them together."

"I like it, Mr. Jensen," Handy Barker spoke up.

Five minutes went by, during which Smoke wondered if the hands had run into a silent ambush, when he heard a muffled shot from the back of the building. Stumpy opened up with his shotgun, alternated with rounds from a six-gun, while Smoke Jensen, Jules Thibedeaux, and Mort Oliver rushed the storefront.

It became a mad scramble for the outlaws inside. Nine hard cases tripped over one another, fired blind shots into ceiling and floor and tried to force their way out the rear. Hot lead from the Sugarloaf hands met them. They recoiled and sought the wider, sliding door entrance on the loading dock. That only served to expose them more. Then Smoke and the two men with him entered the front with six-guns blazing.

Three of the trapped thugs tried to resist. They died before the eyes of their comrades in a swift, deadly duel. One gunhawk, smarter than most of them, laid his Colt on a counter and raised his hands. He spoke sage advice.

"There ain't gonna be any big pay-off for us. Me, I'm quittin' right now. Don't shoot, I give up."

In three minutes it had ended. Stumpy Granger took charge of the prisoners while Smoke had a look around the unnaturally quiet town. He soon discovered that all of the gunmen had either been killed, captured, or had fled. Except for a few, Smoke reasoned, who would hang close to Spectre, Tinsdale, and Buckner. That left Smoke Jensen with only one thing to do: hunt down the three responsible for all this destruction, misery, and death.

Twenty-three

Their attention centered on the Watering Hole saloon While Smoke Jensen made preparations to storm the building from its blind side entrance and the rear, using his Indian allies to pour a withering fire into the front, a stout florid-faced man with a shock of white hair and thin mustache, and a large shotgun, approached in a dignified manner.

"Mr. Jensen. You remember me, don't you?" At Smoke's hesitation, he went on, "I'm Issac Spaun, the banker. I helped you the last time you had to do this."

"Oh, yes. You did well, as I recall. It looks like you put in a hand this time, too."

Beaming, Spaun nodded vigorously. "That I did. And I came to offer more help if needed. I have fifteen men from town, all well-armed, who want to be in on putting an end to this terrible affair."

"There's not much to do, Mr. Spaun. We're going after the three responsible right now. They and a handful of gunmen are in the saloon over there."

"Well, we came to help. I suppose we could keep an eye on the second floor windows. And there's a door up there on the side."

Smoke gave him a warm smile. "Thank you, I appreciate you doing this. Pick your spots and we'll get started."

Four minutes later the Arapaho and Shoshoni warriors began to whoop and caterwaul, while they sent a shower of arrows in through the shattered casements. Some of the outlaws showed themselves in the window of the upper story, only to be shot away from their vantage points by the townsmen. Smoke Jensen let the softening-up go on for a full ten minutes. Then he ordered the ranch hands forward as the outside firing dwindled to nothing. Smoke personally led the assault on the side door.

Hank Evans used his burly shoulder to smash through the thin, poorly secured portal. Smoke rushed in at once and skidded to a halt. He found himself face-to-face with Ralph Tinsdale, who held a shot-barreled ten-gauge shotgun, pointed directly at Smoke's chest.

Smoke Jensen reacted automatically and instantly. He put a bullet between the eyes of Ralph Tinsdale. The shotgun in Tinsdale's hands discharged into the pebbly, pressed tin cciling as he went over backward. Smoke swung to his right to confront Gus Jaeger and felt a powerful blow in his lower right side. His shot went wide of the mark, only nicking the Prussian gunfighter in his left upper arm. A quick glance showed Victor Spectre on the landing, a smoking revolver in one hand.

At the present, Smoke had no time for Spectre, who had tried to shoot him in the back. He returned his attention to Jaeger, who unlimbered two shots at Smoke, both of which missed. On the floor, Tinsdale shuddered his last and expired in a welter of blood. Smoke fired again, aiming at the center of mass on the chest of Gus Jaeger. The bullet went home and shattered the breastbone of the gang foreman.

Gus Jaeger took two unsteady steps backward and abruptly sat in a sturdy oak captain's chair. He looked down foolishly at his .44 Colt Frontier, as though he did not know its function. Then, remembering, he raised it to aim at Smoke Jensen. From the other parts of the saloon, Smoke heard scattered exchanges of gunfire. He had the position and time advantage over Jaeger and used it fully.

Smoke's bullet slammed into the face of Gus Jaeger to make an exclamation point of the gunhawk's long, patrician nose. The chair went over backward and Gus Jaeger sprawled in the clutches of Father Death. Sudden movement drew Smoke's attention to the stairwell. Victor Spectre had disappeared onto the second floor.

Favoring the wound in his side, and the stinging from arm and back, Smoke limped slightly as he followed after Spectre.

Every nerve screamed caution as Smoke Jensen climbed the stairway. Near the top, he bent as low as his injuries would allow and presented the least silhouette as possible when he edged over the second floor landing. When no bellow of gunfire challenged him, Smoke came upright and stepped into the hallway. To add to his irritation, he found every door closed to him. However he chose to proceed he had the sinking sensation that he would select the wrong one. A quick glance to the rear showed him a narrow, steep stairway now covered by hands from the Sugarloaf. That decided him.

Smoke turned to his right and went to the front of the building. There he began a game of cat-and-mouse, seeking the villainous man behind so much misery. The first door he opened yielded up only three corpses. At the second, the hinges squealed loudly when he flung back the panel. One dead man there. Smoke moved to the next.

He felt resistance. The lock had been set against him. He stepped to the side, raised his left foot and readied himself. With all the force he could put behind it, he drove his boot into the portal beside the cast-iron lock mechanism. Metal shrieked, wood splintered and the door flew inward. From the bed, a thoroughly frightened soiled dove stared at him while she clutched a sheet to her bosom and made little squeaking sounds.

Smoke tipped his hat. "Sorry, wrong room. Are there any more of you up here?"

Mute at first, the lady of the evening eventually found her voice. "Y-yes. Two or three . . . I think."

"Thank you. I hope I don't bother them as much."

Banishing the vision of rounded silken shoulders, Smoke went on with his search. He found the next two rooms empty, then got a look at a pair of scarlet sisters in bloomers and shifts, who hugged each other in the middle of the room and wailed like banshees. Once again he apologized and moved on. Room after room proved to be empty. Smoke had taken only three strides past the last one he had inspected when the door to it silently swung open on well-oiled hinges.

His boots removed, Victor Spectre stepped out into the hallway on silent, stockinged feet. He held at the ready a Smith and Wesson .44, which he raised slightly to make a perfect back-shot on Smoke Jensen. How much he would have liked to make Jensen suffer, but everything was in a shambles and he believed it best to simply get it over and escape. Carefully he lined up the sights.

That flicker of motion, reflected in the glass chimney of a kerosene lamp, alerted Smoke Jensen to the danger. Instantly, Smoke dropped to one knee, his Colt Peacemaker on the rise as he turned toward his would-be assassin. His .45 bullet reached Victor Spectre before the latter's left the barrel. Slammed into the wall, Spectre's slug went wild down the hall. He fought back pain and cocked his weapon again.

Fortune deserted Victor Spectre entirely then. Again, Smoke Jensen's round reached its target before his could be discharged. Shoved back through the open door, Victor went to all fours, and struggled dimly to stay alive. *Smoke Jensen had to die!* He told himself that in a litany of desperation. Obligingly, Smoke presented himself again. Victor was waiting for him and fired a shot that cut meat from the muscular underside of Smoke's left armpit. Then, suddenly, the world of Victor Spectre washed a brilliant red.

Scarlet changed to dazzling white, and then blackness. Shot through the head, Victor Spectre died without ever recognizing the error of his ways.

Not satisfied with the death of his enemy, Smoke Jensen continued to search the upper floor. Alarmed voices called to him from below. He recognized one as that of Monte Carson. Over his shoulder he called to his friend.

"Come on up, Monte. I just killed Victor Spectre. We have to find what else is up here."

Footsteps pounded on the stairs as Smoke went to the next room. Monte joined him after he had checked it. They headed to the last room at the head of the hall. Smoke stood to one side of the door, .45 at the ready. Monte turned the knob and flung the panel inward. Smoke spun around the jamb and into the room. There, a feeble Olin Buckner tried to raise a Winchester and fire at Smoke Jensen. A Shoshoni arrow protruded from his left shoulder and hampered his effort. Smoke crossed the room to the bed and yanked the rifle out of Buckner's weak grasp.

"I haven't seen you for a while, Buckner," Smoke gibed at the wounded man. "Can't say you're looking better than ever."

"You bastard," Buckner panted breathily.

Smoke examined the man. The local doctor had done a good job. Outside of the arrow, it appeared that the bullet wound Smoke had given him was healing well. It showed not a sign of angry red swelling that would indicate infection. That pleased Smoke Jensen mightily. He told Olin Buckner why.

"It looks like you will most likely live to meet the hangman, Buckner. If it's any consolation, I won't enjoy watching that. Public executions have never been my idea of having fun."

"A lot of good that does me," Buckner grumbled.

"I'm sure it doesn't overjoy you. Now, where's the loot your gang accumulated?"

"To hell with you. If that damned Indian had not shot me, I would have killed you the moment you came through the door."

Smoke's eyes narrowed. "You're not good enough. Never mind, we'll find it, and we'll do it before bringing the doctor to deal with that arrow."

Buckner paled. "You can't do that! I'm your prisoner," he squealed like a pinched pig. One look at the stern, unrelenting expression of Smoke Jensen, and his appeal died. "There's a door on the—on the balcony. It's locked. We put everything in there."

"Whoo-eee! Lookie there," Zeke Duncan howled gleefully when the door had been forced on the improvised strong room. "Must be a fortune here. Naw, three fortunes."

A shaft of light through the doorway gave a soft glow to stacks of gold and silver ingots. Bags of coin, and neat rows of paper currency, filled tables jammed tightly together. Enough money to boggle the minds of nearly anyone.

Nursing his wounded shoulder, Ezra peered over the shoulder of his partner. "Ya ask me, I allow as how it's all Smoke's now."

Smoke Jensen surprised and disappointed a number of people with his response. "No. It has to go back to the places they undoubtedly robbed on the way here. The banks, and stores, and stage lines can be identified and what remains divided among them. Which reminds me. Whatever money we find on these trash has to be the wages Spectre was paying them, so we can round that up and add it to this."

Zeke looked genuinely pained. "Sure is a shame to get hands on so much gold and have to give it back," he mourned.

At that moment, Sally joined the cluster on the balcony, accompanied by her bodyguard of Shoshoni warriors and ranch hands. She extended her hands to take one of each aged mountain man. "At least you got to rescue a lady in distress." Then she impulsively came forward and kissed each of them on the forehead.

Crimson rose from the collarless necks of their shirts to the roots of their thinning gray hair. Zeke began to shuffle his moccasins, while beside him Ezra dragged out a huge, paisley kerchief and mopped at his face to hide his blush and rubbed the toe of one boot with the other.

"Awh, gosh, ma'am, we was only doin' what's right," Zeke muttered softly.

Ezra shifted his cud of tobacco. "That's right, ma'am. We was only helpin' a friend. 'Twern't anything special."

"Well, I love you both for it," Sally declared with a sunny smile.

Tension eased and Smoke Jensen took the opportunity to make an announcement. "We'll rest up here a few days, then make ready to return to the Sugarloaf."

"So soon?" Banker Spaun objected. "You've hardly gotten here. We have to celebrate this great victory."

Smoke sighed, indicating his regret. "Sorry, but there's the spring branding to tend to and the herd needs culling for sale. Horses don't wait for people."

Spaun looked hurt, then brightened. Nodding toward the heavily blood-stained clothing of Smoke Jensen, he spoke with renewed encouragement. "Shot up the way you are, you won't be going anywhere for a while. We'll still have a few days to whoop it up."

Smoke Jensen cut his eyes to those of his wife. He saw the anticipatory gleam there and read it correctly. "Yes, I'm sure we will."

ZEBRA'S HEADING WEST!

with GILES, LEGG, PARKINSON, LAKE, KAMMEN, and MANNING

KANSAS TRAIL   (3517, $3.50/$4.50)
by Hascal Giles

After the Civil War ruined his life, Bennett Kell threw in his lot with a gang of thievin' guntoughs who rode the Texas-Kansas border. But there was one thing he couldn't steal—fact was, Ada McKittridge had stolen his heart.

GUNFIGHT IN MESCALITO   (3601, $3.50/$4.50)
by John Legg

Jubal Crockett was a young man with a bright future—until that Mescalito jury found him guilty of murder and sentenced him to hang. Jubal'd been railroaded good and the only writ of habeus corpus was a stolen key to the jailhouse door and a fast horse!

DRIFTER'S LUCK   (3396, $3.95/$4.95)
by Dan Parkinson

Byron Stillwell was a drifter who never went lookin' for trouble, but trouble always had a way of findin' him. Like the time he set that little fire up near Kansas to head off a rogue herd owned by a cattle baron named Dawes. Now Dawes figures Stillwell owes him something . . . at the least, his life.

MOUNTAIN MAN'S VENGEANCE   (3619, $3.50/$4.50)
by Robert Lake

The high, rugged mountain made John Henry Trapp happy. But then a pack of gunsels thundered across his land, burned his hut, and murdered his squaw woman. Trapp hit the vengeance trail and ended up in jail. Now he's back and how that mountain has changed!

BIG HORN HELLRIDERS   (3449, $3.50/$4.50)
by Robert Kammen

Wyoming was a tough land and toughness was required to tame it. Reporter Jim Haskins knew the Wyoming tinderbox was about to explode but he didn't know he was about to be thrown smack-dab in the middle of one of the bloodiest range wars ever.

TEXAS BLOOD KILL   (3577, $3.50/$4.50)
by Jason Manning

Ol' Ma Foley and her band of outlaw sons were cold killers and most folks in Shelby County, Texas knew it. But Federal Marshal Jim Gantry was no local lawman and he had his guns cocked and ready when he rode into town with one of the Foley boys as his prisoner.

Available wherever paperbacks are sold, or order direct from the Publisher. Send cover price plus 50¢ per copy for mailing and handling to Penguin USA, P.O. Box 999, c/o Dept. 17109, Bergenfield, NJ 07621. Residents of New York and Tennessee must include sales tax. DO NOT SEND CASH.

HAUTALA'S HORROR AND
SUPERNATURAL SUSPENSE

GHOST LIGHT (4320, $4.99)
Alex Harris is searching for his kidnapped children, but only the ghost of their dead mother can save them from his murderous rage.

DARK SILENCE (3923, $5.99)
Dianne Fraser is trying desperately to keep her family—and her own sanity—from being pulled apart by the malevolent forces that haunt the abandoned mill on their property.

COLD WHISPER (3464, $5.95)
Tully can make Sarah's every wish come true, but Sarah lives in terror because Tully doesn't understand that some wishes aren't meant to come true.

LITTLE BROTHERS (4020, $4.50)
The "little brothers" have returned, and this time there will be no escape for the boy who saw them kill his mother.

NIGHT STONE (3681, $4.99)
Their new house was a place of darkness, shadows, long-buried secrets, and a force of unspeakable evil.

MOONBOG (3356, $4.95)
Someone—or something—is killing the children in the little town of Holland, Maine.

MOONDEATH (1844, $3.95)
When the full moon rises in Cooper Falls, a beast driven by bloodlust and savage evil stalks the night.